MW00801092

AVI BERNSTEIN

# Death in Dahab

F4F

First edition



Published by Bernstein Press

ISBN 978-0-9926699-2-8

Typeset for print by Electric Reads

www.electricreads.com

*This book is for all those that dedicate their lives to protect the environment, and in many cases, tragically pay the ultimate price.*

## *Contents*

*Acknowledgements*

During the course of writing this book, I have learned a great deal more about the world than I could ever have imagined and yet I realise, that even with all the knowledge gained, I still understand absolutely nothing about life. One thing I have attained, however, is the enlightenment that comes only with the appreciation of the importance of family and friends. I would therefore like to thank my mother, Sue, my father, Gerry, my two sisters, Maya and Tamar, and my brother, Dov. I love you all more than you can know.

To my friends; Jane, Gary, Monica, Gina and Aymen, thank you to one and all for your support, loyalty and love.

In addition, I would like to acknowledge the work of three important organisations: The Sea Shepherd Conservation Society, a group of people prepared to go anywhere and risk everything in defence of the marine environment, Pelagic Life, an organisation undertaking invaluable work in Mexico, and the Black Fish who work hard to uphold European fishing laws in the Mediterranean.

“It’s like looking through a pair of binoculars, observing people on a far off beach, running around in circles fixated on the small area of sand under their feet, as a tsunami races towards the shore… ”

*Pete Posthlethwaite*

“But then… finally, you’re underwater and you see the thing that you were taught your whole life to fear… and it’s perfect… and it doesn’t want to hurt you… and it’s the most beautiful thing you have ever seen… and your whole world changes.”

*Rob Stewart*

“In essence, we’re just a conceited naked ape.”

*Captain Paul Watson*

## *Author's Note*

Despite the fact that it's all bullshit, everything you are about to read in this book is completely true.

A DARK SHARK

# DEATH IN DAHAB

ADVENTURE

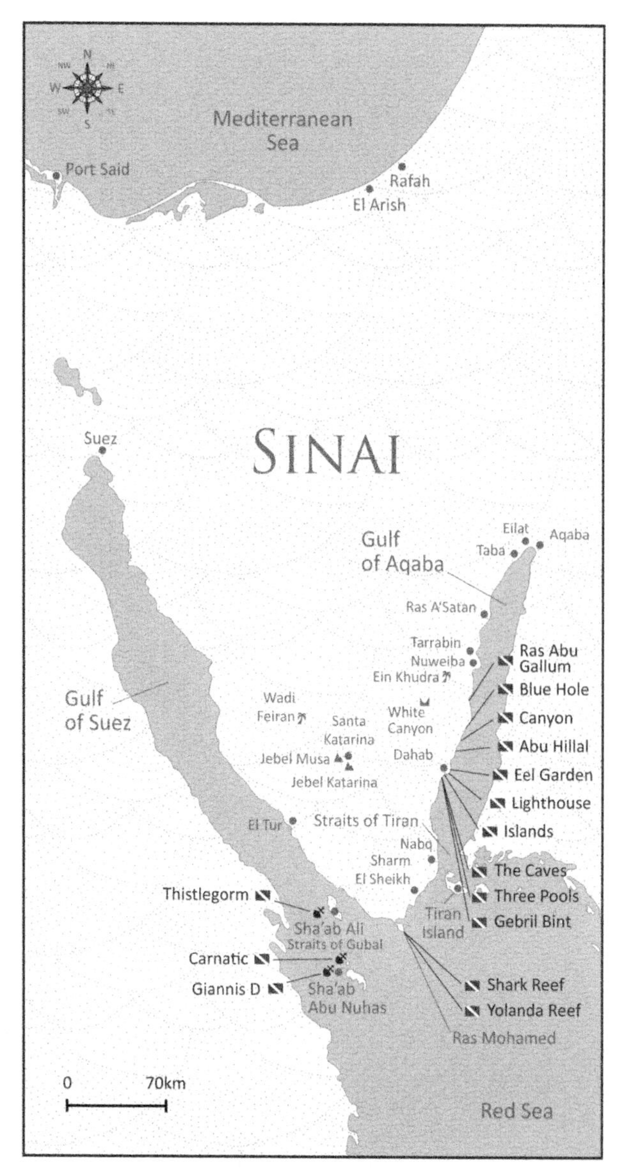


Fig. 1 The Sinai Peninsula

# *Prologue*

Dark Shark and Gastronimica occupied the main room in Dark Shark's half a house. Blue smoke curled slowly up, hitting the ceiling then spreading out in soft waves. The pair sat crossed legged on cushions, Bedouin style. Separating them was a metal box with legs. The box contained warm coals, a pot of tea and two small glasses. For a long time neither companion spoke. It was Dark Shark who broke the silence first.

"Gastro, why do junkies always end up in seaside towns?"

"I dunno. I guess it's because they like staring at empty spaces."

They both laughed. Dark Shark took a sip of tea. Gastro cocked his head slightly to one side and sucked on a joint. On the other side of the metal box, the smile slowly left Dark Shark's face and he stared into space once more. The silence returned. Minutes passed. Gastro waited patiently, sensing what was coming next. Dark Shark sighed.

"I'm bored Gastro."

"I know. What you gonna do?"

"I'm gonna write a book."

"That's pretty cool. Am I in it?"

"Of course. You know every hero needs a sidekick."

"No fucking way."

"Ah c'mon G, it'll be fun."

"Forget it. I aint gonna be no-one's motherfucking sidekick."

"Your use of the English language is highly nuanced."

"Fuck off ya middle class liberal."

"I rest my case."

"Look… I'm willing to compromise, which is something I rarely do. Let's make a deal. I'm happy to be the co-star on condition that when the book gets turned into a film, I want either Daniel Day Lewis or John Malkovich to play me."

"Deal."

Gastro mulled this new arrangement over in his head and presumably liked what he mulled, because he beamed from ear to ear and his eyes lit up with excitement. When he spoke, his voice had increased by several decibels.

"Soo… C'mon, c'mon, tell me… how does is it start?"

"Shhh… you'll wake him up."

# 1

## *One Pax*

Dark Shark woke with a start. He had sensed the weather even before waking. All through the night, he had tossed and turned, dark forebodings invading his dreams. Outside his house, gusts of cold wind had buffeted the wooden slatted shutters covering the windows. At five o'clock in the morning, the Mullah's loud exhortations, the call to prayer, had brought him from deep sleep to light. Dark Shark had stirred, but he'd done nothing more than dribble from the side of his mouth. He'd slept on. At the crack of noon, he groaned. Groggy, from too much sleep and de-hydrated, he pulled aside a dark blue duvet, jumped off the bed, and half stumbling, half running, dashed to the toilet. He pissed. His tongue felt like sand paper, his head throbbed.

Dark Shark showered, rubbing his body down with soap before rinsing off with brackish water. He tried to feel invigorated and cleanse the night's clinging residue, but it wasn't really working. He dried himself off rapidly before throwing on a plain blue t-shirt, a forest green hoodie and a pair of long beige chino pants. Badly needing coffee, he entered the kitchen. He prepared a cup, filled a small, metal pot with water and tried to light one of the rings on the top of a gas stove. The lighter he used, like the majority of the many billions of lighters sold in the developing world, was of the super cheap variety. It was made in a factory in China which no doubt had a 'work-till-you-drop' ethic, a workforce numbering in the several thousand and very little regard for human rights, never mind quality control.

What happened next had happened to Dark Shark on dozens of occasions during his time in the Sinai, and would no doubt happen again. The lighter exploded, shattering into hundreds of pieces and burning his thumb and first two fingers. Fumbling and swearing, Dark Shark reached into a cupboard and pulled out a box of matches. This time he was successful and a few minutes later, was rewarded for his efforts with a cup of piping hot Nescafe. Feeling more confident, he returned to the room containing his bed but which also served as a lounge. He plumped himself down on cushions and flipped open his newly acquired Acer laptop. He carefully sipped the coffee and waited somewhat impatiently for the thing to boot up.

When it had finally done so, he clicked on the media player. From Altec Lansing speakers, Otis Redding's voice sang sweet soul, his velvety tones soothing away the day's tribulations. The speakers worked well. Too well. The bass was booming and it jangled angrily with Dark

Shark's mental state. He turned it down. Having fulfilled the first three chores of the day, Dark Shark felt shaky but victorious. Lighting a cigarette, he completed his daily morning routine.

Outside, the freezing northern wind sent temperatures plummeting to twenty-five degrees Celsius. The wind carried with it molecules of an ancient, but remarkably familiar scent. As well as goat shit, the unmistakable aroma of expensive French perfume wafted through the open window and carried on its journey into Dark Shark's brain receptors. Being a smell, it had activated a memory. A memory he would have preferred remain buried deep inside his dehydrated cranium. Time slipped by. The cigarette was beginning to burn to the halfway mark. A small circle of ash was accumulating on the floor. James Brown was singing:

"This is a man's man's, man's world, but it would be nothing, nothing without a woman or a girl… "

Dark Shark inhaled smoke and blew it out of his nostrils. This was something he didn't do normally. Right now, however, was definitely not normally. *Her* memory, brought on by the smell, dumped him straight back into the past. He struggled to rip off the familiar cling- film effect. He fought to push the painful memory to the deepest recesses of his mind; he tried hard to replace it with something mundane - like falafel. But the pain only got worse. The feeling was dreadful. It started in his stomach, then inexorably rose up, clawing as it did so, rising up, up, up... before finally tearing apart his heart.

Gripped by guilt-ridden angst, Dark Shark was saved by the bell. His new clamshell mobile phone rang. The noise emanating from the tinny speakers was awful; a bizarre mixture of polyphonic nonsense. It had the effect of startling him, snapping him of out of a deeply unpleasant reverie, pulling him back from the brink of a yawning abyss. He flipped open the phone, but all he could manage was a barely inaudible mumble.

"Hello?"

"Salaam, salaam! Dark Shark!"

The caller was loud, gregarious, full of warmth and for Dark Shark in his present fragile state, far too early. The possessor of the boisterous voice was Mohammed, owner of Dahab's newest dive shop, Just Another Dive Centre. He sounded as if he was eating sunflower seeds, drinking coffee and smoking a cigarette at the same time. It was all Dark Shark could do to manage another mumble in reply. The combination of dehydration, lack of quality sleep and memories of *her*, all contributed to make his mouth feel as if it was full of cotton wool.

"Salaam, Mohammed. Kol a tamam?"

"El hamdul'allah! Dark Shark, Walla-he el hamdul'allah! Listen, I have work for you. It's a one pax open water course. She's American, just arrived! Heh, heh, heh, come down and meet her, okay?"

As if to underline the importance of his announcement, Mohammed spat out a sunflower seed, took a last slug of

Nescafe and took another drag on his fag. Dark Shark managed a third mumble to say he had understood and was on his way. He closed the phone. Looking down as he did so, he noticed sudden movement beside his left foot. A cockroach the size of a small mouse scuttled optimistically across the floor. Dark Shark grabbed a can of insect spray, covering the cockroach with liquid death. The cockroach ran around for another few minutes while the chemicals did their deadly work. The roach flipped onto its back, moved all its limbs very rapidly in violent death throes, and was still. Dark Shark was passionate about nature; he worked hard to empathise with all living creatures, yet even he had limits.

"You cockroaches might survive a nuclear war and take over from us humans; but not you pal, not in my house and not on my watch."

He brushed his teeth, pulled on his black coat and stepped out of his house. He emerged onto El Fanar Street. One of only two main roads that led to the Lighthouse, El Fanar Street was vitally important in Dahab. The Lighthouse was the focal point of the eccentric town, the beating heart. When Bedouin town planners designed the layout of modern Dahab, they decided street names and door numbers were surplus to requirements. Why not? After all, although there are those in the West who adhere to the rigidity of Roman roads and grid systems; the Bedouin have been navigating the wadis of Sinai for hundreds, perhaps thousands of years, with nothing more than the sun, the moon and the stars for guidance.

Of course, some expats coming from the West found the system somewhat disconcerting. One particular South African diving instructor, Wesley, pointed out his perceived incongruities to the chief Bedouin town planner, but his observations were met with scathing looks and dark mutterings. The only explanations given, amongst a deluge of Bedouin expletives, were random statements such as: "The oil will run out soon', "Everyone will end up diving on camels", "The Egyptians will go home" and so on.

Being humans, the Western expats adapted. They accorded to the streets the names of their final destinations. The main landmark, as previously mentioned, was the Lighthouse. The mighty structure, well over eleven feet tall, was purchased by the Egyptian government from some camel traders in Shelatin. The traders swore blind the Lighthouse was good quality – "Not from China, but from Japan". Installed on the Dahab Riviera, the indomitable Lighthouse had stood the test of time, a beacon of hope to the small but significant fleet of boats moored in the bay.

Dark Shark glanced at the rambling scene as he ambled through it. Rambling was the word. On the left, just after Dark Shark's house, Hamada and Lynn owned a three-story building. They had purchased the building together. Hamada conducted classes in Akido while Lynn took care of the diving. Business had been slow during the long winter. Due to his need to increase (much needed revenue), Hamada had taken to combining the two different businesses at the same time. He was practicing Aikido on divers in full equipment. Not too long ago, a confused Dark Shark had met Hamada in their local fruit and vegetable shop. Intrigued by the man's business initiatives, Dark Shark had inquired about the success or otherwise of his unusual strategies.

"Great! Saves on costs and they love it!"

"Don't they find it difficult with all that gear on?"

"La, walla-he, yaani, they are tourists!"

In the middle of the street facing Mecca, was a mosque. It was majestic, white, with glowing red and green neon tubes decorating its minaret. All along the length of El Fanar Street, pickups and jeeps ferrying divers intermingled with water trucks, camels, dogs, cats, and the ubiquitous Bedouin kids. It was a noisy, cacophonous orchestra of animals and machines. A fruit shop displayed its wares on the street, a brown awning protecting the fruit from the harsh sun. Palm trees sprang from every available nook and cranny. Ezet and Hani, two brothers, sold pine from a timber workshop. Working eighteen hours a day, they lived at the premises, their business inseparable from their lives. Bedouin kids played a dangerous game of football in the street, kicking a makeshift ball, dodging the vehicles, their brown, bare feet with soles like leather. Even younger Bedouin kids played marbles in the dust, their scraggy, dusty rags clinging to their small brown bodies. Broken glass, bottles and plastic bags littered the street, the bags often picked up by gusts of wind and deposited in the sea.

On the pavement stood one of Dahab's notorious green rubbish bins. Rubbish was a highly contentious issue in Dahab and was generally disposed of in three ways. It could be burned, left for camels and goats to eat, or placed in one of the green bins. These bins were almost never emptied due to lack of government intervention, so in actuality, there were only two ways to dispose of household garbage. All the bins in Dahab were overflowing, sometimes for weeks. For a large resident population of always hungry stray cats, food could be found in abundance at the bins. Consequently, there was a constant presence of cats inside them. Sometimes dozens of desperate cats would congregate, fight and rape each other inside one bin.

On opening the lid of the bin, the wary disposer would have to contend with all the cats jumping out at the same time. No matter how many times over the years Dark Shark had opened a lid - cats jumping out never failed to scare the shit out of him. Like a good horror film that you can watch again and again; you know the scary bit it's coming, you know what is going to happen, but when it comes, it still makes you jump out of your skin every time.

Today, for once, he wasn't thinking about rubbish or cats and barely noticed the skulking felines. He didn't even notice the obligatory, ever present smell which was usually pungent. Today, he still had a certain French perfume wafting through his brain and leading him down memory lane. A taxi driver slowed down close to where Dark Shark was walking, tailing him, gunning his engine and pulling him out of his stupor.

"Hey, you want taxi – a man?"

"La sucran."

Dark Shark was so used to being accosted multiple times on a daily basis by taxi drivers; the reply was automatic and far from enthusiastic. The taxi driver spat out something about Dark Shark being the bastard son of a thousand camels and sped off, kicking up a cloud of indignant dust.

The end of El Fanar Street merged with the Red Beach road and culminated at the Lighthouse. Shops, bazaars, taxis, pick-ups and people all squeezed into a few square meters. A large white building calling itself 'Golden Europe' stood at the junction, its purpose unknown. There was a laundry, 'The King of Clean', a humble but efficient enterprise, squeezed between the 'Why Not?' bazaar and the busy junction. A large, pale blue sign, painted on the white crumbling wall of an old weather beaten hotel, proclaimed the legend 'Taki'. It certainly was tacky, reminding Dark Shark of Portuguese buildings in Goa, faded and ancient, but without the charm of those former colonial houses still gracing the Indian sub-continent.

Despite the wintry weather, the Lighthouse was busy. Dozens of divers came and went, disappearing into the sea or emerging from the blue water having finished a dive. The divers looked cold but they glowed with contentment that only diving brings. The strong wind whipped up white horses in the Gulf of Aqaba. Huge, multi-coloured triangular sails dotted the horizon. Windsurfers zipped across the Gulf, reaching almost halfway to Saudi Arabia. The sun was high and warm in the sky. The top of the coral reef, known as the reef plate, shone a pale green colour, the water being only a meter deep. Snorkelers, their red and yellow tubes contrasting sharply with the deep blue sea, swam along the edge of the reef plate catching glimpses of the underwater spectacle below.

At first glance, Dark Shark didn't recognize anyone at the busy site; unusual in itself - but then he spotted the Walrus emerging from the sea. The Walrus was Dahab's oldest Russian diving instructor; a big, gruff, burly bear of a man. Although the freezing Dahab wind was doing its best and the water temperature was a chilly eighteen degrees, the Russian was sporting his normal attire of nothing more than a pair of Speedos, diving equipment, fins, and neoprene boots. He had a magnificent, two-foot red beard which stretched down to his belly button. The beard was truly epic, but sadly incomplete. Three days ago, whilst the Walrus had been sleeping on the beach decompressing between dives, a goat had decided to take a large chunk out of the poor man's beard.

The Walrus evidently did not believe in using wetsuits, because his two students followed him from the water wearing nothing more than bikinis underneath their diving equipment. Two freezing, dripping wet Russian women trailed in the Walrus's wake. The cold caused their nipples to stick out, which in turn caused the ever present taxi drivers to suck harder on their shisha pipes. Dark Shark turned right onto the bay. If the Lighthouse was the beating heart of Dahab, the bay was the overworked artery. It stretched for one kilometre in a crescent, from the Lighthouse in the north, to Mushraba in the south. Along the bay diving centres, shops, and restaurants vied for the tourist dollar. A row of wooden parasols had been erected all along the water's edge, every spare inch of beach taken by essential beach paraphernalia.

Tourists soaked in the sun on a few feet of beach which separated the sea from the promenade. Egyptians, Bedouin, ex-pats on mountain bikes, tourists, tourist police, rice pudding vendors, waiters, European newspaper vendors, cats, camels, horses and of course, divers, all streamed along the paved perimeter of the bay. A veritable river of life. Palm trees formed the boundary of the perimeter, the only green to be seen.

Many of the shops sold wonderful, multi coloured bottles of perfume, the bottles shaped into long, elegant flutes. Bazaars sold anything remotely connected to Egypt, Sinai, Bedouin or the Red Sea. Dozens of shops sold exotic crap to gullible tourists. Egyptian tourist police lolled about, their radios crackling. Dressed all in black, the police were all bored and all broke. Waiters in front of restaurants bullied the tourists in seven different languages, desperately imploring them to enter their establishments. Tourists, who explained that they would like to 'look around' before making a choice, soon realized that all the restaurants employed the same effective technique. They all had exactly the same menu.

Dark Shark marvelled at the scene before him. He never tired of the colour, warmth and vibrancy of the Dahab Rivera. He was a more than willing spectator to the Middle Eastern carnival. Suddenly, out of the corner of his eye, he saw movement. It was Rambo. A waiter in a restaurant on the beach, Rambo's prodigious talent was wasted serving tourists. Here was a man who truly made the most from every opportunity. When things were slow, and they were very slow now, Rambo's amateur dramatic talents would burst forth. On such occasions, Bruce Lee, Sylvester Stallone and Arnold Schwarzenegger would've felt acute envy had they been present to witness the spectacular displays that had become a regular feature of the Dahab beach in the winter months. Just now, Rambo was wielding a huge kitchen knife, a la ninja, to the astonishment of three Bulgarian medical students, currently on one week R&R from two heavy years of Hippocratic oaths.

Rambo was going for it. He sensed people watching him

and his audience drove him on. Imagining their awe, he basked in the celebrity glow. His fighting moves become more and more animated. Unfortunately for Rambo, the show does *not* always go on. Just then Gastronimica, Poi and her sister Flake turned up riding three horses. Serious riders to a man and woman, they careered down the promenade making straight for Rambo. At the last moment, the three horses sensed the impending danger and pulled up sharply.

In an instant, all hell broke loose. Gastronimica's horse got closest to Rambo and not surprisingly reared up at the sight of a man wildly flailing his arms whilst clutching a twelve inch knife. It was all Gastronimica could do to hold on to the reins. The other two horses managed to pull up short without incident; but Rambo, who was confronted with the sight of a large Arab stallion rearing up its front legs at him, involuntarily flinched. The knife, so aptly wielded only a few moments ago, flew out of his hand and embedded itself into a First Aid Dummy being demonstrated on by Paul, a Kiwi diving instructor. Paul had fallen in love with the dummy two days ago, and wasn't about to let some dumb waiter stick his beloved with a kitchen knife. He picked Rambo up and roughly threw him into the sea. A few seconds later, Rambo burst out of the water, screaming and hopping on one leg. The reason was clear immediately. Sticking out of his groin were three long, beautiful lion fish spines, quite poisonous and very painful. Still, nothing a little boiling Bedouin piss couldn't fix...

Several dogs barked. Four Bedouin girls whooped at the ensuing chaos. The horses whinnied and smarted, forcing Gastronimica and the girls to fight to control the agitated beasts. Poi's horse, Moon

Dance, broke into a fast trot and swept so close to the koshary guy, he lost control of his bike and drove into a shop window. The dogs' barking, along with the Bedouin girls' whooping, got louder. A gaggle of tourists formed a bemused audience, spectators to the theatre on Dahab's bay. The Bedouin girls turned their marketing antenna on the tourists, trying to sell their wares of bracelets and necklaces, exchanging their whoops for shouts and imploring their potential customers to:

"Buy one! Buy one! Buy one!"

Gradually things calmed down. Gastronimica managed to control the horses, Paul administered First Aid on Rambo using boiling Bedouin piss, Dark Shark bought koshary, and the three Bulgarians medical students just gawped. It was a typical Dahab day on the bay.

Dark Shark continued on his way, hunched against the wind, eating rice pudding. Palms trees bent in the freezing blasts and Leonard Cohen blasted out of a nearby restaurant.

"Comforting." he thought.

As he walked along the bay, Dark Shark passed Utopia Dive Centre. Utopia's owner, Shwaya Shwaya, had spent so much money on making Utopia look beautiful, he didn't have any money left to spend on equipment and books. In the middle of the dive centre was a large, leafy area known as the 'Wadi'. A giant palm tree stood proud in the middle of the Wadi. A pine palisade had been built around it, providing an extremely mellow ambiance as well as shelter. Sumptuous cushions placed on brightly coloured Bedouin rugs, lay on the ground. The music of Enigma wafted from speakers and incense burned in the grooves of the palm tree. Candles often burned at night when the chef prepared a delicious Bedouin barbecue of chicken and rice. The Wadi was so relaxed; divers had been known to spend three days there without realizing it.

Utopia was not really a dive centre; it could be more accurately described as a restaurant where diners were offered diving as an extra. Shwaya Shwaya had not yet realized that people came from Europe to dive, and if they wanted just to eat, they could quite happily have stayed at home in Europe. As a result, Utopia was sinking. Shwaya Shwaya reassured himself that all was well; he had the best-looking dive centre in Dahab. However, that did not really help when the rent was due and the monthly bills were coming in. By the end of that year, there would be over one hundred dive centres in Dahab, all vying for a slice of the European bubble market.

Dark Shark paused, hair swept against the gale. He waved to a couple of diving professionals lounging in the Wadi. Peter and Heidi were doing a sterling job of relaxing, protected against the wind and the threat of work. A young couple from Norway, they were blond, suntanned, and healthy. They had perfect teeth and lots of money.

Peter was a DMT (Diver Master Trainee), Heidi his instructor. Right now, she was reviewing his mapping assignment for his Dive Master course, Peter having mapped the Islands dive site the day before. Two bottles of Delta water stood on a small table next to them. Peter clutched a copy of Debelius's Red Sea Reef guide; Heidi was holding his map with long, perfectly manicured fingers.

"Ohhh, Peter it is even more beautiful than the real thing! You have even included these gorgeous little nudibranchs - and so concise! Oh yes, definitely full marks!"

"Thank you, it was really nothing. I am just soo at home down there... "

Peter had a strong, booming Norwegian accent.

" ...Like Jacques Cousteau himself. I am a fish, it is natural. I am a fish with lungs."

"Ohhh... Peter you're my man from Atlantis."

Heidi wore a white tank top, pink surfing shorts, and tan sandals. She had a new henna tattoo of a sea urchin on the back of her neck, three silver rings on her fingers and two on her toes. Around her ankles were two brightly coloured friendship bracelets. Peter dressed in a light blue t-shirt, tan shorts and brown sandals. He also had silver rings, friendship bracelets, and a necklace made from two-tone brown beads. Peter and Heidi were known as 'The Sexy Scandis.' After hearing the conversation that had just taken place, Dark Shark would now forever refer to them as the 'The Vomit Vikings'.

Shwaya Shwaya walked very slowly out of the office and acknowledged Dark Shark with a subtle, but regal nod. He was wearing a green flowing jelibya; a purple kefir, brown sandals and carrying a cup of Bedouin tea flavoured with nana. His age was impossible to judge with any degree of accuracy, but he had the air of a man who'd been around. Shwaya Shwaya looked across to Dark Shark and recognised his friend. In greeting, he held up his hand, open palm towards Dark Shark, and separated his fingers to form a V-shape in the middle - perfectly mimicking Spock from Stark Trek. On his face was a look of relaxed apprehension. Dark Shark acknowledged the acknowledgement by lifting up his hand and trying the Spock manoeuvre but he'd never been able to separate his fingers in quite the same manner, so instead he rather sheepishly held up his hand before continuing on his way.

Mohammed was waiting for him at the Just Another Dive Centre counter. Also present were staff members, Sally the counter chick, Mohammed the compressor guy and Mohammed the driver. In Islamic societies it is customary to name the first born son after the prophet

Mohammed. With a population of eighty million and rising fast, there were a lot of Mohammeds in Egypt. Dark Shark took heart from the friendly, familiar faces at the dive shop.

Just then, he noticed something different and for the first time since waking up that morning, he completely forgot about the French perfume. Looking lost, frightened and out of place, was the second most beautiful girl Dark Shark had ever seen. For the first time in a long time, he found himself not quite knowing where to put himself.

Mohamed the owner opened his mouth ready to offer a greeting, but as was so often the case, Sally jumped in first.

"Darkers, you're here. Great mate. This is Moheet. Moheet, this is Dark Shark, and he is going to be the instructor for your course!"

Before either Dark Shark or Moheet could respond, Mohammed offered them both warm salutations.

"Dark Shark, Salaam! This is Moheet. She has come here to learn to dive. I want you to take very good care of her and give her the best course you can. Tamam?"

Dark Shark could not have agreed more.

"It would be my pleasure."

"Helwa."

Mohammed was in his early forties, large, friendly and robust. He had black hair which was rapidly receding, a black moustache and thick pink lips. Large hands, large legs and a large heart. Big round eyes and a big round belly. Dark Shark liked him a lot, especially as Mohammed had just given him some work in the appealing shape of a one-pax beauty.

At first glance, Moheet appeared to be of indeterminate race, but as Dark Shark looked more closely, he could discern First People's ancestry. She had huge almond brown eyes, high cheekbones and full lips. She possessed a wild look, fierce and intelligent. Dark Shark liked her immediately. She didn't stare at him, but neither did she avert her gaze. She seemed far more relaxed and in control now than when he had first arrived at the dive centre. This was normal. Students were often nervous before meeting their instructors.

When she spoke, her voice was calm, collected and measured.

"Hello. How are you?"

"I'm good. So, you want to be a diver?"

Even as he asked this, Dark Shark cringed inside.

"Yes, it's something I have always wanted to do… ever since my mother died of lung cancer. She was a diving instructor, but she smoked and couldn't stop. Do you smoke, Dark Shark?"

Dark Shark shifted from one foot to another. The young lady was certainly direct.

"Well, yes… but I am trying to quit" he stammered, "Anyway let's get you ready for the course, shall we?"

Dark Shark handed Moheet over to Sally who promptly and efficiently issued the new student with diving equipment, books and materials. Sally had long blond hair and normally bright, sparkling blue eyes. Right now though, they were not sparkling too much. Born in 'Sydneeeeeyyyy!!!' Sally was bubbly and outspoken, sexually indiscriminate and enjoying life. She had left nursing college and

Bondi Beach for a year off. Traveling the world and learning to dive. To be a Dive Master and live the life. On her arrival in Dahab, she had been skint and so had walked into Mohammed's Just Another Dive centre after she had spying an advert on the wall. The advert had read:

**'Wanted: Counter Chik**
**12 hours a day seven days a week no day off**
**Must be woman**
**Must speak 5 languages floontly**
**1,000 le**
**Ask for Mohammed. (The right one)'**

Sally had gone in and negotiated with Mohammed. After a huge argument, which involved many sunflower seeds being thrown at the wall, a coffee glass getting smashed and Mohammed burning himself, they'd agreed on the terms of Sally's employment. Sally would work for one year to get her free Dive Master course before staying on and working as a DM. In the beginning she would receive one thousand Egyptian pounds which would go up according to commission earned, the current dollar/euro exchange rate, and whether Mohammed's accountant in Cairo was on holiday or not.

Now on the counter for over a year, she had only qualified as an Advanced diver, was still earning the same money, and had dived nine times. However, she did get to use a camera. Twice. Sally, her hair in bunches, wore a white t-shirt that had a red spaghetti sauce stain near the bottom, faded blue shorts and a pair of green Dahab flip-flops which, though Sally had bought them only the day before yesterday, were falling apart. She was wearing a Casio G-Shock watch, Baby G; pink, with a missing light button. The light button was lost during a stopover in Singapore, en route from Sydney. Sally had had an encounter with an overzealous customs official who had stripped searched her in his office. She hadn't minded the search too much, but tying her up with noodles was a bit much.

Just now, her eyes looked like saucers; each saucer had red rivers crisscrossing the surface.

"Okay. Moheet, let's see… you are five eight, weighing about eight stones, so you'll need a medium BCD, regs, and about twenty kilos of lead… "

"Seems like a lot of weight!"

"Nah, it'll be fine, you need a lot of weight in the beginning to keep you down."

"I'll sink with all that weight!"

"That's the idea, girl! Don't worries, Dark Shark hasn't

killed anyone in a long time, have you Darkers?"

Dark Shark just sighed. Sally continued on breathlessly, omitting commas from her speech in her haste to explain everything.

"Okay girl here's your mask and fins don't call them flippers coz they aint and here's your manual your forms to fill in and you gonna need insurance for sure don't rinse your regulators without the dust cap on or it's a $15 charge pack your box properly or it's a $10 fine drink eight litres of water a day wear a hat and lets drink together later at the pub cool?"

Sally smiled sweetly and leaned on the counter. Moheet was beginning to look confused. Mohammed was chuckling to himself in the background.

Once Moheet had been issued with kit, Dark Shark began explaining the structure of the course to his beautiful new student. Warming quickly to his subject, Dark Shark lectured her on the success of the course's educational federation, PADI (Put Another Dollar In). He discussed with her the endless possibilities of diving, of how a whole new world would now open up for her. He warned her - with a touch of machismo not unknown amongst instructors - that once she'd taken her first steps on the path of diving, Moheet would probably become addicted and would do nothing else with the rest of her life.

For her part, Moheet was enthralled. Dark Shark possessed more than a little charm and let loose on his favourite subject had boundless passion, dry wit and wry anecdotes. Dark Shark gave Moheet a lesson on equipment, showing her various different items which would provide her with a solid knowledge base for what was to follow. He demonstrated equipment assembly and showed her how to turn on the air. He explained the basic workings of the first stage, the second stage, and the alternate second stage, and showed her the gauge console that displays depth and tank pressure. Dark Shark also taught Moheet how to put on a mask, the theories behind fins and the complexities of the snorkel.

The basics over, and with both instructor and student filled with anticipation (but for different reasons), it was time to get wet. Standing just in front of her, Dark Shark instructed Moheet to put on her mask and place the regulator in her mouth, indicating to her that she should hold it between her teeth. Then making sure she was comfortable, he checked her as she took her first breaths on the strange piece of equipment. Satisfied that she was gaining the hang of it, he held her shoulder with one hand, gave the thumbs down with the other and together they submerged below the surface. They were standing in very shallow water, so when they dropped to their knees, the surface was just above their heads. Kneeling on the sandy bottom, Dark Shark watched Moheet's eyes carefully. He was checking to see that she was breathing properly under water.

The two divers faced each other. Dark Shark was

holding Moheet's hands in order to stabilise her and also to provide her with the reassurance that comes only with physical contact. She had a look of surprise on her face and her brown eyes were wide open. She seemed not to believe that she could breathe underwater. Bubbles sprang from the sides of the diver's regulators producing a crinkly, almost metallic sound as they were expelled. After a minute or two, she was comfortable enough to be able to look around and take in her new environment. Small silversides swirled around them, the sunlight reflecting off their shiny scales. A yellow and black banner fish, momentarily surprised, zoomed off, only to return a second later, his curiosity getting the better of him. A tiny crab crawled past them, scrabbling across the light brown sand leaving behind a faint trail. A puffer fished irritated by their presence, ballooned. Triangular spikes stuck out from its white, bloated body.

Dark Shark and Moheet practiced the first skills needed to dive. They took out their regulators, put water into the mask, and Dark Shark showed her the first steps to achieving neutral buoyancy. They began swimming along the edge of a light brown sandy slope which dropped dramatically on their right hand side, before disappearing into a dark blue abyss. Above them, the sun was warm and strong. Shafts of light penetrated the water, dancing around them. The sun's strong light was the first spark of an extraordinary explosion of life in the tropical sea. Green and brown sea grasses swept from side to side in the surge created by the strong wind. Dark Shark and Moheet swam forward then stopped, waiting for the surge to take them back, and then when it turned, taking them forward, they kicked hard, taking advantage of the forward momentum.

In the blue, off the slope, a large jack swam past searching for silversides, a powerful hunter of the reef. On the slope lay the inevitably sad, discarded rubbish of nearby human activity. Bottles, cigarette butts, plastic bags, and concrete blocks. Greying tires and twisted, rusting, metal bars. Dark Shark and Moheet swam past the debris and turned around, returning to the point on the beach opposite the dive centre. They held hands under the pretence that Dark Shark was helping to stabilize her buoyancy, but they both knew it was more than that. It was whilst they were under water that Dark Shark began to feel something for this girl. For him, water magnified emotions, and his emotions were running high. Their hands touched whenever she felt 'stressed' and it seemed to Dark Shark that her touch was electric. Moheet also felt something, her stress was apparent on every skill and the touching hands became part of the course. Dark Shark demonstrated fining, emphasizing correct body and leg positioning. The two divers played and practiced, Moheet getting to know the water and understanding the way the body moves in a liquid environment. After an exhausting hour under the water, Dark Shark gave the thumbs up and they swam slowly to the surface.

Finishing the dive, they showered and dressed. Each was thinking about the other. Each was wondering where it would go from here and each was speculating what the next move would be. Dark Shark gave Moheet some work to do for that evening. She would read from the manual and test her knowledge of the day's lessons in a quiz, which they would both review the next morning. Dark Shark said goodbye to his student, Moheet, and bade farewell to Mohammed, Sally and the others. Gathering his things, he slowly made his way home.

On the bay, the sun was beginning to drop on the horizon. The stunning red of the setting sun cast spectacular shadows on the water. Brightly coloured streaks of cloud formed hallucinogenic images in the darkening sky. Dark Shark passed Utopia Dive Centre. Peter was not looking very pleased at all. He was lying in a hammock to one side of the Wadi, his feet up and arms crossed, a cold grimace on his suddenly hard, Norwegian face. Heidi appeared to be whimpering. A large female camel stood just inside the entrance of Utopia, the map of the Islands dive site in her mouth. She was slowly chewing the map, digesting it with a look of mild disdain. A Bedouin girl, no more than four years old, perched on top of the camel. She was wearing a pair of torn, dirty red trousers and a faded green t-shirt. She was clasping a plastic bag stuffed full of bracelets and necklaces in one hand and was holding the reins of the reluctant female camel with the other. She jumped up and down ecstatically, shouting:

"Buy one! Buy one! Buy one!"

The female camel nonchalantly took a dump on the ground just outside Utopia, and began walking away with a long, slow, loping gait. Completely unfazed by the new spatial dynamics, the Bedouin girl swivelled completely around so she could continue to face the dive centre. As the camel departed she was riding it backwards, still jumping up and down and still shouting:

"Buy one! Buy one! Buy one!"

Dark Shark walked on.

After another minute or two, he came upon a familiar scene. Rambo was still on the same stretch of beach. After his adventures in the early afternoon; Rambo was now much quieter, but he was still enthusiastically regaling to the Bulgarian students, the famous story of the time Bruce Willis had come to Dahab. Rambo had kicked Bruce Willis' ass, because the Hollywood mega – star had been rude to him when ordering a Sahlab. Dark Shark sighed. It was quite possibly one of the worst stories he'd ever heard. Thankfully, one of Dahab's dogs, Lisa, playfully ran over to Rambo and licked the wounds on his groin caused by the spines of the lion fish. Rambo screamed. Dark Shark smiled imperceptibly and went home. For once, just for once, it had been a very good day.

# 2

## *Reef Shark*

The following morning Dark Shark jumped out of bed at seven o'clock. The alarm on his clamshell had alerted him to the promise of another day with his beautiful new student. After showering and shaving, Dark Shark left his house still shaking off the last vestiges of sleep. On El Fanar Street, nothing stirred. Most of Dahab would not be awake for another hour or so. Only the diving pros could be seen, rubbing sleep from their eyes, lighting cigarettes and praying for a six pax course. In complete contrast to the previous morning, Dark Shark was practically bouncing down the street.

A water truck swept past, the driver shouting: "Sabah el kheer!" to Dark Shark as he sped past. The instructor responded with:

"Sabah el ful!"

Dark Shark was actually smiling. The driver, momentarily stunned, almost drove into one of the two-foot kerbs lining the streets of Dahab. He had not seen Dark Shark smile for a very long time, not since *that* time and the sight of him smiling now was truly a shock. He wasn't called Dark Shark for nothing.

When Dark Shark arrived at Just Another Dive Centre, Moheet was already there, chatting to Sally and Mohammed, recalling the events of the previous day. She seemed much less ambivalent, her shoulders had relaxed, and Dark Shark thought her even more beautiful than the day before. Mohammed was lighting his tenth cigarette of the day. Sally was obviously struggling with a hangover.

Dark Shark and Moheet reviewed the work Moheet had done the previous evening, assembled their equipment and entered the water for the second time. Under the water, things were perfect. The cold northerly wind had died down. The sea that had been whipped up for four days straight was now doing a very good impersonation of a swimming pool.

In the shallows, Dark Shark and Moheet practiced the skills required. Dark Shark was impressed by Moheet's abilities; she was calm and beginning to master the sensation of diving. She was learning fast. As the divers practiced, various coral reef fish played amongst the alien intruders, their impressive colours and inquisitive natures adding to the delight of the visitors. Twenty minutes into the dive and with their air half finished, Dark Shark began to demonstrate the final skill of the session to Moheet. After finishing demonstrating the skill, he then indicated for her to practice it.

Just as she was about to begin, he glimpsed a long,

sinewy body swim gracefully a few metres behind his student. Dark Shark's heart jumped. He knew immediately what it was. He couldn't believe Moheet's luck. Sharks were very rare in Dahab - unheard of at the Lighthouse. He wasn't mistaken; his perception had been good, for there it was. Swimming around in a large elliptical circle behind Moheet, was a white tip reef shark. Dark Shark signed to Moheet to stop what she was doing. Before she could comprehend what was going on, he held her by both shoulders and slowly spun her round so she was now facing the shark. Giving her the sign for 'shark', he first looked at her then pointed off into the blue in the direction of the sleek predator. Moheet followed his finger pointing out into the blue, and then looked inquisitively back at Dark Shark. She hadn't spotted it yet. Holding back his frustration, he again pointed at the shark. Suddenly she had spotted it. A squeal coming from her regulator told him she had finally seen the magnificent fish. The king of the reef. Not wanting to miss this extraordinary opportunity, as much for himself as for his student, the excited instructor grabbed Moheet by the hand and began to fin powerfully in the direction of the circling shark. Lifting themselves off the sandy slope, the two divers, for the first time during the course, found themselves swimming in blue water. Below them the slope dropped off as far as the eye could see. There was nothing below them, or above them, or to their sides, except blue water. Swimming in the blue like this can cause a diver to feel disorientated, even to their point where they arc unable to tell what is up, what is down and what is left and right. There is absolutely nothing with which to provide a reference for the brain to latch on to. It takes some experience to know how to dive comfortably in blue water. Dark Shark held Moheet's hand but despite her best efforts, it was he who was doing all the work.

Although she bravely tried to fin, she was not yet ready for this swim. Dark Shark had to compensate for the inefficiency in order for them to maintain the same depth as they followed the perfectly designed fish. Swimming only ten - fifteen metres in front of them, they could easily distinguish details on the shark such as colouring and markings. They could even make out an interesting looking scar on the tail fin, a notch cut out that may have been the work of another shark or even a boat.

Its large brown eyes constantly searched the liquid world, seeking out both food and foe. The divers could clearly see the incongruous dimples on the shark's snout – the Ampullae of Lorenzini - a channel circumventing the entire shark's body filled with mucus which gives the shark the ability to detect minute electrical impulses in the water. Whereas we humans have five senses, sharks have six. The sixth sense is so acute, they can sense our heart beats.

The adventure lasted only a few minutes before the shark gave a gentle flick of its tail and disappeared beyond sight. For the two divers though, it felt like it lasted many hours yet was over in a flash. Dark Shark had heard this description from other divers countless times over the years. A shark encounter is like nothing else in the sea. As wonderful and vital as coral reefs are, diving with sharks is truly a rare and privileged thing.

Dark Shark took stock of their air supply. Moheet was naturally highly excited by the shark encounter and had sucked her tank nearly dry. It was time to get out. Swimming back to the slope whilst taking in the incredible experience they had just been through, the two tired but extremely happy divers, exited the water. Dark Shark had seen many, many sharks over the years, but he was just as happy and excited by the sighting as Moheet. He was simply very pleased that she had had such a wonderful experience on only her second dive.

They de-kitted, showered and began to tell everyone their wondrous tale. Moheet couldn't hold back. She gushed with enthusiasm, telling everyone who would listen about their adventure in the water. Many of the local residents of Dahab, including some of the professionals, had never seen a shark, so her tales, although on the whole were received with genuine warmth and congratulations by most, also drew envious stares from some. Such is life. Not everyone is happy for others.

Mohammed and Sally were genuinely delighted for Moheet. Sally squealed in delight on hearing the news and Mohammed declared that they would all celebrate with dinner in Slow Down. To top off a truly remarkable day, Mohammed would treat them all.

Established by a former safari legend, Hymen, Slow Down was amongst many other things, different. For a start, the restaurant served bacon. It was the perfect place for infidels and their heathen ways. Three hours later, refreshed, glowing and exceedingly happy, Dark Shark, Moheet, Mohammed and Sally entered the darkened, forbidding interior of Slow Down. Portishead were playing on the stereo, various diving pros lounged about and in the kitchen, wonderful smells wafted out as the head chef, Gastronimica, masterminded the culinary projects. When Hymen spotted the four guests entering his establishment, he let out an almighty shout.

"Mohammed! Sally! Dark Shark! How are you all!?"

Hyman was fat, sweating, with straggly black locks of hair. Currently, he was holding a beer in one hand and a cigarette in the other. Hymen had once been the leading diving safari guide in all Egypt. One day, he had moored both his wooden boats together at the jetty, and to his horror, a freak storm had wrecked his life's work. The boats had smashed against each other during the night, and in the morning, the only thing left was the rope. The insurance company had refused to pay out due to the illegal mooring; Hymen had had to start all over again, this time in Dahab. Hymen was, if nothing else, a survivor and optimist.

Rewarded for his tenacity and ability to score bacon in

the very heart of world Islamic learning, his new venture, Slow Down, was quickly gaining all-important kudos in Dahab's social circles.

In the kitchen, things were not so rosy. Gastronimica was cursing Shanti, his Sudanese co-worker. Shanti was a hard worker, but getting the message through to him was a legendary task. Shanti and Gastronimica made a strange partnership but both of them adored the other and their efforts in the kitchen were the heart and soul of Slow Down.

There were shouts and curses in a few languages. Crockery could be heard being smashed against walls.

"Shanti, can't you see I am busy?! Just boil the fucking spuds and then serve the salad, what's so fucking difficult?"

"Gastro, there's no water!" replied a shaky Shanti.

"No water! No water! What am I? Fucking Jesus Christ?! Go to the water truck man and get some more then!"

Gastronimica had steam coming out of his ears. The steam was having a hard trouble escaping the matted tangle of dread locks that fell from Gastro's head, but somehow they managed to finally dissipate into the cool night air. Hyman decided that it was probably a good time to get Gastro out of the kitchen.

"Gastro! Get out here man! Dark Shark and the gang are here!"

From in the kitchen a moan, followed by a thud

preceded the eloquent response.

"Oh fuck man, I can't! Shaky Shanti has fucked up the salad, the spuds and the soufflé! I have to save the day! Again! Tell them to sit down, chill out, order some grub and I'll bring it out to them!"

The gang from Just Another Dive Centre made their way to the lounge section where a completely different scene awaited them. In the lounge were Simon, an English diving instructor, Wesley, a Safi instructor, Kim an Aussie dive master, Megaphone, Peter, and Heidi. Propped up in one corner, was Paul the Kiwi and his new love, the first aid training dummy. Wesley was talking:

"Why don't they put street names and numbers on the doors? I just don't get it, this is the year 2004, and these people still don't get it!"

"Wes, why don't you try to understand? This is simply a different culture, Egypt is a developing country."

Kim had long ago learnt from her very sensible, open-minded mom, that people were different and it was this difference that made life so interesting. Wesley was buying none of it.

"Ach man they don't get it! They never will! We need a system of separation here."

Simon the English instructor felt a sudden, strong desire to interject at this point in response to Wesley's thinly disguised attempt at promoting a system of apartheid.

"Ah yes the system of separation that worked so well in

your own country, eh, Wes?"

Simon was a political animal. He never allowed the conversation to stray too far to the right (or to the left for that matter) before bringing to bear an Islington upbringing, and anyway, he was trying to impress the multiculturalist, Kim. Simon was from Hertfordshire and had had a career as a dentist back home. He had been earning £100,000 a year, but was finding the experience too stressful. Like so many before him, he decided to take some time out and chill in Dahab. He had become a Dive Master, then instructor and hadn't yet found a way back to his 100K a year job. Wesley boiled and bubbled.

"Listen man, since Mandela and the Blecks took over; the country has gone to the dogs."

The diving pros shifted nervously in their seats. Resisting the urge to shove a bottle of Becks into the politics of Wesley, Dark Shark motioned for his companions to sit down but away from the others.

The conversation on the other table continued but failed to improve even slightly. Heidi cut in:

"But Dahab is so beautiful..."

Her boyfriend Peter was always ready to support his partner.

"Yes, it is an exciting mix of different peoples and cultures."

"Dahab is magical."

Simon was not only politically correct, but poetical too. Kim, liking him more and more, pressed her legs against his thighs. Megaphone spoke up. He was big on volume, but had a somewhat limited vocabulary.

"This is a great place, man, great chicks, man, great diving, man, I love it, mate!"

Wesley harrumphed but was otherwise silent. He wanted all the others to moan and groan about Dahab, but they actually enjoyed being there.

Amongst the pros, was one who had not said anything yet. He was different. He was older, more cynical, calculating. He'd been round the block and then some. After that, he tried to steal the block. You didn't turn your back on this guy even when he wasn't in the room. His name was Bent Bob and he worked for WDD, World Domination Divers. The WDD was based at the Stilton Hotel. He was dripping with money; as well as the gig at the WDD, he received lots of various revenue streams from side-lines in diving equipment, guns and figs. Bent Bob was a big, brash, loud American who loved dripping, bloody steaks and fat gold rings.

When diving, it is very important to maintain depth and control buoyancy. Swimming up and down in a saw tooth fashion causes nitrogen gas to rapidly expand and contract. If this continues, there is a good chance the nitrogen will form bubbles in the body's tissues. DCS - decompression sickness - occurs when the nitrogen bubbles are stuck in the body's tissues causing life-threatening symptoms. DCS can cause extreme pain forcing the patient to double up in agony. This is why divers who are suffering from DCS are also said to have the 'bends'. Bent Bob has been diving for fifteen years and had had the bends twelve times. This was how he'd had earned his nickname. He was the only diving instructor in the Red Sea who called the recompression chamber in Sharm el Sheikh to inform them he was diving, so they could keep the ambulance engine running.

On the other side of the lounge away from the shallowness of the other diving pros, Dark Shark introduced Moheet to Hymen.

"Hymen, this is Moheet, she is my student and started her course yesterday. Today, on only her second ever dive, we saw a shark!"

"Walla-he! Meir meir! Eshta a lay! That is amazing! Pleased to meet you girl, you are very lucky, Dark Shark is one of the best instructors, if not the happiest - welcome to Dahab!"

"Thank you. Dark Shark is very good and I am really enjoying my course! Today was unbelievable!"

Moheet smiled sweetly and squeezed Dark Shark's hand.

Gastronimica came bounding out of the kitchen, his torn, dirty jeans flapping against skinny white legs, dreadlocks everywhere. Teeth threatened to spring from his mouth. Gastronimica was juggling four plates, but grinned a huge, gaping grin when he saw Dark Shark and company. Gastronimica and Dark Shark had been close friends ever since Dark Shark had arrived in Dahab nearly two years ago. A former junkie from Brighton, Gastro had come to Dahab to dry out and start a new life in the desert. Dark Shark liked him because he was not a diving pro; he had a wicked sense of humour and dressed in the kind of clothes that caused middle class people to start charities.

Not drawing his income from diving had forced Gastronimica to seek out other opportunities, and he had applied himself admirably to a variety of different ventures. Chefing in Slow Down, taking tourists horse riding and promoting the famous Slow Down parties, Gastro was a Dahab renaissance man and the desert in the Arab Republic of Egypt had proved a good place to dry out.

Dark Shark introduced his friend to Moheet. He was charmed by her and she in turn was more than happy to relay yet again the events of the day to a willing audience. Sally piped up.

"That was amazing today Moheet. You got some luck girl. I had to wait three months to see my first shark and that was on the Barrier Reef. Good on ya!"

Mohammed corrected her, whilst sticking another handful of sunflower seeds into his mouth, taking a puff on his fag and ordering another Nescafe.

"It wasn't luck, Sally. It was Just Another Dive Centre. We always try to make our guests feel comfortable and at home. Our service is very important! You come as guest, leave as friend!"

They all laughed. For the rest of the evening, the drinks flowed and the food kept piling up on the table courtesy of Gastro and Shaky Shanti. Finally the evening began to wind down and the gang's thoughts started to turn to their beds. It was Sally as always who took charge.

"Okay diver dudes, time to hit the sack. Tomorrow, bukra at the DC. Get plenty of sleep and don't be late. Eight o'clock sharp."

Dark Shark and Moheet both said at the same time:

"I'll be there."

As they left Slow Down, Moheet drew Dark Shark to one side and discreetly asked him to walk her home. Later, outside her hotel room door, they kissed. Saying good night, they reluctantly parted company and Dark Shark bounced back to his half a house. Once there, he threw himself onto the bed, flailed his arms around wildly whilst sporting a big cheesy grin spread across his sun-drenched face. Not since *that* time had Dark Shark felt so happy. Three minutes later, he was fast asleep.

# 3

## *Corpse*

At six-thirty the following morning, the sun emerged over the Saudi Arabian mountains warming the crisp, early morning air. A Bedouin woman, fishing for calamari on the reef plate at the Eel Garden dive site, discovered the body of Moheet.

Two hours later, Sally, Mohammed and Dark Shark sat on the bench outside the office of Just Another Dive Centre. All three were in severe shock. Milling around were numerous officials representing the Egyptian authorities. Sally sobbed deep, uncontrollable sobs. Mohammed with tightly clenched hands, sat rocking back and forth, chain smoking cigarettes. Dark Shark sat frozen. He was hunched over, his eyes staring into space. He was completely unable to speak, to function or even to feel. A cold clammy numbness had encased his entire body.

Moheet's corpse was transported by ambulance to the hospital in Sharm El Sheikh. Up until now, there had not been any evidence to suggest the cause of death. The Egyptian authorities believed they were competent and were convinced they would soon have that answer. An autopsy would be performed and the body would be repatriated back to the US for burial. The shining ray of light introduced to the dive centre only forty-eight hours ago, was suddenly, tragically, no more.

# 4

## *Hooked*

Later that day, Dark Shark and Gastronimica sat on cushions on the floor of Dark Shark's house. Blue smoke was drifting upwards and unusually, there was no music playing. Gastro stared at the floor, his large round eyes fixed on a point in time or maybe a point in space.

"I just don't fucking believe it! It was only last night, that we all had such a good time, Moheet was sitting there in Slow Down, happy as Larry and now this! I don't *fucking* believe it!"

Dark Shark took a deep drag on his joint. Tears had welled up in his eyes and were now making their way down his cheeks. He was still gripped with grief, but he was now able to function somewhat.

On arriving at the dive centre, Gastro had discovered what had happened and promptly dragged Dark Shark away. He knew his friend would need lots of help and support at this time. For the last five hours they had sat motionless. Pangs of pain washed over Dark Shark. The feeling was almost overwhelming. In Japanese the word, tsunami, can also mean a wave of emotion, as well as a killer wave from the sea. What Dark Shark was experiencing at this precise time was a tsunami of emotion.

He desperately sought a stable anchor, something to stop him being swept away in a torrent of despair. Summoning all his reserves of strength, he was still only able to mumble:

"She drowned, man. Apparently she went swimming in the middle of the night and the current at the Eel Garden pulled her under."

"Bullshit, man, yanni, she was a good swimmer, and anyway what the fuck was she doing swimming on her own in the middle of the night? Nah, not this girl, it just doesn't make any fucking sense!"

"You saying it was murder?"

"Something aint right."

"The police think it was an accident."

"More convenient than murder."

"I don't know, Gastro."

"Come on Dark Shark, you know that girl didn't go out there alone to swim, man, she went to bed thinking 'bout you, her hand down there and a smile on her face."

Dark Shark knew Gastro was right.

"What we gonna do, Gastro?"

"Let's find out what the fuck happened last night; we owe it to the young lady, right?"

"Okay, Gastro, Okay… "

"The first thing we should do is take a tank and have

a look at the Eel Garden site, see if we can't find somit interesting."

"Gastro, I am down with this, but we have to be very subtle and discreet, we don't need anybody to know what we're up to."

"Dark Shark, I am the epitome of subtlety."

Dark Shark wiped away the tears and nearly smiled. Gastro was right again. Even if his theory was incorrect, just doing something would be beneficial to both of them. Simply sitting and doing nothing was no longer an option. Dark Shark called Mohammed on his clamshell and informed him he would be taking two tanks for a dive at the Lighthouse.

"Dark Shark, you going diving today? You're crazy man!" He exclaimed when he heard the plan.

"I need to calm down, Mo, and you know the only way I can do that, is if I dive."

Mohammed was nonplussed but he told the compressor guy that Dark Shark and Gastro would be taking two tanks. Mohammed the compressor guy muttered something about coming back with fifty bar of tank pressure. He had never liked Dark Shark and did not trust him with the air.

Dark Shark's plan was simple in theory, but difficult to execute. He and Gastro would swim north around the Lighthouse reef until they reached the place where Moheet's body had been discovered. Since the current ran to the south, they would have to swim against it for a good half a kilometre before drifting back to the Lighthouse. Dark Shark hoped the current was not running strongly, but a new moon and the northerly wind did not bode well. He and Gastro only had two hours sunlight left. Both of them were experts in breathing compressed air and despite being smokers were strong swimmers.

The sun was already starting to dip on the horizon when Dark Shark and Gastro finally reached the Eel Garden dive site. The current had been strong, but Dark Shark and Gastro had persisted, slowing their breathing, kicking long slow kicks and staying shallow. All around them the day shift of reef fish were bedding down for the night, hiding in nooks and crannies within the reef. The night predators were emerging and a marbled ray glided past Dark Shark and Gastro.

Corals took in water, swelled up and spread their tentacles to feast on nocturnal particles floating through the dark blue liquid. A yellow and green unicorn fish, refusing to pass up such a unique opportunity, nibbled on Gastro's flowing dread locks as he swam past the fish's home. Dark Shark and Gastro swam over a large plastic McDonald's sign. The big yellow M was still evident, but it was broken and slowly disintegrating. Three years previously, McDonalds had built a branch in Dahab. A flash flood, unexpected, devastating, swept from the mountains, right through the middle of town and into the sea, taking McDonalds with it. The good people of Dahab had cheered and strangely, McDonalds had not returned.

"Seems like nature can only take so much change and progress." Dark Shark was thinking as he swam over the sign.

At the Eel Garden, they paused, taking stock of their surroundings. The fantastic white sand slope of the Eel Garden lay before them, stretching down to the infinite depths. To their left, the coral reef cast a deepening shadow, to their right, nothing but dark blue and black. Back at the dive centre, the two divers had gone over the plan.

"Gastro, we will be looking for something small when we get to the Eel Garden. So… we will do a circular search pattern with a rope, ten metres should be fine… you've done a search pattern on your advanced course, right?"

"Nope, didn't do my advanced yet."

"Open water?"

"Nope, haven't done my open water either."

"So basically, what you are trying to tell me is that you are not a certified diver? In fact you have never even taken a diving course?"

"Yeah, but you know… I've dived many times. I know what I'm doing."

Gastro smiled. Dark Shark sighed.

Exactly where Moheet's body had been discovered, Dark Shark took out a ten metre rope and indicating for Gastro to stay in one place, gave him one end, motioning for him to hold it tight. Dark Shark swam away until the rope was taut, careful to avoid kicking up the fine sand. He swam in a circle with Gastro positioned in the middle. When Dark Shark had completed a circle, he took in one metre of rope, gave Gastro the sign meaning OK and completed another circle. Each time Dark Shark completed a circuit, he shortened the diameter of the circle, thus ensuring he covered all the ground in the search.

After three complete circles, with his air supply now at half way, Dark Shark noticed something shining in the pale light. Eagerly, he swam towards the object, curiosity getting the better of him. Lying half buried in the sand was a gold necklace. He recognized it immediately. It was Moheet's necklace. Dangling at the end of the necklace was a heart shaped golden locket. Dark Shark carefully placed the necklace in his BCD pocket. Feeling triumphant, he was about to indicate to Gastro that it was time to depart when his eye caught the glint of something else.

This something else was also half buried in the sand, but unlike the locket it was silver. Dark Shark moved into a better position to pick up the new object. Inside, he was fighting a battle to control his impatience and told himself to proceed with caution. Alarm bells were ringing. Something was definitely not right. Even before his hand reached the object to pick it up, he knew something was wrong. Nevertheless, he found himself closing his hand over the object. At first, nothing happened.

Next to him, Gastro had noticed his friend's new discovery and swam over to investigate. Dark Shark turned the object over. It was a hook. A large, heavily barbed, metal fish hook. Whatever fishes this hook was meant to catch, they would have to have been big. Even before Dark Shark realized what the hook was attached to, he felt a sudden, sharp pang of recognition. This was a shark fishing hook! This hook was used to kill sharks! His mind reeled at the thoughts that came next. Shark fishing!? In the Red Sea!? It was unthinkable! No matter it was seemingly impossible, here in his hand was the cold hard proof that someone was fishing sharks in the Egyptian Red Sea.

At the precisely the same moment that Dark Shark was having this realization, a number of things occurred simultaneously and with alarmingly rapid speed. Firstly, a large black shadow appeared directly above them, blocking out what little light there was left. The shadow was accompanied by the sound of an outboard motor.

Next, Gastro began to scream into his regulator, just as the hook was jerked out of Dark Shark's hand. Flying upwards extremely quickly, the hook was pulled across his shoulder and towards his face. Dark Shark jerked violently. Twisting around, he somehow managed to avoid the hook catching his face, but instead the vicious barb buried itself into his left shoulder. Dark Shark screamed into his regulator. His mask filled with water. The water around him turned red with his blood. Directly above on the surface, the occupants of the boat pulled on the line tied to the hook with all their might. Dark Shark continued the long scream as he was hauled up through the water.

He was now five metres off the bottom. Ten metres. Another five metres and he would be at the surface. He was going up much too quickly. The pain was unbearable. He was about to black out but was fighting hard against the inevitable. He knew he had a small line cutter on his BCD strap. If only he could get to it before it was too late! Trying desperately with his right hand to reach the cutter, his efforts were stymied when the motor above kicked into life and the boat began moving off.

Now he was being dragged diagonally up to the surface and at an even greater speed. Just as he was about to give up all hope, a single massive dread lock passed in front of his mask. He felt a tug on his left shoulder and then a strange floating sensation. After all the struggles and all the heartache, he suddenly experienced a moment of absolute peace and serenity. He wandered if this feeling was death. He also realized that if it was, it wasn't so bad after all. Death did not however, come to our hero that night. Death's hand had been stayed. Destiny had other plans for him. No indeed not, for Dark Shark had merely passed out.

Darkness spread its black cloak over Sinai. The bay twinkled with thousands of multi-coloured lights glittering on the surface of the water. They created long streaks of red, yellow, blue and green. In the distance, a light grey mist lay suspended over the water, masking the mountains of Saudi Arabia and dimming the last of the light.

It was another thirty-eight hours before Dark Shark woke up. When he did, the first thing he felt was a sudden, sharp jolt of pain emanating from his left shoulder. He slowly opened his eyelids, afraid that even with this minuscule movement he would aggravate the shoulder. He need not have any fear however; for he was able to see quite clearly. Sitting opposite him on a chair was Gastro. He looked worried but was smiling. Even in his weakened state, Dark Shark could tell that Gastro looked immensely relieved.

"Good morning. You're awake. Excellent. How do you feel?"

"Good morning, Gastro. I feel like shit. The shoulder hurts like hell. Now I know what it feels like to be a shark"

"Ach, it's nothing ya middle class liberal"

Dark Shark grinned despite himself, but immediately regretted it. Pain returned from his shoulder. He glanced down. A large white patch had been placed over the wound. Bandages had been wrapped around his chest in an attempt to keep the patch in place.

Slowly looking up and around, he studied his environment. He saw that he was in a plain white room with just one large window, a door opposite him and a sink on the wall to his right. The only other furniture apart from his bed was the single chair which Gastro was sitting on and a small wooden table. Gastro had a brown leather satchel over his shoulder which he removed and placed down on the table in front of him. Dark Shark was lying in a bed naked except for his underwear and the bandages, covered by a single white sheet.

"Where am I, G?"

"You're in Sharm el Sheikh Hospital. You were sewn up by Dr Adel. He put thirteen stiches in your left shoulder. He said you will be good again in a week and a week after that, he will take out the stiches. He said you were not to have any more adventures and certainly no diving for at least a month. Oh and he says to tell you specifically not to take out the stiches yourself this time. He doesn't believe, as apparently some do, that scars are sexy."

"Mmmm... Okay. Well I'd better do as the Docs says. He knows best."

"I think he's serious, Darkers."

"Yeah. So am I. I need time to recover. What happened to me yesterday was a real bitch."

"Yesterday? Guess you don't know eh?"

"Know what?"

"You've been asleep for thirty eight hours straight."

"Jesus."

"Aye."

"When I woke up, I had trouble remembering what

had happened to me. Now it's all flooding back. The locket. The hook. That fucking boat."

"It was shocking. I've never experienced anything like that in my life."

Dark Shark again smiled at his friend's humour and again felt the pain of the hook. He was bursting for information and the questions tumbled out.

"Gastro, you gotta fill me in on everything that's happened over the last thirty eight hours while I was asleep. What happened with the boat? How did you get me out of the water? What happened with Moheet's body?"

"Yes of course. I know you have many questions, but first, the nurse is going to come and change your bandages. Then I'm gonna go and score some food. We need to eat. I'm going to fix you up a proper salad with some fruit."

At the mention of food, Dark Shark suddenly realized he was hungry.

"Good idea. I am hungry."

"You should be. After what happened to you and sleeping for thirty eight hours, it would be fucking weird if you weren't hungry. It's a good sign - means you're healing."

Just then the nurse came in. She was so quiet, they barely noticed her arrival. She was wearing a simple white nurse's uniform with a patch displaying the legend Sharm El Sheikh International Hospital. She also had on black shoes with white socks. The only jewellery she wore was a necklace which looked as if it was made of leather. Whatever the necklace had on the end of it was hidden beneath her blouse. In her hands she held a white tray which carried scissors, bandages, sticky white medical tape, iodine and cotton wool.

"Salaam Aleichem, Dark Shark. You are awake. That is good. I am here to clean your wound. I also brought you some water. Drink this."

She handed Dark Shark a plastic bottle of water and he drenched his thirst while she looked over the wound on his shoulder.

"We are going to have to prop you up. It's going to hurt, but we have to do it if I am going to change the bandage."

Gastro came over to the other side of the bed.

"I'll help."

Putting his arm underneath Dark Shark's right arm pit, Gastro lifted his friend as gingerly as he could. Never the less the effort was excruciating. He needed a moment to catch his breath and for the pain to subside.

"Okay, I'm off to score some food. I'll leave you guys to it."

Gastro walked out and Dark Shark was left alone with the nurse.

Placing the tray on the bed beside Dark Shark, she asked him to lean forward. Taking the scissors, she carefully cut off the bandage around his chest and slowly peeled off the large patch covering the wound. Congealed blood had left a dark brown circle on the bandage which was beginning to cake. The bandage was disposed of in a bag. She studied the wound.

"It has leaked a bit which is normal. The good news is, it's closing and healing. Dr Adel's work is as good as always. El hamdul'allah."

Dark Shark looked down at the wound on his shoulder. It was huge, a large hole and tear running at least six inches across the top of his shoulder extending almost as far as his collar bone.

Next, the nurse cleaned the wound with cotton wool and iodine. The coldness of the chemical and the softness of her touch felt soothing on the enflamed, angry skin. She dressed the wound with a large clean patch which she secured to his shoulder by winding a length of bandage twice around his torso. The nurse finished by fastening a safety pin to the end of the bandage and covering it up with some sticky tape.

"Try not to move around too much. In a week the wound will close properly and Dr Adel will take out the stitches. I will come regularly to change the bandage and clean the wound."

"Sucran. You are very kind."

"Afwan. You are most welcome. It's been interesting. I have never before cared for a diver who has been hooked by a shark hook."

"Insha'allah, you will never have to again."

"Insha'allah. I will be back soon with Dr Adel. Rest

now and eat something."

Gathering up her items, she placed them on the tray and left the room with the same silence and efficiency with which she had entered.

Half an hour later, Gastro returned loaded with salads and fruits of all kinds. He was grinning, clearly enjoying his new found nurse-maiding skills.

"Compliments of Hymen!"

"Walla."

"Walla-he!"

"Hymen is a good man."

"Yeah, but crap at tying up boats."

Dark Shark smiled, and then groaned.

"Ahhh... Don't make me smile. It hurts too much."

"So don't smile."

"Come; tell me what's been happening?"

"Wait. First we eat."

Dark Shark sighed, but was far too weak to argue.

Gastro prepared the food. He produced a first rate salad within a few minutes and by the time he was finished, Dark Shark was more than ready to eat. With only his good right arm, he shovelled the food into his mouth as best he could. He was too shy to ask, but Gastro was a wise old soul and helped him with the last few morsels.

They finished the meal with bananas and oranges washed down with water.

"Thank you for that G. The food was wonderful. It definitely hit the spot."

"You are most welcome."

Having finished eating, Gastro cleared away the remains, pulled his chair closer to the bed and got down to business. For his part, Dark Shark elected to remain exactly as he was. Gastro began his reconstruction of events.

"Okay... where to begin? After you got hooked I managed to get to your line cutter and cut the line. That much is fairly obvious, otherwise you wouldn't be here. After I'd cut the line, you slumped in my arms. The boat drove off immediately and left no sign of having been there. The two most urgent problems I was now presented with, was firstly how to keep you breathing and secondly how to keep the regulator in your mouth, until I could get us both to the beach. I turned you upside down, inflated your BCD slightly and kept one hand on your regulator to keep it in your mouth. Your mask was full of water and I was extremely thankful you didn't seem to be breathing the water up your nose. I was fairly confident that I could hold the regulator in your mouth and swim back to the shore, especially with the current to assist. The rest was relatively easy, apart from you being unconscious and having a bloody great hook still stuck in your... "

"I still had the hook in me? Until when?"

"Don't interrupt. Until Dr Adel carefully cut it out under surgical conditions here at the hospital. The hook was barbed. There was no way I could have taken it out without taking a large chunk of your flesh with it. I've seen the film 300, I know about these things."

Gastro smiled and continued his story. Dark Shark listened intently, fascinated yet not believing that these events had just happened to the two of them.

"You wanna see it?"

"You have it here?"

"Of course. I asked Dr Adel if we could keep it. He looked at me like I had just paddled up the Thames on a water biscuit, but he acquiesced to my request."

Gastro pulled the shark fishing hook from his bag. It was wrapped in bandages. Even in that condition, it still looked evil.

"I know why I have a bandage wrapped round me, but why does the hook have a bandage wrapped around it? I thought I was the one with the large hole?"

"You are. The hook is bandaged in case it takes a liking to anyone else's shoulder. Or thigh. Or arm. You get the picture."

He handed it to Dark Shark who took it with a feeling of strong trepidation. A shudder of horror and curiosity travelled up his back. Once hooked, twice shy as the saying goes. As soon as it was in his hand, he felt again a stab of pain in his left shoulder. This time though, it was imaginary. The memory of the 'accident' was still very recent and very raw. Dark Shark slowly took it out from inside the bandage, almost worried that it had a life of its own. The hook was nearly four inches long. Its point was razor sharp and a nasty looking barb curled away from the main hook. Turning it over in his hand, he felt the strength and killing power of this simple, but devastatingly effective and brutal little tool.

"It's a horrible, evil thing"

"Yep. As far the sharks are concerned, it's fucking medieval."

"What happened with Moheet's body, G?"

"They are about to finish the results of the autopsy. It may take another day or two. The Shamandura have predictably been all over this, even sending top brass from Cairo. They questioned me, Mohammed, Sally and the other staff at Just Another Dive Centre. They even popped in here to check up on you. Apparently Adel has a hard on for you."

The Shamandura was the Egyptian secret police. Brutal, ruthless and thoroughly corrupt, they were, never the less, thoroughly efficient. Whereas the normal tourist police carried standard issue firearms, the Shamandura bristled with sub machine guns which they tried to hide under their $50.00 suits. This made them ready for most situations, but detracted somewhat from their ability to remain incognito. With their bristling ballistics, cheap suits and dodgy haircuts the men of the Shamandura made Colombian coke dealers look respectable.

Adel was head of the Dahab branch of the Shamandura. A couple of years back, he had caught Dark Shark smoking a big reefer outside his house. Storming up to him, Adel had grabbed the joint out of the shocked instructor's mouth, broke it into three pieces and threw it on the ground in utter contempt. Apart from getting caught smoking dope by the secret police in a developing country and now possibly facing one of the most brutal prisons systems in the entire world, Dark Shark was slightly taken aback by this behaviour. It was the last of his weed after all. Adel commanded him in a voice that left no room for dissidence. He thundered his order.

"Passport!"

Dark Shark, who had seen Midnight Express, was terrified. He duly brought forth his British passport and handed it to the irate agent of the dreaded Shamandura. Scanning every page in minute detail at least four times, whilst fiddling with the safety catch of his sub machine gun, Adel finally handed back the passport. Fixing him the most furious stare imaginable, he hissed a parting shot before storming off.

"No smoking!"

Dark Shark waited patiently for a few minutes. From nowhere he received a sudden feeling of avian intuition. He looked up at his roof antenna and noticed a large osprey perched casually on top of the thin metal structure. The proud raptor was observing with a detached, dignified air, the goings on below. To the bird, human antics must have seemed like anthropomorphic trivialities.

Feeling emboldened by this sign from the gods of the natural world, Dark Shark disappeared into his house for a moment, before returning to his stoop outside. He was defiantly brandishing a packet of Rizla papers. Gathering up the remains of his joint, he emptied the contents of the three pieces onto a tray. Mixing it all up again, he rolled another joint and proceeded to ignore the fascist with the gun. Dark Shark may have run out of weed but he hadn't run out of Rizla.

"Yeah, Adel and I go back a ways. What else were those social workers from the Shamandura doing?"

"They were checking for signs of that boat or of any shark fishing along the Dahab dive sites but... "

"They didn't find anything."

"Don't interrupt. How you know that?"

"Two reasons. Firstly, shark fishing just off the Lighthouse is too risky. Far too close to far too many punters. Second, the guys that hooked me weren't there to fish sharks."

"What were they doing there then?"

"They were protecting the Eel Garden dive site from snooping visitors."

"Protecting the Eel Garden because of things like that locket of Moheet's!"

"Yep. You got it now."

"They weren't there to fish sharks! They were there to fish people!"

"You've hit the hook on the head."

"*Mother*fuckers!"

"Indeed."

"But who are these people?"

"That is the 100 million shark question. Please tell me we still have Moheet's locket?"

In answer, Gastro reached again into his magic bag of tricks. This time he pulled out the delicate gold locket complete with eighteen inch gold chain. He handed the precious item to a relieved Dark Shark. The wounded instructor examined the locket closely, turning it over before attempting to open it. Despite having been underwater, the locket clasp worked well and within a few seconds he had succeeded in prising it open.

Dark Shark and Gastro stole a glance at each other before they both leaned over at the same time to inspect the contents of the locket. They were disappointed with their discovery. Inside was a photo of a woman, quite obviously Moheet. Her photo occupied one half of the locket. The other half was empty.

"Well, that was a waste of time. We've learnt nothing new so far."

"Not exactly, G, not exactly. Don't be so hasty."

"Explain."

"A locket is a heart shaped container meant to bring together two people's photos. They are joined together by love and this is represented in the locket."

"I believe I know that, Sherlock."

"We know that Moheet had a locket which must mean she had someone special. We also know that when she died, the person who was previously in the locket was no longer so special at the time of her death. Therefore we know there is another person; we just don't know who they are or where their photograph is. I am willing to bet that this person who lost favour with Moheet is going to be able to provide us with lots of information regarding the tragic events of the last few days. We find the photo, we find the person. We find the person; we may find the answers to the questions surrounding Moheet's death."

"Not bad. Not bad at all Darkers. You really hooked on this thing eh?"

"That's not funny."

"Ah... c'mon Dark Shark, you must admit it was mildly amusing."

Dark Shark was fighting back both the pain and a smile.

"Gastro. The place for us to start is the Forty Thieves Hotel. That is where Moheet was staying."

"Yeah, in a week's time when you can leave this place."

"No way, it will have to be quicker than that. We don't have a week. I'll check out early. We'll take things easy. Work only on land. In two weeks, I will come back and let Dr Adel take out the stiches."

"You'd better. Last time he gave you stiches, you took them out yourself. He wasn't best pleased. Also, he says you damaged an integral part of Egyptian heritage."

"I certainly did not! How on Earth could I damage the Thistlegorm? If anything she damaged me!"

"Dr Adel says you swam into a stationary WWII shipwreck."

"I got skewered on the hand rail. The rail went into my leg almost an inch. I felt like I had been spear fished."

"Indeed. And why was the hand rail broken in the first place?"

"Because some Muppet had decided to tie a dive boat with a rope to the hand rail of the Thistlegorm and as a result, the hand rail had snapped. But that particular Muppet was not this one."

"So? What's the plan?"

"I will need three or four days to recover sufficiently to leave the hospital and then we will start our investigations properly. We now know for sure that Moheet did not drown that night. She was murdered, of that there can be no doubt. In the meantime, you can try to get as much information as you can about any shark fishing going on in this part of the Red Sea. Also let me know the results of the autopsy... "

"I can do that."

"You gonna have to be subtle about it. After what happened to Moheet and then the business with us at the Eel Garden, the whole town is going to be talking about us for weeks. A low profile is going to be impossible from now on. We seem to have blown the element of surprise."

"Why do you always have to ask me to be subtle? I have told you I can do subtle."

"Gast..."

"Also, we haven't necessarily lost the element of surprise. Surprises can come in many shapes and sizes.

Anyway, you and I are often the subject of conversation in this town for some reason."

"Sex whilst on ketamine in the toilet at a party with a diving professional dressed in a Nazi uniform, is not exactly subtle."

"I said I can do subtle. I didn't say I did subtle all the time."

"We need to find out how Moheet was murdered and more importantly, why."

"Not to mention by whom."

"Yes."

Their conversation was interrupted by the entrance of Dr Adel and the same nurse who had changed Dark Shark's bandage earlier.

"Ahh... Gastronimica, Dark Shark. Good day to you both. The nurse tells me you are awake and that she has also changed your dressings. Good. I also see that Gastronimica has brought you all important sustenance. Also good. How do you feel?"

Dr Adel ran the recompression chamber in Sharm El Sheikh. He had been doing the job for over thirty years. A former North Sea commercial diver, he had studied hyperbaric medicine and became one of the foremost 'diving' doctors in the world. Dr Adel performed far more than just hyperbaric duties. He was also the Divers Alert Network Director for Egypt, a first rate paediatrician, and a superb diving instructor specializing in safaris. Dr Adel frequently offered his services for free.

Sharm El Sheikh was one of the top diving locations in the world. Over the years it had grown rapidly from a small Bedouin fishing village into a world famous Mecca for diving. The Red Sea was a

spectacular, exotic destination and Dr Adel was the safety net. It made every diver who visited Sinai feel much safer knowing someone like Dr Adel was a continuous presence. Many professionals in Sinai believed Dr Adel *was* the industry. When the horror of suicide bombs arrived in Sinai, Dr Adel had worked for days on end without sleep to administer aid to patients. The words, heroes and legends, are bandied about far too often these days, but in Dark Shark's humble opinion, Dr Adel was both of these. A huge, round man, Dr Adel had straggly receding black hair, a forty two inch waist and the warmest brown eyes you could ever hope to see.

"Salaam, Dr Adel. I feel like a very lucky fish."

"You are. That hook I took out of your shoulder is designed to kill one ton sharks. Let me have a look at it."

Dr Adel strolled over and peered at the dressing.

"The wound is closing. I had to put in thirteen stiches. We will need to keep any eye on it. I trust Gastronimica filled you in on my instructions?"

"Yes."

"Good. Please stick to them. The wound will need a week to close properly. After that I can remove the stitching. In the meantime, the nurse will change your dressings on a daily basis. This is the third time I have stitched you up now."

Dark Shark never had enough money to pay Dr Adel for his life saving work, and Dr Adel had never asked for payment, so the reference to the loyalty card was a moot point.

"Dr Adel, I can't stay in the hospital for a whole week. I need to get out in three or four days. Gastro and I have to get to the bottom of what happened to my student."

"Dark Shark, you won't be strong enough to do anything in three or four days. Leave the investigation to the Shamandura."

"With all respect Doc, you have to be kidding."

"I am not. They will complete their duties."

Dark Shark did not reply to that. There was no use. Dr Adel knew full the corruption within the dreaded secret police force, but was not about to advise or encourage anyone else to interfere with official lines of inquiry. It was essential for Dr Adel to remain a respectable pillar of the community. He continued on.

"If you are strong enough after three or four days, you can check yourself out. *But,* I want you back here in a week to remove the stitching. No arguments about it. Last time you took out the stitches yourself. You can damage the Thistlegorm, but I will not allow you to damage yourself."

A year ago, Dark Shark had been leading a group of divers around the world famous Thistlegorm wreck located in the Gulf of Suez. The wreck was in the middle of the open sea and dive boats were forced to tie directly onto the wreck in order for the divers to make the trip down. Diving the Thistlegorm involved a dive professional jumping in the water and tying the dive boat to the wreck with several lines. It was an extremely difficult and dangerous task. Having finished diving, was necessary for a diver to go down once again and untie the dive boat. These activities were normally shared by the dive professionals on the boat.

Of all the tasks Dark Shark undertook in his role as an instructor, tying onto the wreck was his least favourite. He tried everything he could to avoid having to do it. On this particular occasion it was his turn to untie the dive boat. The task has to be accomplished as quickly as possible. There were three lines to untie and once the first one was off, the dive boat was in serious danger of spinning into the waves. It was also important to avoid the rope which had just been untied. Attached to a one hundred tonne dive boat jumping in the waves, the rope would be whipped up to the surface as soon as it was untied. Woe betide any diver stilled holding on to rope as it sped to the surface. Speed and timing were of the essence. Dark Shark descended to the first rope. He successfully untied it, released it, and then headed off at high speed along the edge of the wreck to the next line. In his haste to reach the line, he failed to notice the sharp, broken hand rail and swim straight into it. He screamed as the rail went into his leg nearly one inch. Gasping his air, he had to actually grab the rail and pull himself off. He was at around twenty metres when this occurred and when he pulled himself off the rail, the blood that floated in the water was green in colour. Knowing the dive boat could be in severe trouble he still had to untie the two remaining lines before surfacing. It had proved difficult, but he had managed it without further incident. Back on the dive boat, blood as well as water had flooded out of his wetsuit when he removed it. At the hospital, Dr Adel had performed the first of the (so far) three operations to stitch up Dark Shark's wounds.

"Doc, I didn't damage the Thistlegorm."

"Dark Shark, you know as well as I do that any diver who visits the Thistlegorm damages her."

Again Dark Shark was stumped. Technically, Dr Adel was right. Tying dive boats to the Thistlegorm was having a detrimental effect on the wreck. Inexperienced and extremely stressed dive professionals often tied the lines to places on the wreck that were far too weak for the strain. Dark Shark's accident with the hand rail was proof positive. In addition, the expelled bubbles from every diver who went inside the wreck, floated up to the roofs of the holds. The oxygen inside the gas mixtures the divers were breathing was oxidizing the metal of the wreck.

The mighty Thistlegorm was not so slowly breaking up. In response to this, the authorities had drilled holes into the metal so the bubbles could escape without doing too much harm. The strategy worked up until a point. Dark Shark concluded there was no point in arguing with a legend. Especially a legend that regularly sewed him up.

"Now, I must be going. I have a diver in the pot, a woman about to give birth and a meeting with the Governor of South Sinai."

For a man with such a large girth, Dr Adel was surprising nimble. He did a quick turn and with a few steps was out the door. As he was leaving he gave Dark Shark a parting warning:

"Remember my instructions. Be back here in a week or else. And leave the investigation to the Shamandura."

"I will Dr Adel. Good bye."

Dark Shark was only half lying. He fully intended to comply with at least half of Dr Adel's instructions. For the next three days, Dark Shark was content to allow himself time to recover. His strength gradually returned, the pain in his shoulder began to subside and the wound continued to heal. Each day the nurse returned to change the bandage. Gastro supplied food, water and titbits of Dahab gossip. The results of the autopsy came in. The cause of death was officially drowning. A verdict of accidental death was recorded and arrangements were made for the repatriation of Moheet's body back to the States. As far as the Shamandura and the police were concerned, the case was officially closed. This suited Dark Shark. He didn't need the Shamandura to think he was interfering in an investigation.

During this time he was also visited by Mohammed and Sally of Just Another Dive Centre. It was great to see them, but they fussed over him until he could take no more and he shooed them away. On the fourth day, Dark Shark felt strong enough to check out of the hospital. Dr Adel arrived in the morning, checked the wound and agreed that his patient was free to go. At ten o'clock, Gastro arrived in a taxi and an hour later, Dark Shark found himself back at home for the first time in nearly a week. Dark Shark made a pot of Bedouin tea and the two of them sat down to talk shop.

"What's the plan Captain Hook?"

"First thing is a visit to the Forty Thieves Hotel. It's a week since Moheet checked in, but we may still find something interesting there."

"Mershi, I'll come with you. We'll swing by the internet café at the Forty Thieves hotel first. I have to email a Slovakian nymphomaniac and then we can ask the guys at the Forty Thieves if they have any information for us on Moheet."

"Sounds good. We can also have a look at Moheet's room."

"How's the shoulder?"

"Getting better. It still hurts but nowhere near as much."

"You ready?"

"Yalla."

The two detectives walked out on to El Fanar Street and continued towards the Lighthouse. Turning left onto the bay, they continued along the promenade, glancing into Utopia as they passed. Inside the dive centre, Peter, Heidi, and Shwaya Shwaya were getting ready for a night dive. The three of them were excited. It had taken them a week to get ready for the dive, because they had been waiting for tank valves to arrive from Cairo. Utopia had Egyptian tank valves on their tanks. There was nothing wrong with the valves except they only fitted Egyptian regulators. The problem was that Egypt didn't manufacture regulators. Shwaya Shwaya had reluctantly ordered some new valves from Cairo, which arrived promptly, only for him to then find he had run out of O-rings.

An O-ring is small black rubber ring, inserted in a metal ring inside the valve. It is the only way to connect the regulator to the valve with an airtight, watertight connection. Shwaya Shwaya ordered some O-rings. After waiting four days for the right equipment and Shwaya Shwaya approaching bankruptcy, they finally got the chance to do their night dive. They were laughing and happy, they even had different coloured chemical lights strapped onto their new tank valves. Peter, Heidi and Shwaya Shwaya, impatient, but professional, did a last minute check before the dive only to find that their torches had failed. A second later, a scream was emitted from the dive centre that was so loud; it could be heard around the whole bay.

Dark Shark and Gastro entered the internet café connected to the Forty Thieves hotel. The café was small and cramped, rows of clapped out machines whirred loudly. Electric cables zigzagged across the floor; crumpled reams of print paper were stuffed into boxes. On the wall were notices selling second hand diving equipment, adverts for safari operators, flyers for a Slow Down party and personal notes. One note said:

'I am truly sorry for what happened at Taba. I hope we can all live together in peace and happiness. Dahab is a place where everybody can come together to be mastool. Ahmed, Dahab.'

A year ago, on the final day of the Jewish holiday, Sukkot, Al Qaeda (allegedly) had set off five bombs targeting Israelis holidaying in the Sinai. Two large bombs exploded at Nuweiba and two in Ras a Satan. The biggest was saved for the Stilton Hotel at the Egyptian border-town of Taba. A massive suicide car bomb destroyed one whole side of the Stilton hotel, killing thirty seven. That very day, Dark Shark had planned to cross the border on his way to Eilat. He had wanted to buy nicotine patches, but had decided to postpone the trip at the last minute. Later, he reflected on the irony of quitting smoking only to be blown up at the border.

In the middle of the internet café was a long wooden table, stacked high with books from all over Europe and Egypt. Guide books on Sinai, maps and works of fiction. Crap romance, naff crime books, and dodgy military stories. Amongst the rubbish, the internet café also contained a few gems. Like the books written by one of Egypt's best writers, Naguib Mahfouz. He is world famous for his wonderful stories of ordinary Egyptians and was honoured with a Nobel Peace Prize for Literature in 1988. Mahfouz's books are genius; skilfully twisting plots and containing wonderful, descriptive insights into the world of the Egyptian street.

Gastro settled down to email his Slovakian nympho. Dark Shark checked his emails; found nothing interesting, so got up, nodded to Gastro and walked outside.

Turning into the foyer of the Forty Thieves Hotel, he strode over to the reception desk. Behind it a man sat diligently reading the Koran. The man, absorbed as he was in the great book, failed to notice Dark Shark approach until he was already at the desk.

"Salaam, Mohammed."

The receptionist glanced up hurriedly from his studies. He was in his late thirties, had black hair with brown eyes, a long face which supported a thin black moustache. He wore dark grey trousers, a striped, pale yellow shirt, black waist coat and black tie. For a hotel receptionist, he didn't look too welcoming and he became decidedly nervous when he realized who was standing in front of him.

"Ah... Dark Shark. Salaam, salaam. Kol a tamam?"

"Aiwa, Mohammed, how are you?"

"Hamdul'allah, Dark Shark. I heard about your accident and what happened to your poor student. Terrible, sad news. It is so good to see that you are okay."

"Mohammed, I am here about my student, Moheet. She was staying here and I need some information"

At this, Mohammed went pale, his hands trembled and his moustache quivered.

"Dark Shark, mishkela... walla-he.... very bad... Moheet was so nice, very sweet girl... I am very sad... this very bad thing what happened."

"I know Mohammed, I know."

Mohammed looked like he was going to start crying.

"I need some information. I know you have already talked to the Shamandura, but there are a few things I need to know as well."

"Mershi, Dark Shark, mershi."

"How long did she stay here?"

"She was here for one week; she told us she might be staying a few more."

"You talked to her a lot?"

"La, I worked most evenings when she came back from her course, yanni, we spoke a couple of times, yanni, she was very friendly, very sweet."

He sniffed and wrung his hands, nervously playing with a string of dark brown worry beads.

"Did Moheet always sleep alone?"

"La, once, somebody else stay in the room with Moheet."

"Who was that and when was that?"

"A blond man called Nemo, he wasn't nice man, very arrogant, yanni, he argue and complained."

"About what?"

"The air-conditioning."

"Mohammed, can I look in the room where Moheet was staying?"

"Okay, Dark Shark, mershi."

"Has the room been cleaned since Moheet stayed in it?"

"Of course. We always clean up after the guests…. "

Mohammed broke off, unable to finish the sentence. He hadn't meant it that way, but what he was about to say didn't feel appropriate.

"Have any other guests stayed in the room since?"

"La. The only people inside the room apart from me and the cleaner were the Shamandura."

"Good, okay. Let's check it out."

Mohammed liberated key number five from a drawer in his desk. As they were about to go to the room, they were joined by Gastronimica who had finished emailing his Slovakian nympho. The three of them walked up a flight of stairs, emerging onto a balcony which overlooked a market below. Walking along the hallway of the balcony, they passed four brown doors. Mohamed unlocked the fifth door. Inside, the room was clean and aired. Two balcony doors swung open at the back, the cold wind making the white net curtains billow in its blasts.

The room was a typical double room. It had two beds, neither of which was big enough to be called a double, but not quite small enough to be classed as singles. In 2004, Dahab discovered pine. It was being shipped from the Nile delta, and everything in town was getting a pine makeover. In this hotel room, the beds were pine with brown sheets and a single brown pillow on each bed. The walls of the room were white. Dark brown light switches adorned every wall and next to each bed, was a small reading table, also pine. It looked like a Swiss alpine chalet in the middle of the desert.

At the back of the room was a discreet balcony, small and quiet with a view over the bay. For the money, the rooms at the Forty Thieves were some of the best value in Dahab. The owners were honest, hardworking and decent. Moheet's personal effects had been removed by the Egyptian authorities, but Dark Shark and Gastro thoroughly searched the room anyway, checking for clues. Dark Shark opened the doors of the wardrobe, checking a small shelf, the floor.

He went into to the bathroom, peering in, checking under the basin, next to the toilet and all around the bath. While he searched the bathroom, Gastro checked underneath the beds. Next he opened each drawer in the bedside tables. He also found nothing. They were beginning to get slightly miffed. There was only the wardrobe left. Dark Shark walked over to it and opened the doors. It was a standard double pine wardrobe. Across the top was a pine hanging rail complete with perhaps twenty hangers (yes, pine). On the left hand side were three shelves on top and three drawers on the bottom. On the floor of the wardrobe was a single sheet of wrapping paper which took up the entire space. This was normal in Dahab. The paper was used to keep dust off the floor and therefore off the clothes. Dust in the desert was a major part of everyday life. Dark Shark checked each shelf and opened each of the three drawers. Still he found nothing. He was about to give up and tell Gastro they were leaving, when something told him to check under the wrapping paper. Before he did so, something also told him to check where Mohammed was. He needn't have worried. Mohammed was still standing in the doorway to the room. Peeling the paper off the bottom of the wardrobe, Dark Shark spotted it. His heart leapt. Lying innocently on the floor of the wardrobe and covered in a fine coat of desert dust, was an oval photograph. Not only that, but it was identical in size to the one of Moheet inside her locket. Dark Shark was sure that he had just found her missing ex-sweet heart. He bent down, picked up the photograph and carefully placed it in his wallet.

Standing up again, he motioned to Gastro that they were done here. He announced to Mohammed that they were finished. Exiting the room, the three of them returned to the reception desk.

"Mohammed, we didn't find anything, but thank you

anyway for all your help and information."

"Afwan, Dark Shark, afwan."

"Just one more thing before we leave. Please don't mention to anyone that we were here, okay? Can you do that for me, my friend?"

"Of course. I will not tell a soul. "Thank you again. Until the next time."

Dark Shark and Gastro left the hotel and made their way back along the bay.

"Well that was a waste of time."

"Not exactly, G, not exactly."

"What do you mean? We didn't find Jack."

"I found something in the wardrobe."

"Did you!? What!?"

"Not here. Let's go to Just Another Dive centre first. I need to talk to Sally. Then we'll go somewhere quiet like the Lagoon and talk."

"That sucks, but okay."

Five minutes later they had entered the dive centre. As usual Sally was behind the counter and orchestrating the diving activities with the efficiency and strength of a Sydney nurse.

"Hey girl how are you?"

"Well, well. It's Captain Hook and the Cook."

"I aint a cook. I'm a chef."

"Really? Let's see some proof then."

Dark Shark decided to put a stop to this.

"Guys we don't have time for this right now. Sally, did

Moheet leave anything here at all which has not been taken away by the Shamandura?"

"Funny you should ask. I found a locker key from another dive centre yesterday. I've asked everyone who it belongs to, but nobody has claimed it. I suppose it could Moheet's."

Gastro and Dark Shark exchanged knowing looks. The day was proving quite profitable so far.

"Can I have it?"

"Of course, but if anyone comes forward for it, I will have to get it back off you."

"You're the best Sally."

She flashed a smile.

"I'm aware of that."

Sally disappeared inside the office and came back a second later with the key. She handed to Dark Shark who placed in his pocket.

"Gastro. Let's go."

The two adventurers walked to the main road to hail a taxi. They stood on the side of road on one of the two foot high kerbs, and Gastro stuck out his hand.

"Taxi!"

In response, four taxis, a mixture of Mitsubishi pickups, American Jeeps, blue and white Peugeot 504s and a mule, all attempted to pull up right next to where Dark Shark and Gastro were perched on the kerb. At the same time a herd of goats, which had been walking across the road close to where they were standing, scattered directly in front of the oncoming mass of metal. Dark Shark and Gastro jumped into the first taxi. After a lengthy argument with the driver about the fare, they shot off at high speed, just missing the remnants of the goats. They drove south in the direction of the lagoon.

The road was busy, cars and trucks zooming along at high speed. The taxi driver 'spoke' to the cars driving past him in the opposite direction, turning his lights off and on in a code, which even after two years, Dark Shark had still not been able to decipher. Leaving the busy evening road, the taxi turned, driving onto a bumpy gravel path, cutting through a large piece of waste ground strewn with discarded rubbish. After another two hundred metres of bumping, the taxi pulled up next to the lagoon just south of Dahab. Gastro was sporting a large round Rasta hat to keep his Medusa locks in one place. He was so tall, his head was right up against the roof of the car. When he clambered out of the taxi, his hat was squashed, like somebody has been sitting on a tea-cosy. They paid the driver and started walking.

The lagoon is just that. It is a large expanse of shallow crystal blue water, almost completely encircled by light brown sand and hundreds of various rocks. Shallow and protected from the north wind, the lagoon is beautiful, quiet, a place to contemplate and reflect. It is also a good place to learn to wind-surf; beginners can practice in the sheltered safety of the lagoon before venturing into the Gulf of Aqaba. When they first begin, windsurfers learn to stand on the board, hold the sail, and ride the wind. They also learn to stop and turn around. This is vital when learning to ride the wind across the sea, on a bit of wood. Sometimes wind surfers fail to understand stopping and turning. These wind surfers have to be returned to Egypt by the stern coastal officers of Saudi Arabia.

Sitting at the side of the Lagoon at night, you notice, apart from the sea and the mountains, the bright twinkling diamonds in the sky - the stars. You have a moved a little distance from the bright, artificial lights of the town and you can now begin to appreciate the amazing, infinite reaches of the night time sky. To marvel; knowing that the light that reaches your eyes, has travelled millions of miles across the universe, has taken millions of years to do so, and that you are staring at the very origins of the universe. The further away you are from the lights of the town, the bigger the stars. To appreciate the stars at night in the deep desert of Sinai is to know wonder and to feel very humble.

Dark Shark and Gastro walked slowly, circling the edge of the Lagoon and looking for a sheltered place to sit and inspect the clues they had discovered. Spying an abandoned building, they ran inside and settled on plastic crates strewn across the floor of the main room. Dark Shark took out the items from his jacket pocket and from his wallet. First he inspected the locker key, before handing it over to Gastro. The key was a standard padlock key, often used by dive centres for lockers. It hung on a small metal ring, a white plastic tag attached to it. The plastic tag had some letters and a number scratched across it: WDD 16

"WDD? What's that?"

"World Domination Divers. They're based at the Stilton. Bent Bob is the head honcho."

"Figures."

Next, Dark Shark carefully inspected the oval shaped photograph. The image was of a young man with blond hair. He had cold, arrogant blue eyes and a straight Roman nose. High cheekbones, thin lips and a jutting chin. He did not look Jewish.

"Gastro, I believe we have found the photograph of Moheet's mysterious former lover."

He passed the photo to Gastro who stared at it intensely.

"He looks Eastern European. Maybe Jewish. Now we just need to find out his name."

"I know it."

Gastro nearly fell of his seat.

"Pray tell!?"

"Whilst you were emailing your Slovakian nymphomaniac, I was asking the receptionist at the hotel some questions. One of those questions was, had anyone stayed in the room with Moheet? He told me that she had indeed had a guests stay over on one of the nights she stayed at the hotel. The receptionist had met the gentleman in question and didn't have very nice words to say about him. Turns out he wasn't such a gentleman after all. The receptionist called him harsh and arrogant. He mentioned that he complained a lot, particularly about the air conditioning.

"Did you get a name?"

"No."

"So we are looking for an Eastern European, possibly Jewish, definitely arrogant and who doesn't handle the heat too well."

"He's not Jewish."

"How do you know that?"

"Trust me, I know."

"Okay. Scratch the Jewish part."

"He has the classic features of an Aryan."

"Where do you think we will find this cold blooded blonde Aryan?"

"At this point I don't know. What I do know, however, is that we should go and sneak a peek at WDD sometime soon and have a look inside locker number sixteen."

"Dr Adel was just a little bit wrong about the abilities of the Shamandura."

"Nah, he knows they're full of shit. He was just saying what he had to. The Shamandura are useless and he knows it."

Deep into their conspiratorial conversation, both Dark Shark and Gastro jumped when Dark Shark's phone suddenly rang. The combination of the abandoned building and the quietness of the desert outside caused the sound of the phone to be amplified many times. Recovering sufficiently, Dark Shark opened his phone.

"Aiwa?"

Speaking in a low tone and sounding half scared to death was Mohammed, the owner of Just Another Dive Centre.

"Dark Shark, you'd better get back down here right now, there is someone here to see you."

"Mershi, Mohammed, on my way. Give me half an hour."

In a nondescript white office with only one window, deep within an unassuming building located in the heart of Dahab's official district, a large man sat behind a desk. He wore a grey suit, white shirt and shiny new black shoes. Inside his jacket, a sub machine gun was clumsily holstered. The get up was standard issue. The man brushed back greasy, black hair with one hand whilst holding a phone to his ear with the other. The conversation was being conducted in Arabic.

"Did he find it, Mohammed?"

"Aiwa Adel-sir."

"Good. I will be watching. You did excellent work, Mohammed. Now, be a good Muslim and get back to your studies."

The man with the grey suit closed the phone. He leaned back in his chair, rested his elbows, put his hands together and brought the tips of his fingers to his lips. He contemplated events as he stared out window.

Dark Shark and Gastro ran to the main road, jumped in a taxi, and sped home. A shower, a coffee and half an hour later, Dark Shark entered Mohammed's office. The owner of the dive centre sat behind his desk looking very nervous. Sitting to one side, crossed legged, hair in a ponytail and aggressively smoking a cigarette, was a woman. Dark Shark stared wide eyed, not believing what he was seeing. Surely, his eyes were playing tricks on him? For the third time in a week, he felt as if he had been hit with a sledge hammer. He legs felt like jelly. He went weak at the knees and he collapsed into a chair. The woman took a long drag on her cigarette, blew the smoke into Dark Shark's face and spoke for the first time.

"Hello, Dark Shark."

Dark Shark breathed out a deep, deep sigh.

# 5

# *Jamila*

Dark Shark sat in the chair and stared at the woman who had come back into his life. He was truly shocked. He never imagined he would ever clap eyes on her again. Sitting in the office here and now, she looked different to the Jamila Dark Shark had known oh so well only a year before. She appeared older, wiser. She was wearing a dark grey suit and a white blouse with black shoes. Jamila looked neat, tidy and officious but she still had the same effervescence that had so stirred Dark Shark's heart. Her eyes still glowed with light and determination. Her brown silky hair, tied up in a familiar pony tail, shone in the pale light of the dive centre's office.

"What are you doing here, Jamila?"

"PADI."

"PADI? What have you got to do with Put Another Dollar In?"

"I work for them. QA."

Dark Shark shivered, but it wasn't cold.

QA (Quality Assurance) was the internal police of PADI. For every diving instructor in the world-even non

-PADI instructors- those two letters sent fear cascading down their spines. Jamila and QA. Dark Shark wondered if things could get any worse. As he was learning fast, of course they could.

"You're under investigation, Dark Shark. QA want a report on this. They sent me here to write it. You are now on indefinite suspension until this matter is cleared up. You're to hand in your card ASAP, is that understood?"

Dark Shark pulled out a cigarette, lit it and smoked intensely.

"You look like shit, Dark Shark."

"It's been a rough week."

There was a heavy, loaded silence.

Mohammed, who until now had decided it was wise to be the forgotten man in the room, took the opportunity of the break in proceedings to offer refreshments.

"I am sure you two would like some tea?"

They both nodded, but said nothing.

Mohammed busied himself making tea. The silence returned to the office, only briefly interrupted by the crashing sounds of crockery being prepared by a nervous Mohammed.

Jamila is the Arabic word for beautiful. She was born in Kuwait to English expatriates, but grew up in South London. Jamila. Dark Shark had met her on his arrival in Dahab. She was working on the counter of The Dive Centre (Mohammed's original enterprise), when Dark Shark arrived from England with two students in tow.

After only two days back in the desert, Dark Shark probably got heat stroke because he had fallen in love. Deeply in love. Dark Shark had met some characters in his time, but he'd never met anyone like Jamila. She drove him nuts. Effervescent, intelligent, sensitive and very funny, Jamila possessed a personality to die for. She was the heart and soul of the dive centre. Although only the counter chick, she ran the show.

Three weeks after his arrival, Dark Shark had organized a trip to the Canyon dive site for his two students. Upon hearing this, Jamila had pleaded to join the trip. Dark Shark agreed and the four of them set off to make the dive. On the beach, as they had assembled their equipment, Dark Shark had briefed them on the course of action to take underwater. However, once on the dive, he had been forced to deviate from the dive plan due to changing conditions. A disorientated Jamila was confused by this and by her lack of experience at the canyon. At the bottom of the thirty metre cave, Dark Shark and Jamila had had a minor argument, conducted only with hand signals. Despite the fact there is only one canyon at the site, Jamila was now insisting that they'd entered the wrong one. She was telling Dark Shark this by forming her hands into a V-shape then rapidly moving her right index finger from side to side. The V-shape symbolized the Canyon; the finger indicated that Dark Shark was wrong. Being in thirty metres of water definitely wasn't helping Jamila's judgment. Dark Shark's two students just hovered above them, their regulators almost falling out of their mouths as they looked on in patient bewilderment. The argument was only settled when Dark Shark shook his head and led the group out of the Canyon and into shallower water.

Now that she was back in blue water and at a shallower depth, the disorientation Jamila was suffering dissipated. She realized her mistake and swam over to Dark Shark to apologize. He just smiled through his regulator and inwardly he was laughing. At that moment an attraction had formed between the two of them. An attraction that Dark Shark believed would last forever. Before finishing the dive, the divers swam to a sandy white slope to make a three-minute safety stop. This stop allowed the divers to further decompress before surfacing, adding a layer of safety to the dive plan.

Despite being under water, the four of them were giggling as they settled down on the slope. The adventures in the canyon had been hilarious. Looking at each under the water, Dark Shark and Jamila felt an overwhelming urge to kiss. Without any signals necessary, they took out their regulators and kissed for as long as they were able before they were forced to breathe again. Jamila later told Dark Shark it was one of her best dives ever.

A month later, Dark Shark had gone into the office to ask Jamila something. Whilst there, Mohammed received a call from a friend of his who just happened to be watching a wild dolphin swimming in the Blue Hole.

Acting on the tip, and after pleading for time off, Dark Shark and Jamila raced to the Blue Hole. Once there, they donned mask, fins and snorkel and joined the exuberant cetacean. The large male bottlenose dolphin, taking time out from its adventures in the open sea, had come into the hole and was happily swimming in playful circles, delighting in the attention it received from its human audience. Watching Jamila in the Blue Hole, swimming with a wild dolphin for two hours, Dark Shark's spirit had soared. There were few spectacles more beautiful to the eyes of the love-struck Dark Shark.

After eight months of working in a dive centre, Jamila had failed to see a turtle. She was about to get her chance. Dark Shark had organized a diving safari on behalf of another dive centre. The boat, a twenty eight metre Live-Aboard, was moored on a 'shamondora' at Travco jetty in Sharm El Sheikh. The venerable old boat was owned by a prominent doctor living in Cairo. For the last five years Dark Shark had regularly run safaris exclusive with the good doctor on the Live- Aboard, so he pushed for the boat to do more than the usual two-day trip. And more it did, visiting Ras Mohammed, the Straits of Tiran and the Thistlegorm – an extraordinary itinerary for a mere two days.

On the very first day, Jamila looked over the rail of the boat, spying a turtle popping its head out of the water. She was thrilled, the only passenger to see the spectacle. It was a good omen; she was to see five more turtles in the next two days. The divers, all professionals, thrilled to the diving. The sheers walls of the Straits of Tiran, the eerie magnificence of the Thistlegorm and the stunning reefs of Ras Mohammed provided a wonderful two days.

It was at Ras Mohammed, swimming between Shark and Yolanda reefs, that the divers witnessed a very rare spectacle indeed. A whale shark arrived. It was the biggest fish in the sea, growing to over eighteen metres in length. The behemoth glided only a metre above Dark Shark's head before swinging out into the open sea. It was one of his best moments underwater ever. At the back of Dark Shark's group, a student had managed to capture the event on camera. Digital cameras were a new phenomenon in the diving world and this student possessed one. The instant image capabilities of the camera allowed the student to immediately swim over and show the image to a delighted Dark Shark. Not only was the shark in the picture, but it also featured Dark Shark celebrating as the behemoth swam above him. The trip had been a major success. The divers were ecstatic and Dark Shark treasured his photo, showing it to everyone in Dahab until they were sick of him and the picture.

It was around this time that Jamila was studying for her Dive Master exams and she asked Dark Shark for help. For his part, he was only too happy to oblige. Sitting on his bed, Dark Shark lectured from his manual, explaining the finer points of Physics, Physiology and

Diving Equipment. Jamila listened eagerly, interrupting to ask questions or seek clarification. She was the ideal student and received 100% in all her exams.

In bed, Dark Shark found that he had never been more comfortable with a woman. Jamila fulfilled all his desires. He felt, for the first time in his life, a very deep, spiritual love. Just as Dark Shark was beginning to think this was it, it wasn't. From the beginning there'd been problems. Jamila, despite having strong feelings for Dark Shark, was frustrated by his moods, which swung wildly. He was emotional, confused and angry. He retreated inside, causing further tensions. Dark Shark was passionate about the environment. He loved Sinai and the Red Sea. He was continually upset by the damage being done in the name of tourist dollars.

Being emotional and strung out on spliffs, he constantly harangued against the world, projecting his anger on everyone and everything. Jamila, fun loving, sociable and hardworking, couldn't understand his behaviour. Eventually after many heated arguments she'd left Dahab, returning to England and the comfort of her parents' home on the South Coast. Dark Shark was devastated. During her time, Jamila had made a lasting impression on the people of Dahab, especially the Bedouin, and especially on him.

She loved the Bedouin kids, spending hours playing and laughing with them, teaching them English and helping them make bracelets and necklaces. She could often be seen riding a pickup or jeep, covered with a whole gaggle of Bedouin kids, all shouting, laughing, hooting, and hanging on for dear life. Seeing Jamila on top of the jeep with the Bedouin kids was one of the treasures of the Sinai, comparable to the sea and the desert. Even a year after Jamila had left Dahab, the Bedouin girls still attacked Dark Shark from time to time with shouts of:

"Where's Jamila!? Where's Jamila!? Where's Jamila!?"

With Jamila gone, the desert seemed a truly barren place to Dark Shark. Despite Jamila coming to see him at the end, Dark Shark decided to make sure she never contacted him again. He needed to move on with his life, to try to forget her. Being emotionally challenged, he emailed her two months after her departure, telling her he now hated her. And that was that. Dark Shark continued on a downward slope and it was only Harmonica who had jumped in, saving his hide. She provided him with work and support. Dark Shark had been ready to hang up his regs until Harmonica had given him a reason not to.

For months he languished in a no man's land of depression. Finally after much effort on the part of his friends, he began to slowly move past his failed relationship. He began enjoying his work again and organized more safaris. He was more active. Life, however, is not called a roller coaster without reason. Just as he was beginning to get it back on track, Jamila was here to put a bloody great spanner in the works.

All the effort Dark Shark had put in trying to forget her evaporated like so much steam into the cold night air.

"There is something I don't understand, Jamila."

"Go on."

"The autopsy on my student Moheet concluded that she died from drowning. The coroner returned a verdict of accidental death. As far as the Shamandura is concerned the case is closed. Why is PADI still investigating this at great cost?"

"PADI investigates every diver's death, especially if the diver was on a PADI course at the time. In this case, however, we at QA do not believe Moheet's death was accidental. We have information that suggests otherwise."

"What information? And why hasn't it been passed on to the Shamandura?"

"This conversation is for another time. Right now, I am beat. I've been travelling for sixteen hours and badly need some shut eye."

She stubbed out her cigarette and tightened the knot in her ponytail. Dark Shark imagined a noose being tightened around his neck. Tea was served by Mohammed and the three of them drank in silence. None of them wanted to continue with this meeting any longer than they had to. As soon as she finished her tea, Jamila thanked Mohammed and without more than a cursory look at Dark Shark, bid them goodnight. Dark Shark did the same and soon was back in his house and in the company of friends.

Back in his home, Bob Marley sang No Woman, No Cry. Gastro was sat on the cushions staring at the photo of Moheet. From time to time he got up, went over to Dark Shark's laptop and fiddled with Adobe Photoshop Ver.7. Yanni Mechanicy was Dark Shark's landlord and had come to lend moral support. He busied himself with making tea and asking Gastro to roll a joint. Dark Shark was in the toilet.

Finishing his business, he flushed the chain. A low rumble started in the depths of the toilet. The rumble became a whine then turned into a full blooded scream, the shrill sound resembling a cat being shafted on a Dahab roof in the middle of the night. The scream lasted a good six minutes before finally dying down to a barely audible gurgle. Dark Shark came out of the toilet and re-joined his guests. Without looking up from the photo of Moheet, Gastro spoke first.

"Who was at the centre?"

"Jamila."

Gastro, who had just taken a large drag from a spliff, spluttered and choked, the spliff flew out of his hand and landed in Yanni Mechanicy's lap.

"Sucran a man."

Yanni calmly picked up the joint and inhaled.

"She's working for QA at PADI. She's here to investigate Moheet's death and I am suspended until the investigation is over."

Both Gastro and Yanni took in a deep breath. Yanni exhaled blue smoke and Gastro spat a tooth onto the floor.

"Oi vay."

Dark Shark's clam shell blared its polyphonic nonsense.

"Dark Shark, its Jamila. You and Gastro get your shit together and meet me at Just Another Dive Centre tomorrow morning at six. We're diving the Blue Hole. Don't be late."

Dark Shark closed his clam shell, closed his eyes, and passed on the message to Gastro who again responded with an:

"Oi Vay"

Yanni Mechanici smiled and mentally thanked Allah for blessing him with so much entertainment, not to mention money, from Europe. Gastro continued:

"Dr Adel told you not to… "

Dark Shark cut him off with a tired wave of his hand.

"I know what Dr Adel said. But if I don't co-operate with Jamila, I don't think I am going to have a career to go back to in a month."

"True"

"Guys, it's time to crash. It's been a long day and I have a feeling tomorrow is going to be even longer."

With slow, stoned movements Gastro and Yanni got their things together and said their goodbyes. That night, Dark Shark slept a troubled sleep. Tossing and turning, dark dreams returned to haunt him. He slept sideways on his bed, his arms flat out and his head propped against the wall. He dribbled slowly from the side of his mouth. The nightmares got worse. In his mind's eye, he was swimming in the Blue Hole with Jamila and the wild dolphin. Jamila was concentrating on the dolphin and didn't notice the trouble her companion was in. Dark Shark was drowning. He was fighting to stay up, swimming furiously only to be inexorably dragged down. He tried to scream but the words never came.

"Jamila! Jamila!"

Water entered his lungs, he spluttered and coughed. Struggling, he kicked with legs and arms against an unseen force, but to no avail. He sunk, pulled under by the incredible strength of invisible hands. He was being dragged down. Down, down, down… to the very bottom of the Blue Hole.

# 6

## *Blue Hole*

Dahab was still cold and dark when Dark Shark and Gastro stumbled into Just Another Dive Centre at six o'clock the following morning. The dive centre was empty except for Jamila. She had already organized her equipment and was now smoking a cigarette and drinking a coffee. She had changed from her office clothes and was back in Dahab mode. She wore beige cargo pants, brown sandals, blue t-shirt and a dark green hooded top. She looked tired and haggard, but Dark Shark recognized immediately the woman he fallen in love with so long ago. Jamila dispensed with the niceties and got down to business.

"We are going to the Blue Hole to look for clues into the death of Moheet. She dived there only the day before starting the course with Dark Shark."

Dark Shark was stunned.

"How could she dive the Blue Hole? She wasn't even a diver!"

"Her mother was a diving instructor and she taught Moheet many years ago."

"Then why... ?"

Jamila cut him off before he could finish his question.

"That's one of the things we are going to find out. After your adventures at the Eel Garden, I figure that the next logical place to start is at the Blue Hole. Hello Gastro, it's been a long time."

"It's great to see you again Jamila. Welcome back to the 'Hab. How are you?"

"Frazzled. I need at least four more coffees."

They hugged. During Jamila's time in Dahab, she and Gastro had become good friends. Despite all that had happened between her and Dark Shark, the bond with Gastro remained strong. With equipment preparations over, Mohammed the driver turned up in his American Jeep. Dark Shark, Jamila, and Gastro loaded the Jeep with tanks, an Oxygen bottle, a first aid kit, a set of spares, and their own equipment. With Dark Shark sitting up front, Gastro and Jamila in the back and with all of them holding on, the Jeep lurched forward and the journey to the Blue Hole began. The Jeep pulled out of Just Another Dive Centre, drove fifteen meters down the road and spluttered to a halt. Mohammed the driver jumped out of the Jeep, apologizing profusely. The Jeep had run out of gas. Dark Shark sighed. Mohammed flagged down a passing pickup which stopped next to the Jeep. After a heated debate between the two drivers, and an exchange of money, Mohammed pulled out a one foot length of rubber piping and sucked out enough gas from the pickup to get the divers to the Blue Hole.

Located twelve kilometres north of Dahab, the Blue Hole was a wonder of nature. A giant hole in the reef, dropping to over one hundred and forty metres straight down, the Blue Hole had become one of the most famous dive sites in the world. The world famous reputation of the dive site was not built on its beauty, however, but on something far more sinister. The Blue Hole was a study in diver stupidity. Over the years, dozens of divers had perished in its forbidding depths. The reason is that at fifty six metres, a spectacular arch could be seen in the reef wall, the beginning of a cut in the reef that extends to the open sea. Diving through the arch was to risk the very edge of recreational limits. Many divers had tragically paid the ultimate price for going over the edge. When Dark Shark had first arrived in Dahab, the road to the Blue Hole was no more than a dirt track. Tourists bounced along its length and the journey was an adventure in itself. But now asphalt had been laid and the journey was not quite as exciting.

The road wound its way north, hugging the harsh Sinai Mountains and following the spectacular coast of the Gulf of Aqaba. All along the road to the Blue Hole, huge, ugly, sprawling hotels had sprung up. Each hotel sat in the middle of a five hectare plot of land. Each plot of land hugged the coast, attempting to claim as much of the beach as possible. Building such vast concrete nightmares changed the feeling of the place.

They destroyed the ambience of a unique environment. The whole point of the Sinai, the reason for its fame, was the starkness, the emptiness and the silence. By building these monstrosities, the desert's beauty had gone forever. Even worse than this, was the damage inflicted on the coral reefs by having building sites within such close proximity. Pollution, light and noise were all consequences of the development and were all detrimental to a unique and fragile eco-system. Most humans are stupid enough to believe that developments such as these are positive. That they represent change and progress. Dark Shark was always being told that change and progress were inevitable. Dark Shark thought the only thing inevitable was that some rich fucker always got their own way - while the environment just got in the way.

At the end of the Blue Hole road, just before the Hole itself, the road went up, took a sharp left and passed through an extremely narrow crack in the rock, barely wide enough for the jeep. Although he had executed this manoeuvre thousands of times, Mohammed still slowed the jeep almost to a halt. He gunned the throttle gently and inched the heavily loaded vehicle through the narrow gap in the rock. The jeep made it, but not before taking a couple of scraps and losing some paint work. Mohammed swore in Arabic and continued down the other side. The road swung down and to right carried on for another one hundred metres and then shuddered to an inelegant stop.

They were at the Blue Hole. They jumped out, stretched their legs and looked around. On their right hand side was the Hole itself. In the grey early morning light, the Hole seemed more like an abyss. It was huge, over one hundred metres across and one hundred and forty metres straight down. Around the Hole, the shallow water covering the reef plate was grey-green in colour. In front of them, huge mountains came right down to the water's edge. The road hadn't just stopped, it had finished entirely. The mountains came down so close to the water, a road was impossible. The only way to continue was on a camel or on foot. On the left hand side of the road was a string of restaurants. At such an early hour, they were empty except for the staff that lived there. The restaurants resembled Bedouin hooshas but they were not. The waiters were mostly Egyptians who had emigrated to Dahab looking for work. Their wages were so low and they were so far from home, it made sense for them to sleep at the restaurant they worked in. Most of the workers were from Cairo or Luxor and had family back there.

They would work for weeks on end without a break then take time off and visit their families. They had little opportunity to spend the money they earned in Dahab and it was expected that they save most of it for their wives and children back in Egypt. In each of the restaurants, the waiters were waking up. Drawing back blankets, rubbing sleep from their eyes and making coffee, they were getting ready for another day of making money. Seven days a week, the Blue Hole was a place of frenetic activity. Camels and Bedouin kids, snorkelers from Sharm El Sheikh, divers from Dahab, jeeps and pickups loaded with equipment, Egyptian waiters running around shouting and tourist police trying in vain to keep everything orderly. At this time, however, the Blue Hole was very quiet, almost eerie. As the three divers fixed their equipment, the sun popped up over the mountains of Saudi Arabia on the other side of the Gulf of Aqaba.

Slowly, light filled their world and the warmth crept back into their bones. There was very little wind; the sea was glass and the temperature perfect at thirty degrees. Jamila took charge.

"We'll go in at the Bells, swim along the reef wall and finish by swimming across the top of the Hole. Mohammed will pick us up. Let's stay shallow. The maximum depth will be thirty metres. There's no reason to go deeper. We need to conserve our air supply and make sure we have the time to search properly for clues."

The Bells is a twenty eight metre, three-sided shaft, cut into the reef. It is located twenty metres north of the Blue Hole and can only be accessed by traipsing over a small outcrop of rock. Steps had been cut into the rock to make the passage more accessible. The outcrop was the base of a mountain. Just before the steps, were fixed plaques bearing the names of dead divers. The plaques told the grisly stories of those who'd perished in the depths of the Blue Hole. Dark Shark and Gastro followed a sprightly Jamila over the rocky outcrop and down to a small hole, no more than a meter across that was the entrance to the Bells shaft.

"Jesus, it was only a year ago I was taking her diving."

Dark Shark thought again how Jamila had changed during the last year. She was more composed, more mature, but she was still Jamila, even if she now got paid by QA. Gastro wondered if Shanti had got it together to replenish the stocks of water in Slow Down. Jamila wasn't thinking about anything except the task at hand. Standing on a rock at the entrance to the shaft, Dark Shark put on his mask, inserted his regulator into his mouth, held onto his weight belt and stepped off the rock.

He landed with a splash, went down half a meter and then popped back up to the surface. Gastro and Jamila followed suit. When all three were in the hole, they deflated their BCD jackets and descended into the gloom below. The Bells shaft was still dark, the morning sun not yet high enough to completely penetrate its close confines. Shoals of tiny transparent glass fish, with their big bulbous eyes, scattered past the divers' field of vision, greatly disturbed by the intrusion of the clumsy aliens. Bubbles from the divers' regulators slowly floated up before popping at the surface. Every meter or so, they equalized their ears to the increasing pressure in the water.

Sea urchins, their brittle black spikes sticking out in dangerous balls, dotted the walls of the shaft. Patches of red algae spread across the wall, a living patchwork of fish food. There was not enough room in the shaft to go down in a group, so they descended one by one and upright. Dark Shark went first. Jamila may have taken control, but old habits die hard and he was determined to lead the dive. Occasionally he would look up and check on his fellow aquanauts, but they were comfortable and the descent was completed without incident. At 26m the shaft closed to four sides. The divers had to squeeze through the remaining two metres and emerge…

Into the deep, deep, blue of the early morning Red Sea. After the gloomy constraints of the shaft, they were bombarded with light, colour and space. The divers were on a sheer wall, stretching down to an invisible bottom. An eagle ray glided past. It boasted a two metre wingspan, brown and white dots on its wings and a three metre whip like tail which it trailed behind in an elegant arc. Schools of jacks and snappers swam past the divers, oblivious to their presence. With their backs to the wall, the divers could see nothing but blue.

Dark Shark, Jamila and Gastro inflated their BCDs approximately half full. At this depth, they needed plenty more air to keep them stable. With Dark Shark in front, Jamila and Gastro followed behind swimming side by side. The group swam horizontally, streamlining their body positions to reduce drag. They turned right and swam directly underneath a massive over-hang of coral.

Under the coral, the water was dark blue, almost brown, murky and ominous. Huge white Gorgonian corals adorned the roof of the over-hang, their delicate white branches forming huge, intricate fans. Orange, purple and white sea stars intermingled with the Gorgonias. Glass fish and Klezinger's wrasses fought amongst the fans and corals. A large red tube coral protruded upside down, two feet from the ceiling. The divers carried on past, their bubbles forming pools of air on the ceiling of the dark over-hang.

Passing into the blue again, Dark Shark began slowly swimming up diagonally. All three divers changed positions slightly, expelling air. The water pressure was now decreasing and less air was needed. At fifteen metres Dark Shark levelled out and kept swimming. Behind him, Jamila and Gastro followed. All three were in different worlds. The inability to speak forced the divers to concentrate on their own thoughts and emotions. Dark Shark was thinking that Jamila was beautiful and with a sigh, he knew he still loved her. Jamila, despite the last email, was glad to see Dark Shark and, annoyingly, realized she still felt something. She promised herself nothing would happen again between them. Gastro wandered if his remaining teeth were enough to keep the regulator in his mouth. He kept his hand on it, just in case.

The sea had turned a much lighter and brighter blue. The early morning sunlight streamed down, lighting up the bright colours of the reef wall. At this depth the water absorbed less light, consequently the spectrum of colours on show increased. Because of the increase in light, the coral reef changed at this depth. The colours become more radiant; the corals basked in the warm rays of the desert sun. Black fire corals, bright green cabbage corals and pale blue Gorgonias adorned the reef wall. Luminous blue, pink and purple soft corals swayed gently in the slight current. Brightly coloured orange fairy basslets formed spectacular clouds around coral pinnacles. Red Sea coral grouper, decorated with bright blue spots, stalked the corals, waiting for the chance to snatch an easy meal. Large round beams of sunlight danced across the reef wall, like spotlights on a stage. Schools of silversides shimmered, as they darted around, forming large balls to protect themselves from being hounded by ravenous jacks. The predators herded the silversides onto the reef, making it easier to pick off individuals.

A nocturnal Red Sea octopus, a very clever, powerful hunter, lurked deep inside a crevice. The nocturnal animal only emerged at night to track down its unfortunate victims. Not surprisingly, Dark Shark's all-time favourite TV was the BBC's epic natural history series, the Blue Planet. The beauty of the reefs he was once again witnessing reminded him of an eloquent dissertation given by David Attenborough on the life of a coral reef.

"In all the seas of the world, the warm waters of the tropics contain the richest and most colourful communities. They may seem like underwater paradise, but they are perpetual battlegrounds for space. Even the corals have to fight for it. In this crowded, frenetic community every individual has to find its own place, its own way of surviving. If a coral larva settles on a suitable spot and survives, a new reef will be founded. In just a few days the larva changes form, and becomes a polyp, similar to a sea anemone. Identical copies bud off, gradually a colony develops. Each polyp surrounds itself with a hard skeleton, and from this solid base begins to grow. It increases in length by an impressive fifteen centimetres a year. A mature reef can be many thousands of years old. Corals provide the foundation on which the entire reef community relies. Some organisms, like the multi-coloured Christmas tree worm, actually live within the coral. Others climb out, away from the reef, to filter their food from the water. As the community grows, intimate relationships are formed, and different creatures become increasingly dependent on one another. The extraordinary maze of the reef is built, layer upon layer, of millions and millions of individual animals, polyps. Each polyp's flesh is supported by the limestone skeleton.

Below the gut is where most of the growth occurs. Here the living tissue, deposits an intricate lattice of limestone, beneath that, the limestone skeleton is bare, having been vacated by the living coral tissues. This is the hard structure that forms the foundation of the reef, and a single reef can extend for many miles. Coral reefs are only found in the clear, warm, shallow waters of the tropics. Sunlight is vital to them, even though they're animals, because inside each one of them live millions of tiny single cell-algae, plants. All plants need sunlight to photosynthesize sugars.

Ninety five per cent of the food eaten by the coral is provided by the algae. Without them the reef would not exist. Like any other plant, algae, need just the right amount of light, not too much, not too little. The corals regulate that with pigments we can only see when they are illuminated under ultra violet light. Most corals, for their protection, spend the day withdrawn into their stony fortresses, but even then they are not safe from the jaws of butterfly fish and others.

At night, the corals take in water, expand their tentacles and emerge to feed. They collect plankton. Each tentacle has batteries of stinging cells, which fire on contact. Once the prey is caught, it is passed down to the polyp's mouth. It is at night when the polyps are extended, that they add to the limestone foundations beneath them. Inevitably, the corals begin to overgrow each other, and that means trouble. When neighbours get to close, they detect one another, chemically. The polyps extrude their guts, and simply digest their rivals alive.

A no-man's land, a band of white skeleton, is the only

evidence of the night's border dispute. Coral reefs can be home to astounding numbers of fish. Here you can find the smallest and the largest fish in the sea. Whale sharks are only visitors; when currents bring nutrient rich water up from the deep, they come in to feed. Even animals that spend much of their time traveling the open ocean return to the reef for a clean. Turtles and sharks take advantage of the cleaning stations on the reef, allowing the reef's inhabitants to pick off fungal infections. In the entire world, the bio-diversity of a coral reef is matched only by the tropical rainforests."

In 2004 President George W. Bush refused to sign the United States' inclusion into the Kyoto Protocol. This is very sad, because in 2005, the world's foremost marine biologists declared that within thirty years, all the corals in the world will cease to exist. And the overwhelming, number one reason for the apocalypse was global warming. The build-up of harmful emissions in the atmosphere is heating the planet. As a result the world's oceans are warming and becoming more acidic. The polar caps are melting. The change in conditions is killing the coral reefs of the world. America is the overwhelming, number one contributor to global warming, with twenty five per cent of the total world output of harmful emissions. A large percentage of these emissions come from cars. So, it all makes sense, because Bush is an oilman. Dark Shark wondered what America would think if somebody mentioned to them, that they would all cease to exist in thirty years' time.

Nevertheless, despite the looming apocalypse, Dark Shark remained hopeful, which is why he still took people diving. He wanted to show as many people as possible the beauty of the reefs. His hope was that inspired by their experiences in the Sinai, they would one day make decisions that benefited the environment.

Throughout the dive, the marine detectives had searched the sandy slope for clues. Up until now they had found nothing out of the ordinary. There was plenty of man-made rubbish in the water, but that was nothing unusual. Dark Shark, Jamila and Gastro swam on, kicking long, slow kicks, regulating their breathing with long, slow breaths. After a few minutes Dark Shark spotted something large and torpedo shaped lying on the sand. He swam closer, puzzled. At first, he thought it must be a man-made object, so unusual was it to see something so large on the sand. It was at least two meters long.

Beckoning for the others to follow, he increased his speed. Gastro and Jamila followed behind, struggling to keep up with Dark Shark's powerful fin kicks. At the same time, all three of them realized that there were many of the same objects. Dozens, no hundreds, of large torpedo shaped objects littered the sand as far as the eye could see. They swept south, they went north and they disappeared down the slope to the depths. Dark Shark reached the object he'd spotted first. With a sinking heart, he knew instinctively what it was, but prayed he was wrong. His prayer was not answered. Lying on the sand was a dead white tip reef shark.

It was similar to the one he and Moheet had swum with at the Light house. The shark was not only dead. Each of its fins had been hacked off. The shark was a female. She would never give birth, never reproduce her own species. Dark Shark was crushed. He was beside himself with rage. He had never felt so outraged in his whole life. He breathed out, dropped down and knelt by the corpse of the finned shark. Gastro and Jamila reached him. Dark Shark could hear Gastro gasp and Jamila scream as they realized what they were looking at.

Dark Shark prodded the body of the shark. Gingerly he picked it up. The mouth, located under the head, was slack jawed and he could clearly see the magnificent rows of teeth. Where the fins should have been, were crude slash marks made by a deadly blade. The blood had long ago left the writhing creature, its heart beat forcing its precious life force into the surrounding water. Without looking up from the shark, Dark Shark knew that all the other objects littering the slope were also sharks and that they too had suffered the same fate. They had come here to look for clues and had stumbled onto a massacre. The horror of what they were witnessing could not be comprehended. It was simply impossible to take in. Never before had they seen such cruelty and such waste.

For a long time, Dark Shark knelt on the sandy slope, holding the body of the shark. When he had been hooked at the Eel Garden, Dark Shark's friend had cut him loose. A doctor had removed the hook and sown him back up. He had survived the ordeal. No one had come to help this animal. No one had cut her free. Dark Shark's anger mounted. He clenched his fists and bit deep into his regulator, breaking the mouthpiece. He swore revenge. He promised himself and the shark in his hands, that whoever had done this was going to pay the price. He made a pact with himself that he would never again rest until the brutal practice of finning sharks had become nothing more than a tragic footnote in the pages of history.

After what seemed an eternity, Jamila placed a hand on Dark Shark's shoulder. He looked up at her, his eyes filled with tears. She pointed to her gauge and indicated it was time for them to go up. Dark Shark nodded and put the shark down again on the slope. Slowly, the three divers made their way across the top of the Blue Hole and back to the beach. They exited the water and trudged over to the jeep and Mohammed the driver. At first he smiled when he saw his divers coming back, but when he saw the look on their faces, his smile was wiped from his face. They stripped their equipment down and took off their wetsuits in silence. Gastro ordered coffee for all of them. Dark Shark spoke to Jamila.

"Jay, you'd better call Adel of the Shamandura and inform him of what we have just seen."

The tension that had existed between Dark Shark and Jamila had evaporated. The terrible vision they had experienced together had put their personal troubles into perspective. Their differences no longer seemed important. All that mattered now was the plight of the sharks.

"I know. I will do it now."

Whilst she was calling Adel, Dark Shark flipped open his clamshell and called Just Another Dive Centre. Mohammed answered the phone in his office.

"Mohammed, its Dark Shark."

He couldn't hide the emotion in his voice. Mohammed picked up on it immediately.

"Dark Shark, you finished the dive already? What's up? Why do you sound like that? What happened?"

"We found dead sharks, Mohammed. Hundreds of dead sharks. They have no fins."

Back in his office at the dive centre, Mohammed dropped the phone and began shaking.

"Mohammed, are you there?"

Mohammed picked up the receiver. He was trembling from head to toe.

"Walla-he this is very bad... mishkela, kateer ka-teer..."

"It's the worst thing I have ever seen Mohammed. There is a major shark finning operation going on in

Dahab and it's been going on right under our noses."

Mohammed was beside himself.

"Why are they doing this? They are fucking mad! They are killing the sharks and destroying the sea! How stupid can anyone be?!"

"I know, Mohammed, I know."

"Walla-he Dark Shark, this has to be stopped. It has to be stopped now. What has happened to Dahab? First Moheet and now this. It's madness, I tell you, madness!"

Mohammed's description was apt. It was sheer madness.

"Listen, Mohammed. Jamila is right now calling Adel of the Shamandura. I need you to call all the dive centres in Dahab. Speak to all the owners. We need to first of all warn them about what is going on. Tourists cannot be allowed to dive where there are finned sharks. It would kill the industry. Secondly, we need to try to find out if any of the dive centres have any information about what is going on. Somebody in this town knows something. Before we leave here, we will speak to the waiters and ask them some questions."

"Mershi, Dark Shark, mershi. I will do as you ask."

"Thank you Mohammed. We should be back within the hour."

"Insha'allah."

"Aye, Insha'allah."

Closing his phone, Dark Shark turned his attention back to Jamila who was also finishing her conversation with Adel.

"What did Adel say?"

"He's in Cairo. He says he is going to jump on a plane and come down here with a specialist team. It will take him a few hours to get here. He also says we are not to go too far away. He wants to ask us some questions later."

"Great. Just what we need. Interrogation by the Shamandura."

"It was to be expected. You know that. What are we going to do now?"

"We need to talk to the waiters. We need to find out if they saw any boats during the night. "

Dark Shark explained his plan to Gastro who had returned with the coffees. They drank in silence, and then proceeded to visit all the restaurants one by one. Their efforts were in vain. None of the waiters had seen anything during the night. To a man they were all sleeping.

Dark Shark couldn't believe that one or more shark fishing boats had pulled up off the beach of the Blue Hole dive site, finned hundreds of sharks and departed without anyone being none the wiser. Dark Shark didn't know whether to believe all that he was told by the waiters, but he had little choice in the matter. The news of the dead sharks brought great consternation to the waiters who formed agitated groups to discuss the news.

Many of them donned mask, fins and snorkels before plunging in to see for themselves. Dark Shark decided no more could be done and it was time to leave. As far as he was concerned, they couldn't get out of there quickly enough. He didn't like the Blue Hole at the best of times, and this was most definitely the worst of times. Loading the equipment back into the Jeep, the intrepid adventurers began their journey home. Not a word was spoken the entire way back. All three were thinking about the vision of horror on the slopes of the Blue Hole.

Half an hour later, Mohammed's Jeep pulled into Just Another Dive Centre. Leaving the equipment to the staff, Dark Shark, Gastro and Jamila strode briskly into Mohammed's office. Inside, Sally was sitting on a chair and looking nervous. Mohammed was behind his desk and on the phone. Looking up, he waved the gang to sit down before returning to his conversation.

"Yes, that's right… at the Blue Hole…yes… hundreds… all finned. I have no idea. I will talk to him now… yes… he's just walked in… Mershi, we will do that… yes… okay… good… Salaam for now."

Mohammed slammed the phone down.

"The town is in uproar. All hell is breaking loose, my friends."

"Fill us in."

"Mershi. As you know the Shamandura is on its way. They plan to check all the dive sites for shark carcasses. They also plan to inspect every boat along this part of the coast. The Egyptian diving federation has banned all diving for now. I have spoken to more than thirty dive centres since I got the call from Dark Shark. They are going to ask around and collate information. Anything interesting comes up, they will let me know. The whole town is up in arms and is outraged."

"They should be."

"Walla-he Dark Shark, this news is so bad. Not only are they killing the sea, they will kill us too, walla-he"

"Yep. When sharks are killed in such numbers, the eco-system that relies on them to keep the balance also dies. When that happens we can all pack up and go home."

"This is my home, Dark Shark. I don't have anywhere else to go, habibe."

"I was speaking figuratively, Mohammed. I also don't have anywhere to go. This too, is my home."

A silence followed this brief exchange as the occupants of the office took in the enormity of the situation. It was Gastro who spoke next.

"Dark Shark, show Jamila the photo and the key."

Jamila was perplexed.

"What key? What photo?"

Instead of answering, Dark Shark pulled his wallet out and handed Jamila the picture of Nemo he had found in the Forty Thieves hotel.

She took the photo and stared at it.

"Nemo! This is a picture of Nemo!"

Dark Shark was stunned.

"You know him!?"

"Yes. I know him. He owns a dive centre in Sharm el

Sheikh. Why have you got a photo of him and where did you get it from?"

"He is Moheet's ex-boyfriend."

"What? How do you know that?"

Dark reached into a bag and produced Moheet's locket on a gold chain.

"From this… "

He gave her the locket. Jamila opened it and saw the oval picture of Moheet. She took the photo of Nemo and placed it in the empty compartment. It was a perfect fit.

"They were lovers."

"Yes."

"How did…?"

"Gastro and I went for a dive at the Eel Garden to look for clues. You know about my subsequent attachment to a shark hook. Just before that unfortunate incident occurred, I'd found Moheet's locket and chain buried in the sand which I squirreled away in my BCD pocket. Later in the hospital, Gastro and I opened the locket. We found, as you did, Moheet's photo in one compartment but that the other one was empty. We now knew that Moheet had had a lover and that it was important to find out who he was. Yesterday, when I checked out of the hospital, we checked Moheet's hotel room at the Forty Thieves and I found the photo of Nemo under the dust sheet on the floor of the wardrobe."

"Nemo… we'll I'll be damned."

"Who is he?"

"I know little of him. All I know is that he is a dive centre owner and that he is an Austrian."

"Does he have a surname?"

"I don't know. I will check back with the QA office."

"Try to find out his address too."

"I can't access personal details, Dark Shark, you know that."

"Yeah, right."

"I will see what I can do."

"Please. As much information as you can find on this guy would be useful. We need to find out what his game is."

"What about this key?"

"Sally found a WDD locker key in the dive centre a couple of days ago. Although she asked everyone if it belonged to anyone, she drew a blank. It's possible the key belonged to Moheet. Gastro and I are going to try to find out."

"How are you going to do that?"

"We're gonna check it out later this evening"

"The hell you are, Dark Shark. WDD and the Stilton Hotel are big players in the diving world. Bent Bob hates you and he's definitely not going to let you go snooping around in his lockers."

"Which is why we're going after WDD is closed."

"Dark Shark, I'm gonna make sure you never work in this town again!"

"Does that mean you're not coming with us?"

"There are two investigations going on, Dark Shark, the one conducted by the Shamandura and mine. You have nothing to do with this and neither does WDD or the Stilton Hotel. Why do you always see enemies and conspiracies?"

"You're wrong, Jay. Moheet was my student and she came to me for a reason. I'm gonna find out what that reason was."

Jamila became agitated.

"I'm investigating it, for fucks sake!"

"So investigate, Jay, come with us."

Jamila shook her head slowly and sighed.

"You haven't changed, Dark Shark, you're still an asshole."

Dark Shark smiled inside, knowing she would go with them. Mohammed chuckled behind his desk; this was just like the old days.

"How did you know Moheet was already a diver?"

"PADI. Whenever there is an accident or a fatality during a diving course, its standard procedure for the Egyptian Authorities to contact PADI. As soon as PADI learned of Moheet's death, they put me in charge of the investigation. One of the first things I did was check Moheet's name on our database. The computer returned some interesting results. Apparently, she was already certified as a Dive Master. Her mother's name is on the application as the certifying instructor. I jumped on the first flight out here. On my arrival, using a photo

I had of Moheet from our database, I started asking the taxi drivers at the Lighthouse some questions. A young Bedouin told me he had taken two divers to the Blue Hole last Sunday, and one of them was the young woman in my photo. I'd got lucky. She'd started the Open Water course with you on the Monday and was found at the Eel Garden on Wednesday morning. That same evening I called most of the dive centres in Dahab, though many of the managers had already left. When I called Mohammed, I learnt the strange news that she had started a course with you."

"But why did she start the course with me, why was she diving in the Blue Hole, who is finning sharks and what is the connection between Moheet and the sharks?"

No one said anything. None of them had answers to Dark Shark's questions. The phone on Mohammed's desk rang and he picked it up.

"Aiwa? Salaam. Mershi… aiwa… aiwa... mershi… aiwa… mershi."

Mohammed replaced the handset on the receiver.

"That was Adel from the Shamandura. He has been delayed and won't be arriving until tomorrow morning. He wants us all to be here at ten o'clock on the dot."

"Let's get some lunch. Then I need to sleep. This evening we go to the Stilton Hotel. Can you arrange transportation, Mohammed?"

"Of course Dark Shark. Is not the Pope Catholic?"

Dark Shark, Jamila and Gastro walked out onto the

bay. They had decided to eat in the Wadi at Utopia dive centre. The food was good and Jamila wanted to catch up with Heidi and Peter. The bay was deathly quiet. The diving had been forced to stop and it was as if this ban had extended to all aspects of life in the town. Shops were closed. Bars were shut. Only internet cafes seemed to be open. At the Lighthouse dive site, they saw a group of people standing watching the sea just off the reef. A boat was out there and divers were falling over the side. The boat belonged to the Egyptian Navy and the divers were checking for dead sharks along the bottom. Pausing to watch for a moment, the three friends carried on towards Utopia.

As they did so they were approached by Frank Zappa. He had a finger in one ear and was staring straight ahead. He was stumbling a bit, listing from side to side. Frank hadn't just come ashore and he wasn't drunk. He was just finding it difficult to balance. Frank Zappa was a typical Dahab character; he'd arrived six months ago and had made an immediate impact, becoming an integral feature of daily life on the bay. He was a much loved figure, lolling along, not remembering why he'd left A to get to B. In his late 40s/early 50s, he had long, manky brown hair, which frizzed out in all directions.

Frank was thin and gangly, always smoking and always smiling. He was smiling now as he passed by. He was wearing black ripped jeans and a black and white faded Frank Zappa t-shirt he'd bought at a concert way back in '73. He'd fallen in love with it, never again to wear another. Frank Zappa had tattoos in places most people don't have places. To say he'd been around was like saying a cube is a square. It's true, but a cube is so much more than a square and Frank had been more than around, he'd been an interstellar wanderer.

Frank was the archetypal rock fan, attending thousands of concerts in his time. Over the years, his ears (and his balance) had taken a pounding from the volume. Occasional mishaps, such as the time back in '86, didn't help. He'd gotten so drunk, he'd fallen asleep with his head inside a bass bin during a Motorhead gig at the Hammersmith Odeon. Motorhead are in the Guinness Book of Records for being the loudest rock band in the world. When Frank woke up later that night, he had ringing in his ears which had never quite left.

"Hey, Frank, what's up?"

Frank listed to the left, put his right hand down the front of his jeans and peered down. He giggled.

"Nothing yet... heh, heh... maybe when I meet that Spanish girl later...Yeah, man...she's foxy, man... big brown eyes, big brown tits....Yeah... cooool man... Yeah... I gotta go man... going to my camp...see you foxes later... "

Frank rolled down the bay, smiling and waving to the waiters who were standing outside the restaurants and imploring what few tourists there were to enter their establishments. They didn't bother with Frank though.

Just before they entered Utopia, Dark Shark informed Gastro and Jamila that he was going to talk to the Navy.

"Please order some food for me. I'll be back pronto."

On entering Utopia, Gastro went to find a good place to sit, whilst Jamila took the opportunity to catch up with the dive centre's owner. Shwaya Shwaya was in his office, sitting behind his desk.

"Salaam, Salaam, Shwaya, Shwaya."

"Walla, Salaam Alechem, walla-he, Jamila, you are back!"

"Aiwa. How are you?"

Shwaya Shwaya knew Jamila from her first time in Dahab, and although not close, the two of them had always liked each other.

"What brings you back to Dahab, Jamila?"

"Work… PADI. I work for PADI now."

"In England?"

"Aiwa."

"Meier, meier, and how is the life in cold England?"

"It's good, I miss Dahab, but I have a good job and a nice house in Bristol."

"Quayas."

"What about you, Shwaya Shwaya? How is family, business and life in the desert?"

"Hamdul'allah, the life is good, the family healthy, hamdul'allah, but we are finding business is a little difficult right now… money is tight… "

"I am sure things will get better for you."

"Insha'allah, Jamila, Insha'allah."

"You've heard about the dead sharks at the Blue Hole?"

"Walla he Jamila, of course. The Federation ordered us to stop diving. A very terrible business. First there was the tragic death of Dark Shark's student, then his accident at the Eel Garden and now this. These are very dark and troubling times. You and Dark Shark must be very careful where you put your feet."

"I know Shwaya, Shwaya, I know."

Just then, Heidi rushed into the office.

"Jamila! Its sooo good to see you!"

"Heidi!"

The two of them hugged warmly. They had been good friends in the 'old days', a force to be reckoned with. They had spent a lot time together getting drunk, going diving and breaking hearts.

"Come Jamila; let's sit with Peter and Gastro."

Before she could reply, Heidi had dragged Jamila out of office. Jamila said good bye to Shwaya, Shwaya as she was pulled away and the two friends, giggling like school girls, went to find the men. In the centre of the Wadi, Peter was lounging as he only could and Gastro was smoking a joint. Peter stood up when he saw the girls approaching.

"Ah, Jamila. How are you again?"

"I'm great; it's so good to see you both again after all this time!"

The three of them settled down in the Wadi and ordered

chicken pizza and Delta water. Heidi was shaking; she was so excited and emotional.

"Sooo, when did you land? How long you here for? Have you got a boyfriend? Where do you live? Why didn't you reply to my last email?"

"Whoa girl! Hold on! One question at a time!"

"But I want to know…!"

"Well, first of all I landed last night, as to how long I'm here for depends on… "

"On what?"

Jamila took in a deep breath.

"I am working for QA. I am here to investigate the death of a diver, Moheet, who was found dead at the Eel Garden."

"We heard about that… "

Jamila continued.

"She was Dark Shark's student, which doesn't help matters, as I'm sure you can understand. He's on suspended status right now."

There was a long pause.

"Today, Dark Shark and I dived the Blue Hole. We went in at the Bells as usual, and then swam along the reef wall. When we got to the sandy slope we came across hundreds of dead sharks. It was truly awful. The sharks had had their fins cut off. I don't think I have ever seen anything so awful in all my life."

"The sharks! Yes! Yes! This morning! We saw the same thing! At Abu Hillal!

"Did you!?"

"God yes! It was terrible. Horrible. Ugly and brutal! There were dozens of dead sharks everywhere. All without their fins. After the dive I couldn't stop crying."

Peter concurred with his partner.

"It was truly appalling."

"Did you report it?"

"We told Shwaya Shwaya when we got back. He assured us he would report it to the authorities."

"I need you guys to keep your eyes peeled to see if you notice anything else out of the ordinary happening in Dahab."

"That's not gonna be that easy, honey, this whole town is out of the ordinary."

"I know, Heidi, but I mean at the dive sites… look out for anyone lurking with intent, you know what I mean… I am gonna give you my mobile number. If you see something, you can call me or call the Shamandura. There's a special team flying in from Cairo and hopefully they'll find these shark fishermen.

"Okay, Jamila."

"Count on us, honey."

"In the meantime, Dark Shark and I will carry on with my investigation into his student, Moheet."

"What's happening there between you two, it must be awkward, all those emotions, trying to stay professional, the past always there… lurking in the background… "

"It's hard. Dark Shark is stubborn and moody. You

know how he is…"

Peter voice boomed, a deep Norwegian baritone.

"He's a dark one, that Dark Shark."

Heidi offered some advice to her friend.

"He's a loner, never get serious about a loner, honey, they always hurt you in the end, no, nah ah, never fall for the dark mysterious ones, they're the worst. You want rugged stability, like Peter."

"Heh, heh. Thank you."

Jamila bit aggressively on a slice of chicken pizza and washed it down with some Delta water.

"I know. That's why I left him."

"But you still love him, don't you?"

"No!"

"You do! I can see it all over your face, you gotta be careful of that honey… "

"I don't love him, Heidi."

"Yes, well, you keep telling yourself that and you'll get back on the plane."

"Heidi, you're impossible!"

"So, how's life in Blighty? Where you living?"

"Bristol."

"Bristol? Where's that? Sounds boring."

Jamila laughed.

"No, it's not boring, it's nice"

"Good, and have you got a nice man, yet?"

"No… not yet… there have been some, nothing serious… you know, I want to wait for the right guy."

Jamila shifted slightly in her seat and finished the pizza she was holding. Heidi stared at her perfectly manicured nails, still perfect despite life in harsh desert conditions.

"Don't wait too long, girl, you're biological clock is ticking"

"Heidi!"

"It's true!"

"Even so… "

"I'm sorry."

"It's okay."

"Sooo… where you staying?"

"At Dive Splurge."

"Ah okay, cool. Listen when you have some time, lets the three of us have dinner."

"I'd love to, Heidi."

"Cooool!"

"So, how are things with you two?"

"They're good" Heidi replied "The dive centre is quiet at the moment, but I am giving Peter his Dive Master course and we are going to Hurghada with Megaphone and Paul in a few days' time. We'll party in Hurghada for a couple of days; there is a good DJ from Prague - DJ Czech! Then we're all going diving for two days, so you know, we got it all to look forward to. Next month I want to do my EFR, DPV, MSDT, and IDCS for PADI, join SDI and TDI; sign up with HEPCA, SSDA and RSDASS. Peter wants to do his IDC at WDD, oh… and last night we watched a lovely DVD from the BBC… "

Jamila translated the acronyms in her head. Gastro had said nothing up until this point. He was content to let Jamila catch up with the other two. He took a lull in the proceedings to ask where Dark Shark was. Before the others could respond, the answer to his question showed up. Jamila looked up and scolded him.

"Dark Shark, where have you been? Your pizza is getting cold."

Heidi, Peter and Gastro smirked. Jamila's concern belied her true feelings for the moody instructor.

"I've been talking to the Navy."

Gastro chimed in.

"What did they say?"

"They didn't find any dead sharks at the Lighthouse, but they found plenty at Abu Hillal. They are moving up to the Canyon next. Another patrol boat is at the Blue Hole as we speak. Navy divers are removing the dead sharks from the water. Checks are also being made on all the boats in Dahab. They are trying hard to find the shark finners. Once the sharks have been removed from the Hole and Hillal, and if there are no further incidents, there is a chance they may reopen the dive sites and allow diving to start up again."

Dark Shark was starving. As he was talking, he wolfed down his pizza and washed it down with a Coke. For the next half hour, the friends discussed the events of the day. Jamila and Heidi caught up with more gossip and then it was time to leave.

'Guys, it's been great, but we have to be going."

"So soon?"

"Aiwa, we need to catch up on some sleep."

Heidi sighed. She was enjoying spending time with her old friend.

"Jamila, honey you take care of yourself now..."

"Yes, look after yourself, Jamila"

"I will guys and don't forget to call me if you see anything suspicious."

"We will."

"Bye Heidi."

"Bye, bye darling."

"Good bye Peter."

"Good bye Jamila."

The three of them hugged. They were still good friends. Peter and Heidi waved good bye and Jamila, Dark Shark and Gastronimica started to make their way home. Before they reached the exit, however, Jamila asked the other two to wait outside while she quickly checked something with Shwaya, Shwaya. In his office, the owner of Utopia was relaxing in his favourite chair. He looked up when he saw Jamila enter and spoke to her in a low, level tone.

"Ah... Jamila. Come in."

"Thank you. Shwaya Shwaya. Forgive me for bothering you again, but I wanted to talk to you about the dead sharks found at Abu Hillal this morning."

"Ah yes... terrible... terrible."

"Did you call the Shamandura or the Navy about the sharks?"

"The Shamandura or the Navy? No, no. The Shamandura actually got in touch with me first. Before I could ring them."

"Why did they do that?"

"They were calling all the dive centres as part of their investigation."

"Ah, okay. Fair enough."

"Don't worry Jamila, the Shamandura are competent and I am confident they will clear up this terrible mess."

Jamila was far from convinced and something inside told her Shwaya Shwaya felt the same.

"Thank you for your time, Shwaya Shwaya."

"Mafish mishkela, Jamila. Take care of yourself. "

"I will. Good bye."

Jamila re-joined Dark Shark and Gastro on the bay.

"What did you ask Shwaya Shwaya?"

"Later. Let's get some sleep for a few hours."

The three friends agreed they would meet outside the Stilton Hotel at sunset, which today was at six o'clock. Saying their good byes, they each went their separate ways. Dark Shark and Gastro reached their houses and crashed out immediately. At Dive Splurge, Jamila wearily opened the door to her room and collapsed into a chair. Her legs crossed, she sat in the chair for a while, smoking a cigarette, staring at the wall opposite and running a hand through her shining brown hair. She was trying to collect her thoughts, thinking about all that happened to her since her return to Dahab.

In particular she thought about Utopia, Heidi, Peter and the sharks in Abu Hillal. She also thought about Shwaya Shwaya. He seemed different to her now. He was more stressed - older, but not wiser. After ten minutes contemplation, she picked up her mobile and dialled a number, placing a call to QA in England.

"Hi, Melanie, Yeh, it's me, Jamila. Hi, how are you…? Yeh… I'm good thanks… Listen… Can you bring up Utopia's file and email it over to me…? Good… thanks, Mel. I appreciate it… How is Malcolm..? Ah okay good. Yeh… I will… No worries… I'll call you later tonight… Yep… Okay… Bye."

Jamila stubbed out the cigarette, undressed and took a long, hot shower. She lathered the soap well, washing away the salt, the emotions and all thoughts of that incorrigible loner, Dark Shark. Drying herself off, she set the alarm on her mobile, switched off the light, laid her head onto the soft pillow and promptly fell asleep.

# 7

## *The Dhow*

Every town in the world has their big cheeses, and in Dahab the big cheese was the Stilton Hotel. The Stilton represented the antithesis of everything Dark Shark loved about Sinai. At the Stilton, the idea was that no matter where in the world the hotel was located, the guests received exactly the same 'service.' What this actually meant was that the Stilton was the 'Starbucks' of hotels. It was the exactly the same everywhere. Guests arrived in air-conditioned cars and spent two weeks in their air-conditioned rooms.

The hotel catered to their every whim; there were multiple swimming pools, bars, restaurants, saunas, gyms, water sport activities, and of course, the own private 'beach'. The Stilton had its own private, de-salination plant. The swimming pools were so large it was ridiculous, a tasteless flaunting of excess in the desert of Sinai where ordinary people still made do with salty well water. The waiters were rigid and cold. The prices in the restaurants and bars were astronomical. The private 'beach' was not natural. When they built the hotel, the geniuses decided that the beach didn't have enough sand on it, so they imported some, dumped it on the beach and smothered the offshore section of reef. The coral died and the reef fish disappeared. The Stilton 'beach' was the worst place to dive in Dahab. The visibility was always bad because of the sand and instructors hated working there.

The two-week package tourist who stayed at the hotel never gained any understanding of where they were in the world. They never sampled the town, the people, the culture or even the food. Worse still, was the fact that the hotel brought almost no benefit to either the people of Egypt or the environment. The Egyptian staff was paid next to nothing and the Bedouin were excluded entirely. The hotel was just a machine to make money and this money was being siphoned off to either America or Europe. After Sinai and the Red Sea have been destroyed by the big cheeses; they will go off and count their dollars on their money farms, no doubt drinking beer with their close friend, George Dubya Bush.

In perfect harmony and close alliance with the Stilton Hotel was the dive centre, World Domination Divers. The manager, Bent Bob, first met Dark Shark a year ago at Slow Down. Within thirty seconds of introducing himself he had tried to sell Dark Shark some knocked off diving equipment, no doubt from his own customers. The American and Dark Shark took an instant dislike to each other and hadn't spoken since that first showdown in Slow Down.

In the intervening months, rumours had circulated in the darkened corners of Dahab's watering holes. Revealing rumours. Whispers of mischief. Dark tales told, of an American selling not just air or equipment, but figs and guns. World Domination Divers was a factory. It was huge, boasting one hundred sets of equipment, its own day boat at the jetty and of course rich customers from the Stilton Hotel. The philosophy was "get 'em in, get 'em out." The diving pros working there were simply tea bags, working long hours, receiving little pay and having to work the crappy beach. Bent Bob ran the dive centre like his own personal fiefdom, a big bad baron.

At six o'clock precisely, Dark Shark, Jamila and Gastro met up outside the main entrance to the Stilton Hotel. Dark Shark told them it would be best if he reconnoitred first. It would be far easier with one than with all three. It was agreed. Gastro and Jamila would get a coffee and pretend to be tourists (harder in Gastro's case than Jamila's) whilst Dark Shark did some tactful snooping. They parted company and Dark Shark was left alone.

He steeled himself for the task ahead. He hated the hotel and wanted to get in and out as fast as possible. He told himself to relax, pretend he was a tourist and to go for a walk around. Silently he padded through the vast expanse of the hotel, past the ridiculous swimming pools, the restaurants, the lobsters from Europe still on the beach, and on to the far side of the complex. Reaching the dreaded dive centre, he resolved to play it cool. As he strode past, he glanced into the interior through the huge glass doors, taking in as much of the scene as possible. Inside, leaning on the counter, was a counter chick Dark Shark didn't recognize. Standing next to her was Bent Bob.

The slimy American was talking to a Bedouin dressed all in black. The two men appeared to be having an argument and had no idea Dark Shark was strolling past the outside of the dive centre. Also inside were a group of German students just arrived back from a boat trip at Gebril Bint. Dark Shark knew this because the Germans were watching a video of the diving, sitting in front of a screen and laughing, recalling the days adventures on the boat. Evidently, WDD considered itself too important to take any notice of the diving ban.

Dark Shark continued walking quickly round the building, skirting the edge, looking for a place where he could remain out of sight, but still watch the events within… Ten meters further on, he spied a clump of palm trees squashed against the window, providing exactly what he was looking for. Making sure no-one saw him, he ducked into the clump, turned around and sat down. Immediately, he bit down hard on his lip. A six inch palm thorn had dug into his left cheek, breaking the skin and causing blood to trickle down his chin. He swore, wiping away the blood and leaned into the palms, looking through the glass and into the dive centre.

Inside, Bent Bob had finished with the Bedouin and was shaking his hand. The Bedouin turned swiftly, his black Jelibya flowing dramatically behind him, and left. Bent Bob said something to the counter girl, who acknowledged him with a nod and took out something from the desk. The Germans were getting louder watching their video, and a phone rang on the counter. Bent Bob took whatever he had asked for and disappeared into his office at the far side of the dive centre. Dark Shark looked around the interior.

Apart from the counter in the middle of the room, there was also another counter on the left which contained the dive centre's equipment. On the same side of the building, there was a door three feet from Dark Shark and to his right. It opened into a room, but the view inside was obscured by a wall. Dark Shark guessed it was the classroom. Looking back inside the main room, he saw the divers' lockers, stacked up row after row, starting at the edge of the main counter and continuing the entire length of the dive centre to the front door. There were dozens and it took Dark Shark a few minutes to guess the location of locker number sixteen.

Feeling sure he had a good idea of where it was, he wiped away some more blood, checked outside the clump to make sure no-one was watching, and pulled himself clear of the palms and their thorns. He walked quickly back to the front entrance of the Stilton and searched for his friends. Inside his office, Bent Bob was on the phone.

He was ordering a large, dripping steak from the Stilton restaurant. Dark Shark found his two friends in one of the many coffee shops and ordered a drink that was at least five times the price it would have been in town. Jamila pressed him immediately.

"What happened?"

"I found locker number sixteen, but the dive centre is still open. Bent Bob and the counter chick are there, as are some German guests. We'll have to wait a few hours before we can make our attempt to get inside the locker."

Gastro's smile was wicked.

"Good. I have a friend of mine who has just rocked up in town with some killer acid."

"No way, G. We need you to be compos mentis."

"Not fair."

"What's not fair are hundreds of dead, finned sharks. What's not fair is one of my students lying dead in the morgue. What's not f… "

"I get the picture. I will do compos mentis."

"Gee. Thanks G."

Jamila acted as peacemaker.

"Guys, we don't have time for this. Let's go chill out for a couple of hours, then we can finish this story with the locker. We don't even know whether or not this is even Moheet's locker key."

Not for the first (or last) time in human history, the men had to respect the logic and sense of a woman. Jamila carried on.

"If we are going to meet up here again later, I'm going to get some more sleep. The travelling, diving and stress of what we've seen has knackered me more than I realized. What time should we meet up again, Dark Shark?"

"Let's meet at ten o'clock. There won't be anyone at the dive centre at that time except the cleaners. Insha'allah."

"Insha'allah."

Jamila caught a taxi home. Dark Shark and Gastro lit out for Slow Down with Gastro promising to remain compos mentis.

Whilst Dark Shark was seated at a table and Gastro had gone to check up on Shanti, he pulled out a cigarette. Leaning back in the chair, he remembered what he had seen at WDD. He recalled the layout of the dive centre, the lockers, doors, the classroom and the counters. The dive centre would be closed at ten when they planned to go back, but it wouldn't be locked. Access would be possible; guests at the hotel could walk through the dive centre to get to the beach at any time. Gastro soon returned. He and Dark Shark chatted away the hours, waiting for the right time and the promise of discovering what lay inside locker sixteen.

At nine thirty Jamila's alarm sounded, rudely awakening her from the siesta she desperately needed. She groaned, slammed off the alarm, and staggered to the bathroom. Still rubbing sleep from her eyes, she showered, dried off and dressed putting on a blue hooded sweatshirt, dark blue jeans and white trainers.

She picked up her mobile phone, keys and some money, but left behind her hand-bag, opting instead to put the items in her pockets.

Walking onto the main road, she got into a taxi and arrived at Slow Down ten minutes later. The three of them got into a taxi, heading for the Stilton Hotel. The plan was that Gastro would walk in first and create a diversion. Dark Shark and Jamila would follow, pretending to be a married couple from England; they were guests and had forgotten something in their locker. The only person who knew all three of them was Bent Bob and he would be at home, watching his beloved Dallas Cowboys on satellite. Simple.

The taxi arrived at the hotel and the three of them hurried around to the dive centre, trying not to appear as if they were hurrying. As they approached they could see that the dive centre was indeed closed. A lone cleaner was mopping the floor. Dark Shark and Jamila waited outside while Gastro went in. Gastro opened the main doors and strolled up to the cleaner.

"Salaam, habibe. Where is the toilet?"

"Salaam. Toilet? There, there."

The cleaner pointed to the far end of the dive centre and continued to mop the floor.

"Sucran a man"

Gastro walked across to the toilet door, pushed it open and went through. After a few seconds, he screamed. The cleaner jumped, as indeed did Dark Shark and

Jamila. Gastro's scream was most realistic. The cleaner dropped the mop and ran into the toilets. Dark Shark and Jamila waited. Outside, they could here Gastro shouting something about cockroaches and the cleaner responding frantically.

"Mershi, mershi."

After a few minutes there was silence from within the toilets. Gastro came out followed by a much shaken cleaner.

That was the cue. Dark Shark and Jamila walked into the dive centre, holding hands. The cleaner looked up and they smiled, looking around like lost tourists.

"Salaam, we left something here earlier, in our locker. Can we get it now please?"

"Aiwa"

The cleaner pointed to the long rows of lockers. Dark Shark let go of Jamila's hand, went over to the lockers and after a quick search, located locker sixteen. He pulled out the key, placed it into the lock and turned. Opening the door, he peered into the darkness. It appeared to be empty apart from a few sheets of paper. Dark Shark picked up the papers and looked underneath them, searching with his hand into the furthest reaches of the locker. Underneath the papers, his fingers felt something plastic. Sheeting. He peered inside the plastic sheeting. Folded up, were a map and a log book. He took the items, stuffed them into his jacket pocket. Finally he locked the door of the locker and popped the key into another pocket. Turning to the cleaner, he smiled, said thank you, and taking Jamila's hand they both made their getaway. The cleaner who was glad to be rid of his strange interruptions, carried on cleaning. The old man cut a lonely figure in the darkened interior of the closed diver centre. Outside the dive centre, Gastro was making sure the brick wall he was leaning against wasn't going to fall down. He was smoking a cigarette and smiling.

"Halas?"

"Aiwa. Let's yalla."

Fifteen minutes later, they were back in Dahab. Another ten minutes after that and all three were fast asleep.

The next morning at ten o'clock, Dark Shark, Gastro and Jamila met up at the entrance to Just Another Dive Centre. Sally was leaning on the counter talking to four Korean students who were interested in taking some photos of the underwater world and needed an expert to help them. Sally picked up the yellow phone on the counter, dialled a number and waited.

"Hi, Megaphone, how are ya mate? It's Sally at Just Another Dive Centre…Yeh that's right the new counter chick… yeah, yeah we were talking last night at the Furry Cup… nah that's all right mate....! Nah, I accept your apologies… ah no worries, mate! Listen, I have some guys here who wanna take some shots… Yeah, Okay, so we'll see you shortly, yeah? Cool… See Ya! Bye!

Megaphone was a big, strapping Aussie videographer. He was also a long-time Dahab resident and popular local character. His favourite party trick was to execute a handstand and drink a pint of beer without spilling a drop. Like many locals, Megaphone rode around town on a mountain bike and like many of the other locals, Megaphone's bike was Egyptian. He had never been able to fix the spokes adequately and had to ride the bike around town in a very wiggly line, desperately avoiding the oncoming mass of people, machines and animals. Megaphone's bike was bright yellow and it was called the Golden Eagle.

As he entered the dive centre, Dark Shark could hear the booming voice of Megaphone coming down the telephone. Megaphone was loud, very loud. Behind Sally, Paul the Kiwi instructor was preparing some PADI materials for his course. Sitting next to him with some newly acquired black marks on its face, was the EFR dummy. Everybody looked up when they saw the sombre faces of Dark Shark, Jamila and Gastronimica walking into the dive centre. Sally put the receiver down and without saying a word, pointed to the office. Sitting inside, talking to a very nervous looking Mohammed, was Adel.

He was wearing a dark grey suit, white shirt and shiny new black shoes. The get up was standard issue Shamandura uniform. Also standard was the bristling sub machine gun stuffed inside his jacket. As was his want, Adel was fiddling with the safety catch. Dark Shark idly wondered what would happen if someone took the gun away from Adel. Quite possibly the man would be lost without his favourite penis extension.

Adel didn't stand up. He merely raised his eyebrows slightly and waved for everyone to sit down. Mohammed was more welcoming.

"Ah guys, Sabah el Kheer. How are you all?"

Dark Shark, Gastro and Jamila muttered their good mornings and found themselves each a chair to sit down on. Moments later, Sally brought them coffee and then left them to it. The meeting began.

It was Adel who started proceedings.

"Dark Shark, Gastro. Good morning. I trust you slept well last night?"

Neither one replied except by nodding their heads. They didn't exactly feel particularly sociable dealing with a fascist sporting a gun at ten in the morning. Adel continued anyway.

"Jamila, it's good to see you again. How is it working for PADI?"

"Hi Adel. It's good, thank you."

She wondered how he knew she was working for PADI but then he was the branch head of the Dahab Shamandura.

"QA is quite a responsibility, but I am not at all surprised. I could see the potential in you the first time I met you. You have done well, but you have not of course exceeded my expectations as my expectations are always correct."

He laughed at his own rather pathetic joke, but was alone in doing so. Adel was slimy. Oooh, he was so slimy. The man was so oily, he literally secreted corruption. Not for the first time, Dark Shark wandered how the Shamandura hired its staff. What did they put in the adverts announcing vacancies? Something like this perhaps:

'The Dictatorship of the Arab Republic of Egypt is looking for a few corrupt men to join the Shamandura. Prospective candidates must be oily, corrupt thugs, also uneducated, ignorant and thoroughly dodgy. Must be willing to ruthlessly suppress dissension, protest and freedom. Please go to the Ministry of Justice to pick up and fill in an application form.'

Composing himself again, Adel continued.

"Mershi. Let us, as the Americans say, get down to business. There have been a number of very worrying developments happening in Dahab during the last week. First there was the unfortunate case of Dark Shark's student, Moheet, being found dead at the Eel Garden. Second, Dark Shark and Gastro are involved in an unfortunate incident at the same dive site. Lastly, a few days later, the Blue Hole and Abu Hillal dive sites are full of dead sharks. I will begin by discussing Moheet. The autopsy report indicated that she had drowned and the coroner returned a verdict of accidental death. Arrangements were made for Moheet to be returned to her family in the United States. However, I must inform you all at this time that Moheet's body did not actually return to the US. She is still in the morgue at the hospital in Sharm el Sheikh."

Adel paused for effect. He didn't need to. The office was filled with a stunned silence. Adel went on.

"Before we could send the body back, an orderly working at the hospital noticed marks on Moheet's neck. Being a dutiful man and a good Muslim, he immediately called me. I went to the hospital to verify the information and found to my shock that the orderly was correct. I then had a rather interesting conversation with the coroner who had conducted the autopsy and of course, I asked him why he had failed to miss such obvious marks on the neck of the deceased. He couldn't give me an explanation but apologized profusely and begged forgiveness. Needless to say, I don't do forgiveness, especially when it comes to the reputation of our beloved nation. Sadly the coroner is no longer with us as he met with a rather unfortunate accident a few days later. Poor man."

Adel smiled, but again was the only one to do so. Dark Shark was furious but was trying hard to not show it.

"So are you saying there is evidence to show that Moheet was murdered?"

"Oh yes, Mr Dark Shark. Oh yes indeed."

"So what happens now?"

"We are conducting another autopsy. This time we will find out exactly what happened to her. We have also launched a full scale murder investigation. We are putting the full resources of the Egyptian government into this. There is pressure coming from the US Embassy to deal with the crisis and return the body as soon as possible."

"Do you believe there is a connection between Moheet's death and the dead sharks?"

"Quite possibly Mr Dark Shark. We are, of course, looking into it."

Dark Shark hated being called Mr Dark Shark. He knew that Adel knew he hated it, but as he hated Adel he tried hard not to show Adel that he hated it. Who knew that hate could be so complicated?

"Let us move on to your 'accident' at the Eel Garden."

"It wasn't an accident. The guys on the boat tried to kill me."

"Yes they did. El Hamdul'allah they did not succeed, eh Mr Dark Shark?"

Adel flashed an evil grin. He had all the warmth of a Komodo dragon. Dark Shark said nothing.

"The Shamandura, in partnership with the Navy, is currently scouring the coast looking for the shark fishing boat or boats. We know that once the fins are removed from the sharks, they are transported to Hong Kong for the shark fin soup market. We also know that the fins need to be dried before this can happen. Somewhere around here, the criminals are drying the fins before exporting them and we are looking for that too. So far our investigations have turned up nothing, but we are more than competent and we are confident that we will soon have the culprits in custody and facing Egyptian justice."

Dark Shark thought that if anyone else mentioned that the Egyptian authorities were competent, he was going to scream out loud. Adel continued.

"Can you give me a description of the boat that tried to hook you at the Eel Garden?"

"No. It was getting dark at the time. All we saw was a dark shadow appear overhead and the sound of a boat engine. Everything happened so fast, it was impossible to know what was on the surface. Gastro was focused on rescuing me and I had passed out. The boat disappeared before anyone could describe it accurately. No one on shore noticed anything unusual occurring."

"Would you say the boat was a small one? Perhaps a Zodiac?"

"Yes, that's possible."

"Good. We will include the Zodiacs during our inspection of all boats in the Sinai. Now if you would be so kind, please will you describe the scene at the Blue Hole as you found it, Mr Dark Shark."

"After coming out of the Bells shaft and swimming under the overhang, I, Gastro and Jamila came to the sandy slopes just before the saddle of the Blue Hole. It was horrible. There were hundreds and hundreds of dead sharks everywhere. Their fins had been sliced off. The fishermen had been indiscriminate. They had killed all species and all ages of shark. There were even babies and pregnant females."

"Did your group or any of the waiters at the restaurants notice any boats in the area?"

"No. Whoever had done it was long gone by the time we got there."

"It is looking more and more likely that the culprits are committing these crimes at night."

Dark Shark had reached the same conclusion.

"Good. That concludes our meeting for today. I must attend to urgent business. Before I go, I must say a few words to all of you."

Dark Shark couldn't wait.

"Please leave this investigation to the Shamandura and the Navy. That includes you Jamila. I know that PADI sent you to here to investigate the death of a PADI student, but we are the official representatives here in Egypt and we will be the only ones doing the investigating. I have the utmost respect for PADI so I will fill you in from time to time, but only on a strictly need to know basis only. You can then report back to your superiors. Mr Dark Shark, I suggest you spend more time recovering from your accident at the Eel Garden. You must stop your meddling in these affairs at once. That especially means no more visits to the Stilton Hotel. Needless to say, you may not see me, but you can rest assured I will be watching the three of you."

With that, the meeting was over. Adel got up from his

chair, adjusted his ballistics and left the occupants of a now relieved office.

As soon as he was out the door, Gastro pulled out a joint. He lit it, breathed in deeply and exhaled smoke for a long time.

"That guy has all the charm of the Spanish Inquisition."

Dark Shark agreed with his friend.

"He's a Nazi."

Jamila spoke up next, asking Dark Shark a question.

"What did you find in the locker last night?"

"Good question. Let's find out."

Reaching into his bag, Dark Shark pulled out the items he had obtained from locker number sixteen at World Domination Divers. He placed them on Mohammed's desk and they all gathered round to get a closer look. Sitting on the desk were a pile of papers, a single folded sheet of what appeared to be vellum and a small, dark blue book. Dark Shark immediately recognized the book as a diver's log book. He picked it up and opened it on the first page. Not only was it a log book, he realized with a start, it was Moheet's log book.

"Sally was right. The locker key did indeed belong to Moheet."

He studied the log book carefully, turning each page slowly and examining the entries in detail. Never before had he read from a log book whose author was deceased. It felt strange and made him more than a little uncomfortable. Inside were descriptions of dozens of dives Moheet had made in the Sinai. Reefs, wrecks, shore dives, Moheet had certainly been around.

"Our Moheet has been busy."

None of the descriptions mentioned who she dived with. They did not contain any stories. The entries only noted the dive site, the maximum depth and time underwater. Dark Shark gave the log book to Jamila and picked up the papers. They turned out to be invoices. Dozens of invoices. They listed quantities of items and amounts of money but without descriptions. The invoices were neat and complete except for the all-important descriptions. Strange. Whoever had complied the invoices, didn't want the details of the items known. Whatever they were buying, the amounts were large. Hundreds of this, thousands of that. In addition, the money changing hands was also large. Thousands of dollars were being spent on items unknown. Each invoice did include, however, a company name, address and official stamp. Each document stated it originated from the Golden Wadi Massage Parlour.

The address was in Dahab. Gastro, who was feeling left out asked to see the papers. Dark Shark, happy he could ascertain nothing further from the invoices, passed them on to Gastro. Lastly, and most intriguingly, he picked up the folded piece of vellum. The parchment made from sheep's skin was folded twice and when Dark Shark unfolded it, the parchment showed creases dissecting it into four quadrants. Placing it on Mohammed's desk, he bent over and studied the parchment in detail. It was a map. It was crudely drawn with what looked a child's crayon, but he knew instinctively that it was a map of the Dahab coast and in particular, all the major dive sites.

Gastro, who was looking at the invoices, suddenly exclaimed:

"The Golden Wadi Massage Parlour!? That's a knocking shop!"

"Yes and a very good one!"

At exactly the same time, Dark Shark, Gastro and Jamila all looked up at Mohammed with six raised eyebrows.

"Well... apparently. So I have been told. I wouldn't know myself."

Mohammed looked sheepish. Eyebrows were lowered and Dark Shark returned to the map. Along the coast depicted on the map, the names of the dive sites were quite clearly written. Dark Shark had of course seen many dive maps of Sinai, but this one was curiously different.

The names of the dive sites were in German. Next to each name was a number which Dark Shark took to represent the depth at that respective site. At the Canyon dive site was the number thirty, at the Islands, the number fifteen and so on. Gastro and Jamila finished looking at the invoices and the log book. Now, along with Mohammed, they joined Dark Shark in studying the map. All four of them were bent over the desk, gazing intently at the symbols, lines and numbers in front of them. The map did not appear to have a key, but beside each dive site name was drawn a crude picture of a boat. Stretching away from either side of each of the boats, were two semi circles drawn as simple lines.

All along the length of the circles were small squares, regularly spaced out. Beside each boat was also a date. Some of the dates were circled in red and some in blue. The dates made little sense. There were written in standard fashion, day followed by month followed by year etc., but instead of only one day, the date contained two. The only other information on the map was the letter N. The letter was drawn inside a circle and both were in large, thick, red lines. The letter inside the circle was located at the top right hand corner of the parchment.

Gastro was confused.

"What are those lines and boxes coming away from the boats?"

"Those represent nylon fishing lines. The lines have hooks at the end of them which are baited with live fish. The boxes represent buoys which keep the lines floating. What we are looking at, my friends, is a copy of a shark fishing map."

"What about the dates?"

"I was just thinking about that. Mohammed, what's the date today?"

"The 19th."

Dark Shark traced his finger along the dive sites and the corresponding dates. The other three followed him transfixed. At Abu Hillal dive site the date was written like this:

17/18/12/2005.

It was exactly the same date and written in the same way at the Blue Hole dive site. Both dates were circled in red.

"Why are there two days in each date?"

"Remember what Adel said to us. These guys are fishing sharks at night. These dates represent the night between the 17th and 18th of December. Circling the date in red probably means it's already been done. You can also see that the dates were previously circled n blue and then somebody went over them again in red later. These dates are only a day or two ago. That means that somebody has updated this map even as soon as yesterday."

Dark Shark continued tracing with his finger the dates. When he reached the Canyon dive site he saw that the date read:

19/20/12/2005

The date was circled in blue.

"Guys, I believe they are going to kills sharks at the Canyon tonight."

There was an audible gasp.

"What's the letter N in that circle mean?"

"That probably just means north, every map has a compass with at least north marked on it."

"How does the Golden Wadi parlour knocking shop fit into all of this?

"The Golden Wadi is run a by a respectable Chinese family. It may well be a front. If they are buying equipment and supporting the shark fishing industry it would make sense. They may well have connections in Hong Kong to facilitate the illegal and horrendous trade in Red Sea shark fins."

"*Mother*fuckers!"

"Indeed."

It was Jamila who articulated what all four were thinking.

"So, we know that Moheet was murdered. We now also now know why she was murdered. Clearly, she stumbled on this information and was killed for it. Moheet died because she knew too much."

"Yes. It's true. We now know. We are going to find who was responsible for Moheet's death. We are also going to put a stop to the shark fishing. Fuck Adel. We will ignore his warning to stay out of it. I keep hearing the Egyptians authorities are competent, but that guy couldn't organize a piss up in a brewery. Does everyone agree?

They all nodded.

"I don't want to involve anyone who doesn't feel right with this. It's going to be difficult and very dangerous. Shark fins are big money and as we've already seen, lives are lost over them. Anybody who wants out at the stage, I will more than understand."

But nobody wanted out. They all felt the same and they all wanted to remain in.

"What's the plan?"

"We need to get to the Canyon dive site tonight and stop these guys or at least have a look. We need to figure out a way to spot the boat and then try to get close enough to find out what is going on. Zodiacs are noisy, but it would be a good idea to have one on standby just in case we need a quick getaway."

"How do you propose to get close to the shark fishing boat without them hearing us?"

"On kayaks."

"Kayaks!? You're crazy Dark Shark."

"Yes. Kayaks will do the job perfectly well. Mohammed can you get hold of three kayaks?"

"Aiwa. I can go and see Mustafa the kayak guy and order three for rent."

"Don't mention to him what they are for. You'll need to rent them for two whole days so he doesn't suspect anything. Don't even tell him we are going out there at night."

"Mershi, my lips are sealed Dark Shark."

"Can you also get the Zodiac ready to have on standby?"

"Aiwa."

"Excellent. We have time to kill before going to the Canyon. I need to go down to Sharm el Sheikh and get my bandages changed. What are you going to do, Jay?"

"I am going to catch up with Heidi and Peter."

Gastro felt left out again.

"What about me?"

"Gastro, whilst I am in Sharm, go back to WDD and use your famous charms to make friends with the lovely counter chick. She is new and doesn't know you. Get her talking and try to find out anything you can about Moheet and that locker. We need to act quickly. Whoever made that map will by now realize somebody is on to them. You will need to be careful, Gastro. Things are moving fast. The people behind this will do everything to protect themselves and I have a feeling they'll stop at nothing."

"If I stroll into WDD the morning after the map was taken, Bent Bob is gonna make a connection and skin my dread-locked ass… "

"He won't hurt you, not in public."

"… and he's also gonna know it's you who is onto him."

"Good, you can see his by his reaction whether or not he knows about the map. If he is acting strangely when you arrive, we know he's involved. Bent Bob likes you. You are gonna make good bait, Gastro me old mucker."

"Cheers mate."

"It's settled then. I'll go down to Sharm. Jamila will go to Utopia. Mohammed will get the boats ready and Gastro is going to turn on the charm. We'll meet back here at sundown which gives us a chance to prepare properly. Remember, the Shamandura is watching. Let's try and go about our business like dumb tourists."

"Shouldn't be hard."

Having agreed on a plan of action, the four conspirators

left the office. Each one was determined. Each one was on a mission. Jamila walked out onto the bay, turned left and made her way to Utopia dive centre. She strolled past Shwaya Shwaya's office which was empty and spied Heidi and Peter lounging in the Wadi. They looked bored and frustrated. The diving ban was still on. Heidi was reading from her instructor manual and Peter was twirling a silver ring on his thumb.

Looking up from her book, Heidi squealed her delight when she saw her friend approaching. Jamila plumped down on the cushions to join them and ordered some Bedouin tea.

On the other side of Dahab, deep in the midst of Assalah, Mohammed pulled up at Mustafa the kayak guy's house. Mustafa had never been kayaking in his life. Originally from Cairo, he owned property in Dahab. Two years previously, he had rented the property to an English kayak instructor who had gone stark raving mad. Waking up one morning, the instructor had announced to the world that he was giving up all his worldly possessions and going to live in the deep desert with the Bedouin.

No-one in Dahab blinked an eyelid, least of all Mustafa who still had the deposit and had inherited twelve spanking new kayaks. Mustafa now had a new income renting the kayaks to tourists. The English instructor was never heard from again.

Mohammed and Mustafa knew each well. For the next

half an hour, they ate lunch together and at the same time, negotiated on the price for renting the kayaks. The diving ban had caused a surge in business for Mustafa and he only had two kayaks left. Mohammed dialled his mobile phone and called Dark Shark. Speeding in a taxi towards Sharm, Dark Shark answered his phone.

"Aiwa, Mohammed."

"Dark Shark, Mustafa has only got two kayaks left."

"Mmmm... Okay. No problem. I'll get in one and Gastro will be in the other. Jamila will stay in the Zodiac with you. Is everything good with the Zodiac?"

"Aiwa, Dark Shark. Mohammed the driver is right now blowing it up."

"Is he? I thought the electric pump was broken?"

"It is. Mohammed is blowing it up manually."

"Manually?"

"Aiwa. He is using his mouth."

"Walla-he. Okay. I will be back soon. Sucran as always habibe."

"Afwan."

The line went dead. Mohammed resumed his negotiations and Dark Shark arrived at the hospital. As he got out of the taxi and went in, he wandered how Gastro was getting on with the counter chick. He also thought about Jamila and realized how much he longed to kiss her once again. He cursed and went into the hospital. Gastro hadn't yet had any luck with the counter chick. On his arrival at WDD, Bent Bob was working on the counter and there was no sign of the chick. Gastro walked in, hoping she would put in an appearance. Bent Bob looked up from behind the desk. He didn't appear to know anything about the locker. If he did, he wasn't letting on.

"Hey Gastro, how are you man!?"

"Yeh man I'm cool, how are you?"

"Good, good, business is very good. You wanna buy some diving equipment?"

"No thanks Bob"

Bob knew Gastro was skint but he just couldn't help himself.

"So, what brings you to WDD?"

"Err… well; believe it or not…I decided it was time to learn to dive… I know WDD is the best place to do a course and I was hoping you might give me a good discount."

Bent Bob looked rather cross at the mention of the discount.

"Err, well, yes, maybe… okay, well, you'll need to speak to Simone the counter chick. She's lunching right now at Slow Down, you can speak to her there or she'll be back here in an hour."

Gastro couldn't believe his luck and he exclaimed joyfully:

"I'm gonna go and talk to her right now!"

"Yeh talk to Simone and if you're still serious, we'll get you some gear too."

"Cool, Bob, thanks man!"

"No worries, Gastro."

"See ya later, Bob!"

"Bye Gastro."

Gastro jumped in a taxi and instructed the driver.

"Slow Down, sucran!"

Inside Slow Down, Hymen was tucking into a large plate of spaghetti bolognaise. He was shovelling food as fast possible, slurping the pasta and dunking Pitta in the sauce. In front of the food was a bottle of Sakkara beer and a dirty ashtray. Hymen was working hard; large red patches had splashed onto his white shirt. He looked up at Gastro; a thread of spaghetti trailed from the side of his mouth, hanging down over his chin and swaying from side to side. Standing at the bar was Simone. She wore a tight pair of brown shorts, a pink T-shirt and tan sandals. She had light brown hair swept back in a ponytail, brown eyes and light brown skin. Simone was also wearing a wooden whale necklace. She was from New Zealand, and she had very large breasts. Gastro was in heaven. Bringing to bear all his experience, he waddled over to the bar and ordered a beer. He leaned across the bar getting closer to Simone.

"In all the bars, in all the world, why did you have to walk into this one?"

Simone laughed.

"Nice one. Aint heard that before, mate, what's ya name?"

"My name... young lady... is Gastronimica... and I am at your service"

Gastro swept an arm across his waist and bowed low. A bit too low. He banged his head hard on the bar.

"Fuck!"

It wasn't part of the act, but it sure did work. Simone laughed again. "Wow that hurt. What is your name?"

"Simone, honey."

"Well Simone, I would very much like to buy you a drink."

"I would love that. Thank you."

Simone was new in Dahab and found Gastro charming and different. He was certainly at least one of those. For the next few hours, Gastro bought drinks for Simone with money he'd borrowed from Dark Shark. Simone got drunk, enjoying Gastro's company and completely forgetting she was due back at work. Gastro succeeded in gaining the information he was seeking. Just as the sun was beginning to set in the western sky, Simone asked him to take her home.

"I am quite drunk and need help to get home, honey"

"Simone, I would love to, but I have an important meeting with a moody diving instructor."

Gastro put Simone in a taxi and ordered the driver to take her home.

He then jumped in a taxi himself and within a few minutes was walking into Just Another Dive Centre. Dark Shark and Jamila were already there. Mohammed made an appearance ten minutes later.

When they were all assembled, Dark Shark laid out his plan of action.

"Tonight we go to the Canyon where we are expecting a shark fishing boat to turn up. If it does so, Gastro and I are going to paddle out it to see what we can see. Mohammed and... "

"Where exactly am I going to be?"

"You will stay in the Zodiac with Mohammed."

"The hell I will. I'm coming with you in the kayak."

"There are only two kayaks, Jay. I need you to stay in the Zodiac. I don't want you coming over to the shark fishing boat, it's far too dangerous."

"Harrumph."

"Thanks. I knew you'd understand. The moon is very new, so there should be almost no light. We will wait close to the restaurant and stash the boats behind it, so they're out of sight. If anyone does see us, they'll probably think we are just tourists. We'll only use the Zodiac if we really need it. I'll take a flare with me. If I or Gastro get into trouble, I'll fire it as a warning. Obviously the flare will light up the whole area. At that point, Jamila and Mohammed will launch the Zodiac and come on over to help. I don't think it's a good idea to try and stop these guys. We should just try and find out who they are and identify the boat. Then we can hand the whole caboodle over to the Shamandura. Anyone have any questions?"

Jamila did.

"What happens when Adel finds out we went to the Canyon?"

"Depends on what happens when we get there. We will fall off that bridge when we get to it."

There was nothing more to be said. The only thing left was to go and do it. The four companions got into two Jeeps that were parked outside the dive centre. In one Jeep, Mohammed the driver had a trailer at the back with the two kayaks strapped on top. In the other Jeep, Mohammed the owner had a trailer with the Zodiac. With lights blazing, the convoy trundled down the road towards the Canyon dive site. Night had fallen on Dahab. The sounds of a vibrant, noisy town filled the air as they drove through the town.

Barking dogs, kids playing in the streets, taxi honking and camels bellowing all told the raucous tale of Dahab settling down for another evening. As the Jeep pulled away from town, the sounds gradually faded to a whisper. The occupants were left with the roar of the engines, the howling wind and the waves of the Red Sea crashing on the rocky coastline. The journey to the dive site took twenty minutes. It was along the same road as the Blue Hole, but closer to Dahab.

As they approached the restaurant, the two drivers turned off their lights at a pre-arranged signal from Dark Shark. They needn't have bothered. The restaurant was closed and empty. There were no boats offshore. The two Mohammeds parked the Jeeps behind the restaurant out of sight. The four companions settled down on the cushions inside. Cigarettes were lit and Mohammed the driver produced a flask of hot coffee from the Jeep.

"What do we do now?"

"Now, we wait."

Away from the town, the stars were exceptionally bright and piercing. Gentle waves lapped the shore. A cool sea breeze washed over the adventurers and the hours passed slowly by.

It wasn't cold, but it wasn't that warm either. Thick Bedouin blankets had been brought in preparation for a long wait. Pretty soon they all huddled beneath the blankets. As the hours slowly dragged by, Gastro and the two Mohammeds gradually fell asleep.

Dark Shark was still wide awake, as was Jamila. They realized that, inexplicably, they found themselves snuggled up together under a blanket. Dark Shark put his arm around Jamila for the first time in nearly two years. The feeling was electric to both of them. They lay there motionless for a long time, staring up at the stars and out to sea. For a brief, perfect moment, they felt absolute peace and contentment.

"They know that someone found the map, the invoices and the log book. Do you still think they will come out here tonight?"

"I do, Jay."

"Why?"

"They know that whoever took the map, it wasn't the

Egyptian authorities. That being the case, they have nothing to worry about. They are probably hoping we will show ourselves and then they will know who they're up against."

"I hope you're right."

"Yeah, me too."

Jamila's head lay on Dark Shark's chest. He gently stroked her soft hair whilst drinking in the wonderful smell.

"I missed you very much, Jay."

"You didn't exactly show it in your emails."

"I know. I'm sorry about that. You know how I can be sometimes."

"Yeah. Incorrigible."

"Jay, do you think… "

"I'm trying not to think at this time. I have a job and a life back in England."

"I understand."

"Maybe it just wasn't meant to be between us."

"You're probably right."

There was a long silence. Time ticked by. Slowly, first Jamila then Dark Shark succumbed to sleep. The waves continued their relentless pounding, but otherwise the Canyon was still. It was Dark Shark who awoke first. He heard a noise and lifted his head with a jerk. He scanned the horizon. He saw nothing unusual, but could quite clearly hear the sound of boat engines coming from just offshore. Jamila's head was still leaning on his chest.

Whispering in her ear, Dark Shark told her to wake up. She rose, stretched her arms and heard the noises too. Dark Shark shook Gastro and Mohammed awake, urging them to remain quiet. He hissed to his friends and then ran to the beach.

"It's here! The shark fishing boat is here!"

A moment later the five companions lay by the water's edge, watching the activities out to sea. A boat had anchored just outside the Lagoon which was the entrance to the dive site. It was large and at night appeared completely black. The crew on the boat could be heard barking orders to each other and preparing for the night's gruesome work. As yet, there were no lights on the boat and the five companions could see little. The boat appeared only as a sinister, black, hulking form, a complete contrast when set against the spectacular star spangled back drop. The engines of two smaller Zodiacs could be heard zooming around the 'mother ship'. Occasionally, there was the slap of plastic lines hitting the water, or the tinkling of small metal objects. Jamila squeezed Dark Shark's hand.

"What are they doing?"

"They're getting ready to fish sharks. They're laying out lines and baiting the hooks with live fish. Probably reef fish."

Just then, someone switched a light on and the boat was lit up from bow to stern. The 'mother ship' was similar to a traditional Arab sailing dhow but with an engine instead of a sail and made from fiberglass instead of wood. It was approximately thirty meters long. It had a simple cabin at one end and a long, single wooden beam running down the middle. Attached to the beam were dozens of rolls of fishing line. The boat probably had thousands of kilometres worth of line on it. Also on the beam were hundreds of very large metal hooks. Piled up randomly in ones and twos along the deck of the boat were the buoys which were used to keep the lines floating. The tools of the trade.

This was definitely the boat. The crew members were working flat out. Some of them drew out lines and attached buoys. Others attached hooks. First they tied the hooks to the line, and then from a wet compartment on the boat, they grabbed live reef fish and speared them on the hooks to be used as bait. Bathed in the sickly yellow light of a cheap light bulb, the dhow took on the macabre appearance of a horror film. Having assembled the lines, the crew piled them onto the Zodiacs. With engines gunning, they zoomed out to sea. Nearly a kilometre from the 'mother ship' the Zodiacs dropped the lines into the sea, forming two large semi circles. Having completed their task, the Zodiacs returned to the dhow, tied up and the lights were switched off again. The whole operation had taken only twenty minutes from the dhow turning up, to laying the lines.

"What now?"

"Now they will wait for a few hours. Just before

daybreak they will go to check the lines. Any shark they find still alive, they will club to death. They will slice the fins off all the sharks and throw the sharks carcasses back into the water."

"*Mother*fuckers!"

"Dark Shark, we need to call the Navy. They can stop this."

"We will, but first I want to get a closer look."

"Don't go out there. It's too dangerous."

"Don't worry. Danger is Gastro's middle name."

Dark Shark smiled and looked into Jamila's eyes.

She said nothing but her eyes told him she wanted him back alive and in one piece.

"Guys, let's break out the kayaks. Mohammed, as soon we start paddling out to the dhow call the Navy. By the time they get here Gastro and I should be back from our little recce."

"Mershi, Dark Shark. Insha'allah."

Running round the back of the restaurant, Dark Shark, Gastro and the two Mohammeds untied the kayaks. Forming two pairs, they carried the kayaks quickly down to the water's edge. They couldn't enter the Lagoon for fear of damaging the coral, so they set the kayaks in the water just to the south of it. Gingerly, Dark Shark and Gastro slipped quietly into their kayaks. Once inside, they donned buoyancy jackets and tied splash guards to the rims skirting the cockpits of the kayak. Safely ensconced, the two Mohammeds pushed Dark

Shark and Gastro out to sea.

They paddled as softly as they could, steadily making their way towards the black ship of death lying just off shore. Luckily there was no current on the surface and the waves were almost non-existent. Back on shore, the three remaining crusaders watched with a mixture of dread and fascination. On the lead kayak, Dark Shark judged the distance to be only two hundred meters or so to the dhow. Kayaks were probably the slowest device ever invented for traversing the sea, so he estimated it would take them a good fifteen minutes to cover the distance. He just hoped the crew didn't spot them.

On the other kayak, Gastro was struggling. He had never paddled in a sea kayak before and was finding the going tough. No matter how much he battled with the small boat, it simply refused to go in a straight line. He wanted to explain this to Dark Shark, but his friend had moved too far up ahead to tell him without being heard from the dhow. He would just have to persevere. Throwing his locks back, he set his face into a fierce, determined grimace as he re-doubled his efforts.

Back on land, Mohammed called the Navy and explained what was going on, but omitted the information about Dark Shark's clandestine operation at sea. Closing his phone, he informed Jamila that the Navy would be here in thirty minutes. She breathed out for a long time, acutely aware of the sound it made.

"This is going to be long thirty minutes."

Out to sea, Dark Shark reached the dhow without detection. He was at the bow of the dhow, but wanted to go to the stern. He reached up and holding onto the fiberglass hull, he slowly pulled himself along the entire length. He was too fearful that the crew would hear him paddling. The fiberglass was horrible material and he felt his hands being scraped by the sharp protrusions running along the outer skin of the boat's hull. Reaching the stern, he carefully turned so he was positioned right next to the large rudder. Above him, he could hear the crew members laughing and joking as they waited for dawn in the cabin. He would wait for Gastro. He couldn't see his friend just yet, but he was certain he wasn't far behind. He couldn't have been more wrong. Gastro had put in a magnificent effort, paddling furiously for fifteen minutes. When he looked up however, he realized he was back at the beach. Gastro cursed silently. Dark Shark was by himself.

At the dhow, Dark Shark was getting impatient waiting. The waves were getting stronger and it was all he could do to stop the kayak banging against the side of the dhow. This was dangerous. The longer he stayed around, the more chance there was of being spotted. He had now been on the water for twenty minutes. Life on the shark fishing dhow was pretty Spartan. The owners had little interest in luxury. The toilet on the boat was a simply a wooden box which hung over the stern. In the floor of the box was a hole. Crew members would squat over the hole to complete their business.

Dark Shark didn't realize it, but his kayak was right underneath the hole. As he was fighting to control the kayak against the waves and wandering what had happened to Gastro, a crew member went to the toilet. Normally, the mess would hit the water. On this occasion, it hit the front end of kayak, just missing the paddler. It made a rather different noise than normal. Instead of a plop, it was more of a splat. The crew member was confused. He peered over the side of the dhow, but could see nothing in the darkness to indicate why he should have heard a splat instead of a plop. He shrugged his shoulders and was just about to go and wash his hands, when suddenly, he heard an extremely loud bang. Dark Shark's kayak had been pushed against the dhow's rudder by the force of a very large wave.

Now the crewman was certain something was down there. He shouted a warning and uproar broke out on the dhow. The crew started running about. Weapons could be heard being readied. The light came on and everyone rushed to the side of the boat. On the beach, Gastro, Jamila and the two Mohammeds held their breath. They were horrified. They could do nothing, knowing all too well that their friend was now at the mercy of brutal, ruthless shark finners.

On the kayak, Dark Shark decided it was time to get the fuck out of there. Pushing the dhow with his paddle, he backed away from the boat and looked up. The crew was staring straight down at him. They were mostly dressed in white cotton shirts, but one man stood out from the rest. He was wearing all black. He had on a long black jelibya. A black kefir was wrapped tightly around his head. He also had on a solitary black eye patch. Only Bedouin wore the Jelibya, but Dark Shark had never seen a Bedouin dress like this before.

The Bedouin in black was tall and thin. He stood unmoved on the deck on the dhow and glared with intense malice down at Dark Shark. His one good eye bore into the instructor who instinctively repulsed from it. The one-eyed Bedouin in black smiled and Dark Shark thought he had never seen anything so malevolent in all his life. At that moment, he realized two things. He knew that this man was the captain of the shark fishing dhow. He also understood, somehow, that this was the man who had buried a hook into his arm at the Eel Garden. Turning the nose of the kayak, he began paddling hard towards the beach. The crew laughed and threw bottles at him, but luckily they all missed.

Next they launched the Zodiacs and Dark Shark realized he was in serious trouble. He paddled harder still. It would take him a good ten minutes to reach the beach. He knew he would never make it. The Zodiacs throttled their engines and came straight for him. In another few seconds they would reach him and it would all be over. In each Zodiac, there were at least four men all armed and dangerous. Dark Shark was just considering letting off the flare gun as a last resort when a most peculiar thing happened. The Zodiacs turned round and headed back to the dhow. What was going on? Dark Shark looked around him and realized what was happening.

Approaching from the South was the Egyptian Navy. He was saved! A patrol boat was fast approaching. Looking back, he saw the Zodiacs return to the dhow. The one-eyed Bedouin in black stood on the deck staring at Dark Shark. Then he turned and gave the order for the anchor to be lifted and for the engines to start up. With a mighty roar, the dhow was almost lifted from the water by the power of the engines. Dark Shark watched in amazement as the shark fishing dhow disappeared at an impossible rate of knots.

"Fuck! She is getting away!"

As the shark fishing dhow departed, the one-eyed Bedouin in black stood on the deck staring back at Dark Shark. He made a slashing gesture across his throat and then pointed towards the object of his hatred. Wearily, Dark Shark paddled the rest of the way back to the beach and into the arms of his very relieved friends. Jamila particularly, hugged him tightly.

"Jesus Christ, you idiot. I thought I had lost you."

"It's okay, Jay. You didn't lose me. You have never lost me."

An hour later, Dark Shark, Gastro and Jamila were sitting on cushions on the floor of Dark Shark's half a house. Blue smoke was snaking slowly upwards and into the kitchen. Aretha Franklin was singing:

"You better think! Think about what you trying to do to me! Think! I aint no doctor or psychiatrist with no degree, but it don't take much IQ to see what you doing to me! Think! You better think about what you doing me to me! Think!"

Dark Shark, Gastro and Jamila were thinking. After a few minutes, Dark Shark spoke:

"We know that Moheet was murdered. We know why she was murdered. We know that she had a boyfriend and we also know who the shark fishing captain is, but we don't know their names. We're getting closer, but we need more information."

Jamila looked deep into his eyes.

"If we want to know what is going on in this town, then we need to speak to the Bedu. Dark Shark, you have to go and talk to Sheikh Hassan."

# 8

## *Bedouin*

The next day found Dark Shark in the office of Just Another Dive centre. It was eight thirty in the morning. Mohammed was sitting behind his desk as usual. He was slugging coffee, piling sunflower seeds into his mouth and smoking. Gastro and Jamila were also there, sitting on chairs and rubbing sleep from their eyes, both of them nursing coffees. Sally popped in and out, running messages from the counter to the office. Jamila looked up Dark Shark. She was pensive, mulling over the previous night's close call and trying to put it into context.

"I am so glad we managed to stop that dhow from killing any more sharks."

Dark Shark returned her gaze, trying hard not to think about how beautiful her eyes were.

"Me too. That was too close for comfort. Gastro, when you finally take a diving course, you really ought to think about kayaking lessons as well."

"My apologies, brother. I had no idea paddling a bloody kayak could be so complicated."

"No worries. Shit happens."

The phone on Mohammed's desk rang. He picked it up.

"Aiwa."

A voice on the end garbled away in Arabic, too fast and too quiet for the others to make sense of. Mohammed finished the conversation and hung up. He looked around at his friends, before speaking.

"Bad news, I'm afraid."

"What happened?"

"That was Hosni from Utopia. Apparently, last night, Frank Zappa fell down a ten foot well over in Assalah."

"Holy shit. Is he okay?"

"He's a little shook up, but otherwise fine."

"Phew. That guy has issues with balance. Thank God, he's okay."

Just then Adel of the Shamandura strode purposefully into the office.

I won't tell you what he was wearing, you should already know by now. Tension filled the room.

"Salaam Alechem."

The four friends returned the greeting. Mohammed offered him a drink and got up to arrange another chair for Adel, but the man from the Shamandura told him we would stand. What he had to say wouldn't take long.

"I want an explanation as to why the four of you were at the Canyon dive site last night. Mr Dark Shark, perhaps you would care to explain please."

"We went to the Canyon to paddle sea kayaks. We

were bored because of the diving ban, so we decided to go kayaking."

"At night?"

"Why not? The Canyon is beautiful at night."

"Really. Why did you have the Zodiac there?"

Mohammed answered this question.

"The Zodiac was back up, Adel–Sir. We had it there for safety reasons."

"Mohammed. When I want an answer from you, I will ask you a question. Is that understood?"

"Aiwa, Adel-Sir."

"So, let me get this straight. The four of you and Mohammed the driver decided to go paddling kayaks last night at the Canyon dive site, which just happened to be getting a visit at the same time from a shark fishing dhow. Is that your story?"

Adel glared at Dark Shark. Dark Shark glared back at Adel.

"Yes. That's right."

The man from the Shamandura looked as if he believed the story about as much as he believed the result of an Egyptian general election.

"I hope you are telling me the truth, Mr Dark Shark. I hope that you heeded my warnings to stay out of my investigations. The consequences for disobeying me are extremely serious. Do we have an understanding, Mr Dark Shark?"

"I believe we do Adel, I believe we do."

"Excellent. I trust we will not be meeting like this again."

Dark Shark did more than trust. He hoped with all his might.

Adel fiddled with the safety catch on his huge tool and strode as purposefully out of the office as he done coming in. The tension left with him. Silence followed. After a few minutes to make sure the security man had really gone, Dark Shark sighed, stood up and went over to the desk. He reached inside his bag and pulled out the vellum shark fishing map. He carefully unfolded it and laid it flat on the desk.

They crowded around and bent over the map.

"The Canyon was last night. According to this map, the next target is Ras Abu Galum."

"Surely they won't try again?"

"They might well do, despite knowing we are on to them and despite the Navy turning up. Shark fins are big business. These guys are desperate."

"What are we going to do?"

"We need to get this map to the Navy. The dhow has such big engines there is no way a Navy patrol boat can catch her. The only way is if the patrol boat is already at the site. They may not try Ras Abu Galum next as they know we have the map, but somewhere out there these guys are going to fish sharks."

"Who was the guy that attacked you on the boat?"

"That was the captain. A very nasty piece of work

indeed. He wore a black Jelibya, black Kefir and sported a patch over one eye. Whilst I was taking a peek inside the main hold, he tried to separate my head from my body with a machete. I get the distinction impression that he is also the same dude who tried to fish me at the Eel Garden. I have only met this guy twice and on each occasion he has nearly killed me. Until now I've been lucky. I sincerely hope my luck continues to hold out."

Gastro put his hand on his friend's shoulder.

"Next time, it will be me that meets the one eyed Bedouin in black."

Dark Shark smiled.

"What did you find out from Simone?"

"Bent Bob is in it up to his neck."

"What did she say?"

"The day after we took the map from the locker at WDD, Simone told me she saw Bent Bob open one of the lockers and explode with rage. She couldn't tell which locker it was, but she clearly remembers the incident because of his reaction. She is lovely that Simone, I may have to meet up with her again."

"I gather that after you spent a few hours at Slow Down with her, she is now unemployed."

"She is. She told me she is looking for a new job. The experiences she'd had at the WDD were not exactly positive, so she wasn't bothered in the slightest when she got fired."

Their discussions at the desk were suddenly interrupted

by a noise coming from the doorway to the office. All of them spun round and looked up at the same time. Standing there was a woman. She had long brown hair which fell about her shoulders, high cheekbones and, it seemed to Dark Shark, very familiar large, oval, brown eyes.

She was in her forties and wore light brown slacks, reddish brown sandals and a light green hooded top. When she spoke, she had an American accent. Her voice was soft and warm.

"Hello. My name is Mojave."

Dark Shark had a sudden realization that he knew exactly what was coming next.

"I am here about my daughter, Moheet."

No one said a word. They were all in total shock.

It took some time for Dark Shark, Gastro, Jamila and Mohammed to regain their composure. All three of them were still staring at Moheet's mother. She looked so much like her daughter it was uncanny. Mojave had the same almond brown eyes, the same high cheekbones and the same full lips. In every way, except one, Mother and daughter looked the same. The only difference was age. Mojave possessed Moheet's features, but in her face were etched the lines of wisdom and experience that only come with age. Mojave was tall, graceful, regal, and as Dark Shark duly noted, not in the least bit dead.

"I flew out here as soon as I heard the news of my daughter's death from the Egyptian authorities."

Apart from her words, there was absolute silence in Mohammed's office.

"I came here because I want to take Moheet back to her family on the reservation in Arizona and because I also believe my daughter was murdered. I want to find out who is responsible for her death. The Egyptian authorities have told me they believe Moheet drowned going for a late night swim after drinking in a bar with her friends. I know my daughter. It was not an accident. Moheet was born in the desert but could swim before she could walk. Somebody killed my daughter and tried to make it look like an accident."

Mojave was trembling, her voice wavering as she struggled to retain her dignity and composure. The effort was plainly visible to everyone present. Dark Shark stood up and approached Mojave. Taking her in his arms, he hugged her tightly.

"My name is Dark Shark. I was your daughter's instructor. Since her death, we have been trying to find out everything we can. We are determined to get to the bottom of this and find out the truth of what happened to Moheet. I am so very, very sorry for your terrible loss Mojave. She was very special."

Mojave held Dark Shark tightly. She didn't know this man, but her daughter had gone to him for a reason and she instinctively felt she could trust him. Tears fell from her eyes. For a long time, they held each other. When their embrace was ended, the others all came forward and offered their condolences. Mojave sat in a chair and proceeded to share with them the story of her daughter.

"As Moheet told you, I am a diving instructor. I am now a Course Director in Arizona and run my own dive centre. I introduced Moheet to the underwater world at a very young age. As soon as Moheet could hold a regulator in her mouth, I took her diving in the lake next to our reservation. Like many children, Moheet took to it like a fish to water. She loved it. She constantly asked me when we could go diving next and gleefully looked forward to every diving adventure. At school she spent many lessons drawing pictures of the many fish and animals she saw in the lake with her diving mom. The other kids were jealous of Moheet, and it was because of them that I set up the first Native Peoples Diving Centre."

Mojave paused, took a deep breath and continued.

"When Moheet was fifteen, I organized a school diving trip to Bonaire, the best location for diving in the Caribbean. Moheet and her school friends were absolutely delighted and spent all winter talking about nothing else. They read up on the Caribbean reefs, drew pictures of the fish they would see, and practiced new moves in our lake back home."

Her audience were completely engrossed in the story and hung on every word. You could have heard a tooth drop.

"The trip to Bonaire was a huge success. Moheet and the other kids absolutely loved the diving. The weather was excellent the whole week and as usual the locals on Bonaire were great. The only shadow cast that week was when Moheet and I, walking along a path on the remotest part of the island, spotted some fishermen returning with their catch of the day. On the jetty was a pile of dead sharks. Each of the sharks had been finned and was lying in a bloody pool. The blood trickled over the jetty into the sea. Moheet was shocked as indeed I was. Although shark fining is still prevalent all over the Caribbean, it is not only highly illegal in Bonaire, but strictly enforced by the well-armed coastal police. Heavy punishments are meted out to those who fin sharks. Hurrying back into the main town, I telephoned the office of the coastal police to inform them of the crime. The fishermen were arrested and their catch confiscated later that day. The incident left a deep impression on young Moheet. If anything it strengthened her love for the aquatic world. On her return to the United States, Moheet kept up her underwater passions, but now her attentions were beginning to turn to conservation as much as exploration. Not long after, Moheet announced she wanted to become a Marine Biologist. Her father and I were very happy for her. It seemed like a great thing for her to do. She was talented at science and was obviously in love with the sea. When she was eighteen, Moheet graduated from high school with honours. She was accepted to the best Oceanographic Institute in America and planned to spend the summer before university diving in the Red

Sea. However, her father became ill. Instead of going to the Egypt, Moheet spent the summer helping me look after my husband. It wasn't until her second year at the Oceanographic Institute; Moheet got her chance to dive in the Sinai. The Institute was conducting a survey of coral reef populations in the Gulf of Aqaba and needed lots of pairs of fins. Moheet signed up immediately and spent the first three months of her assignment based in Sharm El Sheikh. Whilst there, she met a diving instructor from Austria called Nemo. He had first come to Sinai three years previously, an unskilled immigrant. At first, he worked on and off in restaurants and bars, getting work where we could. Time passed. He saved up some money and managed to get himself a diving instructor license. Soon he started working in the dive centres. He met Moheet at this time. Romance blossomed. He was Moheet's first boyfriend and she was thrilled. To her, he was exotic, adventurous and passionate. I was calling Moheet once a week. At first the relationship went well. They were happy together. Soon though, things started going pear shaped. I knew something was wrong. Their relationship was strained by perpetual arguments concerning money. Nemo was an angry young man, and as a result was finding it difficult to find stable work. He would work in one place for a short while, get fired and move on to another. Moheet was supporting both of them with her university allowance and was evidently impossible to sustain for long. It was only after a tearful

Moheet got on the phone to me one night, that I got the whole truth from her. Nemo was becoming more and more aggressive towards her. In turn, she became more afraid of him. Nemo was not only frustrated by a lack of work. His anger was much deeper than that. When he was only seven years old, his gardener in Austria caught him sexually molesting his pet hamster. I begged Moheet to leave him, but she refused, saying it would be the worst thing for him. Finally, for the first time in her life, the tensions caused problems between me and my daughter. A week ago, after another big argument on the phone, Moheet told me she was going to Dahab to as she put it, chill out and get away for a while. That was the last time I spoke to my daughter. Five days ago she left a message on our answering machine saying she had seen something terrible on her arrival in Dahab. I waited for her to call back, but she never did. I think whatever Moheet discovered in Dahab, got her killed."

Mojave sighed.

There was a long silence.

"What else do you know about Nemo?"

"Not much. Only what you already know. I spoke to him once on the phone. It was a short conversation and little was said."

Somewhere deep inside the nitrogen saturated cerebral cortex of Dark Shark's dehydrated cranium, a light bulb went off.

"Does he have blond hair?"

Mojave was surprised.

"He does, yes. How do you know that? Do you know him?"

"No. Gastro and I found some items belonging to Moheet. Her log book and a gold locket. Her photo was in the locket, but the other half of the locket was empty. Two days ago we paid a visit to the Forty Thieves hotel where Moheet had been staying. In the wardrobe, on the floor, I found this photograph. It fits perfectly inside the locket. We are convinced the man in the picture was Moheet's boyfriend."

As he was speaking, Dark Shark reached inside his bag and retrieved the items belonging to Moheet. He gave them to Mojave who examined each one slowly. Looking at the photo of the blond man, she nodded slowly.

"Yes, that is him. That is Nemo."

When she came to the locket containing the picture of her daughter, she stared at it for what seemed like an eternity. Finally she brokedown, unable to hold the pain in any longer. She cried, tears streaming down her cheeks. Jamila put her arms round Mojave and hugged her tightly. Mojave's body racked from the pain. Her mind screamed, reeling from the information it didn't want to accept.

"I want to see my daughter again. I want to see her one more time. Will you come with me Jamila?"

"Yes. I will go with you. I am here for you."

There was a long silence in the office, punctuated only

with the sounds of Mojave's heartache. The four friends respectfully gave her the space she needed.

Finally, Mojave composed herself and the five protagonists discussed the next step. It was agreed that Jamila and Mojave would visit the morgue in Sharm El Sheikh. Mohammed had to somehow get the shark fishing map to the Navy without them knowing who had sent it. That just left Gastro and Dark Shark.

"Gastro, we should try to get some information about what is going on at the Golden Wadi Massage Parlour. I trust you can handle it?"

"Piece of cake. I will pretend to be a customer."

"Be careful."

"Don't worry. I am the epitome of… "

"Yeah we know. Subtlety."

Mojave looked confused and turned to Jamila with a questioning look on her face. Jamila answered her.

"Don't worry. You'll get used to them."

For the first time since entering the office, Mojave managed a weak smile. Gastro lit a cigarette, exhaled and did an impersonation of Dark Shark's favourite man from the Egyptian security services.

"So, Mr Dark Shark. What will you be doing during this time?"

"I am going to Musbat."

Jamila and Mojave took a taxi to the morgue in Sharm El Sheikh, The taxi driver, Osama, was a huge, friendly man. Over the years Dark Shark and Jamila had gotten to know him well and they liked him a lot. He had become Dark Shark's main taxi driver. Whenever they took taxis to a destination outside of Dahab, they used Osama. The big, burly taxi driver used to smoke sixty cigarettes a day. Unusually in Dahab, he had managed to quit. He had succeeded by replacing each cigarette with a banana. It was a strange strategy, but it worked. The only drawbacks were that Osama weighed one hundred and three kilos and two people were known to have died after slipping on discarded skins outside his house.

Osama was an excellent driver. He drove a 1932 blue and white Peugeot 504. The car had long been banned in Europe, but was perfect in the desert.

"Ha Ha! Gamila, you and Dark Shark are together again eh?"

He laughed heartily, throwing a banana skin out of the window. The skin flew directly into the face of a passing Bedouin riding a donkey. The furious Bedouin shook his fist at the taxi and promised civil war.

Osama was Egyptian. The dialects of Bedouin Arabic and Egyptian Arabic are slightly different. In Bedouin Arabic there is no hard G sound, only a J. The Egyptians, on the other hand, do not say J but G. "No, we are not Osama!"

Jamila liked Osama, but he frequently strayed from the path of tact. Osama grinned.

"But Gamila, you love him!"

"Osama!"

Jamila was only a tenth of his size, but despite this, she nearly knocked him out.

When they arrived in Sharm El Sheikh, Osama dropped off Jamila and Mojave at the morgue, promising to pick them up an hour later and drove off to the fruit market in the district of Old Sharm Maya. Mojave was trembling again and Jamila had to help her to the front entrance of the morgue. Once inside, the two of them made their way to the front desk and explained to the seated official who they were, and the purpose of their visit. The official picked up a purple phone and dialled a number, indicating Mojave and Jamila take a seat. Five minutes later, a door to the right of the front desk opened and three men walked out. They were wearing dark grey suits, white shirts, black shoes and moustaches. All three had large, automatic firearms partially hidden under their clothing. One of the men grunted a greeting.

"Salaam Alechem"

Despite being a Muslim, he did a great impersonation of a pig.

"Alechem salaam."

Mojave replied. Jamila said nothing.

The man grunted again.

"Please follow me."

Mojave and Jamila followed the three men through the door to the right of the front desk. They entered a brightly lit corridor perhaps thirty meters in length. There were broken black and white tiles on the floor.

Dirty brownish-white paint was falling off the walls, and on either side of the corridor were a row of black doors with small barred windows. There was the smell of damp in the air and although she wasn't cold, Jamila shivered. As the three men of the CusAmac led Mojave and Jamila down the corridor they passed a door on their left which had, underneath its barred window, a small sign saying 'Political Opposition.' Inside a man screamed. Jamila and Mojave jumped. A pungent, acrid smell hung in the air.

As they passed the long corridor of horrors, they could clearly hear the sounds of wails and groans. Mojave gripped Jamila's arm and whispered a question to her new friend.

"What is this place?"

Jamila didn't answer. She felt physically sick. At the end of the corridor was a door without a window or a sign. The man who had grunted earlier opened the door and led in the others. They walked slowly into a large, cold room. On the floor, the black and white tiles were new and shiny. Big neon bulbs bathed the room in a cold white glow. There was a single, large, metal table in the middle of the room. Next to the table was a rack containing various surgical instruments. The only noise in the room was the ever constant whirr of the air-conditioning. Opposite the table were rows and rows of square metal doors sticking out about an inch from the wall. Mojave gripped Jamila's hand tightly as they walked slowly passed each door, looking for the one that contained the body of Moheet.

Back in Dahab, Dark Shark walked along El Fanar St. Instead of continuing to the Lighthouse, he turned abruptly left and disappeared into the rambling maze that was Musbat. The Dahab Bedouin occupied two areas. Musbat was one and the other was Assalah. The Bedouin lived in their own self enforced apartheid. They didn't live with the Egyptians who had their own areas, and they didn't live with the ex-pats, who couldn't remember where their own areas were.

The Bedouin not only lived separately from the other residents of Dahab, they also lived in a different era. They had made only partial concessions to the onslaught of change and progress. They'd agreed to give up their nomadic existence, but not their camels or goats, their culture or their Jelibya. (If you don't know what a Jelibya is, Google it!) The Bedouin had a hard time dealing with the modern world which was forcing them to work. Bedouin men believed the day time was for sleeping, not working, especially during the winter months.

Once Dark Shark had stepped off El Fanar Street and entered Musbat, he had taken his first steps into a different world. Between shoddy houses made from crumbling cement blocks, palm trees sprang from the ground. The palms were sacred in Bedouin culture. Their fruit of dates was much prized and it was forbidden to cut one down. Rather, the houses were built around them. Palm trees sprang from the middle of roofs, interrupted walls and formed elegant centrepieces in courtyards. Crude cement block walls divided the space and surrounded each humble abode. Camels were tied up, some sitting, some standing. Most were chewing on tires and rubbish, sometimes a Bedouin. Pick-ups and Jeeps sat in the gaps between dwellings. They were the favourite method of transportation for the men, who mostly worked as taxi drivers ferrying tourists to the dive sites. A Jeep outside a house invariably meant the man had no work and the household could expect less money that day. In amongst the houses, running through flocks of goats, teasing camels and generally creating as much mayhem as they could, Bedouin kids played in the dirt, their bare feet testimony to their poverty. Bedouin women both young and old rushed between the houses, always on a mission of some sort or other. They perpetually shouted, scolded and fussed over the younger children, the goats and camels. Dressed in black and faces heavily veiled, the women worked incessantly to provide for their large families and lazy husbands.

As with all cultures the world over, it was the women who kept it all together. Bedouin culture was a curious mish mash of tradition combined with modernity. It has not always been this way. The plural word Bedu, from which the singular Bedouin is derived, simply means 'inhabitants of the desert.' It refers primarily to the tribes living on the Arabian Peninsula and in the deserts of

Sinai and the Negev. The traditionally romantic Western notions of proud desert peoples sitting astride camels whilst crossing great wastes of burning, shifting sands are not too far from the truth.

The desert provides little agriculturally, so historically, the Bedu moved from one area to another, therefore allowing each area to regenerate. Where ever they went, the sheep, goats and camels went with them. In the harsh conditions of the desert, the environment is an unforgiving place. Violations of territorial rights were considered most uncool and it was a hallmark of Bedouin culture that they neither forgave nor forgot. The deep solitude and barren wastes of the desert imbued the Bedu with much respect and care for strangers and it was that this that gave rise to their famous hospitality. The mere presence of another face was so rare as to cause great excitement amongst tribal members. Once a stranger had entered their camp, he was treated as a guest and could expect to stay so for three days before even being asked questions as to his back ground. During this time the family would share with him whatever they had, even offering him delights usually kept for special occasions. In addition, the guest would receive the complete protection of the clan.

The traditional Bedouin tent the stranger would have found himself in would have been separated into two areas. The first was for the men and male guests. Its Bedouin name was mag'ad, which means 'sitting place'.

The second area was where the women cooked and was also for female guests. This area was called the maharama or 'place of women'. Guests were served either coffee spiced with cardamom or sweet black tea. Music, songs and sayings were very important in traditional Bedu culture. Music offered not only entertainment, but was a reliable way of keeping tales, traditions and continuity. Traditional musical instruments included the shabbaba, a long metallic flute, the rabbaba, a type of violin and most importantly, the voice. Most of the singing was done by women who would sit in lines opposite each other and sing in a style that was almost sung dialogue. As they did so the musicians would play, whilst the other clan members would join in by clapping and dancing.

Today there are Bedouin tribes in Arabia, Israel, Syria, Jordan, Egypt and Libya. In the Sinai there are approximately ten tribes. The oldest, the Aleigat and the Sawalha inhabit an area from Suez to El Tur, taking in Wadi Feiran and Sarabit El Khadim in the south-western corner of the peninsula. The Muzeina tribes occupy the area from St. Catherine to El Tur, taking in South Sinai and the coastal towns of Dahab and Sharm El Sheikh. The Aleigat, Sawalha and Muzeina tribes emigrated to the Sinai from Arabia in the 14th Century.

Much later came the Tarrabin who arrived in the 18th Century and occupied the coastal area north of Nuweiba. The exception amongst the tribes is the Jebeliya, who live in the high mountains around the monastery of Santa

Katarina. The Jebeliya also arrived in the 18th Century, but originated from Eastern Europe, most likely either Romania or the former Yugoslavia. The word Jebeliya means 'mountaineers'. Purity of blood is most important to the Bedu, so needless to say the other Sinai tribes look down on the Jebeliya who cannot trace their ancestry back to the sands of Arabia.

Today, many of the Bedu have exchanged their nomadic existence for a more modern way of life, although in some areas of Sinai the old ways still persist and Bedu continue to live as they have always done. The tourist industry they now work in may be a new kind of tourism, but if the truth be told the Bedu have acted as tourist guides since the advent of Islam. In the old days, the Bedu would guide pilgrims on their journeys to the great holy places; to Mecca, Jerusalem and Santa Katarina. The road taken by the pilgrim processions crossing Sinai was known as the Darb el Hajj (pilgrim's road).

Even today, the modern Bedu organize their society along ancient tribal lines. A family comprises of a tent, a camp of tents make up a clan and kindred clans make up a tribe. Each clan member takes pride in knowing that all members of the clan are of one blood. The tent and its items are individual, personal property, whilst water and pastoral lands are considered tribal property. Bedouin clans demand complete loyalty from each member and each clan considers itself to be of pure blood and superior. It is the strong support structure offered by the clan, reciprocated by unswerving loyalty from each member, which enables the Bedouin to survive in such a harsh environment.

Each clan is represented by a Sheikh who is the leader but does not have absolute authority and must consult with a counsel of tribal elders on matters of importance. Although Bedouin society is polygamous and patriarchal, with the man as master, Bedouin women have a degree of liberty. They are free to choose husbands and divorce is common in Bedouin society. There is no stigma attached to the process and many Bedu remarry. When the husband is away, which in the old days would have been for considerable periods of time, the wife is in charge of the house, children and animals.

Traditional Bedouin laws protected women by making penalties for crimes against them four times worse than for equivalent crimes committed against men. Bedouin laws are strict and as harsh as the desert. Blood calls for blood. If a member of the clan commits murder inside the clan, nobody will defend him. If he escapes he becomes an outlaw and is banished from the tribe. Banishment for a Bedouin amounted to death. Without the tribe, he would be lost and unable to survive in the desert for long. If a murder is committed outside the clan, a vendetta is established. Any clan member is liable to pay the debt and in this situation it becomes a blood feud. Feuds may go on for many years, although vendettas can be settled by payments of blood money.

Traditionally, the Bedouin considered agriculture to be beneath them. Theirs was a life of freedom, adventure and banditry. The modern world has given them new challenges and today the Bedouin farm the land and have planted gardens. The majority of these are situated in the more arable lands of the north where the Sinai meets the Mediterranean Sea and the town of El Arish is located. Modern Bedouin have exchanged a simple, healthy diet of dates, milk and fish, a life of walking and a society without currency for a faster, more modern and ultimately unhealthier lifestyle. Despite all the changes, however, the camel remains the favourite animal of the Bedouin. Camels were not only modes of transport but the means of exchange. For the Bedu they are not just ships of the desert, they are Atta Allah-'the gift of Allah'.

Dahab was the only place in the world where you could find 'geep'. A geep is a goat crossed with a sheep. In Musbat they were everywhere. It was strange indeed to see a fat sheep with the climbing abilities of a lean, mean desert goat. One more than one occasion, Dark Shark had witnessed geep flying off the roof of the nearby Mosque, twenty feet above ground level, land perfectly, and run across the road to Musbat. But today, Dark Shark wasn't thinking about geep.

Today, Dark Shark was thinking about his visit to see Sheikh Hassan. He picked his way amongst the debris, trying to remember where the old Bedouin lived. He'd been to the Sheikh's house many times, but Musbat was an extremely confusing place. Every building looked virtually the same. Sheikh Hassan was probably the poorest Bedouin in Dahab. He was also one of the most influential and popular, and nothing went on in Dahab without Sheikh Hassan knowing about it. He was also Dark Shark's dealer. Sheikh Hassan didn't do any other work and he didn't deal to anyone else except Dark Shark, which was why he was so poor. Also, he wasn't really a Sheikh and had earned the moniker for a completely unknown reason. It probably had more to do with contacts than with influence. Dark Shark spied a familiar looking battered blue gate which was leaning precipitously on one rusty hinge. He had arrived. Good.

He carefully swung open the blue door and entered into a large yard. Walking in he carefully skirted a large camel which had been tied by its knee and was sitting slowly chomping a large piece of cardboard. The ground inside the yard was covered in gravel. In one corner, a large Hoosha had been constructed which provided refuge from the strength of a harsh, beating sun. Palm leaves had placed across the top of a wooden frame. Underneath, cushions, rugs and palm logs were positioned around a pile of blackened coal, the evidence of a recent fire.

Clothes lines were strung across the yard and various t-shirts, underwear, robes and headscarves dangled in the wind. At the far end of the yard, was a house. It was very much like all the rest in Musbat. It was old, crumbling and dirty. Irregular pine wooden slats made up the roof. In the middle of the front outer wall was a thick brown wooden door. The door was closed. To the left there was a single window without glass. Two dark brown shutters were closed over the gap. Dozens of large black flies hovered around the shutters, excited and attracted by sugary morsels dropped by the human inhabitants within.

As Dark Shark approached Sheikh Hassan's house, he wondered if the old coot was awake. Sheikh Hassan took the Bedouin sleeping philosophy to new heights, and most times Dark Shark saw him, he looked like he had just woken up. To Dark Shark's mild surprise, he could hear voices coming from inside. The old coot was very much awake. Dark Shark raised his hand to knock on door but before he could connect, someone had already opened it.

"Salaam, Salaam, Dark Shark. Come in. We have been expecting you."

At precisely the same moment that Dark Shark entered the house of Sheikh Hassan, Gastro was walking into the Golden Wadi Massage Parlour. His long, grey dread locks were tied up in a bunch. He was wearing an old Clash t-shirt, beige sandals and torn denim blue shorts. On his eyes was a pair of large, round, deep red sunglasses. In many ways, he was the archetypal anti-establishment traveller freak. Gastro felt like he had travelled back in time and was visiting a decadent establishment during the Ming dynasty. The overwhelming colour was red. There were giant red Chinese lamp shades hanging from the ceiling. Red couches lined the walls and red lamps bathed the room in a luxuriant, soft glow. Plants sat in huge, ornamental metal pots. On one wall was a large poster. The lettering on the poster was in English but painted in Chinese style. The poster declared the legend:

"Golden Wadi Massage Parlour – We will stroke away your stress."

A huge desk made from an exotic black hard wood sat directly opposite the front door. Next to the desk was a doorway. Luminous gold and silver beading hung down from the top of the frame. The beading had rippled invitingly with the draft when Gastro had opened and closed the front door. The door way was flanked by two large, Chinese stone lions. The lions' mouths were wide open, revealing huge, frightening teeth. They dared anyone to enter, fierce guardians to the forbidden pleasures that lay within.

There was no one present. Gastro looked over to the desk and spied a small, silver bell. He picked it up and rang hard for a few seconds. Pushing aside the glittering beading, a woman stepped into the room. The woman was Mandarin in origin. Gastro guessed her to be in her late fifties. She had long, silky, black hair which she was tied into a bundle and held in place with a long, black needle. The woman wore a long, green Chinese dress, similar to a Kimono. The outfit was lavishly adorned with beautiful, sweeping dragons. Each dragon was sown with silver thread and depicted in intricate detail. The whole ensemble came almost down to her feet which were wearing elegant black shoes. On seeing Gastro, she smiled warmly and bowed low.

"Greetings sir. You have come to sample the delights of the Golden Wadi Massage Parlour?"

"Oh yes."

"Excellent. My name is Pai Mai. I am the proprietor here. I offer you our services and warmly welcome you to our respectable establishment."

Pai Mai turned on a dime and disappeared through the wall of shimmering gold and silver, beckoning her guest with one hand.

"Come with me sir."

Gastro followed like a puppy chasing a ball, his tongue hanging out and bounding along. Pai Mai and Gastro walked down a long corridor. Every few feet, there was a door with a red handle and a number painted in black. Pail Mai walked slowly, her back was perfectly straight.

"Who would you like to give you a massage? Do you want a man, a woman or someone in between?"

"A woman. Definitely a woman, please."

"Yes, I thought so. You look like a lady's man. What kind of woman do you like?"

"I like my woman to have the hips of a fourteen year old boy."

"Ahh... How interesting. Yes... I have the perfect one

for you. You will enjoy a lot. She is very professional and very talented."

Pai Mai stopped outside one of the doors. She knocked once then opened the door and went inside. Gastro breathlessly followed. He could hardly wait for what was to come next. The room was furnished in a similar fashion to the reception, but with one exception. In the middle of the room was a long, massage table. Next to the big table was a small round pedestal which had four red towels neatly folded and piled on top of it. Along the walls, incense burned in wooden holders, filling the room with the strong scent of musk. Tall candles were lit and shadows flickered across the walls in erotic convulsions. Pai Mai gave instructions to Gastro.

"Take off your clothes and put on a towel. Then lie down. The girl will be along in just a moment."

"Thank you."

"You are most welcome. What kind of massage would you like?"

"I don't really know. What are the options?" "When the girl arrives, she will bring two menus with her. One is for massages, the other is for extras."

She said the last sentence with a knowing wink and before Gastro could say any more she was on her way out the door.

"You are going to have a wonderful time, sir. This girl is very good. She will take you to places you have never been before."

Gastro believed every word she said. He stripped off his clothes, threw them onto one of the chairs and covered his naked form with one of towels. He lay on the table, crossed his hands and lay his head on top of them, thinking as he did so,

"This place is funky. I am going to have to come back here and do some more research."

Gastro waited patiently, but he didn't have to wait long. A door opened and he heard footsteps approach. A young voice with a soft Chinese accent said to him:

"Hello sir. My name is Qigong. I am here to give you a massage. Would you like to have a look at the menus?"

Gastro looked up and behind him. Standing there was a beautiful young woman. It was difficult to guess her age but she couldn't have been more than twenty five at the most. She had the same black hair as Pai Mai, but it was more vibrant and shimmered when she moved. She was slim, with big, beautiful black eyes. She wore a simple white blouse and skirt decorated in black embroidery. Her elegant hands were holding two booklets which Gastro took to be the menus.

"I would love to."

He took the menus from the masseuse and opened the one marked Massage. Inside, written in English but with letters in Chinese style, was a list of exotic massages. Customers could sample such delights as Indian head massages, a Thai full body experience, Japanese Reiki and many more. Gastro was in heaven.

"One Thai full body massage please."

"An excellent choice. You will enjoy very much. Please give me ten minutes to get prepare."

"No problem baby. I am here."

Qigong left the room to get ready. As soon as she had closed the door, Gastro got up and walked over to one of two windows on the far side of the room. He peered through the first one, making sure no one could see him looking out. In the courtyard he could see Pai Mai talking to a large man. They were conducting a heated conversation outside a door marked Stores. The man was fat and spoke with an American accent. He was standing partially concealed by a palm tree and from his position; Gastro could see who it was. When he heard the voice though, he knew who it was. It was Bent Bob.

The owner of World Domination Divers was trying hard to calm down his host.

"Don't worry Pai Mai. The invoices don't prove anything. There are no descriptions on any of them. Nothing will get back to you. The Golden Wadi is safe for now."

"Bob, how you can be so sure!? Gastro is inside right now! How do we know the Shamandura isn't going to turn up next and put us all on a boat back to China? I'll be fucked if I'm going back to Beijing. The place is a shit hole. My family has not been able to make money since the Cultural Revolution!"

"Relax Pai Mai, relax. It will all work out fine in the

end, don't you worry, just wait and see. We have got a little surprise for Dark Shark and his pathetic friend. Soon they won't be around to bother us anymore."

"I want him out of here right now! Get that fucking smelly hippy out of my establishment right now!"

"No. Let's not get him suspicious. Give him the works. We will deal with him later."

The debate between them trailed off as they moved out of ear shot and inside the room, Gastro could hear no more. He went over to the chair and picked up his clothes. He still had a few more minutes. He took off the towel, threw it on the bed and dressed quickly. Quietly padding out of the room, he checked to make sure the corridor was empty. He half ran, half walked down the corridor and came to a door. He opened the door and went into the courtyard, heading for the storeroom. He walked quickly to the door marked Stores praying it was unlocked. His prayers were answered.

Inside, the room was black. Fumbling, he found a light switch and flipped it on, closing the door behind him. He looked around quickly, taking the whole room in with one glance. Boxes were piled up, nearly taking up all the available space. On the boxes were labels in Chinese. Gastro couldn't read Chinese, but on some of them the words Hong Kong were printed in large English letters. He opened one of the boxes. It contained nylon fishing line rolled up in a huge bundle. Metres and metres of fishing line. He opened another box. Inside were hooks.

Hundreds and hundreds of shark fishing hooks, exactly the same as the one Dark Shark carried as a memento.

Gastro had seen enough. It was time to get back. He flipped off the light, closed the door and half a minute later was back on the massage table with a towel around his waist.

"I'm so sorry to have kept you for so long, sir. Are you ready?"

Qigong had returned, carrying a bottle of warm oil.

"That's okay. Yes, I am ready."

Pouring oil into her hands, the Chinese masseuse began to massage Gastro's body. She poured oil onto the middle of his back, his shoulders and his legs. She rubbed the oil all over, her light sensitive hands kneading the muscles and working the sinews. Gastro relaxed immediately. Her touch was electric and his muscles jumped involuntarily at the sensation.

"Do you like sir? Is it working?"

Gastro could only grunt in response.

"If you are satisfied with my service, perhaps you would like to choose one of the extras from the menu?"

Gastro grunted an affirmative.

"Here you are sir, you have a look at that and choose."

Gastro took the menu and studied it hard as the masseuse continued to work her magic on him. As he read the list of pleasures on offer, his eyes grew wider and wider.

"Oh my God. Ermm.... Well... Gosh... Let me see... I

think I will have one of each please."

Qigong laughed.

"Very good sir. I want you to relax as much as you can. You are in excellent hands. I will take you to places you have never been."

Gastro believed every word.

Taking off his shoes as was the local custom, Dark Shark entered the dark house of the Bedouin, Sheikh Hassan. Inside a group of Bedouin men were sitting on cushions in a semi-circle. The men lounged around a small, metal box on legs. Inside the box, hot coals warmed a teapot and Dark Shark could smell the sweet Bedouin tea percolating inside. In the centre of the group of men was Sheikh Hassan. He was in his early sixties. He wore a light green Jelibya and a white Kefir which was the same colour as the rough stubble on his chin. In his eyes danced a mischievous smile. He was warm, friendly and thoroughly trustworthy. He could frustrate Dark Shark at times, but on the whole, he loved him to bits.

When Sheikh Hassan and the other men saw Dark Shark enter, they all salaamed him and made room for him on the cushions. On the floor next to the box, a large sheet of newspaper was spread out. Long sticks of Marijuana crisscrossed the newspaper, each stick heavy with flowers. A huge joint was passed to him by a Bedouin with extremely bloodshot eyes. As usual, Dark Shark felt immediately at home. He smoked and drank tea, cementing his reputation as an honorary Bedouin.

At such meetings, the Bedouin are most relaxed. They talk in low tones, if at all. Sometimes nothing is said for a long time. They appreciate silence and only speak if they feel it adds something to the atmosphere. Life in the desert has taught the Bedouin to appreciate silence. This was probably just as well. It was often interesting for Dark Shark to watch tourists in this situation. They did not understand the value of not talking and struggled with silence.

An awful lot could be learned from watching tourists react to the Bedouin and the desert. An hour later, no-one had yet said anything and after drinking two cups of tea and smoking another joint, Dark Shark decided it was time to get down to business before he forgot why he'd come here in the first place.

"Sheikh, I came to see you because there is some very strange things going on in Dahab and I need some information from you"

"Aiwa, I know, Dark Shark."

"You know about the shark fishing? The dead sharks at the Blue Hole and at Abu Hillal?

"Aiwa."

"You know about the death of my student, Moheet?"

"Aiwa."

"So maybe you know who is behind all this and why?"

"Aiwa."

"How do you know all this, Sheikh Hassan?"

"The Bedouin know everything."

"So, will you tell me who killed Moheet?"

Sheikh Hassan took a long, deep drag on a joint. He stared long and hard at Dark Shark from under his white kefir and said:

"La."

Dark Shark sighed.

"What will you tell me, Sheikh Hassan?"

"Go and see my brother, Sheikh Awad."

"Sheikh Awad in Ras Abu Gallum?"

"Aiwa."

Dark sighed again.

"I will go in the morning."

"Good. I will make all the arrangements with my brother, Sheikh Awad. Be at the Blue Hole at seven."

"Sucran, Sheikh Hassan."

"Afwan, Dark Shark, afwan"

# 9

## *Harmonica*

At six o'clock the following morning Dark Shark, Gastronimica, Jamila and Mojave packed their equipment into the Jeep, ready for their journey to Ras Abu Gallum. The adventure would take them back all the way as far as the Blue Hole, before the mountains made any further travel with the Jeep impossible. The previous day, whilst Jamila and Mojave had been in the morgue and Dark Shark was busy talking to the cryptic mystic in Musbat, Gastro had finished up at the Golden Wadi Massage Parlour.

Stumbling out of the palace of pleasures, he'd jumped into a taxi and a few minutes later he'd met up with Mohammed, the owner of Just Another Dive Centre.

"Did you send the map to the Navy, Mohammed?"

"Aiwa. The officials have received it and are delighted. They don't know how or why the map reached them, but they are very happy that it did. Apparently, they will be present at all the dive sites featured on the map. It is highly likely we have closed this criminal operation down for now."

"Inshallah, Mohammed, Inshallah."

"Aiwa, Inshallah. How did it go at the Golden Wadi Massage Parlour?"

"I found out two things. Firstly, it is being run by a madam from Beijing called Pai Mai who has connections to the shark fin trade in Hong Kong. Pai Mai is using the Golden Wadi to order and then store all the tools needed for shark fishing. Lines, hooks, buoys, the whole enchilada. Whilst I was there, I over head the charming Madam Mai arguing with Bent Bob and sounding less than happy about the invoices being discovered. She is terrified about getting deported back to China. For all we know, she is also the conduit for the shark fins to the Hong Kong market. I snuck around the place and discovered a room full of evidence."

"What was the other thing you found out?"

"Heaven is Chinese."

"Ha-ha! You'd better phone Dark Shark and tell him the news. Tell him also about the map reaching the Navy."

"Good idea."

Gastro opened his phone and called Dark Shark's number. The English instructor was coming back from Musbat. He answered the phone just as he was reaching El Fanar Street.

"Aiwa."

"Hey, it's me."

"What's up?"

"Can you call me back please? I am low on credit."

"You're always low on credit. Why don't you go and get some before calling me?"

"I can't. I'm skint. Give me some money and I can go buy credit."

Dark sighed.

"I'll call you back."

Dark Shark closed the phone and returned the call. Gastro pressed the green button on his phone and answered.

"Aiwa."

"What's up?"

"It's me."

Dark Shark sighed again. This was getting old fast.

"I know it's you Gastro. What did you call me for?"

"Two things. I am here with Mohammed. He tells me that the map is now in the hands of the Navy. They are going to be present at all the dive sites listed on the map."

"Excellent."

"Indeed."

"What's the other thing?"

"What other thing?"

Dark sighed for the third time.

"The other thing you were going to tell me."

"Ah yes. I have just been at the Golden Wadi Massage Parlour."

"And?"

Gastro repeated what he had already told Mohammed.

Dark Shark was impressed.

"Wow. Great work Gastro. You're the man."

"Cheers. I'll tell you something else too."

"What?"

"I've just been to places I have never been to before. Places I didn't even know existed."

"Ha! That is saying something. I thought you had been to *all* the places by now."

"Yep, me too."

"Your experiences at the Golden Wadi were that good, eh?"

"Fucking eshta mate."

"Heh-heh. Catch up with you later brother."

"Ciao, amigo."

Once at the Blue Hole, the only way to progress to Ras Abu Gallum was by camel. Dark Shark was ambivalent about the camel part of the safari. One hour on a camel in the hot desert sun always left him a bit cold. After coffee and cigarettes, the four divers said good bye to Mohammed and Sally at the counter, jumped into Mohammed's Jeep and lurched down the Blue Hole road. The trip lasted for five minutes before spluttering to a halt. Mohammed jumped out of the jeep.

"Mershi! Dark Star, mershi! Mafish mishkela! This time I am prepared!"

Mohammed frantically poured a jerry can of gas into the tank, then jumped quickly back into the Jeep. He turned the key to the ignition and lit a cigarette.

Unfortunately he still had some gasoline on his hand which immediately caught fire. Dark Shark sighed and hoped the incident wasn't an omen. Fifteen minutes later and with his hand bandaged, Mohammed was again driving down the Blue Hole Road. Dark Shark noticed he was driving without his lights on and in almost total darkness. A puzzled instructor turned to Mohammed and inquired why he hadn't turned on the lights.

"La, la, mishkela, battery. Halas."

Dark Shark sighed and wished it was the Omen.

Despite the best efforts of their driver, the four divers reached their destination on time. As arranged, Sheikh Awad was waiting for them at the top of the mountain next to the Blue Hole. He was the oldest Bedouin they had ever seen. He was ancient. The lines on his face lines on top of them. He was so wrinkly when he moved the wrinkles seemed to move independently of him. Sheikh Awad was eighty-three, but he moved like a man of thirty-three. Living the traditional way in a Bedouin hoosha, raising a large family on the shores of the Red Sea and ignoring modern trappings, he'd retained much of his health, vitality and vigour. His left arm was permanently crooked; the hand was nothing more than a claw. The fingers were short and the hand bent in, as if he were in constant pain.

When he was just a young child, a donkey had fallen on and crushed his arm. Unable to afford a doctor, the arm had never set properly. For most of his life, this brave, dedicated man had endured the hardship and humiliation of his afflicted arm with the dignity that made the Bedouin what they were once were and sometimes still are, proud survivors in one the harshest environments known to humans. He wore a white jelibya and a purple kefir, standard clothing for a Muzeina Bedouin.

Accompanying Sheikh Awad from his home at Ras Abu Gallum, were four large camels. Dark Shark and the others unloaded the equipment from the Jeep and placed it evenly in sacks which were then strapped to the sides of the reluctant, argumentative, ships of the desert. Sheikh Awad also helped load the equipment, despite the protestations from Dark Shark - who should have known better. The ancient Bedouin would lift an item with one arm and balance it with the other. Even with his impaired arm and advanced age, the man worked faster than everyone else.

The path up the mountain and down the other side was too steep to ride the camels. They would be led up by the humans on foot. The four divers and Sheikh Award trudged up the mountain following an ancient path. They cut through a wadi intersecting the mountain and reached the summit. The view out into the Gulf of Aqaba was astonishing. They could see far into Saudi Arabia from their vantage point. The sea, a long finger only twenty kilometres across, glittered in the early morning sunlight. The sea was the deepest azure blue. Dark Shark had stood on this mountain many times, but had never failed to be in awe of what he was experiencing. There was nowhere else in the world like this. The silence in the desert was total. Only the wind howled amongst the jumble of rocks and shale.

It was still early, but the sun was already high in the sky and beat down on them without mercy. The travellers walked the remainder of the way down a narrow path. The camels, always eager when they knew they are going home, had to be restrained. In their hurry to get down, they almost pushed their human masters off the path to an unwelcome fate on the rocks below. As the strange convoy walked, Sheikh Awad controlled his camels with the skill of a man in total control of animals he had lived with since the womb. He whistled, scolded, prodded, slapped, swore at, cajoled and constantly talked to his camels. Always he urged them forward and always they obliged. Well, mostly. At the bottom of the mountain they reached a small, flat clearing.

Sheikh Awad forced the camels to the ground and tied their knees. He thanked them for their patience and rewarded them with water and straw. The adventurers took the opportunity for a break and tea was served. A half hour later it was time to move once again. The four divers jumped on the camels. Sheikh Awad untied the camel which, freed from the rope, lurched forward and then up. A camel rests by first putting down its back legs, then kneeling on the front ones. When it stands up, it uses the rear legs first and a rider sitting on top is jerked forward violently. The wooden pommel at the back of the saddle digs into the spinal column. For the uninitiated camel rider, it hurts like hell. (Hence Dark Shark's ambivalence towards camels.)

The safari slowly wound its way along a winding path at the edge of the multi-coloured Sinai Mountains. The sun traced its daily arc across the sky casting lurid orange and yellow streaks across the Red Sea. On their right, as far as they could see, the Saudi Arabian coastal mountain range was still steeped in shadow. On their left, the early morning light glinted on sheer walls rising straight up. The walls comprised of granites and limestone, shaped over time into incredible structures by the wind, waves and salt. Nobody spoke; everybody was taking in the atmosphere of the desert.

No matter how many times he traversed this path, Dark Shark never tired of its beauty. To him the beauty that existed all around was evidence that humans still resided in the Garden of Eden. Humans had misunderstood the Bible. Heaven and Hell were not in the afterlife. They existed on this plane. Humans lived in Heaven. The planet Earth was an infinitely beautiful world which provided everything needed to sustain life. Human beings had a choice. They could continue to live in Heaven or turn it into Hell. Dark Shark hoped he was wrong about the direction he believed the human race was heading. The desert and the sea also represented a contrast. The seemingly barren and endless wastes of the desert, met the almost infinite riches of a unique sea. This mirrored the contrast of humans. Some humans gave a shit and some didn't. Dark Shark wasn't a politician, but he figured that all the problems in the world existed because someone somewhere, wanted it that way.

Half way to Ras Abu Galum, the four camels stopped and knelt on the ground. Everybody jumped off, eager to let the blood circulate around their legs once more. Gastro pulled out bacon sandwiches and handed them out to everyone except Sheikh Awad who politely declined. He did, however, accept Jamila's offer of a Marlboro Light. Mojave was impressed by the desert and mentioned how different it was to the one back in her home state of Arizona. Sheikh Awad was particularly interested to hear all about it. In eighty three years, he had never left the Sinai.

Mojave had been riding side saddle on her camel and hadn't quite worked out the differences between a camel and a horse. Comparing deserts was easier. After getting off the camel, Dark Shark had collapsed onto the ground. The unholy trinity of early mornings, adventures and his wounded arm were beginning to exert a toll. He badly needed a break. All he wanted to do was sleep. For a few days. Or even a week. Yes, that sounded good right now. He would close his eyes and sleep. Rest a little on the shores of the sea and succumb to the hypnotic noise of waves breaking onto a rocky shore.

Sheikh Awad missed nothing. He noticed Dark Shark falling unconscious and went over to him. From inside a hidden pouch he brought forth a gourd made from dried goat's skin. He spoke quietly into Dark Shark's ear. The old Bedouin's voice was barely a whisper.

"Dark Shark, wake up. It is not the time to sleep yet. Wake up my friend. You will have time to sleep later. Here, drink this."

Slowly Dark Shark stirred from his drowsy condition and taking the gourd in both hands leaned back and drank. The liquid was thick, warm and slightly salty. It flowed into his stomach and immediately tried to jump straight back out again. He almost retched.

"Jesus, Sheikh. What is that!?"

"Fresh camel's milk. I milked them this morning before dawn."

"Thank you, but I can't drink that. Sorry."

"Neither can I. Tastes like shit. So warm. Ichsa! At least you're awake now."

Sheikh Awad cackled demonically, evidently finding his joke hilarious. As he laughed, his wrinkles rippled. Dark Shark failed to find the humour in the situation. He had to concentrate instead on fighting to keep the milk from launching itself at the mountain.

It was mid-morning by the time the intrepid explorers roused themselves to continue onwards. Sheikh Awad untied the camels and they were off. The strange caravan continued on its way along the path where the desert met the sea. On their left, the huge mountains formed an impassable barrier to the desert. At times, the mountains came right down to the water's edge. In other places, they retreated almost two kilometres away. Always they were a constant presence to the riders, as ubiquitous as the sun, the wind and the sea.

Occasionally, they spotted eagles and once, a black and white osprey, which thrilled momentarily by swooping down and plucking a large fish from the sea. The journey was spiritual, beautiful and surreal. An hour later, the caravan arrived at the large, sandy headland that was Ras Abu Gallum. The headland stretched for more than five kilometres in a gentle, golden crescent. Dozens of ramshackle Bedouin hooshas fanned out along the edge only a few meters from the water. Hundreds of camels were dotted around, tethered to posts or their own knees. Bedouin kids, sometimes no older than two years old, ran amok, harassing the camels, playing games in the sand and receiving shouts or curses from older members of the tribe.

The deep blue waters of the Gulf of Aqaba lapped gently against the headland. Bedouin women, dressed from head to foot in black and veiled as ever, zigzagged slowly across the top of the reef plate, searching for anything they could find to put on the plates of their hungry families or sell to the tourists. The whole place looked like a western movie, the Indians supplanted by Bedouin. Dark Shark kept expecting to see tumbleweed roll past. Some did. Ras Abu Gallum looked like Sinai used to, before it became a two week package nightmare. It is still part of the old Sinai wilderness, the Sinai you only read about in guide books, not the one you visit now.

Sheikh Awad's hoosha was at the far end of Ras Abu Gallum, the quietest spot on the headland. That was because Sheikh Awad wanted his business to be the quietest on the headland. Dark Shark squinted against the strong desert sun to the far corner of Ras Abu Gallum, towards the hoosha of Sheikh Awad.

But for once, Sheikh Awad's hoosha wasn't very quiet, it was in uproar. Sheikh Awad's seven children and one of his wives appeared to be struggling with a Bedouin man. Dogs were barking at the commotion and camels were grunting. The Bedouin wore all black and across one eye was a black patch. It was the Captain of the shark fishing dhow! He was shouting and lashing out at the children with available legs and arms. One Bedouin kid was swinging off his right arm, but the one eyed Bedouin in black still managed to send another of the kids flying with a well-aimed kick.

The kid picked himself up and started crying, a large cut evident over one eye. At this, Sheikh Awad's wife and the mother of the child went berserk. She picked up a large cooking pot and with the biggest swing she could possibly muster, hit the monster squarely on the head with the pot. A thunderously loud clang was heard across the entire headland. The man's two feet came off the ground and up as far as his head. He landed in a crumpled heap on the ground and moaned. Sheikh Awad's wife ran over and brought the pot down on his stomach as hard as she could. Again his legs went up and this time his entire body doubled up in pain. He screamed and crawled away as fast as he could. His Jeep was only two meters away, but by the time he had reached it, Sheikh Awad's wife had managed to hit him four more times.

The one eyed Bedouin in black pulled himself up and began to climb into the Jeep. As Sheikh Awad's wife lifted the pot and came in for yet another blow, he weakly raised his leg and pushed her away. The one eyed Bedouin in black stood in the Jeep and looked up. His head was covered in blood. Both his black kefir and eye patch had fallen off and were hanging down across his shoulders. His black jelibya had patches of blood splattered across it. Just at that moment, he saw the approaching riders. With a snarl, he thrust the key into the ignition. His one good eye contained a maniacal glint.

Dark Shark took all this in and made to spur on his camel, determined his enemy would not escape. Sheikh Awad had already started moving and slapped Dark Shark's camel with a length of cane. The camel shot forward and galloped straight towards the red Jeep, the other camels following a head behind. A second later, the one eyed Bedouin was turning the key in the ignition and Dark Shark thought he would never make it. Sheikh Awad, eighty three years old and on foot, outraced the camels and jumped onto the roll bar of the red Jeep. As he did so, the Jeep's engine started and the vehicle lurched forward. Sheikh Awad put his crooked arm around the roll bar and held on for dear life. The one-eyed Bedouin cursed the ancient Sheikh, who held on grimly. Dark Shark's camel was almost on top of the jeep. From nowhere, Sheikh Awad produced an ancient curved sword with which he now attempted to decapitate the one-eyed Bedouin.

The Sheikh had never been so angry in his eighty three years. The evil, one-eyed Bedouin had violated the most ancient customs of the desert. Sheikh Awad was going to make sure Allah judged him straight after the one eyed head had been separated from the body. The sword travelled through the air with frightening speed, making a swooshing noise. Just before the sword connected, the one-eyed Bedouin yanked the wheel of the Jeep sharply to the right and hit a geep. Instead of the sword cutting off his head, it slashed deeply across his arm. He let out a long, blood curdling scream.

Thrown completely off balance by the impact and the swing of his own sword, Sheikh Awad flew out the Jeep and landed heavily in the dirt, only a few yards from his own hoosha. The sword clattered to the ground nearby. The one-eyed Bedouin roared in victory and sped off north, the red Jeep kicking up a cloud of dust as it departed. The geep, momentarily shaken, staggered onto uncertain legs and after a few moments carried on with its favourite meal of plastic bags. Dark Shark and the others quickly dismounted and rushed over to Sheikh Awad who was dusting himself down saying:

"Mershi, mershi"

An hour later, life returned to some kind of normalcy in the hoosha of Sheikh Awad. His wives prepared Nescafe, the kids were patched up and the animals had quieted down. Dark Shark, Jamila, Gastro and Mojave sat on cushions inside the hoosha, the desert sun burning the air outside. Sheikh Awad explained what had happened in a mixture of Arabic, Hebrew and English.

"This man comes to Ras Abu Gallum, mishkela, Yanni, we kill him, he makes mishkela in the maya, bad Bedouin, eza shtiot, we kill him, mishkela kateer.

"Do you know this man, Sheikh Awad?"

"Aiwa, he is very bad, mishkela, mishkela. His name Salah, he kills sharks. He smoke opium. Very bad man. Walla-he."

"Who does he work for, Sheikh Awad?"

"He work for new dive centre, he work for Neptune."

"Who is the owner of this new dive centre, Neptune?"

"Nemo."

Pretty soon, Bedouin from all over the headland came to discuss the traumatic incident and what it meant for them. After much back and forth, Dark Shark was able to get a better handle on what had transpired. The one eyed Bedouin had turned up at Ras Abu Gallum and headed straight for the hoosha of Sheikh Awad, demanding to know where Dark Shark and the Sheikh were. He had cursed and ranted, accusing Dark Shark of costing him money and Sheikh Awad of helping him. Things had turned nasty when the Bedouin in black insulted Sheikh Awad's wife. For a Bedouin man to go to the house of another Bedouin man and insult his wife was simply unthinkable.

The Bedouin all agreed that this behaviour was unacceptable. They would find the perpetrator and administer traditional Bedouin justice. Dark Shark was quite sure it wouldn't involve a jury.

The four companions spent the rest of the day relaxing. They spent money with the women and the children buying Bedouin trinkets. They also dived the pristine reef skirting the headland and Dark Shark tried to get as much information on Nemo and Salah as he could. Towards evening Dark Shark and his friends decided it was time to head home. There followed an emotional farewell and many promises of return trips to Ras Abu Gallum. They bid farewell to Sheikh Awad and his family.

Once the four camels had been laden with diving tanks and equipment, they roared their disapproval, struggled up and the caravan began snaking its way back along the Red Sea coast. Looking back at Ras Abu Gallum as he left it, Dark Shark saw a French tourist coming out of one of the small toilets which stand back from the hooshas. The French tourist staggered a few feet and passed out. Sheikh Awad's seven kids skipped over to the French tourist, laughing and giggling. One small girl carried a bucket of well water which she threw over the tourist's face to revive him. The tourist came to, spluttering and coughing. The Bedouin kids, screeching wildly, shouted:

"Buy one! Buy one! Buy one! Buy one!"

The sun was disappearing over the Sinai Mountains and pink clouds streaked across the electric blue sky.

Before their departure from Ras Abu Gallum, Sheikh Awad had talked to Dark Shark alone in the desert. They had squatted, Bedouin style, around a small fire deep inside a Wadi. The fire crackled, a waft of thin smoke curled its way up towards the stars. Black shadows leapt and danced on the wall of rocks behind them. Apart from the fire, there was complete silence.

Sheikh Awad was very tired. The deep creases in his face resembled the cracks etched into the desert rocks, carved over time by wind and sand. Despite his antiquity, he still possessed great strength. His brown eyes shone with hidden mystery. He had seen many moons, he was very wise, he had fathered seven children, and he knew the secrets of the deep desert where only the Bedouin choose to walk. Sheikh Awad picked his nose.

Looking around to make sure they were alone, he began speaking. He was using a different tone and his English had improved dramatically.

"Dark Shark, the shark finning in the Red Sea is a matter of great distress to the Council. As well as being incredibly cruel and wasteful, the abhorrent actions by Nemo and the one-eyed Bedouin to kill sharks show a deliberate attempt to de-stabilize not only the local economy of Dahab but the whole of Sinai. The geopolitical, not to mention biological, ramifications of such actions are unthinkable. Not only are the Bedouin threatened, but Egypt, Israel, Palestine, Jordan, Saudia - the whole region."

Sheikh Awad paused, sighing deeply, his action as much for dramatic effect as for breath.

"The Bedouin have walked the sands of Sinai for thousands of years. The desert is our Mother. She gives us all that we need; food, shelter, camels... and peace. We Bedouin have survived many different invaders over the years. The Romans, Byzantines, Phoenicians, Ottomans, Israelis. All have come and all have gone; only the Bedouin have stayed. When it was necessary, we have bent with the wind, helping some, fighting others. In modern times, our brothers across the water in Saudia sold their black gold to fuel the engines of industry. The world has changed and the change has reached Sinai; the Bedouin no longer wander the desert. We must live in houses, working for money, slaves to the onslaught of change and progress. We have witnessed the time of the hippies, the divers, and the two week package holiday makers. Now they are developing the desert. Our Mother is being developed! Roads cut through the desert. Hotels spring up along our coasts destroying the sea. Jeeps, cars, and trucks pollute the pure air with their foul smoke. Air conditioning and standing water have changed Sinai's climate, the air becomes humid, and for the first time ever, there are mosquitoes, attracted by the water and by imported plants. The fish are killed in huge numbers, served up in the restaurants for a few precious dollars. The reefs are dying, killed by the activity of humans. Sinai is crying out, she is in pain! But we Bedouin are patient. This time of change is insignificant compared with the time we have walked the desert. When all the black gold has run out, the Bedouin will still have their camels, when the Jeeps have stopped, we will walk in the desert again and when the pale ones beg us for help, we will laugh in the faces of the stupid infidels!"

Sheikh Awad was now in full flow. He jumped up, striding purposefully around the fire with his hands crossed behind his back. He shot fierce looks at Dark Shark.

"Behind the façade of his new dive centre Neptune, Nemo threatens to destroy the entire Red Sea. Using his influence over the shark fishing Bedouin, he grows powerful this Nemo. Without the sharks, the reefs and therefore the sea will die. The lifeblood of all is dependent upon the health of the sea. The sea is unable to sustain this level of destruction. Sinai cannot resist this latest attack. The Bedouin have decided Nemo must be stopped; the time to act is now. For the first time in nearly forty years, the Council has convened an emergency meeting to decide on a course of action. Almost definitely, the

Council will decree that you will stop him, Dark Shark. The meeting will be in three days when the moon is full."

"Three days!? By that time… "

"The meeting will be in three days, it cannot be sooner. Remember, you are the one. You have time to prepare, but you will need help and there is only one person who can help you. You must go and see Harmonica."

"But it's been a very long time, Sheikh Awad; I don't think she will want to see me."

"Harmonica wants to see you and she is expecting you."

"How do you know that Sheikh Awad?"

"The Bedouin know everything."

Back in Dahab, Mohammed flew out the door of his office, beaming with delight when he saw his four friends returning from their adventures in the desert.

"Salaam, Salaam, how was Ras Abu Gallum?"

"Informative. We found out that Sheikh Awad's wife is very talented with a cooking pot."

The gang packed away their gear and took a much needed hot shower. In the office over coffee, they discussed the events of the last few days. Dark Shark commenced proceedings.

"Sheikh Awad told me that the one eyed Bedouin Salah went to Ras Abu Gallum to complain about the help we are getting from the Bedouin. Our enemies are very angry. Apparently we are making some progress and have already cost the shark finners a lot of money in lost revenue. We are succeeding. However, the gloves have now come off. They are going to come after us with everything they've got. They've become desperate. The bad news is that things are going to get a lot more dangerous around here. The good news is I believe their desperation is going to lead them to make mistakes. When that happens we need to be in a position to take advantage.

"What do we do now?"

"I will go to see Harmonica. What is happening with the autopsy, Mojave?"

"They are nearly finished. Almost for sure the new coroner is going to deliver a verdict of homicide. The Shamandura has launched a murder investigation. They have given me permission to travel to Sharm and get Moheet's body released. I will finally make arrangements for her to be returned to the United States. I want to go down there tonight and am hoping Jamila will go with me."

"Yes of course, I will go with you Mojave."

"Good. What are you going to do Gastro?"

"I'm organizing a party at Slow Down. I need to go and put up flyers around town. I hope you guys can make it to the party. It'll be a great opportunity to relax and let your hair down after all that has happened recently."

Jamila wasn't convinced.

"I don't think this is the right time for parties, Gastro."

Dark Shark didn't agree with her.

"I don't know Jay. I think Gastro is right. We need to unwind badly. A Slow Down party might just be the thing."

"Okay. Let's see what happens and how I feel later."

It was agreed that they would all meet up again later at the bar and bade each other fare well. A few minutes later, Dark Shark found himself picking his way through the rubble of Assalah. It was much bigger than Musbat and had the space behind it for further development. Over the years, expatriate tourists had built houses for rental. Investment in Dahab was moving away from dive centres and into property. As well as Europeans, Egyptians and a few Bedouin had invested in a new buy-to-rent market. Assalah extended to the far edge of Dahab and Harmonica's house was right on the far edge of Assalah. Dark Shark weaved his way amongst the motley array of houses, trying to remember which house was the correct one.

Being a rambling maze in the manner of Musbat, Assala's houses all looked the same. It had taken Dark Shark eighteen trips to the house before he remembered the location. That had been the time when Dark Shark was training. Turning a corner he swore he had just passed a minute ago, Dark Shark recognized the unmistakable outline of Harmonica's house. He walked tentatively to the front gate which was slightly ajar and pushing through, walked into the front garden.

All around him was a green jungle, thick and deep. In the arid conditions of Sinai, the amount of foliage was nothing short of miraculous. Palms, ferns, and bushes of every description randomly, and quite naturally, grew in lush profusion. Dates and figs hung from nearby trees. Dark Shark caught the scent of citrus, the wonderful aroma of nana. Birds flew amongst the trees, and geckos ran across the path and up the walls. He breathed in the smells and drank in the sights; the beautiful garden assaulted his senses, forcing a feeling of peace on the troubled instructor. Dark Shark reached the front door which was round and dark green. It had a mysterious small oval carved into the wood, its significance unknown. Dark Shark raised a clenched fist ready to knock on the door, but it slowly opened of its own accord. Deep from within the interior of the house came a woman's voice.

"Come in, Dark Shark."

Harmonica's house was much smaller on the inside than it appeared on the outside. This is typical in Assalah. But it was beautiful, and she had decorated it with some weird and most fascinating objects from around the world. On one wall, a giant Yin/Yang poster adorned the wall, side by side with a huge Ganesh Throw from the deserts of Rajasthan. Harmonica was sitting cross legged in a lotus position in the lounge. Her eyes were closed and she was breathing deeply. She inhaled for a few seconds and her stomach rose slowly as it was filled with air.

Using sublime control perfected over many years of practice, Harmonica drew the breath up from the stomach and into her rib cage. The air was caressing each rib, oxygenating the internal organs, healing anything damaged and cleansing the body. From there it entered her throat and was dispelled from an open mouth. Behind Harmonica, incense was burning. Amber-scented smoke rose in wisps towards the domed ceiling, its sweet smell filling the room. Dark Shark knew the breathing technique well. Harmonica was doing Prananayamamahamawama, the ancient Indian Yogic meditation technique.

It had been the first thing Harmonica had taught him when he had started his training. After Jamila had left Dahab, a devastated Dark Shark could no longer see the point of training and had ceased attending the weekly sessions. Harmonica came slowly out of the lotus position, stretched, and with sublime grace, control, and power, lifted her feet up. A second later, she was pivoting upside down on the little finger of her left hand. Her right eye slowly opened and she spoke in a soft, soothing tone.

"I know what you seek, Dark Shark."

Dark Shark steadied himself.

"I need your help, Harmonica."

"You left the teachings, Dark Shark."

"I know. I am sorry, Harmonica."

"I will help you, Dark Shark, but you must return to the teachings first."

"I need to find Moheet's killer."

"You must complete the teachings and finish your training."

"I cannot, until I have helped my friends."

"Then I cannot help you Dark Shark. You are on your own."

"The Austrian Aryan Nemo is dangerous and powerful. How do I defeat such a man?"

"You must look deep into your heart, Dark Shark. Find the truth, and be brave in the face of death."

Dark Shark did not feel brave, he felt like a spliff.

"Nemo is psychotic. He is severely lacking in empathy, unable to feel anything. For over 420 million years, sharks have swum in the oceans of the world. They predate the dinosaurs. They have shaped all life in the seas and therefore all life on Earth. Remaining basically unchanged in all that time, sharks are nature's perfect design. Taking sick and weak animals, sharks clean the sea. Their function is to maintain the balance, keeping the sea healthy. Reducing shark populations is extremely detrimental to the marine environment. It is not only the sea that depends on sharks. The Bedouin receive their main source of all important protein from the sea. The Sinai economy depends on the health of the reefs. Nemo cares nothing for any of this. His only concern is to make money. He will not rest until he has achieved his objective of killing all the sharks in the Red Sea. Nemo threatens the environment and the balance of nature in his pursuit of money and power. He has formed an unholy alliance with the Golden Wadi Massage Parlour, the Stilton Hotel, Bent Bob and another man, a one eyed Bedouin who dresses all in black and captains the shark fishing dhow. The Bedouin is the traitor in our midst. Hate consumes him. He spends all his time plotting destruction and suffering. Never before has Sinai been so threatened! Mother Nature is crying out for justice and I feel her screams in my blood. The evil must be stopped before it is too late!"

Dark Shark wondered if a hobbit was going to run into the room, but he continued to listen in respectful silence.

"I have known Nemo for over three years. He was working in McDonalds for six months before Mother Nature turned angry; sending a flash flood from the mountains and sweeping McDonalds into the sea. The manger of McDonalds was Bent Bob. He and Nemo had become good friends and even after the 'accident' of Nature, they kept in contact with each other. They both received compensation from their former employers. Bent Bob used his loot to take over the dive centre at the Stilton, renaming it World Domination Divers, whilst Nemo went to Sharm. He used his money to become a diver, took his professional qualifications, and eventually worked as a freelance instructor for the big dive centres. Not long after commencing her research, Moheet met Nemo and tragically fell under his spell. Seemingly a strange match, Nemo was evidently attracted not only by her striking beauty, but also by her kindly nature and innocent disposition. In Moheet, Nemo recognized traits which he could never possibly hope to attain, hopelessly damaged as he was by deep mental scars. For her part, Moheet was disingenuous, trapped by his snake-like charms, attracted to a darkness she mistook for mystery. Six months ago, Nemo's mother died and he received a large inheritance. Nemo decided to start his own dive centre in Dahab. He wanted to take Moheet with him, but her mother was against the idea, pleading with her daughter to continue her studies in Sharm El Sheikh. When he heard this, Nemo threatened to kill himself unless Moheet went with him. She relented and they came to Dahab, setting up Neptune dive centre. Right from the start, things were tough. The dive centre struggled to find enough customers. It was losing money hand over fist. Nemo had spent the majority of his inheritance on the business and was now under tremendous pressure. The relationship turned tense when Nemo became aggressive towards Moheet, but she remained loyal. Unknown to Moheet, Nemo had joined forces with Bent Bob who introduced him to the one-eyed Bedouin Salah and to the Chinese madam, Pai Mai. The four of them hatched a plan to start fishing sharks and sell the fins in Hong Kong, where they would be turned into shark fin soup. A week ago, Moheet realized something was very wrong when she discovered hundreds of shark fins drying on the roof of a building at the back of Neptune. She was truly appalled by what she saw. As you know, Moheet loved the sea and sharks in particular. She could scarcely believe that she had given up her studies in Sharm El Sheikh, dropped out of university and got together with a man who was killing sharks for a living. She confronted Nemo about the fins, but he shrugged off her protests and told her he didn't care. He was making lots of money and was more than happy about it. She threatened to go to the authorities. Nemo threatened to kill her if she did. Moheet became desperate. She was beside herself with fear and anger. She needed some help immediately. That's when I advised her to sign up for a diving course at Just Another Dive Centre. I made sure you got the course, Dark Shark."

"You...!?"

"Moheet needed a professional. Somebody who shared her love for sharks. Someone who was crazy enough to help her against the scheming Nemo. Somebody like you, Dark Shark. I met Moheet the first day she arrived in Dahab. I was in a shop buying twelve kilos of bananas for Osama. The taxi driver was taking a Russian Dive Master, suffering from decompression sickness, to the re-compression chamber in Sharm El Sheikh. The Russian had got the bends after downing eleven vodkas and going diving in the Blue Hole. He was wearing a seven litre steel tank and wanted to go to the bottom of the Blue Hole, but came up after only three minutes with blood coming out of his eyes... "

Dark Shark was familiar with the scenario, having worked in Dahab for the last two years.

" ...Anyway, Moheet was in the fruit shop, trembling like a leaf in the wind. My spirit soared with hers, we had a spiritual connection.

I sensed the fear within her. Moheet's spirit cried to mine and I responded. I introduced myself and we became good friends. Moheet kept me informed of events and I advised her on what to do."

"When does your advice turn to action, Harmonica?"

"My teachings forbid it, Dark Shark"

Dark Shark walked slowly home. Night had fallen and he found it even more difficult to remember the way back. Familiar objects disappeared into the gloom. Dark muttered to himself as he stumbled over rocks and avoided lethal water wells.

"Fucking Hippies."

Harmonica was one of the deadliest martial artists in the world. She possessed a supreme fusion of deadly technique, incredible speed and a light touch. Yoga, Ninjustu, Aikido and Tiddly winks, Harmonica was a master. Dark Shark needed her help badly against the Austrian Aryan anti-Christ, but Harmonica was having none of it.

Finally, with very sore toes, he reached his house. Opening the door, he went inside. He took off his coat and shoes, then called Gastro and told him he wouldn't be attending the party at Slow Down, explaining he was far too tired. Closing the phone, he went to the kitchen. He muttered again as he attempted to light the gas on his stove with a lighter.

"What is the point of being Bruce Lee if you don't use that shit from time to time?"

The lighter blew up, burning his thumb. Dark Shark sighed, turned off the light and went to bed.

In the back of Osama's taxi, Jamila was holding hands with a tearful Mojave. They were on the way home from the morgue in Sharm El Sheikh. Mojave had finished all the formalities with the Egyptian authorities and Moheet's body was now on its way to their ancestral homeland in Arizona. Mojave stared out the window, breathing deeply. Her exhaled air settled on the windows' cold glass. The light mist coagulated into rivulets of water and streaming down the glass they dropped to the floor, mingling with the salty despair of Mojave's tears. Her head drooped slightly and she appeared as if in a trance. Her mind struggled with the unreality of her situation. She was experiencing flashbacks, snatches of dreams and visions, tormented by memories of her daughter. Mojave, dignified and proud, shook with fierce emotions, her stoicism, and courage tested to the very limit by the devastating events which had rocked her world. At the base of her spine, Mojave felt the rising tide of pain, the Tsunami, a huge wave, rising up, threatening to engulf her in its destructive wake. She struggled to stem the black tide, the mental anguish physically manifesting itself. She spoke, the words as much for herself as for Jamila.

"She is with her people again"

Jamila hugged her tightly. Osama's taxi sped on through the desert, the dark, brooding mountains silhouetted against the night sky. Determined to force herself into the present and remove, albeit temporarily, the overwhelming sense of loss, Mojave breathed out deeply and changed the subject.

"You love him, don't you, Jamila?"

"He's an asshole."

"He's a man."

"He's an emotional idiot."

"He's Jewish, and a Scorpio."

Jamila fell silent. Her face was set in a scowl, the bright jewels of her eyes hard and piercing.

"He loves you very much, Jamila."

Jamila's reply was a barely audible whisper.

"I know… Mojave… I know."

Tears rolled down her cheeks.

# 10

## *Shipwrecks*

The next morning over coffee and a spliff, Dark Shark inspected Moheet's logbook. A logbook is a diver's record, similar to a pilot's log. Moheet's logbook was a marvel. She was not just a sport diver; her experiences underwater had become professional. The logbook recorded all her activities. From her earliest days in the lake with her mother, right up to her scientific research in the waters off Sharm El Sheikh. As Dark Shark read her journal, he became more and more fascinated by the material. A diver's log doesn't just record the dive, it tells a story. The diver often records emotions and feelings alongside the details of the dive.

Of particular interest were the entries concerning Moheet's experiences in the Red Sea, the descriptions filled with scientific notes and observations. Her knowledge of sharks was impressive. She described their hunting strategies, methods of reproduction and distribution. Her work had proved to be both enlightening and entertaining, but her conclusions were laced with foreboding. She gave stark warnings for the future of sharks. Moheet confirmed shark numbers were in reasonable condition now, but with fishing, global warming and increased human activity, they were ultimately doomed, perhaps as soon as in this lifetime.

Much of the material Dark Shark was familiar with, but it was strange to read her work. He was struck by the irony that this was the very same Moheet who only a few days ago, had so ingenuously listened to his lessons. Dark Shark felt stupid at the memories, somehow suckered, though he could never have guessed the extent of her deception, so ably did she play her role.

As he read on, Dark Shark began to conceive an abstract, but important notion. On her arrival in Sharm El Sheikh, Moheet had informed the dive centre she wanted to plan her diving itinerary herself, preferring to dive in a way that optimized the efficiency of her work. It was her choice of sites that intrigued Dark Shark the most. The usual sites were there such as Ras Mohammed, Tiran and the shore dives around Sharm, but there were others, more interesting, less obvious. The wreck of the Carnatic at Sha'ab Abu Nuhas. The Thistlegorm at Sha'ab Ali. What was Moheet doing diving wrecks? She was studying sharks, not wrecks. What was the connection? All of her entries gave a thorough explanation of her activities at the sites except the wreck dives.

Only the minimum details of these dives had been noted. Depth, time, and visibility. Nothing about why she was there. Moheet's time was limited, she wasn't just diving these wrecks for fun. The entries didn't even mention whom she dived with or what boat she used. More mysteries. More unanswered questions. Dark Shark's stoned head reeled from all the information, from the frustration. The more he found out about Moheet, the less he knew about her. Walls behind walls behind walls. Russian dolls within Russian dolls. Just then, deep inside his head, a voice said to him:

"The boat, schmuck."

Dark Shark finished his coffee, picked up his clamshell, and called Dr Mustafa. The owner of the Live-Aboard Etoiles, Dark Shark had known him for five years and had organized many safaris on his boat.

"Salaam, Salaam Dr Mustafa, how is the life?"

"Dark Shark! El Hamdul'allah! The life is good! What do you need?"

"I need the Etoiles for a couple of days."

"No problem! Where are you going?"

"I want to dive Abu Nuhas and the Thistlegorm."

Dr Mustafa whistled.

"Mershi, mershi, I will call Captain Salah. When do you want to leave, Dark Shark?"

"We leave this evening. Six o'clock. Myself, Gastro and Jamila."

"Jamila is back!?"

Dr Mustafa whistled long and hard, beaming a huge grin back in his office in Cairo. It would be more than entertaining to have those three characters on his boat again.

An hour later, Dark Shark, Gastro, Jamila, Mojave, Poi and Flake were eating breakfast at Slow Down. The meal - an English fry up, was being cooked and served by Hymen's new partner, Sparky. An English electrician who'd arrived in Dahab; Sparky had wandered into Slow Down and forged a strange friendship with the owner. Sparky wasn't just an electrician. He was happy, amiable and psychotically passionate about food. Back in his home town of Romford, Sparky had shot a waiter in his local Indian restaurant. The unfortunate young man had served up an inadequate curry. It was not even close to Sparky's exacting culinary standards.

"Three years I spent studying fucking curry in Udder fucking Pradesh! Don't you dare tell me how to cook a fucking curry!!"

He had shot the waiter, walked home, got his passport, and promptly jumped on a flight bound for Sharm El Sheikh.

The only being in Dahab more psychotic about food than Sparky, was Hymen's Rottweiler, Spike. The dog ate anything with a pulse - or anything that used to have a pulse. Sparky and Hymen had become partners, an unlikely alliance if ever there was one. Together they plotted, schemed, and had dreamed up a completely new concept. The new development would be called Stop! They believed the new enterprise would take off in such a big way that both of them could finally retire. Well, at least make it official. Red Beach were going to shit themselves.

The site would be on the bay, behind a dive centre. It would have a swimming pool, a flash new restaurant (complete with water trickling down a glass roof), shops, and wooden bridges. Customers would be served drinks whilst relaxing in the pool. Russians in skimpy bikinis would waitress at the restaurant; taste would be of utmost importance in the new Stop! However, by far the most interesting new development was the decision to make Gastronimica the general manager of this new establishment.

Back at the old Slow Down, Poi was complaining. She had met a gorgeous young diving instructor called Ben and did not know whether to jump right in there or wait. Gastro was trying to make up her mind for her.

"Look, just take some MDMA and shag him… then tell him it was a mistake… it was the drugs and you guys really shouldn't have… "

"But I can't… He's got a girlfriend and she's coming out here next week… "

"Like I said, blame it on the chemicals, it's the Dahab way… "

"Oh I do sooo want Ben's big bulge. Do you think I could… Do you think I should?"

Everyone in Slow Down replied to her question at the same time.

"Yep!"

Flake put in her bid for a share of the limelight.

"Gastroooo, should I go back to England for this gig tonight, then fly to Thailand for a party over the weekend and be back here by Tuesday?"

"Of course, girl! Enjoy it while you can!"

Neither Poi nor Flake seemed bound by space and time like other mere mortals. Their jet set lifestyles never ceased to amaze Dark Shark. Most Dahab residents couldn't even afford to make it across town. Dark Shark decided it was a good time to announce his intention of diving the wrecks the following day. Gastro was up for it. Jamila definitely was not.

"Why on earth do you want to do that?"

"I want to try to understand why Moheet dived these sites whilst conducting her studies in Sharm El Sheikh. It doesn't make any sense. Why would somebody who was studying sharks and whose time was limited dive these wrecks? I need to find out and I need to dive those wrecks… are you coming, Jay?"

"I don't know why… but yes."

"Good, because I'm hoping QA will pick up the bill for the boat."

"You really are an asshole, Dark Shark"

Dark Shark smiled.

"I try, Jay, I try."

Sparky hovered near the table.

"How's the food, guys?"

"Excellent. Yeah, really good. Delicious."

Even if it wasn't, nobody was going to tell him.

Dark Shark, Jamila, and Gastro spent the remaining time preparing for their impromptu safari. The first day would be spent diving Sha'ab Abu Nuhas, the second, the Thistlegorm. Dark Shark called Osama and informed him they needed his driving skills. After loading all their bags and equipment, the three divers waved goodbye to Mohammed and Mojave. They set off for Sharm al Sheikh, their destination Travco port. The journey would take an hour and a half. Dr Mustafa had already phoned Captain Salah, the Etoiles would be ready on their arrival.

Speeding through the grey twilight desert, Osama's car ate the miles, while Osama ate his bananas. In the front seat next to him, Gastro smoked spliffs, turning the taxi blue. In the back seat, Dark Shark stared out the window at the mountains. Jamila had fallen asleep, her head resting on his shoulder. Osama smiled when he looked into his rear view mirror at the sight in the back seat. Dark Shark, catching Osama's grin, frowned. When Osama's taxi reached Sharm El Sheikh, he turned right instead of continuing to the city, skirting along the edge, driving south, past the city and on to the port.

It was six o'clock when they finally pulled into the car park. They had just two hours to unload the equipment, board Etoiles, and get police permission to depart the jetty. Boats were unable to leave the jetty after eight. The jetty was quiet. The day boats had returned hours ago and most of the Live-Aboards were out on safari. Etoiles' crew had come ashore to help the divers with their equipment and together they loaded the boat, using a wooden plank to traverse the gap between jetty and boat. Etoiles was built in 1998. A typical Red Sea Live-Aboard, she was big and basic. Fitted with thirty-five tanks, two compressors and a huge lounge, she was perfectly suited for diving in the Red Sea. Now in her eighth year, she was beginning to show her age, but she was still a wonderful boat and her crew was second to none. Dark Shark warmly embraced Captain Salah.

The Etoiles' Bedouin captain hailed from El Tur, the administrative capital of the Sinai. A son of a famous fishing community, Captain Salah had worked on the Red Sea for forty-two years. He had two wives and nine children. Despite diving very rarely, Captain Salah knew more about the Red Sea than any diver alive. Dark Shark couldn't imagine working with another captain on his safaris and frequently consulted Captain Salah on the best course of action. Now they sat in his cabin discussing this latest adventure, the exploration of the best wrecks in the Northern Red Sea. First, there would be a journey to Seven Reef to moor overnight. Then, in the early hours of the morning, Captain Salah would head to the Straits of Gubal and the wreck of the Carnatic. Dark Shark, Jamila, and Gastro unpacked their equipment with the help of the crew. It had been nearly two years since Jamila had been on the boat, two years since that memorable safari.

She sighed at the recollections; the whale shark, the turtles. She even smiled as she remembered threatening to head-butt a curvy instructor who had shaken her tits for two days at Dark Shark.

Having thrown his bag into the first cabin, an excited Gastro skinned up to the delight of the crew and a cackling Captain Salah. Perched on the prow of the Live-Aboard, his legs dangling over the edge, Dark Shark stared into the blackness ahead, eyes fixed on the horizon. As was customary at the beginning of a safari, Dark Shark raised both hands in the air, his arms straight - ala Titanic. The foghorn wailed and Etoiles moved slowly forward, away from the jetty and away from Sharm El Sheikh, heading directly into the Gulf of Aqaba.

After fifteen minutes, she turned towards the south, engines noisy, and the propellers churning the waters behind her. The Live-Aboard was heading beyond Ras Mohammed, to an unknown future, a future as dark as the sea, as uncertain as the weather in the Straits of Gubal. Dark Shark revelled in the salty freshness. There was a wind, as ever from the North, but tonight it was not cold. He was never happier than when he was on safari and it had been too long since his last excursion. The wind pushed the boat, and Etoiles made good progress, her prow, first high then low, rising and falling in perfect time with the rhythm of the sea. Jamila brought Dark Shark some fresh coffee and together they drank and smoked.

"What do you hope to achieve by going on this wild wreck chase Dark Shark?"

"I really don't know Jay. However, I think we'll find out when we get there. Moheet definitely had a good reason to come out here."

"Which wreck are we going to dive first?"

"Moheet's entry on the Carnatic was straightforward except for one thing. At the end of the log, she writes 'Found it!' Whatever she found was probably on the wreck and we may find some evidence of her search, despite the fact it was over two months ago. In addition, Moheet dived the Carnatic and then the Thistlegorm in that order, so that's what we'll do. This trip is not only about looking for clues, but also about trying to understand what was going on in Moheet's mind in the months leading up to her appearance at Just Another Dive Centre. Our first wreck will also be the Carnatic."

They sat close together, gazing up at a huge, white luminous moon, both of them immersed deep in their own thoughts. Pale moonlight shimmered on the surface water. A school of flying fish jumped from the sea, disturbed by an unseen predator lurking below. The fish skimmed the surface, travelling many meters before splashing down again. They passed families of squid, their colours luminous in the lights of the boat. Many millions of people have eaten squid but it is not possible to say that you have seen one properly until you have seen it underwater. A dead squid on a plate gives you absolutely no idea what they are like.

Below the water, squid are highly intelligent and inquisitive; their large, bulbous eyes regard you with curiosity. They live in highly complex family groups and can often be seen with babies hovering close by. They have flashing lights of different colours; red, blue, white, yellow and green. The colours are created by bioluminescence and they use it to attract prey. With their lights flashing, they resemble space craft. Little aliens who've come to explore our world. To see a whole family of squid hovering close to your mask, flashing different colours and staring back at you, is an incredible experience.

Etoiles was now in the open expanse of sea and the wind was picking up. The bow waves got bigger and cold spray came over the railings, forcing them inside and the shelter of the lounge. After another forty-five minutes, Etoiles reached Seven Reef. Captain Salah carefully maneuverered her around the reef till he found the mooring buoys. At the back of Etoiles, a Zodiac was tied up. During the journey it was dragged behind, rocking and rolling in the Live-Aboard's wake. Now it was used by two crew members who took the Zodiac and drove it close to the reef, searching. They were looking for the mooring buoy. On the bottom of the Zodiac lay a huge rope. Finding the buoy, one of the men jumped into the warm water and tied the rope to the buoy. Etoiles was now safely moored over night in the lee of the reef, protected from the elements.

Inside the lounge, Dark Shark, Jamila, and Gastro watched the Blue Planet series by the BBC, together with an astonished crew who had never seen anything like it. Neither had anyone else when the Blue Planet had been aired on television for the first time. Dark Shark and Jamila settled down, falling in each other's arms and eventually allowing sleep to catch up with the many events of the day. Nobody managed to make it to the cabins.

At five o'clock in the morning, Captain Salah started the twin engines of Etoiles, beginning the two-hour journey to Sha'ab Abu Nuhas. The sun had yet to come up over the horizon. Cold winds blasted Etoiles. The early morning sky was still grey, dark, and foreboding. The crew scurried about, pulling in ropes, securing anything that wasn't tied down, preparing for the rough journey across the top of the Red Sea. Dark Shark, Jamila, and Gastro slept on, disturbed, but reluctant to fully awaken before their arrival at the reef.

They slept in fits and starts, the rocking motion making it impossible to completely relax. Spray whipped the windows, forming long trails of water flowing down and off the decks. Etoiles lurched forward, down, then abruptly up again, the motion causing Gastro's stomach to turn somersaults; the acrid taste of bile filling his mouth. In the mouth of the Gulf of Suez, near the Egyptian mainland, lie the treacherous Straits of Gubal.

Here there is a small cluster of reefs and islands, one of which is called Shadwan Island. Hugging the eastern shore of Shadwan, the last reef on the edge of this cluster is Sha'ab Abu Nuhas. The reef is a menace to ships that ply these waters, since they find themselves in a narrow channel, Abu Nuhas on one side and Beacon Rock on the other. The water here flows faster and faster, like a river in flood, creating eddying currents and violent waves. There is plenty of evidence of its perils, carcasses of modern ships that have run aground and been broken up by the sea, litter the whole Eastern and Northern sides of Abu Nuhas.

The perilous reef has a nickname, The Graveyard of Wrecks. A splendid English steamer, Carnatic was a mixed steam-sail vessel, launched in 1862 to travel the East Indies route. Built by the Peninsula and Oriental Steam Navigation Company at the Samuda Brothers Shipyard in Sunderland, she entered the Register of Shipping on March 2, 1863. With a length of 89m and width of 9m, she had an overall tonnage of 1,776 tons. The engine, built by Humphreys & Tennat in Deptford, produced 1,870 horsepower, fired by a steam boiler and giving her a top speed of 12 knots. Carnatic made her maiden voyage on April 27 1863, from Southampton to Alexandria.

Soon after, she entered service on the Suez-India route and right from her first voyage round the Cape of Good Hope proved fast and reliable, taking only forty nine days to make the journey from Southampton to Ceylon. She started out on her last voyage from Suez bound for Bombay on the evening of September 12, 1869, just two months after the opening of the Suez Canal. Her cargo had arrived from Liverpool on the steamship Venetian and was then loaded onto Carnatic in Suez. She left the port around 10p.m. on a fine Sunday in September with 230 people on-board including both passengers and crew. The sea was calm, there was a light northerly wind, and the ship made good progress until 1.15 am when Captain P.B. Jones was suddenly woken by shouts.

"Breakers at the bow, Captain!"

"Helm to the left! Full speed astern!"

There was a great crash, the sound of breaking coral and two thirds of the hull lurched onto the reef and remained there, stuck fast. Everybody on-board remained calm. An inspection was made by torchlight and as the damage did not appear to be too serious, it was decided to wait until dawn to try to re-float the ship. The captain never gave the decision to lower the lifeboats and the next day, life went on as usual. Meals were served at the usual times. By evening the tension and concern were growing among the passengers and a delegation was sent to speak to the Captain. However, the delegation accepted the Captain's argument that the ship was safe and like it or not they spent another night on-board, waiting for the rescue ship. During the night of September 14th, however, at around 2a.m. water came pouring into the engine room, extinguishing the boiler. Too late, the Captain realized Carnatic was lost. At 10.50 a.m. disaster struck; weighed down by the water it had taken on and weakened by the pounding waves, the hull broke in two and sank, taking with it twenty-seven passengers and crew members.

Lloyd's very quickly organized an expedition to salvage the ship, led by Captain Henry D. Grant. This expedition was one of the first times ever that use was made of a deep-sea diver. Stephen Saffrey, an English diver, succeeded in reaching the mail office, broke his way through the locked door and, within a few days had recovered 32,000 gold sovereigns of the 40,000 reportedly held in the safe box. Divers continued their salvage operations on the Carnatic until March 1870, when a stormy sea sent the bow section down to join the stern on the sea floor, and Carnatic was consigned to oblivion for over a century. To this day, there are still 8,000 gold sovereigns buried in the bowels of Carnatic. At seven o'clock, the crew of Etoiles informed Dark Shark they had arrived at the final resting place of the Carnatic. Dark Shark groaned and got up. After a quick wash, he consulted Captain Salah. The news wasn't good.

"Dark Shark! Mishkela! Currents! Kabeer!"

Dark Shark sighed. He would need to jump into the sea and check the current before making the dive. He walked to the back of the boat and went down to the diving deck to check the water. Etoiles was moored and not happy about it. A surface current, easily two knots, was causing Etoiles to strain her moorings. Normally Etoiles could manage with only one line, but the Captain had been forced to order three lines secured due to the rough conditions. The strong wind was stirring up white horses and the sea churned. Not for nothing was this reef known as the Graveyard of Wrecks. Dark Shark climbed into his wetsuit, put on his mask and fins, grabbed a tag line and jumped in, ignoring his snorkel. With waves crashing over his head, a snorkel would be useless. The current immediately took him away from the boat, but the line kept him from being swept away and he clung to it with both hands. As he did so, he peered beneath the surface of the sea, surveying the scene. Below him lay the Carnatic. A magnificent, grim, metal skeleton. She rested on her starboard side, lying on a sandy seabed twenty five metres down. At that depth, they would have plenty of time, but the current was the main issue and therefore worth checking. With waves crashing over him and straining against the current, Dark Shark looked for fish.

A giant moray lay curled behind a cluster of twisted metal, menacing and huge. A family of five batfish wove in and out the metal struts, seemingly oblivious to any current. A small group of orange fairy basslets was shimmering near one of Carnatic's two masts in the middle of the wreck. They were hovering in one spot, facing the stern. This is what Dark Shark had been looking for. The direction they faced and the degree of their shimmering indicated the direction and strength of the current. There was clearly a strong current running along Carnatic from stern to bow. They would need a reel. Pulling himself back along the tag line, Dark Shark climbed a metal ladder hanging into the water from the dive deck. Much to his relief, Jamila and Gastro were standing on the deck, waiting for him with hot coffee.

"What's happening down there, D?"

"The water is rough. There's a current flowing from stern to bow. This means we can swim with the current in the beginning, but we'll have to swim against it on the way back unless conditions change. We'll descend on the mooring line directly onto the stern. The current is strong, but I don't know for sure how strong until we get down there, so be careful not to be swept past on the way down. Once on the wreck, I'll tie a reel to the ascent line, then we'll swim towards the bow. I'll go first, swimming backwards and reeling out the line. You guys follow me, pull yourself along the line if you have to, and watch my back. When we get to the bow, we'll turn around and head back to the stern, reeling in the line. On the way back, the two of you need to be in front of me, using the line to pull yourself forward. The wreck is not very wide, visibility is good, and we should be able to cover the whole wreck in this way. Stay close to each other and stay close to me. Any questions?"

"Wicked!"

"That's not a question."

"Wicked?"

Ten minutes later, Dark Shark, Gastro, and Jamila were fully kitted and standing on the diving deck of Etoiles. Dark Shark was staring at Gastro's regulator.

"What the fuck is that?"

Gastro had placed a rubber ring around his regulator and was going to place the ring around his head when he put the regulator in his mouth, just before descending.

"It keeps my regulator in my mouth; I'm not as young as I used to be."

"You mean you don't have the teeth you used to!"

"Wanker."

Captain Salah sounded the horn, the crew threw a ring into the sea, and the three divers jumped into the swirling waters. Clinging onto the ring, they half swam, half crawled along the line close to the mooring buoy. The buoy, bright red, a metre across and made of a heavy rubber was bouncing up and down in the waves. The line to the wreck was jerking violently at least two meters at a time. Ascending and descending the line would be risky if not impossible. Just going near the buoy was dangerous, so the divers stayed a couple of feet away, holding the line, assessing the situation.

They would have to descend in mid-water, fast, and hope to catch hold of the wreck before being swept past in the swift current. Dark Shark had anticipated this and back on the boat had instructed Gastro and Jamila to add extra weight to their belts. Equalizing their ears would be problematic on a fast descent, but they had no choice. Dark Shark gave the descent signal and the three divers dropped like bricks. Immediately the current carried them towards the metal skeleton. Equalizing fast, they each grabbed a metal strut – the bones of the skeleton - adding air to their BCDs to stabilize themselves.

Once on the stern, Dark Shark tied his reel line onto a metal strut close to the mooring line. In the event of an emergency, they could use the line to get them back to Etoiles. Dark Shark put more air into his BCD and turned around; sitting in the water and swimming backwards. Ten metres down and to his right, the giant propeller lay on the sand, covered with a profusion of colourful soft corals. Alongside him were large openings, the windows of the first class saloon. Dark Shark reeled out more line. Jamila and Gastro followed, using the line to stop them from being swept along and scanning the area directly in front of Dark Shark. He gripped the reel, but it was easy to keep the line taut in such a strong current; the trick would be getting back. The dark menacing outline of the wreck stretched before them. Imposing its will, the wreck gripped them with a macabre fascination, curiosity increasing as their eyes scanned the belly of the marine dinosaur. Swimming to Carnatic's mid-ships, the divers glided over a twisted tangle of metalwork; not surprisingly, this was the part of the ship that gave way on the morning of September 14th, 1869. Her two masts lay perpendicular to the wreck, the rigging covered in stony coral. On either side of the wreck lay a lifeboat davit, the one on the left adorned with a wonderful formation of coral.

The diver's bubbles were being forced horizontal by the current, giving the surreal impression the divers were breathing sideways. Another surreal image was of Gastro, holding the line, eyes bulging. He was swimming behind his own dreadlocks that were completely blocking his field of vision. Because of his locks, the bubbles were taking their time to get clear, bunching up just past his mask, and then slowly wafting away from his hair as the locks moved in the current.

Jamila was having a much better time of it, her eyes shone with fierce determination and she moved slowly but surely, scanning the wreck for clues. She had become an excellent diver, confident, calm, and composed. Looking down, the divers could make out the engine area, the huge boiler and further on, the funnel. A giant grouper suddenly shot out of the funnel, disturbed by the alien intruders. After another ten meters, the divers arrived at the bow. With the wooden planking from the bow long gone, they were able to enter the hold. Dark Shark tied the reel to a strut and the three of them descended into the hold.

On her final, fatal voyage, wooden boxes containing wine had been stored here. Now little remained, except twisted fragments of metal. The three divers left the hold and Dark Shark untied the reel. Conditions had remained constant until now, and he felt confident about the return journey. Dark Shark turned around, keeping the reel in front of him. Taking their cue, Gastro and Jamila began to pull themselves along the taut line. Behind came Dark Shark, reeling in the line, all the while careful to avoid snagging.

After another five meters, the current began to get stronger. Gastro, just in front of Dark Shark, struggled with the current, almost twisting completely around in his effort to hold the line. Jamila turned to okay Dark Shark and momentarily let go of the line. She was caught by the current and came hurtling towards Gastro. She crashed into him, managing to catch one of his locks. He screamed through his regulator, but to his credit, he held on grimly. Dark Shark could do little; he wanted to keep the line taut. Jamila climbed over Gastro and much to his relief, found the line again. She okayed her friends and continued pulling towards the stern. Dark Shark could have sworn she was smiling.

The three divers arrived back at the mooring line. Conditions on the surface had died down and the line was no longer jerking quite so much. Dark Shark finished winding in the reel and decided to risk an ascent on the line. He gave the thumbs up and the three divers slowly made their way to the surface. The ascent was uneventful and ten minutes later, they were all safely back on the boat, drinking coffee and smoking cigarettes. After showering, the three divers ate breakfast. They discussed the dive, the wreck, and the difficult conditions. Gastro passed Dark Shark the tomato sauce.

"We go in again?"

"No, that was enough for one day; we'll head over to Sha'ab Ali and moor up for the night. We've achieved all we can here."

An hour later, the crew untied Etoiles, the engines rumbled into life and the Live-Aboard turned into the waves, heading north to Sha'ab Ali and the wreck of the Thistlegorm. The journey would take three hours. Dark Shark used the time to study Moheet's dive log. Gastro and Jamila slept in the cabins below, exhausted after their underwater adventures. Outside, the wind had died down. Streaks of white cloud shot across the deep blue sky. Captain Salah scoured the horizon, his hands expertly guiding the wheel. He sucked on a large spliff, concentrating hard. From time to time, he checked his instruments, noting Etoiles' heading, her speed, and the direction of the wind.

The Thistlegorm launched in Sunderland, in England, on April 9, 1940. Built in the shipyards of J.L.Thompson & Sons, the ship was 131m long and had a gross tonnage of 9,009 tons. Owned by the Albyn Line Ltd., it had a triple expansion, three-cylinder engine, capable of producing 1,860 horsepower and giving a top speed of 10.5 knots. The Thistlegorm (meaning 'blue thistle' in Gaelic) registered at Lloyds' in 100 A.1 class. Because of the war, she was armed with a 4.7 inch cannon, an anti-aircraft machine-gun mounted on a tower and a transportable heavy machine gun. Her first mission was to North America, with a cargo of aircraft parts and railway rails. On the second, she sailed as far as the East Indies and on the third to Argentina: both these voyages were made to bring back much needed food. On her fourth mission -tragically destined to be her last- the Thistlegorm left Glasgow in the first week in September, destined for the Red Sea. After a brief stop in Cape Town to take onboard coal, the ship headed northeast; she had sailed the length of the Red Sea and reached the Straits of Gubal when, at 1.30 a.m. on the morning of October 6th 1941, she was attacked by the Germans and sank. The Germans had made a lightening attack; the Heinkel He 111s had no trouble hitting at least one target since there were nearly twenty ships at anchor.

The second squadron of the 26th Kamp Geswader, stationed in Crete, was in action along the Sinai coast and in the light of the full moon; the German pilots spotted the convoy and decided to attack the ship that appeared to be carrying the biggest cargo. They probably had no idea the importance of the freighter they made their target. The gunners on the British ship had not even had time to load the cannon when the bombs dropped by the Heinkels hit the vessel right on No 4 hold. The Thistlegorm was carrying a precious cargo of munitions and supplies for the British Eighth Army, engaged at that time in Operation Crusade, a major offensive launched by Montgomery and his men against the troops of General Rommel. Stacked in her holds were huge quantities of munitions and an assortment of military vehicles: Bedford trucks, Morris cars, BSA motorbikes, plus endless boxes of Lee-Enfield rifles, spare parts, generators, Wellington boots, camp beds, and boxes of medical supplies.

Stowed in holds three and four was a huge arsenal of explosives; anti-tank mines, artillery shells, boxed light munitions and hand grenades. Amid the great freighter's structures on the deck, together with the two paravanes (torpedo shaped protective devices towed at the sides of the sides of the ship in mined areas to sever the moorings of contact mines), were two small tanks, four railway wagons and two railway engines. It was the colossal weight of her cargo that caused the Thistlegorm to sink so fast. The explosives in hold No.4 tore the hull apart and the ship very quickly disappeared beneath the waves, dropping, still upright onto the seabed.

In 1956, Jacques Yves Cousteau came to the Red Sea with the Calypso, on one of the exploratory missions that made such an important contribution to the advancement of scuba diving the world over. His crew had no trouble finding the wreck; all the local fishermen knew of the great ship lying beneath the water and the huge fish that populated it. When they first descended to the ship, the French oceanographer and his men found it practically intact. Masts, rigging, cargo handling booms, everything was still in place, as though the great ship had been 'sleeping'.

Thanks to Cousteau's film the 'Silent World' and the extensive documentation, he put together, the public also learnt the story of this wonderful wreck, its magic and its mystery. Although sixty years on the sea bed and visited by fifty thousand divers a year, the fascination of this huge freighter - crammed with all the supplies a World War 2 army needed - has in no way not diminished. To dive the Thistlegorm properly, to take in the vast ship and all her cargo, requires many dives.

Dark Shark's time was limited. The Council would be meeting in three days and his attendance was crucial. He had dived the Thistlegorm many times, and he knew the vessel well. He hoped two dives on the wreck would provide answers to his many questions So far, they had come up empty handed and Dark Shark was beginning to feel frustrated, his luck had to change. At four o'clock in the afternoon, the Etoiles reached her destination. As always, the dive site was busy. Numerous Live-Aboards and day-boats moored on the wreck and dozens of divers were toing and froing from the water. The site was very busy, but thankfully, the water was relatively calm. Captain Salah carefully maneuvered Etoiles into the midst of the melee, barking orders to the crew as he did so. One of them kitted up and jumped into the water, clutching a large steel cable. He dived down to the wreck, attached the cable to the massive winch chain on the bow, and returned slowly to the surface.

Etoiles would now remain moored on the wreck for the next twenty four hours. Dark Shark planned to make his first dive early in the morning, avoiding the large numbers of divers arriving from Sharm El Sheikh. At that time of the day, they should have the huge wreck to themselves. The light was already beginning to fade, the other boats were heading home, and the passengers of Etoiles settled down for the evening in the comfort of the lounge.

# 11

## *Oceanic Whitetip*

At six o'clock the next morning, Dark Shark's clamshell wailed its polyphonic nonsense. He groaned, rolled off his bunk bed, and staggered to the toilet. He showered and brushed his teeth. Returning to his cabin, he pulled on a pair of shorts, threw on a t-shirt, and then climbed the stairs to the lounge. Gastro had not yet risen from the dead, but Jamila was already making coffee and she glanced up to see a bleary-eyed Dark Shark enter the lounge.

"Good morning." she said.

"Good morning. How are you?" he replied.

"Yeah, I'm good. Got a slight headache, must be dehydrated, but otherwise fine, you?"

"Still waking up. Drink some water; you'll need it on this dive"

"Always the instructor, eh, Dark Shark?"

"Just trying to help Jay"

"I know, I'm joking, and I appreciate your help; despite being a fuck-up, you've got some redeeming qualities."

"Thank you... I think"

Unlike the lounge, the sea was calm. Gentle swells rocked Etoiles slowly back and forth like a very large baby inside a huge cradle.

A cold, grey mist hung over the sea, like a veil, masking the horizon. The sun was just appearing in the east, it's warm rays lifting the veil, drawing back the early morning gloom.

Captain Salah greeted Dark Shark and Jamila with a big smile.

"Mafish mishkela, mafish currents, kol a tamam! El Hamdul'allah!"

"Walla. This dive should be a walk in the park"

Jamila reminded Dark Shark about the absence of their friend.

"You'd better go and wake up Gastro"

"Yeah, I go now."

Half an hour later, the three divers discussed their planned search of the huge freighter. Jamila was talking.

"We should do the usual thing, start at the bow, make our way to the stern, and then return to the winch. We can do a more extensive examination of her holds on the second dive."

"I agree, she's too big to do in one go. We can check the bow, the propellers and then come up to the bridge. That's a good idea, Jay"

Gastro sucked a spliff, and then said.

"Can I take out my regulator in the air space in the toilet, can I, please, please, can I please?" he begged.

"No!" They snapped at the same time.

Ten metres down, in the cold, clear water, Dark Shark, Jamila and Gastro pulled themselves down the metal cable that led to the foredeck of the Thistlegorm. The vast ship stretched out below them, disappearing off into the gloom. Confronted by such a large presence, the divers felt tiny, dwarfed by the enormity of the structure, in complete awe of this majestic tomb.

Diving a wreck is like traveling back in time. Each wreck is a tragedy, the last scene playing to an empty house, the theatre hidden forever beneath the waves. The death of the Thistlegorm was not the end of the story, however, for the sea wastes nothing and over the years she has come back to life. Coral communities are well established and thousands of fish shelter in the safety of the gigantic edifice. The wreck was now a living reef.

There was a current running along her port flank, but it was so gentle it was almost unnoticeable. At eighteen metres, the divers reached the giant winch chains on the great bow, the anchor windlasses still in excellent condition. The three friends settled down on the foredeck, taking a minute to orientate themselves to their imposing surroundings. Dark Shark pointed south in the direction of the stern, okayed his friends, and swam along the edge of the deck, immediately passing over one of the two tank trucks, close to hold No.1. Jamila and Gastro followed. The divers swam over a paravane, and then dropped down to the seabed, on the Thistlegorm's port flank at a depth of thirty-one metres.

Inflating their BCDs, they swam along the bottom, keeping the hull on their right. On their left, intermittent coral formations dotted the seabed along with twisted fragments of metal. After a few minutes, they arrived at the bomb damage. At this point, the ship appears to have been sliced into two at the top of hold No.4, the point where the German bombers struck their target. Scattered all around is wreckage and remains of the cargo, mostly ammunition and assorted explosive devices. They swam on, reaching the stern and the huge propellers. The propellers are so big, the divers swam right in-between the blades, marvelling at the size of these steel monsters.

Turning right, they swam past the toilets -where Gastro had wanted to take out his regulator- and came across some carts lying in the sand a few feet away from wreck. In a previous life, the carts had ferried bombs around the ship, but now provided a home for lionfish, grouper, and moray eels. The divers had now been deep for a long time and they needed to start ascending. They swam over two small armoured vehicles, easily distinguishable from the twisted metal plating of the hull. Made by Vickers-Armstrong, the MK II Bren Carriers weighed only 4 5 tons, and were among the most successful 'all-rounder' vehicles used in World War 2.

Directly in front of them was the large hole that had once been the funnel, and they slowed down somewhat, pausing to gaze inside the darkened interior. A few more meters and they reached the bridge. Dark Shark wanted to check the cabins, and leaving his two friends hovering outside, he went through a gaping hole leading to the Captain's quarters. Visibility inside was bad. It was very dark, despite his torch, and he gave the place only a quick 'once over' before returning to Jamila and Gastro.

Next, was Hold No.2. Split into two levels, the hold contains a number of Bedford trucks on the bottom level and BSA motorbikes on the top. The trucks and bikes are in astonishing condition. Take them out the water, put some gas in them and they may well trundle off into the desert, just as they were intended to do sixty four years ago. The last hold before the winch, Hold No 1, is also divided into two sections. Stacked below are boxes containing medical supplies, Lee Enfield MK III rifles, and spare parts, electricity generators, aircraft parts, camp beds for field hospitals, rubber boots, and tires. Above, on the first level are several Morris cars, no doubt intended for use by the Eighth Army officers.

There was no time to do an extensive search of these Aladdin's caves, so Dark Shark signalled to Jamila and Gastro that it was time to surface. Just as they were crossing the main mast and beginning to swim over Hold No.1, Dark Shark caught something silvery glinting in the darkness below. Curious he stopped, breathed out, and turned around. Signalling his intent to his two friends, he double backed, hovered for a moment over the hold, exhaled, and then dropped abruptly, disappearing into the darkness.

Sinking down, Dark Shark couldn't see anything at first, but after a few seconds his eyes adjusted to the decrease in light and he looked around him. He landed on the floor of the hold, close to the boxes of medical supplies, and only a few feet from a small, rounded object.

Covered in silt, with just the top showing, was a small glass vial. Shaking off the silt, Dark Shark's intuition told him that the object was not an original part of the Thistlegorm's many treasures. The vial was inside a blue cloth bag, providing clear evidence that it had not been submerged for any great length of time. Sown into the cloth in silver thread were two letters SK.

Dark Shark put the vial in his BCD pocket and swam up, joining his somewhat impatient companions. According to Dark Shark's computer, they had about ten minutes left before going into decompression at present depth, so they finned slowly up, over the main deck, back towards the bow and the massive winch chain. Movement on the line to Etoiles was still gentle, indicating surface conditions had remained calm. As they approached the line, they heard the unmistakable sound of another boat's propellers. Equally unmistakable, was the sight of two men, clearly visible to the divers below them, standing on the back of a boat and emptying large quantities of red liquid into the water. Eighteen metres.

The red liquid was oily and viscous. Dark Shark was not happy about this new development at all. Pieces of fish fell around the line, dropping past the divers, littering the deck of the Thistlegorm and the seabed below. The divers continued up. Fifteen metres. A line dropped down from the boat complete with a hooked Tuna. Still alive, the fish struggled to free itself from the hook. The visibility got worse. The water had become a yellowy red soup, flavoured with bubbles. The divers had got close to their NDLs, they were getting low on air, and they needed to do a safety stop.

On the surface, the engines of the boat whined loudly and the men continued to chum the water with their bloody concoction. Ten metres. Jamila gripped Dark Shark's arm so hard it was beginning to hurt. Gastro was managing to look pissed off, anxious and wide eyed, all at the same time. Dark Shark stared past Gastro's locks, horrified by what he saw, suddenly remembering why he did not like this situation. Out the corner of one eye, he saw a white tipped dorsal fin cruise past his field of vision, and circle the divers. At that moment, the plan changed to fuck the safety stop. In the Red Sea, there are two species of white tip shark. The white tip reef shark is small, no more than a meter and a half long and inhabits the reefs of all the worlds' tropical seas. Perfectly adapted to its home on the reef, the shark's long, slim body shape allows it to hunt in surprisingly small spaces. Unusually, it has two dorsal fins, the first being larger than the second. Both dorsal fins, the pectoral fins, and the tail fin bear the tell-tale white marks. The shark is nocturnal, hunting by night and preferring to rest during the day in the safety of the reef's nooks and crannies.

The other whitetip shark is home in the open sea. The oceanic white tip is large; growing up to four metres, it is one of the apex predatory sharks found in tropical waters. It has a distinctive, large, rounded dorsal fin topped off with a splash of white. Possessing a large head, powerful tail and hundreds of razor sharp teeth, the shark is sleek and graceful. Beautiful and deadly. In the tropical seas, only the tiger shark is feared more. Certainly potentially dangerous to humans, oceanic white tips travel far and wide in their search for prey. They are expert, opportunistic hunters of the open sea. Taking sick or injured fish, they perform a vital role in the marine ecosystem, helping to clean the sea.

Both species of white tip are territorial. For the white tip reef shark, this means the reef. For the oceanic white tip, this means the whole sea.

Circling not ten feet from the divers was a fully-grown, female, oceanic white tip shark. Dark Shark and Jamila froze. Gastro started shaking. He let go of the line and began frantically waving his hands and fins, even his dread locks were vibrating. Dark Shark empathized with this behaviour, but it could not continue. Leaning forward, he attempted to grab Gastro's hands and force him to stop. Gastro, his eyes wide, mouth agape, was blowing so many bubbles; it looked like his regulator was free flowing. Dark Shark gripped Gastro hard, but to no avail. Gastro just flapped harder still. Gripped by manic fear, Gastro had unnatural strength and simply pushed Dark Shark away.

The shark's circles became elliptical rather than circular. She zoomed in, and then abruptly out, her dorsal fin arched up, her pectoral fins pointed straight down. Displaying aggressive behaviour, she was clearly agitated and becoming more so by the second. Dark Shark decided it was time to get the fuck out of there. Taking out a small knife attached to his BCD, he cut the line to the wreck, gave Jamila and Gastro the thumbs up, then grabbed Gastro's hands again. At precisely the same moment, the shark decided to find out exactly what was in front of her.

The only way a shark can be sure what anything is, is to bite it. Nobody saw the shark hit, but they all felt it. The huge impact felt like a torpedo had hit them. Boom! The half-ton shark hit at more than forty miles an hour. Dark Shark was almost knocked out by the force of the impact, just managing to keep hold of the line. Jamila winced hard, then coughed and spluttered. She felt the wind knocked out of her and struggled to breathe. On the other side of the group, Gastro went limp. His body sagged.

Dark Shark glimpsed the fish turn, swim down and away, before disappearing into the blue. Half a second later, Dark Shark turned back to look at Gastro. He had lost consciousness. His regulator held in place by the rubber band, but his eyes were rolling up inside his head. His body began turning over, his arms and legs hanging loose. Dark Shark glanced back at Jamila. Luckily, she had been on the outside of the group, protected from the impact by the bodies of her two friends.

They exchanged worried looks, they eyes expressing mutual concern. They both grabbed Gastro's BCD and kicked furiously, fighting their way to the surface only a couple of meters above. Blood trailed from behind Gastro, he was a dead weight and difficult to bring up. Dark Shark released Gastro's weight belt, made sure his regulator was still in place and looked up towards the surface. Two members of Etoiles' crew had jumped into the water, ready to assist the divers. Blood and oil swirled around them, a thick, red soup.

The divers broke the surface a second later. Immediately, Dark Shark threw off his mask and spat out his regulator, shouting for Captain Salah to radio Sea Air Rescue. Luckily, the good captain had already done so and a helicopter was on its way directly. The crew members in the water, together with the crew members still on-board, pulled the divers from the bloody morass. Once on deck, they quickly stripped Gastro's equipment and cut off his wetsuit, desperate to stop the massive bleeding from the shark bite. The blood flowed in rivers. Gastro was moaning. They had to try to stem the bleeding until the chopper arrived. Holding his hand, Dark Shark talked into Gastro's ear, reassuring him it would be okay, his voice soothing and calm. The crew worked fast on Gastro, time was critical. Gastro had been bitten badly; he was in shock and losing a lot of blood. They applied bandages as best they could. They covered him with blankets. They waited and prayed…

After fifteen minutes, they heard the 'whump whump' of whirring blades and a powerful engine. The power of the wind created by the blades was overwhelming. A huge circle of flattened water surrounded the boat as the helicopter descended. The noise of the engine was deafening. The wind made it impossible to stand; a strong spray stung crew and divers alike. A stretcher was winched down to the Live-Aboard and the crew, bending from the force of the wind, carefully placed Gastro on the precarious bed.

Ten minutes later, Gastro was lying at the bottom of the helicopter flying him to the hospital in Sharm El Sheikh. Skilled paramedics worked on him feverishly, but Gastro was still losing a lot of blood. He began to stir, coming to. The pain kicked in. He screamed.

"Please! The pain! I can't take the fucking pain!"

Dark Shark held his hand tightly… talking… pleading… praying…

"Hang in there G… for fuck's sake, hang in there…!"

Gastro continued to scream.

He was very pale, he was shivering violently, and his eyes were wide with terror.

"Dark Shark…please… help me!"

"You'll be alright Gastro… don't worry man… you're gonna be okay… stay with me Gastro… you gonna be fine!"

"I can see the light! Dark Shark, I don't want to die… please… please!"

Gastro's body shook. The paramedics had already given him morphine, but it didn't appear to be working. Dark Shark was frantic.

"We have to do something more for him! Now!!"

One of the paramedics injected Gastro with ketamine. Gastro groaned, but after a few minutes, the ketamine kicked in and his screams gradually turned to gurgles. He passed out. Dark Shark continued to talk to him. Another ten minutes and they were landing at the hospital's helipad. From a nearby building, a team of doctors emerged with a trolley. Gastro's stretcher was set on the trolley and rushed through the doors of the hospital into A&E.

The whole time, Dark Shark refused to let go of his friend's hand. The doctors had to pull him away to allow them to do their work. Confined to an adjacent room, separated from the operating theatre by a large window, Dark Shark pressed his face and hands against the glass; his knuckles white, a helpless spectator to the waking nightmare before his eyes. Gastro. Hooked up to various machines... doctors shouting at junior doctors…junior doctors shouting at nurses… machines whirring, lights blinking.

"Nurse, get an EPG in here!"

"Yes doctor."

"We need an STC; blood pressure is 150/37!"

"Yes doctor."

"Nurse, get me a Snickers!"

"Yes doctor."

"Pump his left lung!"

"Tie a knot in that vein!

"Heart beats slowing, we're losing him!"

"Stab him!"

"Patient has unusually high resistance to opiates!"

"Stab him again!"

"We're losing him!"

"Use the AED!"

"Move those dreadlocks!"

"Clear!"

In the operating theatre, Gastro's body flipped violently from the force of 50,000 volts. In the adjoining room, Dark Shark passed out.

Just outside the open window of the hospital waiting room, perched on the bough of a Mimosa tree and resting momentarily from its migration north to Europe, was a swallow. The small bird was greeting the arrival of the sun with a morning song; her beautiful shrill notes filling the air with joyful vitality and intruding sharply on a certain diving instructor's troubled slumber. Underneath the window, Dark Shark groaned as he slept on a couch. Beams of warm sunlight fell across his face, the yellow shards of light illuminating a deep furrow in his brow and trembling lines of tension etched into the corners of his mouth.

After his collapse the previous night, he had lain on the cold floor for a full twenty minutes until two nurses had discovered him whilst passing the waiting room on their nightly rounds. Checking to make sure he was alright, they had correctly assumed he had passed out due to the highly charged drama unfolding in the operating theatre. Not wanting to disturb him, they had lifted him onto the couch, covering him with a warm blanket and trusting him to the healing powers of sleep. However, Dark Shark had not slept peacefully all night; rather, he had twisted and turned, his mind locked in deadly battle with demons deep in his subconscious. The demons had ridden on horseback, black riders of guilt that bore down on him at frightening speed, their arms held aloft with sharp swords, ready to strike him down with furious retribution. Each of the demons, faceless and eyeless, screeched Gastro! Gastro! Gastro! Over and over and over, until in his mind's eye, the demons, the horses, and the screeches all became a whirl, a maelstrom, a storm which threatened to overpower him, engulf him and prevent him from ever waking up again.

The early morning sun, along with the swallow's joyous musical interjection, finally pushed the demons to the far recesses of Dark Shark' s mind and he gradually emerged from deep sleep to light. The smell of coffee wafted up his nostrils, closely followed by another, very familiar, smell. Dark Shark stirred, stretched his arms, and sat up. The movement startled the swallow. Dismayed by this rude interruption to her one bird show, the swallow abruptly leapt off her leafy stage, flapped her wings, and resumed her epic journey. The proud little Avian Diva was determined not to sing for such riff raff again; but instead save her energies until her return to Paris, where she would perform to a far more cultured audience.

Dark Shark rubbed his eyes, yawned… and remembered. Images of the previous night flooded back as he swung his legs off the couch and stood up. Turning around, he immediately staggered backwards as if hit with an incredibly powerful force. He promptly sat down on the couch… his senses reeling… his face frozen in shock and awe.

Sitting in a wheelchair, gazing nonchalantly at Dark Shark and smoking a spliff, was Gastronimica. His waist, left hip, and leg were heavily bandaged. Behind his wheelchair stood a large machine complete with plastic tubes and a gurgling drip. The tubes connected Gastro's arms, head, and chest to the machine, which bleeped reassuringly. A large hole had been cut into the middle of his seat and Gastro's heavily bandaged backside was currently languishing in the middle of the said hole. His beady blue eyes sparkled with Irish mirth as he watched his friend cope with the shock, a huge toothless grin spreading across his crinkly face.

"Good morning… coffee?" he asked.

The question appeared on the surface so simple -nay, so innocent; yet suggested, in the present context and betrayed as it was by those mocking Irish eyes, a degree of bravado that can come only from one who has so narrowly escaped the cold embrace of Death. Dark Shark's only reply was a slightly strangulated rasp. He sounded like Darth Vader attempting polite dinner party conversation on-board the Imperial Death Star.

After a few moments, Dark Shark cursed softly and pulled himself together, the shock beginning to wear off. He got up and walked over to where his friend was sitting on the far side of the room, his surprise turning to curiosity. Gastro passed him a cup of coffee. The movement caused sudden, sharp pain to shoot up his leg and back.

"Owww… my arse fucking hurts!" he wailed, Irish mirth temporarily replaced with outraged pain.

Dark Shark thought he was still dreaming, this was simply not most people's definition of reality.

"Y… you… you only got bitten on the arse?!?!"

"Well… yeah… one of me hips are in a bad state, three ribs are crushed... but it could have been worse…!"

"I don't believe it… You mother fucker… I thought you were dead!"

"Don't sound so disappointed!"

"But the AED... last night... your heart stopped!?!

"Twice, but the doctors brought me round. Allah is smiling on my scrawny Catholic ass and incredibly, against all the odds, I am still here! Annnd IIIII Feeelll Gooood!"

He winked, and for the first time in a long time, Dark Shark laughed long and hard. The two friends embraced, carefully, Gastro loudly protesting his very low pain threshold to his boisterously happy friend.

A young nurse came in, complete with clipboard, pen and a big smile.

"Salaam! Salaam! Your friend is very lucky, El Hamdul'allah!' We have never witnessed such a remarkable recovery; your friend is a medical marvel! El Hamdul'allah! A true miracle! We are definitely going to write this one up!"

Then she noticed the spliff, the smell, and the ubiquitous smile.

"Allah! Put that out right now! My God! Are you trying to get us all arrested?! You fool, put it out this minute!"

She grabbed the joint from an astonished Gastro, ran it under a tap, placed it into a plastic bag she produced from her pocket, and quickly disposed of the evidence. Gastro looked crestfallen. The nursed fussed over him for a few more minutes, checking the machine and his bandages. The inspection was unnecessary, superficial, but it forced her mind to concentrate on matters other than the criminal behaviour of the patient in her care.

The nurse, hardworking, devoutly Christian, felt betrayed by Gastro and she struggled to retain her composure. She wanted to avoid any further confrontation, so she used the inspection to relax herself sufficiently before continuing her duties elsewhere. Finishing her fussing, she checked one last time the connection on the hoses, ordered Gastro to lift his feet, and wheeled him out the room.

As they left, Jamila entered. She looked unusually tired and unkempt. Long tear tracks stained her cheeks and her normally large brown eyes, often such an inspiration to Dark Shark, now appeared drawn and haggard. She too had received little respite from her worries during the course of the night and her nerves, like her hair, were severely frayed at the edges. She didn't bother with small talk when she saw Dark Shark, but got straight down to business.

"Look where you're stupid safari got us!"

"This is hardly my fault!"

"No, but it is your responsibility! When are you going to finally understand the consequences of your actions and take responsibility for them like a proper adult? I knew your safari was bullshit, but I went along with it, because like an idiot, I trusted you. Not for the first time! Now Gastro has been seriously injured and we have achieved absolutely nothing in the last two days!"

"We found the vial."

"The vial! Hah! Do me a favour, it means absolutely

nothing!"

She pulled the vial out from her pocket and threw it on the couch, her sense of logic outraged.

"There are fifty thousand divers on the Thistlegorm every year. Moheet dived the wreck over two months ago, so between the time she was there and our recent disaster, there have probably been eight thousand fucking divers on that wreck. For all we know, SK might as well stand for Stephen Fucking King!"

Gastro's nurse came back into the room.

"Please, please; for the sake of the patients, try to keep your voices down."

However, Jamila was not quite finished.

"I am finished with you, Dark Shark. Just leave the investigating to me and Adel!"

She stormed out the room, making as if to slam the door, but at the last moment, she closed it very quietly.

Dark Shark slumped into the couch, sighing as he did so. He stared into space, plagued with feelings of guilt, resigning his soul to an eternity in hell. The fires of hell roared, he smelt the gut wrenching smell of his own burning flesh. After a minute or so, he became bored with the concept of hell and consigned it to the bin of Christian superstition. He glanced down next to him. Lying innocently on the couch, the little vial spoke to him, just as it had done on the Thistlegorm. He stared at if for a long time, reached over and picked it up, the glass cold in his hand. He studied it. He turned it repeatedly.

It appeared to be old, maybe hundreds of years old. The letters SK were sown directly in the middle of the blue cloth bag. The vial was heavy for its size, well made, of high quality glass. He stared at it for what seemed like an eternity. The frown line in his forehead deepened. The nurse, still standing in the room, was also staring at the vial, and it was the nurse who enigmatically broke the long silence.

"Stephen King is very rich and very successful. He likes to do many outdoor activities in countries all over the world. He is also an avid scuba diver; however, to my knowledge, he has never dived the Thistlegorm. That vial you hold in your hand, originates from the monastery of Santa Katarina."

Dark Shark was suitably and significantly staggered.

"How do you know that!?"

"I've also got one."

She unbuttoned the top two buttons of her white blouse to display an identical vial, hanging on a thin, silver chain with the now familiar SK sown into the middle of an identical blue cloth bag.

"This vial is the symbol of Santa Katarina. The monks have been collecting the oil in vials for almost as long as the monastery has existed. Over a thousand years. The oil used is secreted from the remains of St. Katharine herself. The vials are famous all over the world. Whoever lost that one must be very unhappy about it. The vials are only given to monks who have passed through the rigorous initiation ceremonies of the monastery. Pay a visit to the Archbishop at the monastery; I am sure he will know this vial. Every vial is unique, and is recorded in the annals of the monastery's library. The secrets are written down inside a secret ledger. Only the archbishop has access to the ledger. You must speak to the archbishop at Santa Katarina monastery."

There are always signs and portents and only fools ignore the obvious. The vial was most definitely more than a clue. It was a sign, an omen of luck. Dark Shark's search would now take him to the high mountains, to the bitter cold of Santa Katarina. He was elated; he had been vindicated, freed, unshackled from the heavy chains of guilt.

Basking in the warm light of his new found absolution, Dark Shark jumped up and bounded across the room. Reaching the door, he grabbed the handle and pulled hard. With a loud thud, the door hit him square on the forehead.

"Owww! Fuck!"

He staggered a few feet and slumped back into the couch, holding his head in his hands. For some reason, he was finding it extremely difficult to get off this couch today. The nurse chuckled, doing up the buttons on her blouse. She was having another entertaining day. Since her transfer from Santa Katarina two years ago, she had been having a lot more fun in the tourist magnet of Sharm al Sheikh. Yesterday, was the first time she had ever seen dreadlocks bitten in half by a shark. What would tomorrow bring? Only Almighty Allah knew the answer to that question.

# 12

## *Santa Katarina*

That night, Dark Shark prepared for his journey to Saint Katharine.

He and Jamila had spent the rest of the day with Gastro, fussing over him, keeping his spirits up, both of them happy to turn their attentions away from each other. Somehow, it had been far easier for them to show their affection towards Gastro than to each other. Both of them were afraid of getting hurt, neither one wanted to open their heart. In that respect, it seemed as if little had changed from the days when they had been together. Gastro, always the child, was delighted by this extra attention, although he suspected, quite rightly, that while their concerns were genuine, his injury was not the only reason for their enthusiastic affectations.

The three friends stayed together until the sun began to make its descent into the western sky and the nurse ordered Gastro to rest, politely asking Dark Shark and Jamila to leave. Bidding their friend farewell, they had taken a taxi from the hospital back to Dahab, but for the whole hour neither had spoken a word. The taxi had dropped Jamila off at Dive Splurge, where she had mumbled some incoherent words to Dark Shark and said goodnight. Dark Shark did not deem it appropriate to mention his intention of traveling to the mountain; instead, he informed her he would call her in a day or two.

Back inside his house, he packed a set of warm clothes, walking shoes, two blankets, rope, a bottle of water, and three books. Wrapped carefully in the depths of his rucksack, secure in its blue cloth bag, was the vial. Gastro was out of action for the foreseeable and Jamila no longer believed in him, so for now, Dark Shark was on his own.

Finishing his packing, he flipped open his phone, dialled Osama's number and informed the taxi driver he would be going to the mountain in the morning. Exhausted and emotionally drained by recent dramatic events, Dark Shark turned off the light, lay on his bed, and gratefully surrendered to the comforting advance of sleep.

The next day, at ten o'clock in the morning, Osama and Dark Shark sat in the infamous blue and white Peugeot 504. The monster roared through the desert towards the mountain, the car consuming the miles as easily as Osama devoured his bananas. In the passenger seat, Dark Shark remained silent. His face was set in a stony grimace, his eyes constantly fixed on the road ahead. His mind was racing. Thoughts rushed in forcing unwanted painful recollections... memories of a huge shark... bloody water... the operating theatre...Gastro's body racked with pain... Jamila; hurt, angry, accusing...

Dark Shark fought the memories, trying to centre his mind, focusing... searching for positive thoughts. He closed his eyes and concentrated all his attentions towards his nose. Calming his mind, he began the ancient yogic technique of Prananayamamahamawama. His breathing slowed. His mind became clear, and after about fifteen minutes, his spirit soared, released from earthly bounds, free to roam both time and space. Dark Shark travelled back, through the ages, witnessing the sands of time shift inexorably through the desert. Empires, religions, great civilizations and tragic wars. He travelled back, back, back. To a time, 1,700 years ago, when the Roman Empire controlled the known world and Christianity was but a young child, only 300 years old and screaming to be heard. There his spirit touched down, landing in the city of Alexandria.

In the garden was a multitude of men. They had come from across the Empire. They were all wise scholars. Every man was an expert in his field. Numbering over fifty, the men had come to persuade the stunningly beautiful, highly intelligent young woman standing in their midst, that she was wrong. For many days and nights, the argument raged back and forth. The men presented compelling evidence, expounded the latest theories, and pointed out the extraordinary success of the Roman Empire in their bid for intellectual and religious supremacy. For her part, the woman countered with the teachings of Christ. Articulate and charismatic, the woman, to the astonishment of the spectators busy taking bets, not only one won the argument, but managed to convert all fifty to Christian doctrine.

Two months later, in the imperial palace, the Roman Emperor Maximus Diabolicus was sitting behind a great marble desk, poring over a map of the world with disturbing intensity. It had been a long day. From morning until late afternoon, Maximus had studied the map hard, plotting and scheming, desperately trying to find a solution to his problem, but to no avail. He was beginning to get restless. He wanted to conquer more land, plunder more wealth, kill lots more people. Unfortunately, according to the map, the Romans had conquered it all. At five o'clock, frustrated by geographical constraints, he ordered a plate of deer liver, a bottle of Chianti, and some olives.

The meal pleased him somewhat, but it was not enough. He pulled out a small package from deep inside his toga and emptied the contents onto the map. A pile of white powder landed on an empty space, a space that would one day become Bolivia. Maximus stared at the powder for a few moments, hypnotized by its sparkling crystalline qualities. He had discovered it only a few months ago, brought to him as a gift from far-off exotic lands by adventurous Roman seadogs. The white powder had become his favourite pastime. He took out a knife and cut the powder into three straight lines. Pulling out a one hundred Dinari note, he rolled it into a perfect straw and sucked all three white lines up his Roman nose. The resultant effect was instantaneous. Maximus Diabolicus began frantically pacing up and down the room, ideas quickly taking shape in his mind. After another thirty seconds, he decided he was God.

He stopped pacing, stood still. He breathed deeply, power surging through his veins. Holding his arms up to the heavens, his eyes like saucers, Maximus addressed the known universe:

"Hear me! I am the Emperor! I am a God! No! I am far more than that! I am the ruler of the Gods! The world will bow down before Maximus Diabolicus! Let all mortal men tremble in fear for I shall ride across the face of the earth and destroy all those who look upon my terrible countenance! I shall have no mercy, no compassion! Let the world know that I, Maximus Diabolicus am the creator and the destroyer!! A -ha-ha ha- ha-a- ha–ha-ha aaa- ha- ha- ha!!!"

He would have continued his maniacal, megla-monologue, but thankfully was interrupted by the arrival of the fifty wise men. They had returned from Egypt to inform him that not only had they failed in their quest, but that they had all converted to Christianity. Their timing could not have been less astute. By the next day, the Roman Empire had fifty less scholars and Maximus Diabolicus was suffering from a very runny nose.

Katherine had been a thorn in the side of the Roman Emperor for many months. Only eighteen years old, she was the daughter of upper class Egyptians; educated, bright, and beautiful. She had become a recent convert to Christianity after a visit by a mysterious Syrian monk and inspired by the teachings, she had travelled to Rome, seeking an audience with the Emperor, Maximus Diabolicus. Once in his presence, she publicly admonished him for his cruel treatment of Christians. Shocked by her bravery and audacity, Maximus had her removed from the palace and returned to Egypt, where she was put in jail. Fearing the spread of this dangerous new religion and not yet wishing to create a martyr, Maximus ordered his best fifty scholars to visit the young woman and convince her of the error of her ways, hoping she would either relent or commit a heretic crime against the Roman religion, a crime punishable by death.

Katharine of course never gave him the satisfaction and in fact was later visited by Maximus' wife, who, on hearing of the extraordinary woman residing in Alexandria, sought out her teachings and of course, converted. She also perished by order of her husband, Maximus. The Roman Emperor, now beside himself with rage, ordered Katharine to be put on the wheel, a horrific torture device which he himself had invented. However, before it could do its deadly work, the wheel miraculously broke, spinning out of control and killing all the spectators who were standing by and taking bets. Katharine was unharmed. It was time for plan C. Maximus ordered Katharine decapitated and this time, the execution went ahead without any further headaches. (Apart from Katharine's)

Sainthood being what it is, her demise was not the end of the story. Angels came down from Heaven, lifted Katharine's earthly remains, and carried them to Mount Sinai, laying them in the exact same spot where Moses had witnessed the Burning Bush. 400 years later, a Bedouin man, unable to remember where he had left his marijuana plant, stumbled across Katherine's remains whilst searching the slopes of Mount Sinai. Her body had not decomposed, but instead exuded a wonderful aroma accompanied by mysterious, slowly secreting black oil. The news of this remarkable discovery reached the ears of the Empress Helena, mother of Constantine the Great, who built a monastery on the site of the Chapel of the Burning Bush in honour of Katharine. By then the Roman Empire had become Christian, splitting into two kingdoms, Rome in the West, Constantinople in the East. In 565 AD, the Emperor Justinian added a chapel and turned the monastery into a fort, complete with high walls and two hundred Roman soldiers ready to protect the monks from Bedouin raiders.

Dark Shark's spirit had gifted him this extraordinary vision during it's out of body experience and now it returned to the physical realm of the here and now. He opened his eyes. Next to him, Osama was quietly whistling as he drove the taxi through the desert on their way to the monastery. The road from Dahab passed between mountains on its way north, wending its way along the paths cut by flash floods as they cascaded from the mountains. These were the famous wadis of the desert, without which travel would be impossible.

The Gulf of Aqaba is the right finger of the Red Sea which is giving the V sign at the tip of Sinai where Sharm El Sheikh is located. The left finger represents the Gulf of Suez, world-famous for the Canal which connects the eastern Mediterranean with the Red Sea and the Indian Ocean. The two Gulfs differ in topographical features. The Red Sea is a continuation of a trench in the Earth's crust, the Great Syrian- African rift which starts in Zimbabwe and continues all the way up to Lebanon. The sea is a meeting place for two tectonic plates, the Africa plate and the Eurasian plate. The trench takes a right turn at Sinai and as a consequence the Gulf of Aqaba is very deep, between 1800 – 2000 meters at its deepest point. Being more of an afterthought, the Gulf of Suez is far shallower, with deepest depths rarely greater than eighty metres. The Gulf of Aqaba is long and thin, at most only thirty kilometres across.

On the opposite shore is the vast Peninsula of Saudia Arabia. When the great continents of Africa and Asia collided many millions of years ago, the collision threw up huge mountain ranges on either side of the Gulf. It was through this range that Dark Shark and Osama were now travelling. In the canter of the range is Jebel Musa, the mountain of Moses, also known as Mount Sinai. At the foot of the mountain is the oldest continuous monastery in the world, Santa Katarina.

Occasionally the mountains were pink. Sometimes they turned white. At other times they became yellow or blue. When one pictures the desert in the mind's eye, it is normally an image of nothing but constantly shifting yellow sand dunes. Deserts are as varied as they are numerous. The Sinai was a red, rocky desert. Sand dunes were rare. In fact outside Dahab, a dune had been used for sand boarding. Yes, just like snowboarding. But on sand. The desert changed colour throughout the day. It all depended on the position of the sun, shadows and the colours of the rocks themselves.

The mountains dated back over 700 million years to an epoch known as the Pre Cambrian, making them some of the oldest in the world. The huge massif of the South Sinai Mountains stretched to the middle of the peninsula. From there a flat plain called 'Badyat eh Tih' or the 'Plain of Tears' ran all the way to the northern coast and the Mediterranean Sea. The plain was so called due to its treacherous and at times, deadly nature. Apart from the burning sun; shifting sands, disorientation and scarcity of water are just some of the dangers facing the unwary interloper. Many a traveller had entered Badyat Eh Tih never to return.

The South Sinai massif was part of a larger entity

known as the Arabo-Nubian massif. Eighty per cent of the rock was red granite and magmatic, meaning it was formed as molten lava deep beneath the earth's surface. 700-600 million years ago, the granite began intruding upwards towards the surface where it slowly cooled and became rock. The other twenty per cent consists of black volcanic material thrown up by explosions which occurred only 20 million years ago when the Red Sea was formed. The black volcanic rocks cooled far more quickly than the red granite and their crystalline structure was quite different.

Here and there Dark Shark could see dark intrusions running horizontally or diagonally inside the red rock. Grey, brown or black, the intrusions, known as dykes, were darker than the surrounding rock. In places they were metres wide and could run for many kilometres. Being more permeable to water, the dykes often supported mini oasis of life amongst the harsh conditions. Underground springs pooled under the dykes and where there is water, there is life. Plants sprang up which in turn brought animals that came to find shelter and food. The Bedouin called the dykes 'Jidda' or 'grandmother'. The word also implies 'nurturer' or 'nourishes' proving the value they placed on these invaluable sources of life.

Far from being barren and lifeless, the Sinai, although a desert in the classic sense of the word, teems with life. There are striped hyenas which are rarely seen, but widely distributed throughout Egypt and Sinai. Balancing life on the treacherous rocks of the high mountains are the sure-footed, regal Ibex. These magnificent animals are completely at home on the highest peaks. Their vulnerability is that unlike other desert creatures, they must drink daily. Extremely rare now, the Ibex currently number only 400 in the whole of Sinai and was classified as critically endangered. However, the good news is that the population appeared to be stable and getting slowly bigger. In addition to large mammals, there are many species of smaller mammals such as bats, mice, foxes, hares and hyraxes. The Sinai also had many species of birds, reptiles, and insects. Too see the life, one needed only to be quiet. To make little movement, and allow the life to come.

In the car, Osama and Dark Shark were silent. Both driver and passenger were happy to simply drink in the magnificent sights they were driving past. Thirty kilometres outside of Dahab, the taxi pulled up to one of the many security check points that control the highways of Sinai. Osama slowed the taxi to a halt. In his way was a long wooden pole which acted as a barrier and stretched across the road. The pole was perhaps twelve feet long. On the other side of the road was a blue, weather beaten wooden box, standing six feet tall. The blue paint had faded over time under the sun's intense glare. The box had only one window with no glass. Inside, officers from the tourist police sweated under a huge fan. They sat on chairs or stood around a large desk, waving around pieces of paper as much to keep cool as to look officious. The officers all wore the standard black uniforms of the tourist police.

Outside, on the left hand side of the road was another wooden blue box, but far smaller. It sat next to Osama's taxi and responsible for a large wooden barrier that on command from the officers in the larger box would go either up or down. The smaller box was manned by the second-lowest ranking policeman in the service. He controlled the wooden barrier with a rope. On command, he would loosen the rope and the pole which made up the barrier and was heavily weighted on the other end, would go up. When a sufficient amount of time had passed, he would pull the rope and the barrier would come down again. He would then rest the pole on a metal holder and sit down in his small, blue box. Next to him, kneeling on the ground was the lowest-ranking member of the Sinai police force. In front of him was a small, blue wooden shield no more than a foot high. In the middle of the shield was a slot and from this slot a long chain emerged. The chain was punctuated at regular intervals by huge spikes. The man's job was to release the chain which would be thrown across the road at high speed. Any vehicles which attempted to driver over the spiked chain would be minus four tires.

As Dark Shark sat in the taxi waiting for the inevitable, "Passport", he glanced down at the man on spiked chain duty. The man glanced back at Dark Shark but his eyes were vacant. He had the haunted look of a man destined never to throw his chain. Dark Shark could sympathize. He had had some pretty awful jobs in his time, but nothing quite like this. Dark Shark wandered at the conversation the poor man had on returning home to his wife each evening.

"Salaam, dear. Did you throw the chain today dear?"

"La. Not today. Maybe tomorrow Insha'allah."

"Aiwa, tomorrow Inshallah, you will throw the chain."

The officers in the wooden box looked up when they saw the taxi pull up. From inside the wooden box, a man walked out but he was not wearing the black uniform of the tourist police. He wore a grey suit, white shirt and black shoes. He had a sub-machine gun inside his jacket. He also sported a rather fetching pencil moustache and black aviator sunglasses. With a subtle flick of his hand, he summoned another policeman to accompany him and together they walked over to the car. Speaking to Osama, the man in the grey suit and glasses asked the taxi driver to present identification. At the same time, he knocked on the glass in the rear door and spoke to Dark Shark.

"Passport."

Assessing the identification of the car's occupants, the officer from the Shamandura asked Osama some questions, rattled off in Arabic too quickly for Dark Shark to catch. He did however; manage to catch the following answers.

"Aiwa. Santa Katarina. Aiwa. British, Yanni. Aiwa

Tourist."

Evidently satisfied, the officer returned the documents before saying another couple sentences. In reply, Osama gave him a bag containing sunflower seeds, bananas, cigarettes, bottles of water and oranges.

The officer smiled said thank you and with a wave of his hand, the barrier was raised. Muttering through clenched teeth whilst smiling to the men outside, Osama drove the taxi through the check point and turned left.

They were on the Santa Katarina road and from now on, it was only going up. As they pulled away from the checkpoint, Osama reached under the front seat and pulled out another bag. Passing it back to Dark Shark, he said:

"Here you are. Drink, eat. There is maya, bananas, oranges and some sunflower seeds."

"Walla, sucran. You always have to pay the check point tax?"

"Walla he, Dark Shark, every time. But you know, they don't get paid very much money and so I help them and in return they make my life easier. You know, it's like a mutually beneficial arrangement."

"Okay."

Dark Shark thought the only party benefiting was the Shamandura but he said nothing more.

All around them, the landscape had changed. It had flattened out and rolled gently in every direction. Scattered around were acacia and tamarisk trees eking out a profitable existence on very little water. The tamarisk tree was particularly elegant, with long, graceful feathery branches clad in tiny leaves. In spring, the tree produced the most extraordinary pink flowers, shaped in delicate spikes. Common in the wadis of Sinai the tamarisk was called 'tarfa' by the Bedouin and in times gone by was used as fire wood. If the tamarisk tree was beautiful, the acacia was key. Like date palms, the acacia was synonymous with the desert. There were four species in Sinai. Able to withstand the harshest conditions, acacia supported a huge range of insect and vertebrate herbivores including Bedouin livestock. They can survive long periods of drought, making them a reliable source of food in an ever changing landscape. The Bedouin name for the acacia was 'seyaal'.

After fifteen minutes driving through this magical landscape, Dark Shark and Osama noticed them at the same time. Up ahead, about 300 meters, sitting on the side of the road with their hands sticking out, was a man and two children. There had been little or no traffic on the road so far on their journey. The taxi had probably passed no more than a couple of cars and the odd truck. The people sitting on the side of the road may well have been there for hours or even days.

Osama nodded as a thought struck him.

"Bedouin. Probably Gebeliya"

"Let's give them a lift."

"Walla-he Dark Shark I don't know. Maybe mishkela."

"La, la it will be okay. Let's pick them up. Please Osama."

"Mershi, mershi. It is you who is paying the bill."

Osama shifted down the gears and the taxi pulled to halt a few meters from the Bedouin. There was a man, a girl and a boy.

Smiling excitedly and with many thanks, they piled into the taxi. The man took the passenger seat next to Osama while the children got into the back seat with Dark Shark. Introducing themselves, the occupants of taxi conducted at least three conservations at the same time. The Bedouin were indeed Jebeliya from the town of Santa Katarina. The man was the children's father and had picked them up from school in Dahab. It was the holidays and he had come to take the children back home for the duration.

An hour from home, his Jeep had broken down. Unable to fix it, he and the children had waited nearly three hours before Dark Shark and Osama very kindly gave them a lift. His name was Jebeli Goma Jebeli. The children chatted incessantly, pointing out the window, squabbling and asking Dark Shark questions in Arabic for which he had no answer. Goma was wearing a white jelibyah. His head was adorned with a purple kefir.

Over one shoulder he carried a bag made from camel and goat skin. The young girl was wearing a pink t-shirts and blue shorts. Both the t-shirt and the shorts were torn and dirty. The boy was wearing a pair of black shorts and an AC Milan football club t-shirt which said 'Hullit'. Ruud Gullit had been a famous Dutch footballer playing with great success for the Italian club. Bedouin kids were extraordinary. They were one the true treasures of Sinai. Without the kids, Sinai would truly be barren and lifeless. Bedouin kids often had large brown eyes which radiated warmth and adventure.

They had tousled brown hair ranging in colour from black to almost a light sandy brown. Common in their hair were streaks of gold a consequence of the strong sunlight. Frequently shoeless, Bedouin kids had feet like hobbits but without the hair. They had leather for soles. Growing up amongst animals and humans in what was still a wilderness, their playground was the mountains, the desert and the sea. They were tough these kids. Vigorous, robust and full of vitality, they withstood frequent hunger, discomfort and disease with the bright-eyed optimism of the young.

Goma asked Dark Shark for his name. When Dark Shark replied, Goma looked slightly startled and frowned. He went quiet, although the kids continued to make a racket in the back. Dark Shark had never met this Bedouin man before, but the man certainly seemed to know his name. Goma lapsed into silence and stared out of his window, scanning the desert with the eyes of a hawk. The road continued on. Since the check point, the road had started to climb, the land gradually getting steeper and steeper the closer they got to Santa Katarina.

Minutes passed and Goma shifted his bag impatiently, clearly thinking hard.

As the car passed a particularly intricate dyke in the side of a hill, a wadi appeared. Goma looked down with the wadi and motioning with his hand, he spoke.

"We need stop here. Stop the car. We get out here."

Osama was confused.

"Why we stop here? We need to get to the town."

The Bedouin persisted however, repeating his urging for them to stop the vehicle. Dark Shark told Osama it was okay and the big taxi driver pulled over to the side of the road. As soon as they came to a standstill, Goma jumped out and beckoned Dark Shark to follow him.

"What about the children?"

"They come too."

Osama was unwilling to leave his taxi, so Dark Shark and the kids got out. The Bedouin Goma indicated for him to follow and quickly walked into the wadi. The kids skipped and danced as they walked beside the two adults. Apart from the humans, there was total silence in the Wadi. Nothing stirred, not even the wind. The sun was shining, but the winter light was bearable. The air was crisp and cool. Dark Shark could already sense the change in climate as they were now at a much higher elevation above sea level. The air here was drier and cooler. Soon it would be very cold. Goma and the children were walking at a furious pace and it was all Dark Shark could do to keep up with them.

Even in the modern age of cars, Bedouin retained the capacity to walk far. Their stamina was astonishing. Goma was in his forties but walked with the energy of a man half his age. The only noise in the wadi was the crunch of sandals on soft sand. The wadi was a small one, no more than 500 meters across. On either side, sheer walls soared up as high as a hundred or two hundred meters. The walls were almost impassable. The slopes were covered in slippery red or black shale which went downhill fast with every foot placed upon it. The only way to progress was to follow the paths made by water, the wadis.

As they walked, the wadi gradually narrowed to less than twenty meters and they found themselves in a canyon. It was no ordinary canyon. The rocks had changed to white sandstone. The surface of the rock was smooth. The floor of the canyon was of the finest white sand imaginable. It was so fine and soft, it almost felt like snow. This was the legendary white canyon. Exquisitely carved by nature over millions of years, formed by erosion from wind and water, the canyon is a stunningly beautiful natural phenomenon. It wasn't just beautiful. The thing about the canyon was the overwhelming feeling of peaceful existence once inside. Even walking briskly at this moment in time, Dark Shark wanted to lie down and stare at the blue sky above or close his eyes and sleep the most contented sleep.

A light breezed whispered through the white

passageway. Dark Shark thrilled at being in the Canyon again. It was an incredibly special place. All at once, the party came to a dead end. The white sandstone came abruptly up from the sandy floor and it was impossible to walk any further. One side, a black metal ladder had been secured to the rock and Goma slung his bag over his shoulder and expertly climbed, nimbly followed by the children and a far less nimble climber in the shape of a middle-aged English diving instructor. On reaching the top of the ladder, the party of four, scrambled over some smooth beige rocks and found a rope which they used to descend onto the other side of the mini escarpment. They found themselves in another passage way similar to the one they had just escaped from. This one though had light beige intrusions running along the wall which gave wonderful warm contrast to the white.

They continued on. Dark Shark took water from his bag, quenched his thirst, and then passed the bottle around. It had been fifteen minutes since leaving the car and he wandered how much farther they were going to go. The canyon was very nice, but Dark Shark was on his way to the monastery with a pressing mission. He hoped that whatever the Bedouin wanted to say, it was going to be worth it. As to how much longer, they were going to walk for, he would simply have to be patient and wait to find out. If it was one thing that had to be learnt when dealing with Bedouin, it was patience. They had their rhythms and their own way of doing things and if you wanted to hang, you'd better get with the plan, man. Dark Shark carried on walking.

Pretty soon, the white canyon ended by opening up into a wide, open wadi. This wadi was completely different to the one preceding the white canyon. The first thing that Dark Shark noticed was the green. It was everywhere, sticking out of every nook and cranny. There was a lot of water here and the water meant life. This wasn't just a wadi, this was an oasis. The oasis of Ein Khudra. There were the ubiquitous acacia and tamarisk trees, but there were also larger Cypress trees. In places, juniper bushes, bean caper, soapwort and Sinai hawthorn sprung from the gaps in rocks or grew alongside dykes. Dotted around were orchards with fig apricot, almond and pear trees all growing side by side in great abundance with wild melons. From rocks and the ground sprung Sinai milkweed, Syrian rue and henbane. In the left hand side of the oasis was a hoosha. Dark Shark took all this in with one glance. It was stunning. To see such a concentration of green was simply marvellous.

Looking to his left, Dark Shark saw the hoosha. It was about fifteen square feet with a roof made from wood and palm leaves. Two camels, tied up by their knees, sat next to the hoosha munching on straw. A small herd of goats nibbled on an acacia tree nearby. Between the camels and the hoosha were four giant black water buckets, white plastic boxes, various thicknesses of rope and a number of tools. There was white sand from the canyon on the floor of the hoosha; whoever had built the structure was keen to decorate it with only the finest materials. Lying on the floor were four large palm tree logs which formed a square. In the middle of the square was the remnant of a fire, smouldering coals flickering from orange to grey, then back again.

Covering the palm logs were large red and blue rugs and on top of the rugs were around twenty or so brightly coloured cushions. On the remains of the fire sat a small silver tea pot. Steam lazily exited the pot, drifting inexorably upwards. Beside the fire were five small glasses. Next to the glasses were tea spoons and a bag of light brown sugar. Another bag contained nana. Between the fire and the cushions, sat a dark blue glass bulb filled with water. The water was bubbling. Above the bulb, the glass closed to a narrow fluke which had a ceramic bowl sitting on top of it. Nestling on the bowl was a lump of apple tobacco. On top of the tobacco was a block of charcoal burning bright red. Smoke, cooled by the water, was being sucked through a long hose made from balsa wood.

Holding the mouth piece of the hose in the corner of his mouth and calming sitting cross legged on the cushions whilst gazing intently back at Dark Shark, was a man. Whilst Dark Shark had stood agog, staring at Ein Khudra like a dumbstruck tourist, Goma and the kids had already gone over to talk to the strange Bedouin man in the hoosha. On the arrival of his guests, the Bedouin man stood up and welcomed them into his hoosha. Goma took off his shoes, hugged the man then took his place on the cushions. The children decided that entertainment could be had by teasing the camels and skipped with delight over to the reluctant dromedaries. Goma and the other Bedouin invited Dark Shark into the hoosha. He took off his shoes and joined his hosts.

The Bedouin's name was Msaad Abu Mased and like Goma he was also Jebeliya. He was slightly overweight and in his early fifties. Flecks of grey speckled his otherwise jet black hair. He wore a spotless white jelibya with a purple kefir, exactly like Goma. On his feet were brown sandals. He was warm, amiable and friendly. He offered his guests tea and shisha. The tea smelt amazing. Abu Mased poured the beverage into one of the small glasses, and then added copious amounts of sugar and nana. The resultant concoction was minty, sweet and thoroughly delicious. The formalities over, Abu Mased began asking question of his guest.

"You name is Dark Shark and you are on the way to the monastery?"

"Yes."

"Why are you going there?"

"I'm trying to find out some information."

"What information do you seek?"

"I want to find out about this."

Dark Shark's intuition told him this Bedouin could be trusted, so he reached into his bag and passed Abu

Mased the vial from the monastery. The Bedouin gasped. He took the vial and stared at it intently.

"Walla-he. Eshta. You have one of the vials. It contains the oil from the body of the saint."

"Yes. You know about them?"

"Yes, I know them well. I worked at the monastery for a long time."

"Can you tell me about this one? Can you tell me who it belonged to?"

"Walla-he, no I am sorry, I cannot. That information is held only by the archbishop."

"Yes, I am going to see the archbishop today."

"Dark Shark, this is why we have brought you here today. To Ein Khudra. We must give you a warning."

"What warning, Abu Mased?"

"You are entering great danger. We Jebeliya have heard about the death of your student. We have heard about the sharks dying in the sea and we know you look for the criminal, Nemo. The news reaches all who know how to listen."

"The things that have happened are terrible, evil, they must stop now. I must visit the archbishop and get some answers."

"Beware the archbishop, Dark Shark. He is new to the Sinai, brought here by the Vatican only a few years ago. He understands nothing of this place and cares even less. He is pompous, vain and corrupt. The Jebeliya have suffered since his arrival. The monastery has restricted our access to medicines and herbs. There is a bad feeling in Jan'ub Sinai. The trees do not give such good fruit in the last years. The water in the ground tastes bad. This is big mishkela. Soon we will make our feelings known to the archbishop and if he does not change his ways, we will make very big mishkela for him."

"What must I do Abu Mased?"

"Be very careful. Trust no one at the monastery, not even Bedouin. If you do not find what you are searching for, look to the mountain."

"Which mountain?"

"Jebel Musa. Go to Jebel Musa."

"I will. Thank you very much for your warnings. Thank you also for your hospitality."

"You are welcome, Dark Shark. Now come before you go, we will smoke."

"Shisha?"

"Nah, fuck the shisha. We will smoke some real shit."

Goma, Dark Shark and Abu Mased laughed hard, while the camels roared their indignation, at the fun the kids were having jumping on top of them. The guests finished their tea, bade their farewells and half an hour later were driving again on the road towards Santa Katarina. Before they had left, Abu Mased had given a present to Dark Shark. It was material of some kind, wrapped up in brown paper and tied up with string.

"Take this. It might help."

Two hours later, Dark Shark, Osama, Goma and the

two kids pulled up into the car park outside the vast, walled complex of the monastery of the blessed Saint Katherine. Osama had been more than willing to take the three Bedouin right to their house in town, but Goma would not hear of it, instead insisting that they would jump in another Bedouin Jeep for the final leg of their journey. He made it quite clear that it was time for Dark shark to enter the monastery. There were hugs and masalaams all round and after agreeing to meet up again in the future, Goma and the kids walked along the road towards the town. Dark Shark and Osama were once again alone on the road.

It was midday. The sun was at its zenith in the sky, right above them. Even though it was winter, they could feel its constant presence. Behind the monastery, the 2,285 metre mountain of Jebel Musa rose up to the sky where over 5,000 years ago, God had given Moses the law. This was the birth place of Judaism, Christianity and Islam. Here was the cradle of the three great western religions, two of which, over the millennia, had struggled for world domination.

Dark Shark took off his coat and put it into the taxi. He then put the package given to him by Abu Mased into his bag and told Osama that if he was not back by four o'clock in the afternoon, for him to call the police. Osama told Dark Shark to be careful and hurry back soon. Agreeing, Dark Shark made for the entrance to the monastery. Osama got back into his taxi, turned on the radio, split open a banana and settled back into his chair.

Dark Shark nonchalantly skirted the wall of the great monastery. The walls were a foot thick and over twenty feet high, hewn from granite and re-enforced many times over their 1,200 year old history. The intrepid instructor reached the end of the wall and turned right. In the centre of the wall was a large wooden gate suspended on metal hinges. The gate was partially ajar. On one side of the gate, a police man stood guard in a blue wooden box. He said hello to Dark Shark and asked to see his passport. Studying it, he returned the document to the tourist and waved him in. Dark Shark passed through the gate and walked into the monastery of Saint Katherine or to give it it's full, official title: 'The Sacred and Imperial Monastery of the God Trodden of Mount Sinai' He found himself in a huge courtyard, nearly half an acre in size. The front courtyard contained orchards and wells.

Opening the door to the church, Dark Shark entered another world. The monastery was the oldest continually inhabited monastery in the world. Its library was the second largest and most important after the Vatican. It has survived so long because it has had the protection of everyone from the Empress Helena to Justinian to the prophet Mohammed through Arab and Turkish rulers right up to the time of Napoleon. The church is one of the only early Christian churches to have survived. It is surely one of the finest and richest in existence.

Dark Shark stepped back in time and gasped in

awe. He was truly gob-smacked. He had been to the mountain many times, but this was his first time inside the monastery. He had the funny feeling that he had absolutely no idea where to begin. The monastery was not that big in size, but its history, richness and complexity were staggering in scope. Dark Shark gazed around him. He took in the scene with the air of one who knows that what he is witnessing would take many, many lifetimes to study before even the surface was scratched to gain any kind of understanding. His head swam with the beauty and the opulence. It was just so unlike anything else on the entire Sinai Peninsula. Here was a temple, a house of God that had been protected by every single ruler of the entire region for 1,200 years. This was a church where the library had been added to by the most fantastic works of art for over a thousand years.

Dark Shark stared transfixed, drinking in the sights around him. He looked down the nave. Six magnificent, monolithic marble columns flanked the wide central isle. The columns' capitals supported arches and the upper walls of the clerestory which was set with rectangular windows. Between the columns sat elaborately carved stone thrones of past patriarchs and bishops. Separating the naïve from the altar was a 17th century golden gilded iconostasis presented to the monastery by the patriarch Cosmos of Crete. Standing in front of the iconostasis were three pairs of giant gold 18th century candlesticks.

The iconostasis was crowned by a giant crucifix bearing

the figure of Christ, the incredible work of art painted in the brightest colours, every detail richly re-imagined. The table on the altar was inlaid with silver mother of pearl, the work of a 17th Century Athenian artist. Above the altar housed the apse, home to possibly the monastery's greatest treasure, an astonishing 6th Century mosaic. The figures stand out in exquisite shades of blue, green and red against a background of dull gold glass. Dark Shark walked down the nave, studying everything he possibly could.

He was fascinated. Every single piece of material in this building had he most incredible story behind it. Whether a piece of stone, marble, gold, wood, glass, parchment or leather, Dark Shark longed to know the hows, whys and wherefores. He slowly, breathlessly approached the altar knowing full well what he would find there. They were in every guide book, every tourist website.

To the right of the altar was a marble sarcophagus or domed canopy supported by four slender marble columns containing two richly inlaid silver caskets. These held the relics of St Catherine: one contained her skull encircled by a golden crown studded with gems, and the other her left hand, ornamented with gold rings set with precious stones. Dark Shark was standing next to what were supposedly the remains of a young woman from Alexandria who 1,700 years ago at the tender age of eighteen, defied the Emperor of the greatest Empire the world has ever seen, won an argument with the fifty greatest scholars in the Empire, converted the Emperor's wife, was placed on a unique torture device that failed to work, before finally being beheaded.

Her body was lifted up by angels who laid it on Mount Sinai and 400 years later, she became a saint. When he was eighteen, Dark Shark was getting drunk in pubs and banging his head to Led Zeppelin. Things had definitely changed over the last 1,700 years. Dark Shark didn't care if the relics inside the caskets did not belong to Saint Katherine. He didn't care if the story of Saint Katherine was completely untrue. Dark Shark loved history and the story of this amazingly brave young woman was a bloody good one.

He sighed and continued his search of the church. To the left of the altar were two votive sarcophagi, wrought in pure gold and studded with precious stones; the two sarcophagi were gifts from the Czars of Russia, Peter the Great in 1680, and Alexander II in 1860. Dark Shark marvelled at the opulence in this place. Monetary value meant absolutely nothing here. It was literally priceless. It was worth so much and was so famous, that there was simply no point in stealing it and trying to sell it. It was impossible. Of course this interesting point of security had little impact on certain tribes from the Eastern Egyptian desert, the Blemmys, who mounted raids against the monastery in the 5th Century, looting the building and even murdering monks. For the entire life of the monastery, it had been protected by one patron after another, thus ensuring its survival until the present day.

Dark Shark walked back down the central isle. He was looking for the library, the one place where he might find the answer as to the origins of the vial. He approached the south-eastern corner of the basilica and entered the Old Refectory. A rectangular chamber over seventeen meters long, it had a long wooden table in the centre. Brought from Corfu in the 18th Century it was ornately carved with angels and flowers in the Rococo style. The inside and outside of the impressive wooden door frames leading into the refectory bore the coats of arms of pilgrims from medieval times. Interesting, but not what Dark Shark was looking for.

Exiting the refectory, Dark Shark approached one of the monks and politely asked where the library was. He was pointed towards the far end of the church, but told that the library was off limits to the general public and could only be accessed by permission from the archbishop. Dark Shark then asked if it was possible to meet the archbishop but was politely informed that the Patriarch was at this moment in Jerusalem, attending a conference of various church leaders. He would not be back at Santa Katarina for another three days. Dark Shark thanked the monk who bowed in return before walking in the direction the monk had pointed.

Soon he came to a room that could only have been the library. Before him stood a spacious and well-built fireproof concrete wing built between 1930 and 1942. The wing was smaller than he imagined, being fifteen meters long and ten wide. In the middle of the main wall, a door, presumably locked, had a sign on it that said Library. Dark Shark needed to get in there, but how was the big question of the moment. He decided on a desperate course of action, but one that might just work. He walked back up to the altar, looking for a suitable place. The monks were busy with the tourists who were mostly standing around outside a mosque near the belfry.

Behind the altar and slightly below it, there was a small, secluded stone chamber. It was perfect. Dark Shark stole in and took off his shoulder bag. Untying the fastening string, he took out the package given to him by the Jebeliya Bedouin, Abu Mased. As quietly and as carefully as he could, he untied the string on the package, unfolded the paper and took out a long brown garment. It was a monk's gown, exactly the same as the other monks were wearing, even down to the large hood. Made from light weight cotton, the gowns were designed to be warm in winter and cool in summer.

Dark Shark quickly undressed. Not wanting to put his clothes on the ground, he looked around for something to hang them on. Next to him was a large bramble bush. Non-descript and without fruit, the bush would do. He gingerly hung his t-shirt, hooded top and cargo pants onto the branches, hoping he didn't add any holes to his duds.

Next, he dressed in the gown of a monk. He placed a rope around his neck complete with wooden cross and the disguise was complete. The conservation-minded Darwinist Jewish boy from West London had turned into a celibate Christian monk living in 'The Sacred and Imperial Monastery of the God Trodden of Mount Sinai'. Quickly stuffing his clothes into his bag, he tied it up, shoved it deep within the gown, pulled his hood up so that it completely covered his entire head, put his hands deep inside the sleeves and stepped out of the chamber. He was just in time. A monk walked slowly passed. Both he and Dark Shark bowed to each in solemn religious respect. The disguise appeared to be working. Who'd have thought it? Steeling himself to the task ahead, Dark Shark slowly walked back towards the library.

As he did so, he reminded himself to stay calm and act naturally. That meant walking slowly, touching the crucifix from time to time and keeping his mush covered. He was within a few feet of the door and wandering how on earth he was going to get inside, when a miraculous thing occurred. The door slowly opened and an elderly Bedouin cleaner emerged carrying a mop and bucket. Dark Shark had to stop himself from rushing forward. As reserved as possible, he approached the cleaner and bowing, indicated his desire to enter the room. The cleaner acquiesced and Dark Shark was in.

Closing the door behind him, Dark Shark surveyed the room he was standing in. The library. It housed one of the richest monastic collections in the world, second in importance only to the Vatican. Lining the walls and stacked up on tables were books. Thousands and thousands of book. Dark Shark walked along the room, staring at the treasures on display. The library contained more than 6,000 volumes and manuscripts, 3,000 of which were ancient, the bulk - more than 2,000 - in Greek, and hundreds of others in twelve languages including Arabic (some 700), Syriac, Armenian, Georgian, Coptic, Polish and Slavonic.

Dark Shark was looking for something specific. He looked for a desk that might contain a ledger or records. Any record that might tell him the origins of the vial. So far, his search had been in vain and he was taking a big risk. Impersonating a monk might not get him stoned to death, but it the monastery wasn't going to take kindly to an impersonator snooping around amongst their thousand-year-old Aladdin's cave. He came at last to a wall at what he thought was the end of the room, but he came to realize was actually the entrance to another, smaller chamber. A heavy, brown wooden door barred his way. Dark Shark held the handle and turned.

The handle squeaked and he held his breath, but the noise was slight and the door swung slowly open. He gasped almost silently but sound escaped. He was inside the Treasury, known also as the Sacred Sacristy. This wondrous chamber housed the Icon Collection and is the monastery's great artistic treasure. The most important single collection in the world, it includes more than 2,000 works, 150 of which are unique pieces dating from the fifth to the seventh centuries. The collection represents some of the finest Byzantine work and includes a large number of icons from the period of the iconoclasm (726-843), when the depiction of the saintly or divine form in art was considered heretical.

In Christian centres elsewhere during this period almost all representations of religious figures in icons, mosaics and wall paintings were removed or destroyed. Several important manuscripts were displayed in glass cabinets. These include a fine collection of icons, including some of the oldest and most valuable owned by the monastery. Also on display was a large collection of ancient and modern vestments embroidered in gold and silver thread, mitres, chalices and trays of the finest workmanship, gold and silver crosses of various sizes and shapes, and illuminated Bibles of incredible beauty in gold and silver filigree containers set with precious stones. Dark Shark was stunned by the objects on display. He wasn't in the least bit religious, but the art here was literally breath-taking. There were no superlatives to describe what lay before him. He wandered from artefact to artefact, enthralled beyond words. He was so entranced, he didn't hear the sounds behind him until it was too late. Footsteps approached. Jerking up, Dark Shark spun around at the exact moment a voice uttered the words:

"Ah, Dark Shark. Are you enjoying our humble house of God?"

Dark Shark froze to the spot. He stared at the men in front of him. There were three of them. Two were senior looking monks wielding large sticks. The third man, the one in the middle who had addressed Dark Shark was the man in charge of Santa Katarina. Here in front of him was the Patriarch of The Sacred and Imperial Monastery of the God Trodden of Mount Sinai, Archbishop Phillip Damieolas Papadopoulos.

# 13

## *Jebel Musa*

The archbishop sat behind his great desk in his office at the monastery. Opposite him, Dark Shark sat in a chair with his hands tied behind his back with rope. He was flanked on either side by the two spiritual monks who could also be heavy when the need arose. Evidently unconditional love was often just that, conditional. The archbishop, let us call him Phil, was deep in thought. He was leaning back and resting his elbows on the arms of the chair. Phil was studying Dark Shark intently. He appeared to come to a decision and with a wave to the monks broke the silence.

"I don't think we need your hands tied. I must apologize. Sometimes, I still think we are in the 12th Century."

Dark Shark smirked with the irony.

"I can't imagine why."

Phil didn't like that one bit. He frowned and stared hard across the desk. His large brown eyebrows rose up, coming together to meet in the centre of his prominent forehead.

"Please don't test my patience, Mr Shark. Your activities here today could well land you in jail. Breaking and entering. Impersonating a monk. Possible attempted theft of priceless religious artefacts. The list is long and impressive Mr Shark. What exactly were you hoping to achieve by dressing up as a monk and breaking into one of the holiest and most valuable rooms in the entire world?"

"I wasn't stealing. I was trying to get information."

"Information about what?"

In answer to his question, Dark Shark reached into his bag and pulled out the vial. Phil looked aghast.

"Where did you acquire that from?"

"I found it."

"I doubt that very much. Vials are not so easily lost and found. Where do you claim to have found this one?"

"I'll do you a deal. I'll tell you the story of how I found this, in return for information as to who originally owned it."

"Impossible. The monastery does not make deals with criminals."

"I'm not the criminal. I am trying to stop criminals from continuing to commit crimes in the Sinai. I am trying to find out who that vial belongs to. I am not asking for much, just a name."

"Where did you get the monk's gown from? No doubt a Bedouin friend of yours?"

Dark Shark said nothing. Phil continued.

"It doesn't matter, I am sure I will find out who it was. I have many eyes and ears in the Sinai, particularly in this valley. As I am sure you are aware, Dark Shark, the Monastery and the Jebeliya Bedouin share a very close and interdependent relationship. In the past, the Jebeliya relied on the supplies and services that the monastery provided while the monastery was dependent on the local people for manual labour and protection. Today the Jebeliya continue to be employed by the monastery as gardeners, stonemasons, grounds men, bakers, blacksmiths, carpenters and general labourers. Traditionally, all disputes not settled by Jebeliya people have been presented to the Archbishop of the Monastery to resolve. The three round objects above the walled-up old entrance are representing bread (libbe), symbolizing that the Jebeliya, Ulad Said and Muzeina Bedouin tribes could go to the Monastery for help. During the seventh century, the isolated Christian anchorites of the Sinai were eliminated: only the fortified monastery remained. The monastery is still surrounded by the massive fortifications that have preserved it. Until the twentieth century, access was through a door high in the outer walls. From the time of the First Crusade, the presence of Crusaders in the Sinai until 1270 spurred the interest of European Christians and increased the number of intrepid pilgrims who visited the monastery. The monastery was supported by its dependencies in Egypt, Palestine, Syria, Crete, Cyprus and Constantinople.

The monastery, along with several dependencies in the area, constitutes the entire Orthodox Church of Mount Sinai, which is headed by an archbishop, who is also the abbot of the monastery. The exact administrative status of the church within Eastern Orthodoxy is ambiguous: by some, including the church itself, it is considered autocephalous, by others an autonomous church under the jurisdiction of the Greek Orthodox Church of Jerusalem, The archbishop is traditionally consecrated by the Orthodox Patriarch of Jerusalem; in recent centuries he has usually resided in Cairo. During the period of the Crusades, marked by bitterness between the Orthodox and Catholic churches, the monastery was patronized by both the Byzantine Emperors and the rulers of the Kingdom of Jerusalem."

Dark Shark shifted in his chair uncomfortably. Much as he liked history, Phil's lecture wasn't exactly sparkling. The archbishop paused for breath. Dark Shark took the opportunity of a lull in the proceedings to ask a question.

"May I have some water please?"

The archbishop paused as he was about to continue enlightening Dark Shark with the internal political machinations of the church. Instead he nodded and motioned for the monks to bring water. Dark Shark drank the water slowly, relishing the refreshment and the respite from the linguistic marathon. The respite was short lived.

"So, having heard of all of that, I hope you can

appreciate that it is not in the interest of the Monastery to upset the delicate balance that exists here. We have a responsibility to the local population and our reputation around the world. It would simply not do for us to get involved in the seedy goings on in the decadent tourist destinations which you work in. In addition, although the one truth religion of our Lord Jesus Christ predates the important, but false religion of Islam, we at the monastery are nothing if not adaptable. The majority of the people in Egypt are of course Muslim and therefore we find ourselves guests in a country we basically created."

Here Phil paused, flashing a warm smile at the Bedouin monks present. He continued for what Dark Shark hoped would not be much longer.

"I am going to read to you an interesting letter. It was written nearly 1,400 years ago, by the Prophet Mohammed himself to the monks of the monastery."

From a drawer inside his desk, Phil reached in and pulled out a rolled up vellum parchment bound with a blue ribbon. Untying the ribbon, he slowly unfurled the ancient manuscript. He carefully placed the open parchment on the desk and proceeded to recite the passage. Although written in ancient Greek, the archbishop translated the verse into English for the sake of his uneducated guest.

"This letter is the Prophet Muhammad's Charter of Privileges to Christians. - A Letter to the Monks of St.

Catherine Monastery.

'This is a message from Muhammad ibn Abdullah, as a covenant to those who adopt Christianity, near and far, we are with them. Verily I, the servants, the helpers, and my followers defend them, because Christians are my citizens; and by Allah! I hold out against anything that displeases them. No compulsion is to be on them. Neither are their judges to be removed from their jobs nor their monks from their monasteries. No one is to destroy a house of their religion, to damage it.'

As you can see, we enjoyed the protection of all the great rulers of the last 1,200 years. We also want this to continue into the future."

The archbishop looked deep into Dark Shark's eyes, sending a warning telepathically.

"I am going to be lenient with you, Dark Shark. I am going to forget this little incident ever happened. In return, I want you to return to Dahab and abandon your quest. Leave any investigation to the relevant authorities. My responsibilities are increasing all the time. I have much work to do here and so very little time to do it in. Most important of all, is to keep good relations with the Jebeliya Bedouin."

The archbishop smiled at him from across the desk, a smile escaping from thin, dishonest lips.

Dark Shark smiled warmly in return.

"The Bedouin are not so happy right now. They tell me that the water has turned bad, that the trees do not produce much fruit, and that they are finding it difficult to get access to safe medicines and herbs."

The archbishop laughed.

"Ha! Don't believe all that you are told my dear Dark Shark. I can assure you that things are quite good around here. You have nothing to worry about and can go back home nice and promptly, knowing that we who have survived out here for 1,200 years are doing fine thank you very much."

"Agreed. I can do that. I've had enough adventures for one lifetime."

"Very good. My humble monks will escort you to the main gate. You may keep the vial, but I would ask that our gown be returned forthwith. You are of course always welcome to return here Mr Shark, but any visit to the library or anywhere else off limits must be done with my express permission. Do we have an understanding Mr Shark?"

"Yes, we do. Thank you very much for your leniency and understanding. I am deeply sorry if I have caused any inconvenience to the church and to you. My behaviour was unacceptable and I can assure you it will not happen again."

"Very good, Mr Dark Shark! Very good! A humble face before God is the path to heaven, to redemption in the afterlife."

"Thank you again. I must get going now."

Dark Shark rose from his chair, but Phil had not quite

finished.

"Just one more thing before you leave, Mr Shark. Did you realize, when you were hanging your clothes on the bush, that is was none other than the Burning Bush?"

"Err no, you're Excellency. I am terribly sorry. I had no idea."

"Ha- ha! Well no harm done. Luckily you did not damage the Bush which is just as well as it is over 5,000 years old and if you had harmed it; you probably would have caused World War III. Ha!"

Dark Shark was escorted all the way to the front gate at the Monastery. The whole way, he told himself that as long as he lived, he would never tell a living soul about hanging his clothes on the Burning Bush. It was now late afternoon. Dark Shark's escapades inside the monastery had taken over three-and-a-half hours. Time was short. He spied Osama in the car park and made his way over to the burly taxi driver and the blue Peugeot 504.

The mood in the valley had changed. The mild winter sun which all morning had basked the land in warmth was gone. In its place, a cold northerly wind had whipped up, gaining in strength, plunging the valley back into winter. The wind brought with it black clouds, imposing giants casting long dark shadows across the valley floor. The pink mountains became black and menacing, the transformation occurring with frightening speed. Dark Shark hurried along, huddled against the freezing blasts of wind, wondering why he had made this journey to

Santa Katarina and if he would ever find the answers to his many questions.

The few tourists who had braved the winter weather to visit the Monastery, now hurried back to the car park, all thoughts of climbing the mountain gone from their minds as they sought the comfort of their warm coaches and the journey back to their hotels. Only Dark Shark was determined to climb the mountain. Osama had returned from the town only minutes before Dark Shark had left the monastery, and was waiting patiently at the checkpoint.

"Salaam Salaam Dark Shark, how was it with the Archbishop?"

"A waste of time. The anally retentive Archbishop proclaims himself 'Keeper of the Secrets' and refuses to disclose anything."

"What are we going to do now, return to Dahab?"

"No, I want you to wait a few more hours. In the meantime, I'm going to climb the mountain"

"Gebel Musa!? In this weather!? You are crazy, Dark Shark. There is a storm coming, it would be very dangerous to climb the mountain at this time. Why don't you come and have a nice coffee with me and then we can go back to Dahab. I am sure Jamila and the police will find the killer."

"Soon, Osama, soon. But first, I am going to climb the mountain."

Dark Shark said this last sentence with such serious

finality, that Osama relented, sighing as he did so, silently cursing Dark Shark for his stubbornness.

"You have your phone right, Dark Shark? And your coat, take your coat, you will need it, the weather gets worse"

"I know Osama. Don't worry its going to be fine, I'll be back soon."

"Insha'allah, Dark Shark, Insha'allah."

Dark Shark stuffed the two blankets into his rucksack, zipped up his jacket, ate two bananas, and said his goodbyes to Osama.

Pulling on the rucksack, he began making his way back up the road towards the monastery. The astonished tourist police gaped at him as he traipsed past, unable to comprehend why this stupid tourist was going back just as the heavens were about to cave in.

Incredulous, they threw jibes at him, imitating London Cockney slang.

"Oi mate! Where you going?!"

Dark Shark ignored them and walked on, a look of fierce determination on his face.

He was in a different world, cut off from reality. From now on, his fate would be decided by the whims of the huge mountain. A light rain had begun to fall. Dark Shark reached the corner of the Monastery wall and turned right, but this time instead of continuing to the main gate, he followed a barely visible, rocky path leading towards the mountain.

The path crossed floor of the valley, heading away from the main walls of the monastery at a forty five degree angle. Dark Shark picked his way carefully along the path, his progress hindered by sharp thorny bushes and slippery, loose rocks. Putting his foot in the wrong place could easily break an ankle. The path, barely discernible in the ground, led him towards the base of the mountain. From there, he had a choice of methods to reach the summit. The usual way was to walk along a camel path which had been cut into the mountain from years of pilgrim's progress. The path wound its way around the outside of the mountain, circling the mountain twice as it snaked its way to the summit. Traversing this path would take two hours, making it too slow. Instead, he decided to avoid the camel path and head for the alternative route, one that would be much quicker but far harder.

The wind was now screaming through the valley, picking up anything it could: plastic bottles, bags, and cigarette butts. The light was fading so rapidly under the advance of the clouds that even though it was only two o'clock, the day had completely turned to night and the path, barely visible under the sun, was now completely lost to view. The rain which until now had been just small droplets was beginning to turn into a deluge, and Dark Shark realized there was a good chance of flash floods. He needed to get to higher ground fast.

Picking up the pace, he stumbled along where he thought he remembered the path to be. For the most part, he managed to stay on the path, but occasionally he slipped on a loose rock, or stumbled into a thorny bush. The going was hard. The wind cut into him despite his jacket, the path was treacherous and the rain whipped against him, but after another ten minutes, he reached the base of the mountain. He looked up. Directly in front of him, large, roughly hewn steps had been laid down, leading all the way to the top of Jebel Musa, providing a near vertical ascent. Each of the massive steps stood between twelve to eighteen inches high, was nearly a meter wide and cut from local rock, weighed many kilos. Every step had been lain down by one devout Bedouin monk, the mammoth task taking him a whole lifetime to complete. There are over 3,500 steps to the summit of Jebel Musa and they are known as the Steps of Repentance. Dark Shark began the long, slow, relentless climb, placing his foot on the first of the huge steps and steeling himself for what he knew would be a considerable challenge to his endurance and stamina.

Back in the warmth of his office, Archbishop Phillip Damieolas Papadopoulos paced up and down, his hands clasped behind his back, his mind lost in thought. The phone rang. He stopped pacing and stared at the phone, undecided as to whether to pick it up or ignore it. The noise cut through the serenity of his office, jangling his nerves. He angrily picked up the receiver.

"Yes?"

A cold, distant voice spoke on the other end of the line.

"It's me."

The Archbishop froze. His breathing quickened. Whoever the voice belonged to had the Archbishop's .full attention.

"What do you want?"

The voice answered with a question.

"Has he arrived yet?"

"He just left my office, half an hour ago. I gave nothing away and he does not suspect a thing. The stupid fool is climbing the mountain right now, why I do not know, but this unexpected turn of events is perfect for us. There is a big storm coming in and I have given the orders to my monks. They will make it look like an accident. Dark Shark will never get off the mountain alive."

"Good, let me know ven it is done."

"You have my word."

The mysterious voice hung up.

The Archbishop put the phone down, settling into his chair. He put his feet up, opened a copy of Fundamentalist Monthly and waited.

On the Steps of Repentance, Dark Shark was already beginning to feel the strain. He had been climbing for just under an hour, but already the dark, the wind, and the rain were conspiring to sap his strength. He paused for a few minutes, sitting under a giant overhang of rock, covered with a huge bush, the combination offering some respite from the harsh elements. He looked down to the base of the mountain and across to the monastery, but the dark and the stinging rain prevented him from seeing more than a few meters away. He was soaked through and cold, his arctic jacket protecting from the worst of the weather, but not enough to keep him completely dry.

He pulled off his rucksack, and from inside pulled out some food and a bottle of water. He hungrily ate the chocolate, happy to receive much needed energy in the form of sugar. He then ate an apple, some pitta and washed down the rather basic meal with water. Finishing his meal, Dark Shark threw the rucksack onto his back and continued the long climb up to the summit.

As he ascended, the air turned even colder. The rain began to ease off, slowing down. It stopped raining altogether, only to be replaced by something else, something entirely different. It was snowing. For the first time in his life, Dark Shark was witnessing snow in the desert. At any other time, he would have been delighted, but for now, he shivered and cursed the mountain, the snow only complicating matters further. The winds howled, whipping the snow into a blizzard, obscuring his sight even further. His hands and feet stung every time he knocked them on the rocks and he was forced to bend over against the force of the icy blasts.

He didn't know what he would find at the summit, but he was beginning not to care, the only thing in his mind was reaching the top, finding shelter and maybe a hot drink. He had been climbing for an hour and he knew he was only half way up. Normally he would have reached the summit by now, but the weather was making progress slow and difficult. He cursed the mountain again, outwardly shouting, but inwardly he was not sure if he was cursing the mountain or himself.

Why was he doing this to himself? Why was he climbing the mountain? What did he hope to find up there? What was his motivation? The questions swirled around his head, adding to the cacophony of noise created by Nature. The answers would have to wait. Dark Shark realized that if he did not seek shelter soon he could well be in trouble. The snow and ice were getting heavier. The temperature was continuing to drop rapidly. With a brief shot of panic, he wandered if he had gone too far this time and taken one too many risks.

Taking a deep breath, and pulling himself together he shrugged off the doubt and resolved instead to find suitable respite until the weather improved. As he climbed higher, he strained his memory for any files that could tell him whether there was a cave up ahead. The mountains of Sinai contained many caves. The Bedouins frequently used them for hiding, storage and shelter. They also made excellent ambush sites in their battles with the Egyptians security forces. Yes! He remembered now. There should be one just up ahead. He could barely see now, but he judged there to be a fair sized cave only fifteen minutes ahead. He re-calculated his estimate to take account for the weather and redoubled his efforts. Buoyed by the thought of dry shelter, a fire and some food, his spirits lifted. He climbed higher.

After half an hour, he could just make out a huge rocky overhang and realized with a happy heart that this was the cave he was seeking. He half stumbled, half ran the last twenty meters. Finally, he was inside. Taking stock of his surroundings, Dark Shark glanced hurriedly around the cave. It stretched back into the mountain only a few meters, but was sufficient for his needs. He was also glad to note that it had remained dry. He may be sharing the cave with snakes or scorpions who also sought shelter from the elements, so he took care to watch the ground as he unpacked his bag. Fire in the desert is rare. Wood is extremely scarce and the Bedouin have learnt to cook with very little fuel. Dark Shark had taken care to bring some of this precious fuel with him.

Taking out paper, thin sticks and a lighter, he arranged the ensemble into a makeshift tepee shape with the paper making up the volume underneath and the sticks stacked on top. He lit the paper, watched to make sure it caught the wood, and then satisfied he did indeed have fire, piled on two large logs. The fire leapt alive, filling the cave with warmth and light. Shadows danced on the walls and for the first time since making his ascent up the mountain, Dark Shark relaxed. He took off his soaking coat, hanging it up to dry. Unpacking the rest of the food and water, he resolved to finish it all so as to have less weight for the remainder of the climb. He wandered how far he had come. Sitting on the sandy floor of the cave, eating, drinking and with warmth flowing again through his aching frame, Dark Shark thoughts turned once again to the events of the preceding days.

Perhaps our hero was looking in the wrong place for his answers? No, perhaps it was not the wrong place, but the wrong time? Maybe the answers lay not at this time, but stretching back a very, very, long way. To a time before Islam, before Christianity, even before the Romans and the Greeks. A time over 5,000 years ago. When the Pharaohs ruled the world from the Nile Delta and a small nation of slaves had escaped the bonds of their oppressive rulers and were making a desperate bid for freedom. As he recovered from his ordeal Dark Shark imagined the ancient scene in his mind's eye.

In his vision thousands of tents filled the valley below. There were hundreds of camp fires burning brightly, and milling around were thousands of people. They looked poor, desperate, and hungry. They were dressed mostly in rags; their livestock looked destitute. At a single command, the entire populace gathered around a huge rock. Between the rock and the people, a giant golden calf proudly stood its ground. On the rock, twenty men, their ages ranging from young to old assembled around a very distinguished looking, heavily bearded elderly man.

The man held a large wooden staff, but he did not need it for support. The staff proclaimed high office. This man was clearly the leader of this sorry looking rabble. He strode purposefully forward to address them. He leant on his staff with one hand and clasped two stone tablets in the other. There was a deathly hush. The crowd had become unnaturally quiet. It was if they had all done something wrong and were standing like naughty school children waiting for detention. Passing his staff to one of the younger men the ancient father figure of his people, the man who had led them from the bonds of slavery into freedom, raised the stone tablets high above his head. Pausing for a moment for dramatic effect, he violently dashed them on the ground below.

The people were stunned, truly shocked. They shrank back in abject horror. They cried, they wept, and they pulled their hair. They begged for forgiveness. They tore down the golden calf, destroying the huge pagan image by melting it down in a great fire. They ran hither and thither, pleading for mercy, imploring the man on the rock to give them another chance. Alas! It was all in vain. Their leader, hurt, angry and betrayed, gave the people the bird, threw his beard over his shoulder and stormed into his tent.

Back in the cave, Dark Shark tried to make sense of the vision. What had it meant? What relationship did it have to the events he had recently experienced? Dark Shark had no idea. The tale of the Israelites losing faith and worshipping false idols seemed to have little relevance with the horrors of shark-finning. Dark Shark stopped trying to analyse his vision and instead returned to his present surroundings. The fire had died low. Outside, the snow storm was increasing in strength. The temperature in the cave was dropping again. Shivering, he put more wood on the fire. The flames leapt high into the air once more, visibly excited by the introduction of more fuel. Shadows created theatre on the walls of the cave. Dark Shark sat on the floor, wallowing in self-pity, a non-believer praying for the storm to abate. He was just about to prepare some more coffee, when he saw it. Or thought he saw it. He wasn't sure what it was, in fact he wasn't even sure whether he had seen anything at all; and if he had seen something, he didn't know if it was real or another vision. He froze. Then he saw it again. There it was!

A shadow, moving cautiously, lurked at the front of the cave. Dark Shark was rooted to the spot. What was it? He didn't know. The shadow made a scratching sound, and then slowly, effortlessly, it glided into the light of the fire. The shadow became a form. He could clearly make out a large, powerful head, then a body and legs and finally, the long sweep of an elegant tail. Dark Shark recognized the animal and gasped without making a sound or moving a muscle. It wasn't through choice. He couldn't have done so even if he'd wanted to.

There were persistent rumours that the animal still stalked the high passes of the Sinai Mountains. The Bedouin occasionally found clues. Dead carcasses of livestock. Blood spots on the rocks from unknown victims. Despite this, no one in living memory had ever seen one. Not the Bedouin, not the scientists and certainly not the tourists. They had even laid out an intricate network of camera traps for hundreds of miles, but still nothing. Doubts crept in about the likelihood that they still existed, the scientists declared the species biologically extinct in Sinai. The existence of the animal passed into rumour. Rumour turned to legend. The memory of the animal became a distant thing, told in stories around camp fires to scare the children. The animal became more than a mere beast; it became a ghost, a wraith of the mountains, some said even a God.

The animal now sharing a cave with Dark Shark was one of the rarest, most elusive predators on the planet. It was an Arabian leopard. Much smaller than its African counterpart, the Arabian leopard is critically endangered - there are only 200 left in the wild and the population is continuing to decline. Found only on the Arabian Peninsula, Sinai and the Negev, a huge effort has recently been made to try to save this astonishing creature. Arabian leopards feed on mountain gazelle, Arabian tahr, rock hyrax, hares, birds, even lizards and insects. Dark Shark was not an expert on Arabian leopards but he knew this individual was a female. The reason he knew this, was because by her side, only a few months old, was her cub.

Dark Shark sat frozen, staring at the mountain spirits that had come to haunt him. He was completely unable to process this information. Thinking right now, would have been about as effective as Mitt Romney on a pre-election tour of Europe. So Dark Shark didn't think. He just sat there, transfixed. As she came closer, the fire reflected in her giant eyes. Orange and red light danced against dark slits set in luminous yellow orbs. She stared at Dark Shark, unflinching and unafraid. Dark Shark stared back, flinching and terrified. He couldn't understand it. She seemed unconcerned by his presence and unperturbed by the fire. Didn't wild animals fear and hate fire? On the contrary, she seemed to be rather comfortable sharing a cave with her cub, a skint Jewish diving instructor and a nice warm fire.

Leading her baby further inside, the female Arabian leopard walked a few paces before lying down on the floor between the fire and the entrance to the cave. Just as a domestic house cat would do, she rolled over, exposing her belly and allowing her cub to suckle. The cub joyfully bounded in, rubbing his tiny paws on her stomach whist finding the source of his food. In the light of the fire, her beauty, grace and power took Dark Shark's breath away. She was clad from nose to tail in a most luxurious golden brown coat. Stunning black and dark brown patches speckled her head, neck and flanks. Her head was characteristically large. Her jaws were frighteningly powerful. Despite her relatively small size, she could easily kill much larger prey, and then drag it up many hundreds of meters where she could eat in privacy. She was a master hunter. Powerful, silent, invisible, she could kill almost anything in the desert, before disappearing without a trace.

At this moment, she was anything but the powerful assassin. Just now she was soft and gentle, as good a mother as she was a hunter. The cub was a perfect miniature of its mother. Already the fur had the distinct golden sheen, the dark spots dotted the body and it moved with the same delicate elegance, frequently supplemented by playful, foppish exuberance. The Arabian leopard purred softly as her cub switched between chasing the shadows on the wall and sucking on her teats. Ever she kept a watchful eye on her offspring, only breaking off to glance at Dark Shark or to look outside, staring into the bleak winter storm for a few seconds before returning to her little bundle of fur.

"Wow this is really, really something" Dark Shark thought. "Not only to see an Arabian leopard... but a cub too! The next generation! Simply eshta!"

The water inside the kettle boiled over, hissing angrily as it touched the hot embers. Dark Shark was unsure what to do. He made a slight motion with his right hand towards the fire and then stopped. He stared at the great cat to see what she would do, but although the movement caught her attention, she did nothing more than gaze at him wistfully. Feeling bolder, he moved forward and prepared himself another cup of coffee. He deliberately made his movements slow so as to avoid disturbing his guests. He was dreading that one false move on his part would shatter this magical moment, that in a flash of gold they would be gone. Sipping his coffee, unable to believe his luck, he continued to stare at the mother and cub for a long time.

Time passed. Dark Shark didn't know how long, had no idea, but he knew that time had passed because the snow outside was finally abating. Sensing the change in the weather, the mother leopard stirred from her maternal duties and stood up. Dark Shark grew instantly sad, realizing with growing inevitability what was coming next. She stretched as only cats do; fully extending her body, digging claws into the floor and tensing her tail. Next, the leopard scanned the entrance to the cave, looked down at her cub and then at Dark Shark, before returning once again to the entrance. She seemed to be making a decision. After another minute, she nudged her cub and proceeded to make for the exit. The cub bounded after her, excited to be following mom on yet another adventure. Reaching the entrance, she glanced back at Dark Shark one final time as if to say thank you, then both she and the cub were gone. Once more, they became legendary ghosts of the mountains, haunting the high passes and low valleys of this ancient, rocky landscape.

It was time for the human to also get going. Taking a last slug of water, Dark Shark emptied the remainder of the bottle over the fire which articulated its reluctance to die by fizzing and sending a plume of dark grey smoke billowing up to the roof of the cave. Dark Shark slung his bag over his shoulder, turned the collar up on his coat and stepped outside. The temperature remained bitter, but the snow had ceased. Now it was possible to make better progress to the summit. Dark Shark, stiff from the cold and inactivity, put one foot in front of the other and began to climb again. He was much warmer and drier, but the ordeal was far from over. The snow may have stopped falling, but the rocks remained treacherous. Taking care not to lose his footing, Dark Shark scrambled up sensing rather than seeing the thin path ahead.

As he climbed, he remembered every moment from his adventure in the cave. The experience of meeting the mother leopard and cub was indescribable. He felt wondrously happy, elated even. He felt truly blessed. Just when things had seemed to have gone beyond hope, when he felt the urge to climb this mountain, he was visited by a divine presence. The sign had to be a good omen. Boosted by his new found elation and good fortune, he redoubled his efforts, more determined than ever to reach the summit. Dark Shark was sure that this lifetime experience in the cave was the turning point in his life, the moment when, after all the recent heartache, all the pain and misery, things could finally improve. Unfortunately for our intrepid protagonist, he could not have been more wrong.

He never even saw the blows. He just felt them.

They came from nowhere. The first blow took away his legs. He didn't even have time to shout out, let alone defend himself. He simply crumpled, falling down and backwards at the same time. He hit the ground hard, banged his head on a rock and slid whilst flailing his arms in a vain attempt to stop the blows raining down on him. A second blow hit him on the left arm. Somebody was tenderizing his flesh with a large stick and it didn't feel like they were going to let up anytime soon. A third blow hit him on the shoulder and by the time the fourth blow struck him on the back of the head, he was already losing consciousness. Just before he passed out, Dark Shark felt rather than heard high pitched screams. They seemed to him to be very loud and close at first, then diminish rapidly. He dimly wandered if it was him doing the screaming, the mountains, or his assailants. After that, he knew only the void of blackness.

# 14

## *Sprilina*

Dark Shark had not felt the strong hands picking him up. Nor had he felt the same hands carry him on strong shoulders to the safety and warmth of the chapel on the summit of Jebel Musa. Instead, he had remained deep in his sleep, oblivious to the world, seeking the safety of unconsciousness. However, sleep is not sanctuary, nor is it an escape. The mind comes awake when the body sleeps and in its own way, it tries to deal with the events which have taken place during daylight hours. So it was that Dark Shark, sick with fever, battled again with the dark demons.

Many times during the course of his long sleep he would cry out, twisting and turning, the images in his mind overtaking his resolve and engulfing him in their violent wake. Despite suffering from hypothermia, his brow was constantly wet from sweat, the trickling beads cold and clammy. From time to time, the same hands that had saved his life by plucking him from the mountain mopped the sweat from his brow with a cloth, soothing his tribulations with soft words of encouragement.

A blanket had been laid across him and a fire burnt in the centre of the room, warming his core, bringing life again to his cold limbs.

For many hours, Dark Shark lay on the bed, his mind gripped with fever, for many hours the hands worked on him, fighting the sickness, exorcising the demons from his mind. Outside, the violent storm spent its anger, the clouds moved on, the winds died down and the stars had appeared, twinkling and merry. Over Jebel Musa, it had turned into a beautiful night.

Two hours later, the sun crept out from the East, dawn came, and Dark Shark's fever broke. Now he lay sleeping peacefully, the nightmares and demons had been banished, and for the first time in a long time, he rested well, his strength flowing back, his mind once again centred. He slept for most of the day and late into the afternoon. As the sun was making its way into the western horizon and casting long red streaks across the dark blue sky, Dark Shark opened his eyes.

He squinted and blinked; there was little light in the room but what light there was caused him discomfort. He decided to close his eyes again for the time being and instead, he tried moving. He flexed the muscles in his hands, moving each finger one at a time. Next, he moved his arms, then his legs and finally his feet. When he tried to move his right ankle, he was hit by sudden acute pain. He cried out.

He laid back, panting, pain shooting up his leg. From a

few feet away, a woman's voice said to him.

"Try not to move, you have sprained your ankle. Your mind had fever and your body became very cold. But now the fever has broken and your body warms. Rest up now, you'll be fine in a little while"

The woman's voice was unmistakably American. It was soft and gentle; it seemed to come from nearby but also somehow to float on the wind. Conversely, the voice was also gravely, raspy, and contained a definite Texan twang, providing the voice with a strange, contrasting texture. Certainly, Dark Shark had never heard anything like it, the voice sounded both earthy and ethereal at the same time. Like John Wayne playing the role of a ghost.

Dark Shark's sense of smell was returning and he noticed strange aromas emanating; spices, herbs, even flowers. His ears could detect the noise of bubbling liquid, and a gentle breeze, slowly banging the shutters of the windows. None of this made any sense. He did not remember what had happened, why he had got here or where here was. His mind reeled, disorientated, confused, and helpless.

He was still weak from his ordeal on the mountain and his first words were uttered in a barely audible murmur.

"Where am I?"

"You are safe. You are on the top of the mountain, in the chapel."

"Who are you?"

"Ha! That is a good question. Who am I? In many

different places,

I am known as many things and I have many names, but for here, for now, you can call me Sprilina."

The woman's voice seemed to move around, changing pitch, her precise location difficult to ascertain.

"Sit up and drink this" she commanded.

He did as he was told, placing his hands on the bed by his side, pushing up until he was in a sitting position, careful to avoid moving his ankle and risking another shot of pain. His body ached from a dozen places all of them protesting his re-alignment. As he sat up, the form of Sprilina came into view and for the first time, Dark Shark looked upon the face of his saviour and his host.

She was old. Very old. Even in the gloom of the room, Dark Shark could make out dozens of lines crisscrossing the weather-beaten, leathered old face. She had large, oval, blue eyes which, even at her age, were lit up, twinkling with energy and vitality. Her long silvery hair was tied into a pony tail and swept down her back all the way to her waist. She walked upright, regal. Despite her antiquity she did not stoop, but carried herself straight. She was thin. Very thin. Folds of suntanned brown skin hung off her remaining flesh. Her cheek bones looked razor sharp and her legs resembled those of a stick insect. She looked like a cross between a concentration camp inmate and an Ethiopian famine victim. So thin, she was wispy; her limbs did not look like they could carry their own weight, but Dark Shark knew her appearance belied the truth. He sensed awesome strength still residing in those ancient limbs.

She was wearing a long, green, faded dress of an unknown material and of a fashion Dark Shark could not place, but looked very familiar, perhaps in a different century. Draped across her shoulders and covering part of her head was a white shawl made from cotton. She had two large, silver rings in her ears, but otherwise wore no other jewellery. In her long thin fingers she was holding a cup which she passed to him, ordering him to finish the contents. He took the cup, first glancing down quickly at the dark brown liquid, and then glancing back up at Sprilina before swigging it all down. The liquid had smelt foul, but when he swallowed it, the taste was even worse and he almost gagged.

"What the fuck was that?!"

"My own concoction. Very healthy. Fig leaves, lemon, honey, nana, sweat from a rabid bat and the skin off a camel's balls."

Dark Shark gagged.

"Don't worry. The soup is good for you. It will give you strength, revitalize your organs."

"It will probably pickle my organs."

"That's great! A joke! I see you are returning to health already, Dark Shark!"

Sprilina chuckled, her eyes looming even bigger, one long hand waving in the air, folds of brown skin flapping.

"How do you…?"

But she cut him off with a wispy wave of one arm, walking away from him, her voice becoming fainter.

"I know many things... Dark Shark... I know who you are... and I know what ails you... "

Her voice trailed off and she was gone.

Before he could say anymore, the potent brew he had drunk started to take effect and Dark Shark suddenly became very sleepy. His eyelids felt heavy, they drooped slowly. He closed his eyes, succumbing once again to sleep. As Dark Shark travelled between the worlds of waking and dreaming, Sprilina's voice floated gently alongside, bobbing gently up and down on his cerebral swells. Her musical Texan inflection, with more than a hint of Marlboro, was soothing, spiritual, and even... cosmic.

"Sleep now...young instructor... sleep... let your body rest and your mind know peace."

Sitting in front of a window, was Sprilina. She was wearing slender silver spectacles, reading a leather-bound book, and rocking to and fro in an antique wooden chair. On her lap, sat a small, tortoise-shell, female cat. A thin, leathered hand was stroking the cat, the feline reciprocating with low purrs of approval. Dark Shark stared at her with impatient intensity. Sensing his questioning demeanour, Sprilina slowly lowered her book. As she did so, she peered over her silver rims, scrutinized him closely, and then said to him:

"Good morning."

Dark Shark mumbled some gibberish in reply, the only thing he was capable of.

"I'll fix you some breakfast" she informed him before rising out of her chair. For an old woman she moved with surprising grace and dexterity.

"While I do that, get out of bed, wash, and get dressed. Make sure you clean your wounds and change the bandage on your ankle. You will find fresh bandages in the bathroom and there is a clean set of clothes on the chair beside your bed."

"Thank you" Dark Shark said.

"We are not our bodies." She responded enigmatically before disappearing into the kitchen.

Dark Shark struggled out of the bed, careful not to place any weight on his sore ankle. The clothes that he had been wearing were now hanging outside, drying in the early morning sun, and as a result, he had been naked in the bed. Not having anything else to hand, he grabbed a sheet from the bed and wrapped it around himself. Holding the sheet in place with one hand, he hobbled over to where Sprilina had indicated the bathroom to be and pushing through the door, he entered.

The bathroom was bare, meagre. White tiles, some losing their colour, some broken, adorned the floors and walls. There was a sink, taps, shower, and toilet. A couple of towels hung off hooks precariously tapped into crumbling plaster. Hanging the bed sheet over one of the towels, Dark Shark turned on the shower and stood underneath. He had turned on the hot tap and after a few seconds, the water came out good and hot, soothing his tired muscles, waking him up with refreshing stimulation. The shower cleared his mind, revitalized his energies.

Drying himself off, he dressed in the clothes provided by Sprilina and headed for the kitchen, his nose following a most delicious smell. Strange smells wafted up Dark Shark's nose as he entered. The kitchen was huge. There were glass jars everywhere, dozens of them, filled with herbs, spices, pastas, pulses, nuts, honey and numerous home-made jams. Cooking books of every description lined wooden shelves along the walls. Garlic, onion, and salami hung suspended from the ceiling. There was a new white refrigerator near the doorway and a giant gas oven proudly stood underneath the only window in the whole room. Knife racks stood on the wooden work surfaces. A large wine rack displayed its bottles in one corner, side by side with a blender, various bowls, a cutlery draw a coffee machine and an assortment of weird and wonderful, crystal, wine glasses. The kitchen was impressive, proof of the importance attached to it by its owner.

Sprilina was currently frying bacon, eggs, and tomatoes. Beans were bubbling in a pan and warm French bread had already been cut up, lavished with melting butter, and set on plates. Strong, fresh coffee was percolating in a pot and cutlery was already laid on a large circular dining table. Dark Shark could not believe what he senses were telling him, he had surely died and gone to heaven. But, no his nose told him he was very much alive. To his delight, breakfast was ready and Sprilina bade him sit and partake of the wonderful breakfast. Dark Shark was only too happy to oblige. He had not eaten properly for two days, the fever had left him weak, and he was ravenous. He could not remember a time when he had enjoyed a meal quite so much as this fry-up on the top of Jebel Musa.

After breakfast, Dark Shark and Sprilina sat opposite each other in the main room of the chapel. Dark Shark sat cross-legged on cushions on the floor; he was holding a cup in his hands and staring nervously at the contents. Sprilina rocked on the chair, her hands folded on her lap, the silver rimmed spectacles perched on the tip of her long, thin nose. She was staring down at him with a look of fierce watchfulness, giving her the appearance of an eagle standing guard over newly-born chicks. She had given him another cup of some foul concoction and she waited patiently while he downed the medicine, no doubt making sure he actually drank the stuff. The mixture was unlike the previous batch, it was merely a mild pain reliever for his sore ankle and aching limbs. When he had reluctantly consumed the exotic cocktail, Spirilina commenced speaking.

“Remember this. Nothing is sure; the future is not set in stone. It is not pre-ordained. The events that befall us are the culmination of actions that we ourselves have taken. The world is a mirror that reflects the images placed in its light."

She paused for effect, flexing her fingers, staring into his eyes.

Dark Shark was not sure he completely understood Spirilina's ramblings but he got the general gist.

Spirilina sighed, long and hard.

"I am old, Dark Shark, very, very old. I was born in Fort Worth, Texas, the year of its completion, 1849."

Dark Shark was almost shocked, but after everything that had happened lately, he was becoming less easily surprised. Nonetheless, he was fascinated by the story and hung on every word uttered by the mysterious Spirilina.

"My father was an officer in the Unites States Cavalry, a Captain, based at Fort Worth. My mother was a Cherokee Indian squaw. Cruel fate had thrown them together when my father was given the order to attack my mother's village. He had ridden with 200 soldiers into the Indian encampment on the shores of Trinity River, and brutally killed all the inhabitants. My mother, young and innocent, watched horrified as the murderous white soldiers destroyed her entire world. She was the only survivor of the massacre and my father, taking pity on her, brought her back to Fort Worth and eventually married her.

My mother fell in love with my father, but in her heart, she could never reconcile the horrendous events she had witnessed in her village. Kind and protective as my father was, their union was a heretic affair in the eyes of the whites, ruining my father's career and placing great strain on their relationship. He had been a good officer, his record exemplary, but his men no longer respected him and his commanding officers did not trust him anymore, making further promotion impossible. Life on the fort was hard for my parents, but their love for each other grew and on the second anniversary of what had become known as the 'Massacre at Trinity River', my mother announced she was pregnant. It was into this complex, difficult situation, that I was born. Right from the beginning, I was hated by the white people living in the fort and despised by the Indian scouts working for the army. I was an ungodly mixture of two races, a living reminder of the conflicts and struggles of the early West. From my earliest childhood I was able to feel the tensions that existed in the household, tensions born from tragic events in the past, events which lingered, skulking like shadows, refusing to depart and finally leave the protagonists in peace. As I grew up, I felt more and more a sense of alienation, a profound detachment to my immediate surroundings, and try as they might my parents could never hope to allay my deepest fears. From my father I gained a strong sense of duty, strength of purpose and conviction. From my mother I gained a powerful connection to the spirit world, healing powers, the ability to read nature and a big nose. I had inherited the perfect tools for independence, and in my eighteenth year, I left my home town and my country of birth. I travelled. I roamed the world, first Europe, then Asia, Africa and South America. For many, many years, I travelled across the face of the globe, learning as much as I could concerning the lore of trees, plants, herbs and flowers. Along the way, I met every race of people, experienced numerous cultures, and learnt dozens of languages. I have witnessed empires fall, civilizations crumble, and wars tear nations apart. Eventually, I tired of traveling and decided to settle down. It could not be just any place; it had to be somewhere special. And so it was that I returned to Sinai, secluded, sanctified, and spiritual. I chose the high mountains of the interior, finding sanctuary in Saint Katharine and living a simple existence amongst the Jebeliya tribe of Bedouin. Years passed. In the mountains I did not age, but continued my life, deciphering ancient scrolls, growing herbs and studying the night skies. The Bedouin did not appear too put out by my seemly eternal condition. They called me 'a-Jinna al-Amrikaneya' or the 'American Djinn Woman' an allusion to the legends of the Djinn, ancient demon spirits which haunt the high mountains, apparently living for ever. I was happy for the most part, but I also became restless. Something inside me was unsatisfied and I searched for the reason behind the imbalance. One night, while gazing at the stars on top of Jebel Katharine and hoping to find answers to my questions, I was approached by a young Bedouin. His name was Hassan and he was, unusually for a Bedouin, a monk from the monastery. He was also looking for answers on the top of the highest peak in Sinai. Hassan originally hailed from El Tur, from the fishing community plying the coast of the Gulf of Suez in their never ending search for fish. Hassan was a young successful fisherman, the most talented in El Tur. He had learnt the trade from his proud father, and after a long apprenticeship, had saved up enough money to purchase his own boat. One night in 1941, the fishing community had watched as a huge convoy of ships pulled up just offshore, at the reef of Sha'ab Ali. The Bedouin knew that a huge war had engulfed the world around them and were used to seeing ship of this size pass by them, but they had never seen any stop here before. The ships, sailing south from the Mediterranean on their way to Aden, had been ordered to stop and hide in the Gulf of Suez by a nervous British Admiralty, worried about the squadron of German fighters based in Crete and causing devastation to British shipping. The convoy of supply ships and their attendant protective frigates had been ordered to stop for three days, maintaining strict noise and light discipline. On the first of these three days, four sailors from the biggest ship, the Thistlegorm, came ashore to seek help from the Bedouin. The British sailors had wanted to meet the best fisherman in the village and were respectfully introduced to Hassan. Sitting together around a camp fire in a

Hoosha, and smoking spliffs, the British sailors had told Hassan the story of the Carnatic. They told him of the sinking, the tragic deaths, the search by the English diver for the gold coins, how he had not salvaged all of them but that there were still 8,000 gold coins unaccounted for. Enough gold to make them rich. They then informed him that they themselves were divers, they had brought with them the latest diving equipment from England, and it was their serious intention to dive the wreck over the next two days and recover the missing gold. They would need a boat, something quiet, and they asked Hassan if he would be willing to help them. In return, he would receive a generous share of the loot. Hassan thought about it for thirty seconds then nodded his answer. He would help them recover the gold. They could trust his silence, his knowledge of the sea and his humble craft. Very early the next morning, Hassan, accompanied by the four British divers and their diving equipment, had sailed across the Gulf of Suez to Sha'ab Abu Nuhas. Over the next two days, the four divers had searched the interior of the ancient steamship, eventually making their way to the cabins and successfully finding the 8,000 gold coins. They had taken the gold back to the Thistlegorm. Being divers and having special status in the Navy, they had no difficulty in secretly stashing the gold in the holds of the huge ship. That night, they had a party to celebrate, the joyous proceedings taking place in the Bedouin village. Hassan was rich beyond his wildest

Bedouin dreams; he would probably never have to work again. The British divers for their part were also delighted. Happy and very drunk they had made their way back to their ship. Back on board, one of the divers, forgetting light and noise discipline, lit a cigarette just as a German Heinkel bomber flew overhead. The four divers never got to enjoy the fruits of their labours. All four perished that dark night in 1941. In the safety of his village, Hassan had watched horrified as the bomber sank the giant ship, the only survivor from the expedition to salvage the gold. Hassan never recovered from that fateful night, believing it to be the work of Allah. He was convinced that Allah had punished the divers for their actions and that he, Hassan, would be next. Fearing Almighty retribution, Hassan fled the coast, finding sanctuary as many have done, in the bosom of Saint Katharine. Hassan made his new life amongst the Jebeliya. He lived well, but in constant fear of Allah. The monastery, source of the Jebeliya's strength, drew him with powerful magnetism and seeking absolution he became a monk, one of the few Bedouin to do so. He passed the initiation ceremonies, made a holy pact of celibacy, and received a vial. Now he lived inside the monastery walls, protected by the teachings of Christ, safe in the blanket of his new religion. And so it was that Hassan lived, until the day when he ascended Jebel Katharine and met me. Needless to say, we fell in love. We kept our affair secret. We did not dare consummate our love, but we knew we were guilty in our hearts, and we tried to keep our relationship away from the all-seeing eyes of the monastery. For a while, we were happy. But soon things changed and we realized that we had come together for a reason. We both knew that we wanted a child, but Hassan's oath of celibacy was proving a stubborn obstacle. He loved me, but he could never break his promise to the monastery. Determined to rescue him from the tenacious grip of the monastic order, I fixed Hassan one of my famous concoctions. That night was wild indeed, and as a result of our passions, I became pregnant. Hassan, blissfully unaware of my scheming, was happy at the news of the infant, but very worried about the consequences. We tried to keep it a secret, but in the small community of the mountain, it was impossible and soon Archbishop Christos Meanos Corruptus learnt the terrible truth. He called Hassan into his office one day and gave him a terrible lecture on heresy, damnation, and hell. A real fucking guilt trip. Hassan, God-fearing and honest, believed he needed to repent his sins and, ordered to do so by the Archbishop, he spent the rest of his life cutting and laying the steps that lead to the summit of Jebel Musa."

Dark Shark murmured a response.

"The Steps of Repentance."

"Yes, the Steps of Repentance."

Sighing deeply, she continued.

"Despite Hassan's biblical punishment and the best efforts of the Archbishop, I gave birth to a healthy baby boy. We named him Salah. The boy grew up strong and happy. His playground was the mountains; his teachers, Hassan and I. When Salah was eighteen, Hassan told him the story of the Thistlegorm, the gold and the death of the four British divers. He gave Salah the remainder of his share of the gold and taking the vial from around his neck, he passed it all over to his son. Salah was extremely moved by the presents of the gold and the vial; he would never forget his father's generosity. Salah grew up happy except for one thing, his father's punishment. Proud and strong, his father's so-called repentance was a source of great shame to the young Salah. He simply could not understand why his father persisted in his mission to lay the steps on the mountain. Salah became angry, raging against Christianity, the Archbishop and the monastery, but despite his son's anger, Hassan continued his work, laying steps right up until the day he died. I tried to soothe Salah's anger, but he only became worse. When his father died, he left Saint Katharine and struck out on his own, seeking work in the newly emerging tourist industry of Dahab. His first job was in McDonalds and he worked there for a few months until the flood came. He became good friends with the manager, Bent Bob, and with another man… a European… "

Dark Shark roared triumphantly. He jumped up, punching the air, the penny finally dropping.

"Nemo! Your son is the one-eyed Bedouin, Salah!"

"Yes, Dark Shark, yes. That vial you are wearing around

your neck belongs to him, just as it belonged to his father, Hassan."

# 15

## *Yoghurt Weaving*

Spirilina rocked gently in her chair, smoking a cigarette and gazing intently at Dark Shark. He sat opposite her on the floor, his legs crossed, elbows pushed on knees. His hands were held together supporting his chin in a classic thinking pose. Neither one of them spoke. Dark Shark was recalling everything that had happened to him since the day he had received the phone call from Mohammed informing him he had a course. So much had occurred since that day. So much had changed in his life, so much which would never be the same again. He felt pain as he remembered Moheet's death. He felt pity for her mother, Mojave, suffering the loss of her only child. He felt guilty when he pictured Gastro lying in the hospital bed and most of all, he felt ashamed at the way he had treated Jamila in the past, ruining their relationship. All of these things he felt and more. Recollections choked him.

Spirilina spoke softly, her voice a gravelly Texan ghost.

"Why oh why must you be so hard on yourself?"

"Is it so obvious, Spirilina?"

"Ha! Your face invokes a Greek tragedy!"

"What should I do?"

"You must go in front of the Council. They will issue a decree and end this nonsense once and for all."

"What about the archbishop?"

She smiled.

"Leave that cretin to me. Revenge is a dish best served cold."

"Oh my God! I just remembered Osama! He is waiting for me at the Monastery. Oh man."

"Don't worry, Dark Shark. I called him yesterday and told him to return to Dahab. I said you had had a small accident on the mountain, but that you were fine and staying with me."

"Did you? Wallah. Thank you."

"It's not a problem. Now you should rest for a while. Sleep. When you wake up again, I am sure you will see the world in a more positive light once again. Here drink this."

"What is it?"

"Amongst over things, it contains pomegranate, juniper and fig. It's very good for you. Drink up."

Dark Shark wandered what 'other things' might be, but he dared not ask. He took the cup from Sprilina and drank down the concoction. It was surprisingly good. Within a few minutes, he felt drowsy. His eye lids felt heavy and pretty soon he was unable to keep them open. He crawled back into the bed and fell asleep.

When Dark Shark woke again, he was truly shocked to discover that he had awoken back in his own bed at home. He had absolutely no recollection of how he had arrived. The memories of the adventure in the high mountains came back to him, but they seemed distant, as if they had happened a long time ago or perhaps to some else. He tested his limbs with small movements before deciding that they were capable of supporting his weight. Everything appeared to be in working order, although he was more than a little stiff and sore in places. He got out of bed and made himself some coffee, then sat on a chair and sipped the hot beverage. The warmth flooded through his body, the caffeine made him alert. For a long time he sat still, cupping the warm drink in his hands and pondering. He needed to talk to Jamila, Osama and Mojave. He also decided to go to Sharm to see how Gastro was doing. After that, he would go to the meeting of the Council, the first of its kind in over forty years. Dark Shark sighed.

It was going to be another long day. He was having a lot of long days recently and it was beginning to make him very tired. He wandered when it would all be over and he could go back to teaching again. He wanted a return to simplicity and normality, at least the kind of normality that existed in Dahab. In the back of his mind, a creeping doubt was telling him that he might never again experience life as it had been before. Something else, however, also told him that this may not be a bad thing. He lit a cigarette and smoked whilst thinking. A few minutes later, he stubbed out the remainder of the cancer stick, threw the remnants of the coffee into the kitchen sink, pulled on his jacket, picked up his bag and walked out the door.

Dark Shark was back on El Fanar Street. He had no idea what day it was, but by the position of the sun, he knew it to be late morning. Despite his weariness from the events of the past week, he felt good. He had a bounce in his stride once more and he felt light, almost optimistic. The hardships in the mountains had taken a toll on him, but he had learnt some important information up there. For the first time since Moheet's death, he was beginning to feel like they were making progress. That soon the shark finning would cease forever and Nemo and his gang were locked up for hopefully a long, long time. Then he remembered something. An image came to him of a mountain deity with a face of gold and black. It wasn't the information that had cheered him up so much. It was meeting an Arabian Leopard. He smiled at the memory of the great cat and marvelled again at his good fortune. No one would ever believe him, but he didn't care. If he died right now, he would die happy having seen the ghost of the South Sinai Mountains.

Dark Shark's first stop was Just Another Dive Centre and a few minutes after leaving home, he entered the house of the bubble makers. He made immediately for the office. Inside, Mohammed, Sally and Jamila were sitting on chairs. When they saw Dark Shark, they all jumped as one, shouting, screeching and whooping with delight.

"Walla-he! Dark Shark! How are you? Salaam, Salaam!"

"Jesus Christ! Dark Shark! Where on earth did you get to?"

"Well I'll be blown by a grey kangaroo, it's Darkers!"

"Ha-ha! Hey everyone! It's great to see you all again and it's good to be back home."

They ushered him into the interior of office, sat him down, made him coffee, peppered him with questions and demanded to know all that had happened to him in Santa Katarina. Dark Shark was happy. He smiled a lot and happily recounted his adventures in the mountains. He left out nothing, except the details about hanging his clothes on the Burning Bush. Since his return to the mountains it was slowly dawning on him that he changed. He felt energized, different. Dark Shark felt like his batteries were recharged and that he could take on the whole world.

Sitting back in the office at the dive centre, he could smell neoprene and it made him feel at home. Here was where he truly belonged; amongst the wetsuits, regulators and divers. He could smell the fresh sea air, it was filling his nostrils and it felt good to be alive. It was also wonderful to see the gang again, especially Jamila. His story was met with "Oohs" and "Ahhs", one or two "No ways!" And even an "Impossible!"

"Trust me, it is all true. I'm having difficulty accepting it myself, believe me."

Jamila shook her head with disbelief. She was transfixed with the story, but didn't know whether to believe a word of it.

"So, Salah, the one eyed Bedouin who tried to kill you, is the son of this woman you met ,who is called Sprilina, lives on top of Mount Sinai and is one hundred and fifty six years old?"

"Yes."

"Do I look like I'm buying tartan paint?"

Dark Shark laughed. He wasn't about to try and argue. He knew the story was true and he didn't care if no one believed him.

"So, what happens now? Are you going to go back to the monastery to become a monk full time?"

"No, Jay. First I'm going to Sharm to visit Gastro in the hospital. This evening is the meeting of the council. It's the first one in over forty years. You want to come with me to visit Gastro?"

"Sure."

"How is Mojave? Where is she?"

"She's okay, keeping it together. She has gone to meet her husband who is arriving at the airport in about an hour from now. His name is Gobi."

"Gobi?"

"Yeah, I know. The family evidently likes deserts."

"Ha-ha! Indeed!"

"That's nothing. Check this out. She has another daughter."

"Wow, really!?"

"Yep. She is older than Moheet. Her name is Sahara and she is pregnant. In fact, not only is she pregnant, she is due to give birth tomorrow night."

"That's amazing. Truly life works in mysterious ways."

"Yes."

"How's Gastro?"

"He's doing great. I went to see him yesterday while you were gallivanting around the monastery decorated in a black dress. He was a bit concerned to find out you had disappeared, but is happy about the fact that he can check out tonight."

"That's very good news. It will be excellent to see him again."

Turning to Mohammed, Dark Shark asked the big man if Adel had been around.

"Aiwa, Dark Shark. He came here looking for you. He wasn't happy to find out that no one knew where you were. He says he is going to talk to you after you have shown up again and he has the time."

"Great. I look forward to it with bated breath."

Sally clapped her hands, stood up and announced she was hungry. Dark Shark realized he was ravenous. Mohammed couldn't leave the office and had work to do, so Dark Shark, Jamila and Sally walked along the bay towards Slow Down.

"So, Jay what is the gossip from Dahab? Has anything interesting happened whilst I was away?"

"Heidi and Peter split up."

"No way!? What happened? I thought those two were destined to spend eternity together. The perfect couple. Is this the end of the Sexy Scandis?"

"Peter told Heidi he was a better diver than she was."

"Oops."

"Tell me about it. It's exactly like you taught me two years ago. Peters has a classic case of the dreaded Dive Master Disease."

"That's bad news. I hope he manages to recover before it's too late."

"Me too. Peter is really not a bad guy, but he is definitely in the grip of DMD."

Every diver who took their professional level certification knew it was a possibility. That it could happen to anyone. It was the risk they all took. They had signed up for it after all. You agreed to the program and you'd better accept what came next. You knew full what could happen. You could do all the preparation you wanted to, but nothing could guarantee you did not get hit with what is known scientifically as Dive Master Disease. The condition struck only when the Dive Master course had finished. Only successful candidates caught it. The signs and symptoms were minor at first. The newly certified Dive Master would talk incessantly about diving. Next, came the parenting stage. This is when the Dive Master would look after everyone he or she came across, even if they weren't diving. They had a pathological desire to constantly make sure everything was safe, that backups existed and everyone was fully up to speed on the latest emergency first response procedures.

Finally the last stage arrived. Here the afflicted victim began to believe they knew everything there was to know about diving. This mixture of bravado and false belief in one's own abilities frequently ended in tragedy. On his arrival in Dahab two years ago, Dark Shark had refused to continue teaching a Dive Master student who was showing early signs of Dive Master Disease. His attitude was simply irresponsible and Dark Shark could not bring himself to sign his student off as a professional who would later be responsible for the lives of other divers. He took some stick for his decision from other diving instructors, but the student finished his Dive Master course with someone else and all was well again. A week after finishing the course, the student did a dive to sixty meters with another diver.

They were only wearing single tanks. Neither of them were trained or equipped to make such a deep, dangerous dive. It was thoroughly irresponsible of them and could easily have led to their deaths. Luckily, they both got away with it and returned to the surface unharmed. Diving in such a manner is akin to playing Russian roulette. It's not *if* it happens, it's only a matter of *when*. Dark Shark was not harsh in his decision not to continue his student's

Dive Master Course. He had been responsible. Dark Shark sighed. Poor old Peter. DMD was a bitch.

The weather was gorgeous on the bay. Small waves lapped the shore. A gentle breeze floated down the Gulf of Aqaba and the sun sparkled diamonds on the surface of a deep blue sea. The three friends walked along, happy to be together again. They entered Slow Down and sat down at the best table. Hymen came out of his office. It was lunch time, but he was already drunk. He was carrying a bottle of Jack Daniels which was a quarter empty. The bottle was shaking and so was Hymen. It was a sad sight, but that was Hymen. He wouldn't have it any other way. He was a monster in the nicest sense of the word. Hymen had a huge appetite. Whether it was smoking, drinking, drugs, sex, music or diving, Hymen tried to consume as much as possible. It had worked for Keith Richards, why not Hymen?

He greeted them all amiably enough and despite his condition was determined to take their orders. Salads, sandwiches and drinks were requested. Soon lunch was served. No one received the food they had asked for, but it was delicious anyway. While they ate their food, Jamila called the hospital to inform Noora they were going to pick Gastro up at six o'clock. Dark Shark called Osama on his clam shell.

"Walla! Dark Shark El hamdul'allah! You are okay! Thank God. Truly I am happy to hear your voice again! What happened to you up on the mountain?"

"It's a long story brother. Let's meet up later and I'll tell you all about it. We need to go to Sharm and pick up Gastro from the hospital. Can you pick us up at five o'clock?

"Mershi Dark Shark, mershi. I will be at the dive centre at five."

"Sucran ya Osama. Yalla. Ma 'salaam."

"Afwan habibe. Ma 'salaam."

Dark Shark closed his phone and turned to Jamila who had also just finished her conversation.

"What did Noora say?"

"She says that she can't wait for us to get down there. Our mutual friend is quite a handful and getting worse by the minute. Noora says he is like a caged animal."

"Sounds like he is back to his old self again."

"Indeed."

"Osama is going to pick us up and take us to Sharm at five. That is two hours from now. Gives me plenty of time to go for a swim along the reef."

"Can I join you?"

"Of course. Can you use a snorkel?"

"Please! Better than you Mr Shark!"

"Ha-ha! DMD right there!"

The three of them laughed. Hymen giggled not far from their table. He hadn't heard the joke, but he was finding it funny anyhow.

Finishing their meal and paying the bill, Dark Shark, Jamila and Sally made their back along the bay. Out in the Gulf, windsurfers rode the waves their resplendent multi-coloured sails fluttering in the wind. Sally had to return to work behind the counter so she said ciao for now and left Dark Shark and Jamila with only each other for company. They promised they would meet at the Eel Garden dive site entrance in ten minutes. During that time, they both went to their respective abodes and collected mask, fins and snorkel. A short while later, Jamila stood on the top of the reef plate at the Eel Garden. She was wearing a blue one piece swim suit and black wet suit boots.

The water on the reef plate was pale green and half a meter high. She was standing on white sand which covered the plate right up until the edge. There were numerous small coral heads dotted around in their hundreds. Just as numerous were black sea urchins, their spikes sticking out in all directions. Dark Shark joined her a minute later. The wind had picked up a little and small waves rolled across the reef. Jamila stood with her back to the waves, legs slightly apart. She put her right hand on Dark Shark's shoulder and with her left hand she put a fin on right foot. Having accomplished this, she changed hands and put on the other fin. Dark Shark did exactly the same, using Jamila for support. This way they could both support each against the waves as they got kitted up. There was far less chance of the waves knocking them over that way. Jamila tightened her pony tail, put on her mask, inserted the snorkel into her mouth and started swimming. Dark Shark joined her and the two of them swam towards the open sea, carefully avoiding the sharp coral and even sharper urchins.

As he hit the water, Dark Shark gasped. The water was cold and he was used to wearing a wetsuit whenever he went into the sea. He snorkelled far less, although he loved it. The water was exhilarating. The way to get warm was to swim and swim hard. They powered through the water, swimming with hands as well as kicking with fins. Every four strokes, they would breathe hard from their snorkels, expelling any water. Twenty meters into their swim, they reached a cut in the reef. There was a long crack with the ubiquitous white sand along the bottom. Reef fish played inside the crack, protected from larger predators. This was the entrance to the Eel Garden site. From here, divers would follow the crack, descend a slope and turn left to see the eels. Dark Shark and Jamila were heading in the other direction, towards the Lighthouse, so when they reached the slope, they turned right.

Below the swimmers, a bright white sandy slope gently rolled down into the abyss. They were in a small 'bay' created by the reef and which they cut across to reach the other side. They headed south along the edge of the reef. As usual, the sights below were gorgeous. Corals and fish of every colour imaginable squabbled, swam, mated and predated below them. They could see at least twenty meters below them to the white slope, sometimes far more. The sun was warm on their backs and lit up the scene below. Shafts of sunlight danced in the shallows. The waves were small; there was a light northerly wind which created a gentle surface current pushing them forwards. The conditions were perfect and they made good progress.

Dark Shark and Jamila were heading towards another 'bay' where the reef retreated towards shore forming a large bowl. There was no point in following the edge of the reef here as it would make the swim far longer. Instead, they cut across the bowl. It was just then that Jamila spotted the turtles. There were two of them. They were hawksbill turtles, a male and a female. They lay on the sandy bottom next to a coral head and were slowly scrapping algae from the coral.

The two snorkelers ceased swimming and floated on the surface, ten meters above the turtles. Dark Shark and Jamila held hands and thrilled at the rare sight below them. The turtles nonchalantly carried on munching, unruffled by the appearance of the two clumsy aliens above them. For almost ten minutes they carried on eating. Then, with an unseen signal, they lifted their heads at the same time, flapped their great flippers and swam gracefully up to the surface only a few meters from the snorkelers. The turtles took large breaths of air and then promptly dived again, this time disappearing into the deep blue depths. Dark Shark and Jamila smiled through their snorkels allowing some of the inevitable sea water into their mouths. It was always wonderful to see turtles. Beginning to swim again, they continued their journey along the edge of the reef.

Fifteen minutes later they had arrived at the Lighthouse and hauled themselves from the water. Dark Shark and Jamila felt fantastic. The combination of the physical exercise and beauty they had just experienced was truly exhilarating. There are few activities more conducive to health than swimming along a reef for nearly two kilometres. It was time to shower, change clothes and return to the hospital in Sharm el Sheikh.

Archbishop Phillip Damieolas Papadopoulos hurried along the corridor to his office. He was thoroughly flummoxed. He had just received word that Dark Shark was back in Dahab, despite the efforts of three of his monks. He couldn't understand it. The three he had sent up were his best. They were trained, hardened and completely loyal. They had always been successful in whatever task he had given them, but only this morning what was left of the bodies had been scrapped off the side of the mountain. Approaching the door of the office, he muttered to himself, cursing his luck. He was holding a great golden ring of keys and he fumbled with it now, trying to find the correct one amongst the dozens hanging down. In his haste and irritation, he dropped the keys. Bending down to pick them up, he noticed the door was slightly open. Alarmed, he shot up to his full height. His long black beard bristled with righteous indignation. He pushed open the door of his office and strode in thinking.

"Who on earth dares to enter my office?"

At first glance there was no one in the room. He looked over to his desk. His high back leather chair was facing the window. Smoke curled up from the chair, but he couldn't see who it was.

"What the hell?"

This was insufferable. As he walked angrily towards the desk to confront whoever it was that had the audacity to commit such sins, the chair swung slowly round to face him. The archbishop stopped in his tracks, rooted to the spot. He froze. He was stunned, shocked. He dropped the keys.

"You...!!??!"

A woman sat in the chair. She was very old, ancient even. She was thin with leathery skin and she was smoking a cigarette. She looked up at the archbishop with big, brown eyes and when she spoke it was with a gravely, ghostly Texan voice.

"Heya, Bish."

At six o'clock, Osama, Dark Shark and Jamila pulled up at the entrance to the hospital. They exited the taxi and went inside. Osama did not come in; he was off to the fruit market and would return to pick them up. Approaching the main desk, they asked for directions to Gastro's room and were pointed down a corridor adjacent to the desk. Thanking the receptionist they hurried down the corridor, turned left, then right and right again, before finding the right door. They knocked, waited for the response from within, then opened the door and went inside. Gastro was lying in bed eating food. Noora was also there, fussing over him. When he saw his visitors, he beamed from ear to ear.

"Well, well. Jamila and the prodigal son."

"Hey Gastro, how are you man?"

"Excellent. Eshta. I am finally getting out of here!"

Noora put some of Gastro's clothes on a chair beside the bed and scolded his lazy attempts at getting dressed.

"You won't go anywhere without first getting dressed. You can't leave here wearing a tunic and not even underwear."

Gastro smiled a wry smile.

"Why not? It wouldn't be the first time I've left a building wearing exactly the same thing. There was this one occasion, a party at Slow Down I believe, when I had been with this girl inside the DJ booth..."

Noora held Gastro's shoulder, pulled him forward and plumped his pillow, probably more in need of getting him to move than improving the pillow.

"Yes well we don't want to hear about that thank you. Please finish eating and get dressed, your friends have come a long way to pick you up and don't want to waste more time in the hospital."

Gastro smiled again.

"I am a very lucky Hawager. Noora is the best nurse in all Egypt."

"Don't be silly! Of course I am not! Now is that shakshuka finished?"

Whilst patiently waiting for the patient to get ready to leave hospital, Jamila was thinking about Mojave. Dark Shark was thinking about Sprilina.

In his office at the 'The Sacred and Imperial Monastery of the God Trodden of Mount Sinai', Patriarch Phillip Damieolas Papadopoulos stared hard at the woman who sat in his chair. He tugged his beard frantically and repeated his exclamation.

"You!? They told me you had died years ago!

"News of my demise has evidently been premature."

"How did you get in here Sprilina? What are you up to? What do you want?"

"I'll get to that in a minute. Listen to this."

She reached forward and pushed a button on a tape recorder lying on top of the desk, which until then, the archbishop had failed to notice. From the speakers a voice came out. It was a voice the archbishop recognized immediately. The knowledge sent a deathly cold shiver that went all the way down his back and on to his feet.

"He just left my office, half an hour ago. I gave nothing away and he does not suspect a thing. The stupid fool is climbing the mountain right now, why I do not know, but this unexpected turn of events is perfect for us. There is a big storm coming in and I have given the orders to my monks. They will make it look like an accident. Dark Shark will never get off the mountain alive."

"Good, let me know vhen it is done."

"You have my word."

Sprilina pressed stop on the tape recorder. She stubbed out her cigarette in an ashtray and returned her gaze to the Patriarch.

"Technology. Can be an amazing thing, don't you think? Surrounded by such treasures from the past, it can be easy to forget the advantages of new technology."

The archbishop said nothing. His was weak at the knees. His legs felt like jelly. He was holding on to his beard and trying to use it to support all his own weight which was in danger of heading towards the floor.

"Take a seat, Phil."

The archbishop slumped into the chair opposite Sprilina. He suddenly looked ten years older. No, I mean he really did look suddenly older. White streaks had instantaneously appeared in his jet black hair. Sprilina carried on.

"Originally, I had planned on making a long soliloquy, you know, a kind of Shakespearean monologue. But then I decided I would rather just get straight to the point."

The Patriarch remained silent.

"Of course, copies have been made. The Bedouin have them. It would be most embarrassing if the copies reached the Egyptian authorities, the Church in Jerusalem, the Vatican etc. etc. Can you imagine the ramifications if it turned out that the Archbishop of the second most important monastery in all Christendom had ordered the murder of a British tourist?"

The archbishop did not answer what was obviously a rhetorical question. In his shell-shocked state, he was desperately trying to find a way out of this hellish nightmare, but realized with an ever growing sense of dread that he could not.

"This is what is going to happen. In order to avoid the seismic fallout from your actions, we are going to make an agreement you and I. Right here, right now. You are going to agree to resign your position as Archbishop, stating ill health. You are going to leave the Greek Orthodox Church and you are going to go back to Greece. If you ever return to the Sinai or Egypt, the copies will end up in the offices of the aforementioned institutions. Is that crystal Phil?"

The former archbishop of Santa Katarina, Phillip Damieolas Papadopoulos could barely mumble his agreement. He had turned pale, his face masked in a sickly pallor.

"What's wrong Phil? You look unwell."

"I'm cold."

One hundred and seventy five kilometres further to the south, a blue and white Peugeot 504 sped along the highway towards Dahab. Behind the wheel in the front seat, Osama was eating a banana. Gastro sat in the passenger seat also in the front. The window was slightly down and he was blowing smoke out of it from time to time. Dark Shark and Jamila occupied the rear seats. Dark Shark was recounting his adventures in the mountains to Osama and Gastro who were giving pretty much the same response he had received back in the dive centre. When he had finished, Gastro who been listening intently spoke up.

"So, Salah is the son of this woman of the mountains, Sprilina? Incredible story. Did you really see an Arabian Leopard?"

"Yes. She came very close, only a few meters away."

"Fucking eshta."

"Indeed."

"What happens now?"

"This evening is the big meeting of the council. There hasn't been such a meeting in over forty years. They are going to issue a decree to do something about Nemo, Salah, the monastery and Bent Bob."

"Not forgetting that intriguing woman at the Golden Wadi Massage Parlour."

"No. I am sure Pai Mai will be in big trouble as well."

"Where's the meeting and who' s going to be there?"

"To both your questions, my answer is that I don't yet know. Apparently I am going to find out later where the meeting is, but I don't even know how that's going to happen."

"Am I invited to this council meeting?"

"I hope so yes. As far as I am concerned, it's important for both you and Jay to attend the meeting."

Jamila squeezed Dark Shark's hand tightly. Gastro took a pull on his joint.

"Cool. What about the Shamandura, did Adel put in an appearance?"

Jamila answered this.

"Adel hovers round like an irritating mosquito threatening to deliver malaria to the unwary. He's been into the dive centre asking what is going on and in particular where Dark Shark was. We didn't know exactly, so our answers were accurate. Adel doesn't seem to be making any progress in his investigation, except to confirm that Moheet was indeed murdered. As yet, they can't say who may or may not have done it. They have no witnesses, almost no evidence and the autopsy revealed that she'd been strangled before being thrown into the sea, which anyway was obvious from the marks around her neck. Meanwhile the search goes on for the shark-fishing dhow which has disappeared without a trace. The Navy received the shark fishing map and placed patrol boats at every site. It must have worked because there have been no further incidents of shark- finning off the coast of Dahab. Bent Bob has been absent from Slow Down and is now seen only in his dive centre WDD."

"How is Mojave? Where is she?"

"Mojave is meeting her husband Gobi, at the airport right now. They're going to meet up with us a bit later. She is okay, bearing up well. She has phenomenal strength that woman."

"It's a special family."

"Yes. We also found that they have another daughter called Sahara. She is older than Moheet and pregnant. She is actually due to give birth tomorrow night."

"Wow. Mojave, Gobi and Sahara. I can understand why they chose to name their second daughter after the Arabic word for ocean. There are a lot of deserts right there. Fantastic news about the baby. That will finally give them something to be happy about. Wonderful."

"It's great news. I'm so delighted for them. They have been through hell."

It was eight o'clock when Osama pulled up outside Dark Shark's half a house on el Fanar Street. He got out of the taxi and promised everyone he would call them when he knew where the meeting was. They were hoping to get something to eat before the council met to decide what to do. The taxi drove off and Dark Shark got out his key to enter his house. He unlocked the door, opened it, went through and closed it behind him. He looked around the room, happy to be home and thinking to make himself a coffee. He took off his coat, hung it up on the door. Turning around to go to the kitchen, something caught his eye and he looked down. There was a folded white piece of paper lying on the floor. He bent down to pick it up. Standing up again, he unfolded the paper and read the thin black handwriting. There were only five words.

'Meeting at ten. Wadi Shag.'

He didn't recognize the handwriting, but he knew what the message meant. He opened his phone and called Jamila.

"Hey Jay. The meeting is at ten o'clock in Wadi Shag."

"Okay, we meet first for dinner at Slow Down?"

"Yes. Did Mojave get back to Dahab yet?"

"Aye. She's here with me now as is her husband. He's looking forward to meeting you."

"As I am him."

"Cool. See you in half hour."

"Ciao."

He closed the phone, dialled another number.

"Gastro. Hey. Listen the meeting is at ten o'clock in Wadi Shag. Come to Slow Down?"

"Yalla brother, on my way there now."

"See you there."

Dark Shark showered and put on fresh clothes. Twenty minutes later, he was sitting in Slow Down at a table with Gastro. They ordered drinks and food, waiting for the others to arrive. A couple of minutes later, Jamila, Mojave and Gobi walked in and came over to the table. Dark Shark and Gastro stood up, said hello to all of them and introduced themselves to Gobi. Mojave's husband and the father of Moheet and Sahara, was in his early fifties. He had a large shock of grey hair which in some places was turning white. He was tall, nearly 6ft 2in with broad shoulders, sparkling brown eyes and a barrel for a chest. He was a man normally full of life and vigour, but today he had an air of great sadness around him. He looked tired and withdrawn, broken by events. Gobi was clearly suffering from his loss. Dark Shark thought again about his student who was no longer with them and his heart twisted with the pain. Gobi smiled warmly at Dark Shark and Gastro, shook their hands and sat down at the table.

Like Mojave, he was quite a presence. He exuded warmth, honesty, integrity and dignity. Dark Shark liked him immediately. What followed was an astonishing two hours of conversation. The more he talked to Mojave and Gobi, the more Dark Shark like them. The way they talked about the land was the same way he felt about the Sinai. Well, about everywhere really. The world was beautiful; it didn't matter where you were. Their passion for the land, for the sea, for life and spirituality touched a deep nerve with Dark Shark. He connected to it immediately and implicitly. The lesson to be learned, the really important point of it all, was to make every human decision bio-centric. That way, we can't really go wrong. The five diners discussed every aspect of what had happened in Sinai, not only with Moheet. Mojave and Gobi were genuinely impressed and grateful for the efforts of Dark Shark, Gastro and Jamila to do something about the situation. As deeply affected as Dark Shark in particular was to them, Mojave and Gobi were also deeply touched by their three hosts. Matters became so engrossing that

Dark Shark nearly forgot about the time, only looking at his watch when it was approaching fifteen minutes to ten.

"Oh wow, guys. We need to move."

They finished their meal and Dark Shark called Osama who was in the middle of eating a huge roast duck with his wife and seven children and was reluctant to come out at that time. No matter, he would ask another taxi driver to pick them up and take them to Wadi Shag. Ten minutes later, Dark Shark, Gastro, Jamila, Mojave and Gobi were walking into the sandy valley of Wadi Shag. The wadi was located on the other side of Dahab behind a hotel called the 'Blue Moon'. The air was cool, and a slight breeze washed through the wadi. The moon was full. It was a huge, white disc emanating light and gravity. The full moon was always an interesting time in the desert. The five walked without talking deeper and deeper into the wadi.

On either side of them, rose sheer walls of red granite and black volcanic rocks. The wadi's entrance was about thirty meters across, but as they moved further inside, the wadi opened up into a large sandy bowl perhaps a hundred meters across. The entire area of white sand was bathed in the light of the moon. It was almost like daytime, but the light was softer. To one side, there were a clump of tamarisk trees together with two acacia trees. Behind the trees, the wadi continued on but dramatically narrowed, then came to a complete halt. After that it was only mountains. Next to the trees was a very large

Bedouin tent. It was huge. Inside the tent were dozens and dozens of Bedouin. Here were representatives from all ten Sinai tribes.

Needless to say, they were all men. They were sitting on cushions which were on top of rugs and date palm logs. They were arranged in concentric circles around a large patch of sand. On this patch of sand were large heavy rugs, complete with twelve larger cushions. These also had occupants sitting on them, but not all of them were Bedouin, and not all of them were men. This was the meeting of the Council, the first in over forty years. The meeting had not yet started. Bedouin and Council members alike were still finding their places. When they saw the latest arrivals, they said little and indicated for them to enter and join in. Dark Shark and his friends entered the Bedouin tent after taking off their shoes and adding them to the many dozens already outside the tent. They found some vacant cushions and sat down to listen to the proceedings. Dark Shark was optimistic that finally something would be done about all the terrible crimes being committed in the Sinai. He sat next to Jamila who had Gastro on her other side, followed by Mojave and Gobi. Just like his companions, Dark Shark took in the scene and studied the twelve members of the Council.

From left to right was Sheikh Awad (Muzeina, Ras Abu Gallum), Sheikh Msallem Faraj (Tarabin, Nuweiba), the Governor of South Sinai Ahmed Said, yoga diving instructor Harmonica, Captain Saul Stetson founder and president of the Sea Slaughterer's Karma Squadron (SSKS), Mahmoud el Faradai Head Master of the International Toddler School of Dahab, Russian free diving legend Rita Menshevik, technical diving guru Eli Trimix, Sheikh Sadallah Hussein (Jebeliya, Santa Katarina), Sheikh Salem Mousa (Ulad Said, El Tur) and finally, Mousa Luxori who represented the Dahab Association of Eminently Reputable Shop Keepers Selling to Tourists (DAERSKST). It was Russian free diving legend Rita Menshevik who began proceedings.

"Everybody please quiet down and listen."

The tent went silent and everyone paid attention to her.

"The meeting of the Sinai Council will now begin. We have gathered tonight, here in Wadi Shag under a full moon, to decide what to do about the terrible events that have occurred in Dahab over the last two weeks. Sinai faces a terrible future if nothing is done about the crimes being committed. As you all know, it has been over forty years since it was felt necessary to hold such a meeting. Now, again, it is necessary."

Rita paused to emphasize the importance of her point. Every one present weighed the enormity of what she was saying and allowed her to continue.

"This is how the meeting will proceed. Each of the twelve council members will contribute to the debate with a short talk. There will be a five minute recess at this point. We will resume the meeting with two guests from the United States, Mojave and Gobi, who tragically lost their daughter recently. We will listen to what they have to say. After that, we will hear from the representatives of each of the ten Sinai tribes. Finally, Dark Shark is going to be given a chance to talk. When everyone has finished speaking, the council will hear any motions that are put forward by any party present. There will be a fifteen-minute recess and we will withdraw to vote on the motions. Refreshments will be served at this time. Once we have finished voting, we will return to announce the result of the vote and issue a decree. I would urge all those who are talking to keep in mind the time, which is short. It is the council's wish that all those mentioned be allowed the proper opportunity to present their case to the Council. Only when we are satisfied that this has happened, will we withdraw to vote. To issue a decree, the vote must be unanimous. The decision of the Council is final and cannot be changed once it has been declared."

One by one the twelve council members put forward their case. The four Bedouin Sheikhs along with Saul Stetson, Rita Menshevik and Harmonica all wanted to take immediate, direct action. Eli Trimix and Mahmoud el Faradai urged caution, arguing that yes, something had to be done, but it was being done and that it might actually be better to leave things up to the Egyptian authorities. The Governor of South Sinai, Ahmed Said and Mousa Luxori (DAERSKST), argued in no uncertain terms that this was purely a matter for the Egyptian authorities and should left in the competent, capable hands of the Shamandura.

After a five minute recess it was the turn of first Gobi and then Mojave. Both Moheet's parents gave a short passionate speech. They talked of the love for their daughter, the terrible pain they felt and their hope and desire that they would get justice for their daughter, no matter where it came from. They thanked all those who had helped them so far and expressed their warm feelings towards Sinai and its people who they said had been wonderful since their arrival. No one present could help but be deeply moved by their eloquent orations. The ten representatives from the Bedouin tribes all expressed much the same as the four sheikhs had. They wanted immediate action and

they also wanted greater inclusion in the decision making process regarding the governance of the Sinai.

There was another short recess and finally it was Dark Shark's turn to talk.

"I first came to the Sinai as a tourist on Christmas Eve, 1992. We crossed the Taba border, my friends and I, getting in a taxi and driving to Dahab. The journey took three hours. We wound our way along the coast, following the edge of a sea the colour of the deepest azure. The entire time, we only saw one of other vehicle. When we arrived in Dahab, there were only a few Bedouin camps and three dive centres. It was the Dahab of the old days. The Dahab of the guide books. There were few cars, only Jeeps. There were no hotels, not even solid buildings except those few left over from the Israeli occupation. The desert, the sea, and the Bedouin. It was a truly magical experience. I felt like I was in a different world. It was like being on a frontier, somewhere exotic. I was. For a week we stayed here, enjoying the hospitality of the Bedouin and the delights of the sea. I fell in love with the place and vowed one day to return. Eleven years later, I did return, coming back to Dahab to work as a diving instructor. When I got back here, I was shocked. The place had completely changed. Now there are big hotels. Hundreds, if not thousands of cars. There are roads, houses, blocks of flats, mosques, shops, even shopping malls. There are horses, swimming pools, industrial units, power stations and warehouses. This was no longer the desert. No longer a Bedouin fishing village. It wasn't even a hippy hang-out any more. It had become a fully-fledged town. A proper resort. Sharm el Sheikh's little brother in every way. Jobs had been created. Money was being made. A hundred dive centres opened where once there had been three. People even stopped investing in diving, the thing that had really made the Sinai famous. They started building property. If you want to make money, property is really where it's at. With all this progress, with all this building, this changing of the desert and the sea, there is a terrible price to pay. A price we simply cannot afford. The environment is being destroyed. We are killing the sea and we are killing the desert. The local people who have lived here for nearly a thousand years in complete harmony with the desert are crying out for justice, for inclusion, to be given the chance to act as the true guardians of this ancient, unique and incredibly beautiful land. The Sinai does not exist for us to get as much out of it as we can. The name Dahab does not refer to gold that has monetary value. The name Dahab is the spiritual gold that you get from being here. It is the atmosphere, the life, the rhythms and the nature that is the real gold of Dahab. In the rush to make money, this all important truth has been forgotten. Well people, the news is not very good I am afraid. This way of behaving cannot continue. It is not sustainable. We cannot take all the fish from the sea. We cannot poison the reefs. We can no longer build and build and build. If the environment is not healthy, if it is not balanced and productive and varied as it once was, we put ourselves in great peril. In fact, I would go even further even that. We will all perish. As a species. It is not the planet that needs saving from us, it us who needs saving from us."

Dark Shark paused for a long time to let this sink in. Then he continued.

"Over the last couple of weeks it has become very clear to me that the lust for money has no limits. That there are people with such little empathy, they will go to any lengths imaginable. Two weeks ago, a wonderful young woman came to me to start a diving course. Three days later, she was found brutally murdered. The same day,

I was involved in an incident where someone tried to kill me. Later, I witnessed with my friends the massacre of hundreds of sharks at the Blue Hole. They had been finned, their bodies thrown back into the water to die a painful and pointless death. At the Thistlegorm, we were attacked and Gastro was nearly killed. At the Canyon and on Jebel Musa, a second and third attempt was again made on my life. The shark-finning business is a terrible one, run by criminals, gangsters and mafia. It is big, big money, easily comparable to the trades in illicit drugs and guns. The perpetrators are utterly ruthless, cruelly finning sharks before exporting the fins to Hong Kong where they are made into shark fin soup. They allow no one to get in their way and live have been lost over fins. We are convinced that Moheet, the beautiful daughter of Mojave and Gobi was murdered because of what she knew about shark-finning in the Sinai. Let us not be under illusions. There is a web of corruption and criminality running throughout the highest levels of Sinai. This web is supporting murder and the illegal finning of sharks. I urge you all, the twelve honourable members of this Council, to come together as one, to truly represent the wishes of the peoples of Sinai and to act now to prevent any more crimes against nature or against the people and to find and bring to justice the perpetrators of the heinous crimes against Moheet and the shark population of the Red Sea. We simply cannot rely any longer on the investigation being conducted by the Egyptian authorities and in particular, the Shamandura. In the fourteen days since Moheet's death, they have turned up little or no evidence in their inquiries and have made no progress what so ever in tracking down either Moheet's murderers or the shark fishermen. I hereby put forward a motion that the Council agree to the formation of and action by, a coalition of representatives from those gathered here today, and to support both financially and logistically all attempts made by that coalition to bring a satisfactory conclusion to the tragic events that have taken place here over the last two weeks. If not, the actions of a few, which have already had a terrible impact on everyone else, will get exponentially worse. I cannot stress enough, the importance of redressing the balance which has been so dangerously altered. We owe it to Moheet's parents Mojave and Gobi. We owe to the Bedouin. We owe to the sea and to the desert. We owe it also to ourselves and most of all; we owe it to our children and our children's children. Thank you for listening."

There was a hushed silence. Then everyone started talking at once. Dozens of different conversations were being conducted at the same time. People were passionately talking across each other, everyone was involved and the giant Bedouin tent hummed with discourse. In the middle of the hullabaloo, Eva Menshevik once again took control.

"People, People! People! Quiet please! Hush! Please be quiet. We must continue with discipline and respect."

Gradually the noise subsided and a silence was observed.

"Good, thank you. Now, everyone has spoken. Everyone has had a chance to put their case forward. Apart from Dark Shark, is there anyone else who would like to put forward a motion for us to vote on?"

Rita waited. There was no answer. Dark Shark's motion would be the only one.

"Very well. There will be a recess for fifteen minutes whilst the Council votes on the motion put forward by Dark Shark. During this time tea will be served. Please do not go far. We would like to finish the meeting on time. Thank you."

The Council of Sinai meeting had now run for over three hours. Everyone was exhausted and took the opportunity to drink the tea or stand up, stretch their legs, and/or go to the toilet. A small clique of Dark Shark, Jamila, Gastro, Mojave and Gobi met up and discussed the meeting so far.

"What do you think Dark Shark?"

"I don't know. I am not feeling that optimistic to be honest. As the talks progressed, I thought that Eli Trimix and Mahmud el Faradai might come over to our way of thinking. That would have left only Ahmed Said and Mousa Luxori against. Being the only two to feel that way, they might be persuaded to vote for the motion. I am not confident though. To get twelve votes is asking a bit much. They really should make it a two-thirds majority vote. A unanimous vote is ridiculous."

The others agreed and it was all they could do but to wait patiently for the result of the Council's vote. A few minutes later, their patience was finally rewarded. The twelve members of the Council return to their giant cushions in the middle of the huge Bedouin tent. Rita Menshevik called everyone's attention. There was a hush of expectant silence.

"The Council has voted on the motion put forward by Dark Shark. The result is 10 in favour of the motion, 2 against. There has not been a unanimous vote on this motion and therefore the Council has no option but to reject it."

With the announcement came uproar as people took in the information. Dark Shark was furious. He jumped to his feet, angrily pointing his finger at the line of Council members.

"This is an outrage! After everything we have been through! After all that has happened, you are not going to do anything at all?! How can a unanimous vote count!? It's ridiculous! Disgraceful! This stupid meeting has been an absolute waste of time. Total Bullshit! Nothing but a right load of old yoghurt weaving!"

Now, Rita stood up.

"Mr Dark Shark! I suggest you hold your tongue right now! The rules of the Council are over a thousand years old and cannot be changed! The motion has been rejected. No action by any coalition will take place. The only action to be taken is by the Egyptian authorities which this Council fully supports. The Council's decision is final. I would advise everyone present to respect the Council's decision, especially you Dark Shark. This meeting is closed."

"Ach, bollocks…!"

Dark Shark would have continued to argue the point, but Jamila pulled him by the arm and dragged him away. He stormed to the front of the tent, put on his shoes and began striding quickly back down the wadi. Jamila ran after him and caught him before he'd gotten very far. She held his arm. They stood still for a while. Together, they stared up at the big, luminous white moon, impossible to ignore in such a brightly lit wadi.

"It's all such bullshit, Jay."

"Yeah, I know."

"The problem is, not enough people care."

"Not true. Enough people do care. They just have to come together and they have to have the heart and the willpower to find a way."

"You think we'll be able to find a way?"

"Absofuckinglutely."

An hour later, Dark Shark was getting ready for bed after an extremely long day. He undressed, got in the shower and turned on the water. Hot water sprung from the shower head and he relished the cleansing. It made him feel good. Alive. After the meeting had ended, the parties had split, wished each other good night and everyone had retired for the night. Everyone that is, except for Gastro, who informed Dark Shark that he was going to meet Simone at the Lagoon. Dark Shark put his mobile phone on charge, got into some funky pyjamas and gratefully sank into a warm, soft bed. He was cocooned inside a large duvet. Snug as a bug in a rug. Dark Shark closed his eyes and waited for sleep to come. But sleep never arrived. For a long time, he just lay there thinking. He was very tired, but he simply couldn't sleep. He could feel the cold, clammy grip of insomnia.

At the Lagoon, Gastro waited patiently for his rendezvous with the gorgeous Simone. Leaning up against a wooden palisade, he smoked a joint, gazed out to sea and imagined the liaison to come. Out to sea, the moon glittered white on the surface. Fish jumped out of the water from time to time, spurred into action by unseen predators. The wind was slight, the stars were incredibly bright and it was a wonderful night, which was surely about to get much better. Ten minutes passed. Gastro was beginning to wander if Simone was going to turn up. He imagined her again and smiled at the images that crawled through the gutter of his mind.

It was while he was in this erotic state of anticipation and arousal, that Gastro saw something out to sea. At first, he thought he was imagining things. He blinked and looked again. It was still there, far out in the distance, but getting closer all the time. Whatever it was, it was moving fast and heading straight for the part of the beach where Gastro was currently in the grip of a Kiwi fantasy. It was black with a single large light. Soon, Gastro could make it out as a boat. A Zodiac. The boat got closer. Gastro could hear the engine and recognized the small, but distinct shapes of four men. What was a Zodiac doing approaching the shore of the Lagoon at three o'clock in the morning? Gastro had a sudden feeling that he was getting a visit from the shark finners. He steeled himself. He made ready to flee. He looked around for a weapon. Gastro became frantic as he realized he might be in an awful lot of trouble. This was stupid. He had only just got out of hospital after surviving an exploratory bite from a four meter oceanic white tip shark. No way was he going to allow anyone to hurt him again. Hospital food just wasn't that good.

He froze, watching the fast approaching Zodiac with the four men on-board. The boat got closer and closer. Now it was entering the lagoon and only a few hundred meters away from where Gastro was standing. Gastro was rooted to the spot. He resolved to fight to the death, no matter how many of them there were. He was determined it wasn't going to be his death. The Zodiac had arrived at the beach.

The four men rode the dingy right up onto the beach which stuck fast on the sand. The men jumped nimbly over the side of the Zodiac, landing on the sand just a few feet in front of Gastro. He saw with growing horror that the men were armed. Seriously armed. They had AK 47s, RPG rocket launchers and bandoliers of ammunition which were slung across shoulders and hung around waists. The men had knives and machetes tucked into belts. They had red and blue bandanas on their heads.

Gastro didn't move a muscle. He stared at the men coming towards him who in turn were smiling back at him. Some had teeth missing, whilst others flashed sets of gold dentures. All four were in the thirties and forties. They were black as night, their skin leathery and weather beaten. These men were rough, experienced and heavily armed. They looked like they meant business. The group of four men stopped in front of Gastro. One of them broke ranks and advanced closer. He was the oldest one; he looked like the leader and now he spoke to a quivering Gastro.

"We have come a long way. We have travelled the whole length of the Red Sea. From the great horn of Africa, we have come. We entered Bab el Mendab and travelled all the way up to here. We have made this journey of 2,000 miles, for we are here to see Dark Shark. We have come all this way and we are here to help."

In his bed, Dark Shark tossed and turned, unable to sleep. So it was that when his clam shell blared its polyphonic nonsense, the English diving instructor found it to be a relief. He opened the phone.

"Aiwa."

"It's me."

"Gastro. What's up? Did Simone turn up?"

"No, someone else did."

"What do you mean someone else did?"

"I mean someone else turned up instead of Simone."

"Who did? Who turned up?"

"They have come a long way. They have come through Bab El Mendab. They have travelled 2,000 miles to see you Dark Shark. You'd better get down right now. These guys mean business, Dark Shark. They've come from the horn of Africa."

Gastro was sounding mighty strange, even by his mystical standards. He was definitely spooked and to top it off, Dark Shark didn't have a clue what his friend was blathering on about at three in the morning.

"Gastro, what is going on man? Have you dropped something?"

"No. I am being deadly serious for fuck's sake. This is real."

"Okay, okay, so these guys just turned up while you were on the beach at the Lagoon and they are asking for me? Who are these guys? Where did you say they were from? The horn of Africa?"

"Yes. The men just turned up on the beach at the Lagoon. They have come looking for you and they have come all the way from Somalia."

# 16

## *Pirates*

There was no transportation at that time of the night, so Dark Shark was forced to walk to the Lagoon. The journey took him about twenty minutes. On his arrival, he made straight for the wooden palisade where he knew Gastro and Co. to be. On his way there, he was trying to imagine who on earth would turn up from the sea at the Lagoon in the middle of the night, ask for him by name and say they had travelled 2,000 miles from the East Coast of Africa to find him. It was a deeply troubling mystery.

As he approached the palisade, he could see, in the bright light of a full moon, the unmistakable outlines of Gastro and the four visitors from Africa. He also saw that they were armed to the teeth. The scene before him was an eclectic mixture of dreadlocks, AK47s, sandals and RPGs. His mind raced.

"Jesus Christ, they've got rocket launchers, assault rifles, machetes. Who are these guys?"

Dark Shark thought he might already know the answer to his question. These guys weren't social workers. They also didn't look like they spent too much of their spare time yoghurt-weaving. There was only one way to be sure. Dark Shark walked hurriedly up to the palisade and introduced himself.

"Salaam Aleichem. My name is Dark Shark. I understand you gentlemen have asked for me."

Dark Shark was having a discreet rendezvous with four heavily armed men from Africa at three o'clock in the morning on the beach of a desert, and he was introducing himself as if he was in an office in West London. The mind boggles.

The four men smiled warmly back. The leader, who had spoken earlier to Gastro, now spoke to Dark Shark.

"Aleichem a Salaam, Dark Shark. How are you?"

"I am good. Sucran awy. El hamdul'allah. How are you? How was your journey? Gastro tells me you have travelled a very long way."

"Aiwa. We have travelled very far. We are very tired, but we come on a mission from Allah. He has protected us, in his infinite power and wisdom and has given us the strength to arrive here safely. El hamdul'allah. We have come all the way from the great Horn of Africa, from Somalia. We have come to help you, Dark Shark."

"But why...?"

"First, please allow me to introduce myself and my brothers. Then we must move quickly from this place. We cannot talk here. There is too much light. Already we have spent too much time here. We have to talk where nobody can see us. Only then, will we be happy to tell you our story and why we have come."

The man flashed a grin at Dark Shark. There was gold in his teeth.

"My name is Sugule Ali; this is Falafel, Shwarma, and Shakshuka. Now come. We must go to our boat."

Gastro looked frantic at this suggestion.

"I can't sit on a Zodiac! Absolutely, no way. I'll die."

"There is no time to waste, we must leave now."

Dark Shark thought for a moment. Sugule Ali must have been reading his mind because he added:

"Don't worry, we will not kidnap you. We know your family has no money. Ha! Come now, please."

He smiled another gold smile, motioned with his hand for Dark Shark to follow, then turned his back and began walking swiftly to the beached Zodiac. The other members of the gang followed him.

Dark Shark asked Gastro to wait on the beach. Gastro had no problem with that whatsoever. Dark Shark walked down to the Zodiac whilst Gastro remained behind. The Zodiac was pushed off the beach until it was in half a foot of water. Dark Shark and three of the pirates clambered into the dingy. The fourth pirate pushed the boat into deeper water and jumped in. Sugule Ali pulled the rope on the 65 HP engine and it roared into life. A second later, the Zodiac zoomed off into the distance.

Back on the beach, Gastro sat watching the dinghy leave the lagoon. Exiting at high speed, it turned left before heading out into the open sea. He was so engrossed; he barely noticed the sound behind him. He spun round, alarmed. But he needn't have worried. It was Simone. She bounded up to Gastro and plumped herself down on the ground next to him.

"Hey gorgeous man, how are you? Sorry I'm late. I have a friend who is going through some issues right now and I really needed to spend some time with her. Poor girl, she is such a mess."

"Hey Simone! No problem. It's great to see you. How's it going?"

"Yeah man, good! So glad you waited around for me, hey!?"

She smiled warmly and gripped Gastro by the arm.

"Of course. I wouldn't miss it for the world. I was really looking forward to meeting you tonight."

"And here I am baby! Anything interesting happen today? What you been up to?"

"Nothing much, just a couple of meetings."

"What you been doing out here, whilst waiting for me?"

"Oh you know, just staring out at the beautiful sea."

"Cool… I love the sea. It's just great isn't it?"

"It is certainly is. Sitting on the beach by the sea, you never know who or what is going to turn up, or even when."

Simone giggled. She gripped his arm harder. Gastro smiled knowingly. Simone looked up and pointed to the great white orb in the night sky.

"Look at that moon! It's fucking awesome, hey!?"

"Yep. It's mental. Full moon in the desert is incredible."

But Gastro wasn't looking at the moon. He was staring out to sea, watching a small, black dot. The dot got smaller and smaller, and then disappeared entirely from view.

Five kilometres out, Dark Shark grimly gripped a rope whilst perched precariously on the inflated outer tube of the Zodiac. The waves were small and the dingy made swift progress, skimming across the surface of the sea. Dark Shark squinted against the cold spray which lashed his face, arms and torso. His wet, tousled brown hair was flung back in the wind. Glistening ribbons of sea water trickled their way down his neck and arms. The black sky, filled with an infinite number of shiny pin pricks, was getting lighter. Dawn was soon to come. Ten minutes later, the Zodiac was fast approaching the invisible barrier that separated the Egyptian side of the Gulf from the Saudi Arabian.

It was then that Dark Shark spied the outline of a boat. It was moored up to a large, bright orange buoy with marked the boundary between the two neighbouring countries. The boat was big, at least forty meters long. Along the length, a motley crew of men leaned on the hand rail of the deck and stared down at the dingy. They were dressed similarly to the pirates in the Zodiac, but with subtle differences in their choices of weaponry. The boat was dark brown, faded in places. Paint was curling off the bow, rust marks splashed across the hull and the boat had a weary, weather-beaten air to it. The tired old pirate vessel also had very familiar lines.

"Oh great." thought Dark Shark. "It's another dhow."

Sugule Ali did not slow the Zodiac down as they approached the dhow. Dark Shark gripped the rope he was holding even tighter. They were coming in much too fast. Dark Shark's mind did some quick calculations and realized they were doomed.

"What on earth is he doing?"

Dark Shark was terrified that Sugule Ali was about to crash head long into the larger boat. Instead, cackling madly, the pirate drove the Zodiac as close to the dhow as he possibly could, then at the very last instant before impact and certain death, he swung the dingy violently to the left and came to a complete standstill only inches from the dhow. Dark Shark sighed. Morbid Somali pirate humour left him somewhat cold.

Sugule Ali cut the engine. Rope ladders were quickly lowered from the boat, landing on the Zodiac below. The five occupants of the smaller vessel clasped the ladders with their hands. They held on tightly and began to climb, hauling themselves over the handrail and landing onto the deck. Wasting no time, Sugule Ali immediately made for the dhow's stern, waving for Dark Shark to follow. Battle hardened crew members, loaded with ballistic paraphernalia, stared at their guest as he was led to the only cabin at the rear of the boat. Dark Shark quickened his pace. One or two of the hardened members fingered the triggers of their ballistic paraphernalia. Reaching the doorway of the cabin, Sugule Ali ducked down and entered, closely followed by Dark Shark. They were in a small, dark cabin. A single, dull yellow light bulb swung from a cord in the roof. To one side was a sink, cupboards, taps and pots. The rest of the cabin was taken up with cushions and rugs, except for a flight of stairs which descended into gloomy darkness. Sitting on the rugs were two men. They were joined by Sugule Ali, who promptly sat down, telling Dark Shark to do the same.

Tea was served and the two men introduced themselves. The younger one was Ibrahim. He was first mate on the Somali pirate ship. The second man was older. His name was Januna Ali Jama and he was the captain. He had white hair, was in his sixties and looked as if he'd been on the sea of all his life. He was so leathery, he had a face like a saddle. Nevertheless, he had a warm, pleasant demeanour and gradually Dark Shark relaxed. Captain Januna Ali Jama looked across at his guest, the man he had come 2,000 miles to meet.

"Welcome on board my ship Dark Shark."

"Sucran, Captain."

"Afwan. Time is short, so I will begin. As you may already have guessed, we are Somali pirates. I, Sugule Ali and most of the crew are from a small fishing village called Harardhere, in the central region of Galmudug, two hundred kilometres north of the capital, Mogadishu.

For thousands of years, my people have made their living as humble fishermen. We worked on the sea in small boats, each day leaving our homes and families to hunt on the open ocean. We fished tuna, mackerel, squid, cod and many others besides. It was a hard life, but we were happy. We received everything we needed from our mother, the sea. When there was no fish, we dried and stored what he had, saving the fish for the lean times. We never went hungry. We were not rich, but we were content. Twenty years ago, terror came to Somalia. The once proud nation of the Horn of Africa experienced brutal civil war. The government collapsed. War lords and religious fundamentalists battled each other for power and control. The international community stepped in, trying to help, but as ever, they were more interested in helping their own corporations than the people of Somalia. It was at this time that foreign fishing vessels began to raid our coast. Huge industrial ships came to fish our waters, taking our food. They deprived us of our living. The politicians were powerless to prevent it, either through lack of money, lack of will power or both. The Navy had been disbanded when the government collapsed and there was simply no one to protect the sea. On land the situation worsened. Famine came and millions died. Men, women and children starved to death. To make matters even worse, more foreign ships came in close to shore, dumping toxic and nuclear waste into our waters. Now there was absolutely nothing left in the water alive. The sea had been raped and poisoned. Even the crabs on the bottom were gone. My people were faced with imminent starvation. Nobody in the world cared. No one came to help. I and many of the people from my region of Somalia were determined not to die on our knees. Banding together with other fishermen, I formed a marine self-defence group called the National Volunteer Coast Guard. We didn't have any fish left in the sea, but we still had our boats. Each day, we went out trying to dissuade the big fishing trawlers to leave our waters, but with no success. We changed tactics, this time going out armed. Our policy now was to attack and board the ships, before taking the crew hostage. We would then inform the owners and demand ransoms. We resolved that if the illegal fishing did not stop, the companies responsible would be forced to pay us something in return. With this new strategy, we had much success. The insurance companies paid out millions of dollars, knowing full well they would make more money in the long term by increasing the premiums paid out by the shipping companies. We had gone from fishermen to volunteers and now became what they in the West call pirates."

Captain Januna Ali Jama paused and smiled. Dark Shark returned the smile, deeply engrossed in the story. He was fascinated by this meeting, the tale being told and the history being learned. Over the Saudia Arabian Mountains, the sun emerged and dawn broke again in the Gulf of Aqaba. In the cabin, tea was served and the Captain asked Dark Shark if he would like some breakfast. His guest nodded. Sipping his tea, the Captain continued.

"Our success was being noted up and down the coast. More and more groups of fishermen became pirates. As you know fifty per cent of the all the world's shipping passes by the Horn of Africa either entering or exiting the Red Sea bound for the Suez Canal. We moved up from fishing trawlers and started targeting cargo vessels, then finally the biggest prize of all, the oil tankers. It was at that point that the world finally sat up and took notice of our actions. We were labelled dangerous criminals. Governments promised to crack down and eliminate us. The biggest countries, the US, the UK, Russia, France, India and China sent their warships to protect the shipping lanes. Marine security companies popped up, providing work for ex-military thugs. These companies charged extortionate amounts of money to protect the ships. Many such industries grew up around our work."

Captain Januna Ali Jama laughed, rolled his eyes and shook his head in disbelief.

"We spent years appealing to all the relevant authorities, begging them to take action against the illegal fishing trawlers. Nobody did a thing. Now they spend billions protecting the ships!"

He laughed again.

"We are just poor fishermen. All we have ever wanted

to do was to protect the fish. It would have cost just a few hundred thousand dollars to stop the illegal fishing. All it would have needed was a few patrol boats and the right motivation. But nobody cared; nobody

did a thing until we threatened their oil. Then they sent the Navies of the world, spent billions, held urgent summits and condemned our actions. Ha-ha Ha-ha! The world is insane!"

He laughed a third time. Dark Shark had every reason to agree with the old pirate.

"In Somalia, our efforts were supported by all the people. They understood what we were trying to achieve. Groups like the Islamic Courts, Al Shabbab and Al Qaeda tried to extort us into paying them a tax. Some of their people tried to infiltrate our groups and partially succeeded. When hostages have been killed, it is because someone from one of these groups did it. We fishermen have tried our hardest to treat the hostages well and always released them if the ransom was paid."

"What if the ransom was not paid?"

"Then the hostages remained as our guests. The ransom is always paid eventually. Governments say they never pay out ransom money, but they do."

"What did you do with all the money you were making?"

"Good question. We put a lot of it into the local economy in Somalia. Whole industries have grown up around our fishing villages. Factories have started up.

Shops have opened. After twenty years of civil war, the people of my village have a school to send their children to. Of course we also invested in new equipment for our work. Weapons, boats, hi tech marine equipment. It helps us to stay one step ahead of the Navies. There was one more thing we did. For twenty years, ships had been dumping nuclear and toxic waste just off the Somali shore. When the 2004 Tsunami hit, the massive waves which battered the coast, stirred up many tonnes of toxic waste, washing much of it up onto our beaches. As you can imagine the population has been suffering tremendous medical issues as a result. According to the United Nations Environment Program, there are far higher than normal cases of respiratory infections, mouth ulcers and bleeding, abdominal haemorrhages and unusual skin infections among many inhabitants of the areas around the north-eastern towns of Hobbio and Benadir - diseases consistent with radiation sickness. Much of the ransom money has gone on toxic clean-up alongside improved medical facilities. As usual, the West is wrong. We are not ruthless criminals. We are not pirates. The ones who come to steal our fish, pollute our seas and raid our coasts are the true criminals. It is the politicians, the security men and the insurance companies who are the real pirates. We, the simple fishing people of the Somali coast are really 'badaadinta badah' - the saviours of the sea."

The Captain paused again. Just then two crew members

entered the cabin carrying trays of food. They placed them on the rugs in front of the three men, then bowed and left. The Captain took some bread, wrapped some onion, tuna and tomato into it and commenced eating.

"What you do make of my tale so far, Dark Shark?"

"It's fascinating, Captain. I can completely understand why you and the other fishermen feel you have no choice but to do what you are doing. The events that have befallen Somalia are truly tragic. The war, the famine, the looting of the environment. It simply beggars belief. I can only pray and hope that the situation improves for you all and that Allah provides you with justice, truth and prosperity once again. However, with all due respect, Captain, there is one thing I still do not yet understand. Why have you travelled 2,000 miles, at great risk, to come and help me?"

The Captain smiled a dry smile.

"Patience, Dark Shark, patience. First, please eat. Relax. After, I will tell you why we have come."

At the mention of the word eat, Dark Shark's stomach growled like an Arabian Leopard. He tucked in, ravenous as a large mountain feline.

Back on the beach at the Lagoon, Gastro and Simone had finished exchanging bodily fluids. Gastro was lying on his back, staring vacantly up at the sky. His legs were partially open, his arms were spread apart and his dreadlocks splayed out in all directions, like a horizontal Medusa. He had a wide, shit-eating grin on his face. He was in heaven. Simone lay partly on top of Gastro and partly on the sand next to him. She rested her left arm on his chest which supported her chin. With her right hand she twirled his dreadlocks in and out of her fingers. She had a dreamy expression on her face.

"Wow, mate. That was pretty awesome, hey!?"

"Yeah pretty good eh? I surpassed even my own high standards."

"Ha! Men! It's always a competition with you guys."

"I could so easily fall asleep right now."

"Why don't you? Let's go crash out in your digs."

"I can't. I am supposed to be waiting for Dark Shark to turn up."

"Dark Shark!? What time is he coming? Where is he coming from? Home?"

"Err… not exactly. I am not sure where he is right now or what time he is going to turn up."

"Mate, that sounds silly. C'mon. Come back with me. We can lie in bed all day and do it again and again. Wake up, make love. Go to sleep. Wake up, make love. C'mon baby. You really need to sleep, hey!?"

Gastro thought about it for all of a millisecond.

"Okay. Yalla."

In the desert just outside Dahab, a meeting was taking place in total secrecy. It was being conducted in a large room inside a dive centre. Attending the meeting were three men and one woman. The woman was Chinese. The men consisted of an American, a European, and a one-eyed Bedouin. The European was talking. The others listened in reverential silence.

"Tonight, I vant the dhow to go out again. I vant fins! Fins! Fins! Ve have lost lots of money lately. This is unacceptable! Ve are going to find the sharks, take the fins and make all our money back! Nothing is going to stand in our vay! If Dark Shark or Gastro turn up at the dhow, I vant them vasted! Eliminated once and for all. For far too long those useless hippies have ruined our plans! I vant their heads on a slate!"

The American made the rather unwise decision to correct his master.

"Plate. You mean plate."

"Vhat!?"

"You said you want their heads on a slate, but the correct expression is you want their heads on a plate."

"Plate, slate, vlate! Who fucking cares!!?"

The large American shifted nervously in his chair. He was skating on very thin ice and his waistline was increasing exponentially.

"I'm sorry, I didn't think to..."

"Don't think! Vhat have I told you about thinking!"

The American held his tongue. The European babbled on.

"Ve are not going to take this lying down! I don't care about the Navy. I don't care about the Shamandura! I vant the dhow to go out tonight and catch as many fins as possible. Do you idiots understand me?"

No one spoke. They all nodded.

"Good. Now get out of my sight!"

On the Somali pirate dhow, Dark Shark, Captain Januna Ali Jama and Sugule Ali were finishing breakfast. The Captain picked up where he had left off prior to the meal being served.

"Walla-he, that was eshta. Now, Dark Shark. Let me explain the reason for us coming here."

Dark Shark wiped his mouth with a napkin. He took a slug of tea, lit a cigarette and listened intently once more.

"In Somalia we have heard about your loss. We have heard of your struggles against the shark fishermen. I decided that since business had been good recently, I would give my men a little break and come up to see about helping you. We hijacked a Saudi oil tanker six months ago and just received the ransom money. $65 million dollars. Apparently, there was 1% of the entire world's supply of oil on that one ship."

Dark Shark gasped. Not for the first time, he thought he might be in the wrong business.

"I know. It's disgusting. The amount of money we are talking about is phenomenal. I would normally have to be a dictator of a reasonably developing nation to make that kind of moolah."

The Captain laughed heartily, before continuing.

"Dark Shark we are going to stay here and help you to get this done. We are going to be here for you. Whenever you need us, all you have to do is call. I will give you my mobile number. When you know the time is right, use it."

Dark Shark was shocked. He didn't know what to say.

"Walla. Thank you so much, Captain. I am deeply honoured and grateful."

"Don't be. There is no need. I know of your battles and I respect your passion for the sea and for the sharks. When I look at you, I see myself twenty years ago. You deserve our help. Now, remember. Don't be a schmuck. Use the number I gave you."

Dark Shark laughed and shook the Captain's hand warmly. He thanked him again, but was waved away. It was time for him to leave. To return to Dahab and find the bad guys. To end this once and for all. Climbing back into the Zodiac, this time on his own, a seed was beginning to germinate inside Dark Shark's head. During the return journey to the beach the seed grew, getting bigger by the minute before finally turning into a fully grown idea.

In his office at the headquarters of the Dahab Shamandura, Adel sat with his polished black shoes resting on top of his desk. He was bored. He fiddled with his moustache. He fidgeted with the trigger of his sub-machine-gun and sighed. It has been so long since he had had the chance to use it. Almost two years now. The man who'd been shot had survived, which was also a good thing. There was far less paperwork to fill in when they lived. He pictured the man lying face down in the street with a small entrance wound in his left shoulder. On the other side, the exit wound was nearly half a foot wide, taking out a large section of the poor man's chest. Blood had flowed into the gutter. The man was a drug dealer, and as far as Adel was concerned, deserved everything he got. Adel smiled wistfully as he remembered one of his favourite past fantasies.

The phone on the desk rang, the sharp ringing jangling Adel back to the present. He reacted without thinking, pulling his shoes off the desk and whisking the phone out of the cradle with one smooth movement.

"Aiwa."

"Is it Adel?"

"Aiwa. Who is this?"

"I am the Madame of the Golden Wadi Massage Parlour."

"Ah… Yes. Pai Mai. How can I be of service, Madam?"

"I want to give you some information. But first I want you to promise me that no matter what happens, you not send me back to fucking Beijing."

"Well, that would depend, Pai Mai."

"Depend on what?"

"The information of course."

"You don't worry about that. This information is very excellent. You will solve this case and get big promotion. I promise you this. Yes. Big promotion. I will give you the evidence of the man who killed Moheet. The same man who is also behind the shark finning. You promise me you not send me back to fucking Beijing."

"Okay, okay. If the information is true, I promise not to send you back to Beijing."

"Okay. Very good."

"Now, if you would be so kind as to give me the name?"

"Oh no. Not on the phone. No way. You come to the Golden Wadi and you bring letter saying you not send me back to Beijing. Come in ten minutes. I be ready."

Pai Mai hung up. Adel slowly put the phone down, thinking. He got up, put on his jacket and walked out the door. As he did so, he radioed for two junior officers to go with him. He walked out of the Shamandura station, got into his car and turned the key. Adel backed the car out of the car park and turned left onto the main road leading into Dahab. A minute later, another black Shamandura car pulled up next to him and together they drove towards the Golden Wadi Massage Parlour.

On the Zodiac, Dark Shark was thinking about all that the Somali pirate Captain Januna Ali Jama had said to him on the dhow. As before, Sugule Ali sat at the rear of the dingy, his legs calmly controlling the throttle. Dark Shark was thinking that the Somali pirates' situation could very easily be repeated at any time and in any location in the world. There were millions of artisanal fishermen around the globe. They were all of them hanging on to the last scraps of a once plentiful ocean. The great fish stocks of the sea had run out. Nearly all the major fish stocks in the world's oceans had completely collapsed. Fishermen, who traditionally hunted only fish, were now killing anything they could find, especially sharks. There were also industries in gill-rakers which were devastating the magnificent manta ray populations. Ninety per cent of all the large species of fish in the Oceans were now gone. All the species of turtle were critically endangered. Even the humble sea cucumber was being fished to the brink of extinction. The cetaceans, of all the creatures in the sea, were the most loved by humans. But even they were not escaping the genocide. Although the whaling nations had agreed in 1986 on a complete global ban on whaling, humans still went out and slaughtered these intelligent, sentient and complex animals.

The animals in the sea were getting wiped out. Then there was the pollution. So much rubbish, mainly plastic, had been dumped into the sea, the world's oceanic currents had assembled the rubbish in one place. In the North Pacific, there was a garbage patch which the vast majority of humanity had absolutely no idea was there. It was called the North Pacific Garbage Patch and it was currently the size of Western Europe. Much of the plastic is so small, it is almost microscopic. Scientists estimate the patch is so vast it would take a global industry many, many years to clean up. Until that happened, the problem would, of course get worse.

There were problems that even exceeded the magnitude of the garbage patch. Global Warming, heavy metal pollution, tourist developments, deep-sea mining, all were going to lead to the death of the ocean. The list was seemingly endless. What could one person do against such reckless destruction? What could one skint, diving instructor do to change things? To actually make a difference. Was it possible? Could anything at all be done?

Dark Shark's idea was to offer the fishermen an alternative to fishing. A way of making a sustainable income from anything other than destroying the sea. Dark Shark was going to help shark fishermen stop fishing sharks and work with tourists instead. Sharks could be become more valuable to the fishermen alive than dead. If the fishermen could make money from the sea without killing it, they would do everything in their power to protect their own environment. Dark Shark wanted to give fishermen a chance to do what the Somali pirates had done. They had provided themselves with an alternative as well, but it wasn't very popular or sustainable. Dark Shark's suggestion would provide something that was. He would help the shark fishermen to put down their lines and their hooks. To replace the shark fins for divers' fins. Dark Shark resolved to start an organization called Fins4Fins.

Fifteen minutes after it left the dhow, the Zodiac returned Dark Shark to the beach at the Lagoon. He jumped off the inflatable with renewed vigour. He was delighted with his new idea and wanted to share it with his old friend as soon as possible. He scanned the beach, looking for Gastro. But Gastro wasn't on the beach. Dark Shark could see nothing, but the usual mid-morning array of life and vehicles. He sighed. Turning to Sugule Ali, he bade the first mate a warm farewell, walked past the palisade and started for the main road. He hailed a taxi, went home and was soon fast asleep in his bed. Gastronimica. A great cook, but economical with reliability.

Outside the Golden Wadi Massage Parlour, Adel and the other two officers pulled up in their black cars. He got out, closed the door and strode up to the front doors. The three security men from the Shamandura opened one of the doors and went inside. They were standing in the opulent lobby. The air was cool. Air conditioning whirred overhead and they could feel the cold blasts of air flowing along their moustaches. Apart from the men, the reception was empty. Irritated, Adel approached the counter and rang the silver bell hard. At exactly the same moment, a shrill; ear piercing scream erupted from inside the corridor on the other side of the luminous gold and silver bead curtain. Even with all his years of experience and corruption, Adel nearly jumped out of his skin.

Pulling his sub-machine-gun from his holster, Adel and his loyal deputies rushed through the bead curtain towards the origin of that primeval sound. The men sped down the corridor as fast they could. Adel briefly wandered where exactly the sound had emanated from. As if to answer, another scream erupted, as loud as the first and just as terrible. The scream came from a door to his right. Followed by the deputies, Adel burst through the door and into the room. The sight that greeted them was horrific. Lying slumped face down on her desk was Pai Mai. Her normally exquisite black hair was a blood splattered mess. Underneath her head, a thick river of blood trickled onto the floor to form a large pool. Her beautiful, green Chinese kimono was drenched in blood, as were her black shoes. Her arms dangled below the desk, white and lifeless. From the side of her neck, a long black needle protruded from deep within her jugular vein. Next to the body of her former employer, and frozen in terror stood Qigong. She screamed for a third time. It was even louder, longer and more guttural than the previous two.

In his half a house on El Fanar Street, Dark Shark had been asleep for three hours when his phone startled him awake. He fumbled, grumbled and mumbled until he had located the phone. Opening the clam shell, he pressed the green button.

"Allo… "

"Dark Shark! You'd better come quickly! Right now! Come, come quickly right now!

It was Mohammed, the owner of the Just Another Dive Centre and he was frantic with terror.

"Mo, calm down man. What happened?"

"The dhow is finning sharks right now over at the Three Pools! You have to come!

"Shit! Are you kidding me!? How do you know that!?"

"Because Jamila just called me! She tried to call you but you didn't answer your phone!"

"How does Jamila know!?"

"Because she is at the Three Pools!"

"Shit! Shit! Shit!"

"Quick, get dressed! I am outside your house!"

Dark Shark fell out of his bed and landed onto his knees which hit the concrete floor with a loud thud. Pain shot up his legs, but he ignored it. For the next few seconds, he had a fight with his clothes whilst he tried to put them back on. The jury was out, but finally he appeared to be winning the battle. Grabbing his phone and keys, Dark Shark opened his front door and ran to Mohammed's waiting Jeep. He jumped in the front seat. Even before his door closed, Mo put his foot down and the Jeep lurched forward.

"What on earth is going on, Mo!?"

"Walla-he, mishkela! Mishkela kabeer!"

Mohammed's Jeep raced south out of town. The Three Pools was one of the southern dive sites, so called because they lay to the south of Dahab. Dark Shark tried to call Jamila, but she didn't pick up.

"Shit. She's not answering."

"She might not have a signal where she is. She kept cutting out when I spoke to her earlier."

"How long ago was that?"

"Walla-he, five minutes before I was outside your

house."

"Where's Gastro?"

"He is at Slow Down."

Dark Shark opened his clam shell and called his friend. Gastro answered the call and Dark Shark filled him in on the news. At the other end, Gastro cursed.

"Meet me outside Slow Down in two minutes."

"Okay."

When the Jeep pulled up at Slow Down, the building was shaking. A huge bass speaker was booming. Mohammed honked the horn. Gastro came bounding out of Slow Down and jumped into the Jeep, a bag on one shoulder and a can of beer in his right hand.

Dark Shark looked hard at Gastro. His friend's eyes were attempting to swap places.

"How's the party going, Gastro?"

"It's amazing man, I took three acid trips an hour ago, drank seven beers, and I've just been with Eva in the toilets. She is something else that girl, right proper Nazi. I never realized I had a Gestapo fetish till I met Eva."

Dark Shark made a mental note to leave Gastro on the beach. Again. The dreadlocked party animal suddenly remembered why he was in the Jeep.

"How are we going to deal with the shark fishing dhow?"

"By getting help from another dhow."

"You mean the pirates?"

"Yes. They said they had come to Dahab to help me,

so I'm going to take them up on their offer. In fact, I'm going to call them right now."

Dark Shark opened his clam shell and called the number the pirate Captain had given him. As he waited for the Captain to answer, Dark Shark turned to Mohammed.

"I think we should call Adel."

"Walla he. I already did. Something happened in Dahab today that is keeping him very busy. I didn't manage to talk to him yet. I can try him again if you want."

"No. Actually, better to leave it. With the kind of help I am getting, it's probably better to leave law enforcement out of it."

Captain Januna Ali Jama answered his phone. Dark Shark quickly informed the pirate Captain what was taking place and where. The Captain seemed pleased. His chance to help Dark Shark had come quickly. They discussed a plan of action; Dark Shark gave him directions to the Three Pools and then closed his phone.

"Maybe we should get the Zodiac ready, Dark Shark?"

"No, Mo. We won't be needing it."

"Mershi."

At the Three Pools dive site, Jamila was squinting through a pair of binoculars at an area of sea two kilometres off shore. She was lying on some cushions, high up on a hill behind a Bedouin hoosha. The hoosha was part of a restaurant that sold refreshments to divers between dips in the sea. In her lenses, Jamila could see the shark fishing dhow as they assembled the dreaded hooked lines. The dhow's two Zodiacs were dragging out the lines in the now familiar giant semi circles. She could also see Salah, the one eyed Bedouin dressed all in black. She inhaled her breath sharply. He was barking orders, directing the activities with lots of arm waving and pointed fingers. Jamila scanned the dhow from left to right with the binoculars. She took in the whole scene, missing nothing. Continuing to keep tabs on the scene below, Jamila silently prayed for Dark Shark to turn up sooner rather than later.

The journey from Dahab to the southern dive sites took twenty minutes. The Jeep containing Mohammed, Dark Shark and Gastro sped along the road, hugging the sea. The entire journey all three occupants nervously stared at the sea, searching for signs of the shark-fishing dhow. As they approached the restaurant at the dive site, they saw it. It was some way off shore. Big, black, ominous. Even from the beach, they could tell it was getting ready to dish out its own particular brand of death. Zodiacs zoomed around, evidently laying out the lines. The shark-fishing dhow sat like the darkest shadow on an inky, black sea, a smudge of evil in the light of a nearly full moon. Mohammed slowed down, trying to keep the engine as quiet as possible. He inched the Jeep behind the restaurant and cut the engine. Just as he pulled the key out, Dark Shark received a text on his phone. It was from Jamila.

"Am behind you, up on the hill."

Dark Shark, Gastro and Mohammed piled out of the Jeep and ran to the hill. They half ran, half stumbled, climbing their way up to the top where Jamila was lying on cushions, spying on the boat of death.

The three friends lay down next to Jamila who handed the binoculars to Dark Shark.

"They're at it again."

"*Mother*fuckers!"

"What do we do this time? Call the Navy again?"

"No. Last time we did that the dhow got away. Mohammed tried to call Adel earlier, but couldn't get through. No, this time we are going to deal with this without the competent, capable hands of the Egyptian authorities."

"Oh really. And how do you propose we do that?"

"Last night, I met some friends at the Lagoon. They are going to help us."

"Really. Well let's hope they are not Yoghurt Weavers like the twelve distinguished members of the Sinai High Council."

"Nope. Nothing like."

Dark Shark reached into his jacket and pulled out his clam shell. Opening it, he dialled a number and pressed the green button.

"Salaam, Captain Ali Jama?"

"Aiwa, Dark Shark. Where are you?"

"We are up on the beach near the restaurant. We are on

top of the hill. The shark fishing dhow is here and she is getting ready to kill sharks."

"Aiwa. I know. I can see her now. We are on our way. The shark fishing boat will never fin sharks again. Come down to the water, I am sending a Zodiac to pick you up. Ma salaam."

The line went dead.

Out to sea, the four friends could see the approach of another dhow. It was far, off but sailing at speed and making straight for the shark fishing dhow. Two Zodiacs peeled off from the 'mother ship'. One kept pace with its home vessel, whilst the other made a Bee line for the beach.

"Who was that? Who are those guys?"

"It will have to wait till later, Jay. You are going to stay here Gastro and Mohammed. Don't get anywhere."

"What are you going to do?"

"Become a pirate."

Dark Shark left a confused Jamila with Gastro and Mohammed on top of the hill. He ran down to the beach, where already the pirate Zodiac was floating in the water a few meters away. Dark Shark jumped in. Sugule Ali turned the throttle on the powerful outboard motor full on. The motor roared into life and the Zodiac shot off towards the action. On the deck of the shark fishing dhow, Salah had just noticed the approach of the other dhow. He was gob-smacked.

"Who were they? They definitely weren't Navy. Who

could they be?"

Salah had absolutely no idea. He stood rooted to the spot, staring transfixed at the other dhow. Salah watch disbelievingly as one of the dhow's Zodiacs peeled off and headed towards the beach.

The men on the other dhow were all heavily armed. Salah had never seen anything like it. He and his crew were only shark fishermen; they had knives and machetes but nothing more. The only gun on board was the 9mm pistol he was carrying in the folds of his Jelibya. Despite the overwhelming strength of the opposition, Salah steeled himself for battle. He was never going to give in. He would rather die rather than submit. Pulling himself together, he reached into his Jelibya and grabbed his radio. He pressed a red button on the side and barked orders into it. A crackled reply told him his crew on the Zodiacs had understood and were responding. He put the radio back into his Jelibya and shouted at the crew on the shark fishing dhow to ready themselves. There was no time for flight. They would stand and fight.

On his Zodiac, Dark Shark watched as the two dhows, one black, one brown, faced each other like two giant maritime gladiators. Each dhow had two Zodiacs which buzzed around their respective mother- ships. On one dhow were the heavily armed, battle hardened Somali pirates. On the other, were the desperate, ruthless, shark fishing criminals. Sugule Ali gunned the Zodiac closer to the shark fishing dhow. Suddenly, one of the enemy's dinghies came sweeping round the mother ship. The crew on the Zodiac were waving machetes and knives. On their faces were fierce, determined expressions. The Zodiac made for Dark Shark's boat at high speed. In the next moment, they would be on top of them. Sugule Ali calmly shouldered his AK47 and took careful aim. Alarmed, Dark Shark cried out.

"No! Don't kill them!"

Sugule Ali had no intention of harming them. He nonchalantly fired off three rounds which slammed into the rubber tubing at the top of Zodiac. The crew men on the Zodiac cried out in feverish panic as their boat began sinking. Soon they were thrashing about in the water, trying to hang onto whatever they could find. One Zodiac was now down and out. One remained, as did the mother ship.

"So, Dark Shark! You have come again. How interesting. And this time you've brought with you some friends. I see that you are not as stupid as you look!"

Sugule Ali swung his AK 47 up and around, keeping it against his shoulder until it was pointing at the one eyed Bedouin who had just shouted from the deck of the shark fishing dhow. Dark Shark also swung round to face his enemy. Salah was standing at the back of the dhow. His left hand was holding the rigging. In his right hand was a 9mm revolver which was currently levelled at Dark Shark's head.

"It's finished Salah. Give it up. The time of the shark

fishermen is over. The time of the shark diver is now. C'mon. Enough blood has been spilt. Put down the gun. This is not the Bedouin way."

On the other side of the shark fishing dhow, the second pirate Zodiac had moved into position only twenty meters away. There were four pirates onboard the Zodiac. Captain Ali Jama was amongst them and now he pointed a RPG rocket launcher at the shark-fishing dhow.

"What do you know about the ways of the Bedouin, Dark Shark? You are just like all the other fucking Hawager who come to Sinai. You smoke a few joints with the Bedouin, drink tea with them and think you understand their ways? You are an ignorant fool! What do you know of the Bedouin? What do you know of our suffering? The injustice heaped on us by foreigners that care nothing for us!

The corporations who rape the Sinai, leaving the Bedouin to starve!"

From behind the crazed, one eyed Bedouin, a woman shouted loudly.

"Salah! This madness must stop right now! It is over!"

The Bedouin in black spun round. He gasped in abject shock and horror.

"Mother! Nooo!! How is it possible?! What are you doing here!?"

"I have come to take you home, Salah. I am here to help you with your anger."

"No!! You will never be able to help me! I don't want

your help!

Salah spun round again and raised his pistol, taking direct aim at Dark Shark's head. At that exact same moment, three things happened instantaneously. Sugule Ali fired his assault rifle. Sprilina, despite her great age, rushed forward at astonishing speed towards her gun toting son. Reaching him, she grasped him underneath his shoulder and pushed him overboard. Sugule Ali's bullet hit Salah in the shoulder, just as he and his mother tumbled headlong into the sea. Captain Ali Jama fired his rocket propelled grenade towards the shark fishing dhow. The grenade penetrated the hull, slamming into the fuel tanks. There followed an almighty, thunderous explosion.

A huge ball of orange flame ballooned out from the dhow. Massive chunks of fiberglass debris flew up into the sky. Razor sharp shrapnel sliced through the air, peppering everything in a fifty meters radius with deadly effect. The huge force of the mighty explosion knocked Dark Shark off the Zodiac and into the water. Sugule Ali fell backwards, landing in the bottom of the boat and crunching his head on the outboard motor. A black mushroom cloud of smoke slowly expanded upwards, filling the night time sky.

On the hill behind the Bedouin hoosha, Jamila, Gastro and Mohammed looked on disbelief. The explosion could be heard for miles around. They felt the shock waves hitting them even at that distance.

"Jesus fucking Christ!"

"Oh my god. Dark Shark!"

"Don't worry, Jamila, I can see him through the binoculars. He's fallen into the water. The explosion did not hurt him. Look! See there! He is climbing back into the Zodiac!"

Jamila grabbed the lenses from Mohammed and looked through them at the unfolding drama out to sea.

"Oh, thank God. He looks okay. Jesus what a mess! I do hope no one else has been hurt."

Suddenly, all three were bathed in the bright headlights of a vehicle that had driven up and stopped directly behind them. Before they had time to realize what was happening, never mind respond in some way, three men jumped out from the Jeep and ran towards them.

"Hey! What the f…!?

Gastro never finished his question. He was forcibly grabbed. A large black cloth hood was roughly placed over his head, shoulders and arms. Suddenly, he was unable to see or move. Strong ropes were wrapped around his body and tightened in a knot. Exactly the same thing happened to Jamila and Mohammed. Jamila was picked up, kicking and screaming, the sounds muffled considerably by the cloth hood. The men threw her over their shoulder, then bundled her into the Jeep. With Mohammed and Gastro left squirming on the ground, the Jeep roared off into the blackness of the desert night.

When the explosion had ripped through the dhow,

a small piece of shrapnel had embedded itself in Dark Shark's leg. Thrown from the Zodiac into the water, he had struggled to get back in. Sugule Ali, who had been rendered temporarily unconsciousness, had recovered sufficiently to help haul his friend back into the boat. Sitting up, Dark Shark looked down at the piece of shrapnel which stuck out from his flesh at an acute angle. Blood trickled down, splashing onto the bottom of the boat. It hurt like hell. Dark Shark wandered if the wound would require more stitches from Dr Adel. Clutching his leg, he looked around at the scene of devastation. The burning remains of the dhow lay close by. Bright orange, red and yellow flames engulfed the entire hull. Inside, the fire reached more fuel and gas, causing a number of smaller explosions. Plumes of acrid black smoke billowed skywards from the inferno. Only minutes after the explosion, the burning wreckage, all that was left of the dhow, began to sink. The shark fishing dhow was no more. She slid quickly below the waves, sinking down to a watery grave.

For the first time since Moheet's body was found at the Eel Garden, Dark Shark had accomplished one of his goals. The shark fishing dhow was destroyed. It would never kill sharks again. It would never again be used to slice off the fins and it would never again be used to turn those fins into tasteless soup. Despite the pain of his latest wound, Dark Shark was elated at he watched the burning ship disappear beneath the inky surface.

A few meters away, Sprilina and her son, the one eyed Bedouin Salah, were being helped in to the pirate Zodiac of Captain Januna Ali Jama. The rest of the shark fishing crew were hauled into Zodiacs at gun point and taken to the pirate dhow. Salah was bleeding badly from his shoulder. After a quick meeting between his mother, Dark Shark and Captain Ali Jama, it was agreed that Salah and Sprilina would be dropped off at the hospital in Sharm El Sheikh. In the meantime, Sugule Ali would drop Dark Shark back off at the beach so he could meet up again with his friends. Casting off the from the pirate dhow, Dark Shark and Sugule Ali drove to the beach. Wishing his pirate friend thank you and farewell, Dark Shark ran to the top of hill. When he reached the summit, out of breath and in extreme pain, the sight that greeted him nearly knocked him over with the all too familiar feeling of a sledgehammer. He rushed over and untied the ropes binding Gastro and Mohammed, then quickly pulled off their hoods. To his horror, he realized Jamila wasn't one of them. She was gone.

Two hours later Dark Shark, Gastro, Mohammed, Mojave, Gobi, Sally, Adel and Sprilina were standing like statues rooted to the floor in the office of Just Another Dive centre. They were staring at the desk. Lying on top of it was a dead, baby tiger shark. The animal was only three feet long, but it already sported the famous stripes of the tiger. All of its fins had been brutally hacked off. Dry blood had congealed on the floor underneath the desk. In the side of the fish, a message had hacked into the flesh with a knife:

'Ich Bin Eine Jamila!

Gebril Bint 8 PM'

No one spoke for a long time. It was Mojave who finally broke the silence.

"What does Gebril Bint mean?"

Dark Shark slowly pulled out a cigarette. He lit the end, inhaled, then exhaled long and hard before replying in a low tone:

"Gebril Bint means Grave of the Daughter."

Mojave let out a startled cry.

# 17

## *Gebril Bint*

Jamila sat in a chair, struggling to breathe. Her mouth had sticky tape across it, with only a single hole to provide her with air. Her head was covered in the black hood. She gagged. She gasped for air. Panic gripped her. She had to act while she was still conscious. Her hands were tied to the back of the chair so tightly, she was sure her wrists must be bleeding. Her ankles were tied just as roughly. She struggled against her bindings, but only managed to lose balance, topple over and crash to the floor. Jamila moaned more in despair than pain. Behind her, a cold Germanic voice reached her ears.

"Vhy, Jamila. Vhat on earth are you doing?"

Footsteps approached and she could feel strong hands pick her up and set her down again.

"I'm sure ve don't need these anymore."

The man removed the hood, and then with a quick flick of his wrist, ripped the sticky tape from her mouth. Jamila flinched from the pain and gasped for air. She was still bound hand and foot, but at least she was able to breathe again. Jamila looked up at the man in front of her. He was tall, at least six feet two inches. He was well built, fit and trained. On his head was a shock of blond hair. His eyes were grey, cold and arrogant. He had thin, blood red lips and a long Roman nose.

"So, you must be Nemo."

"Indeed I am."

"Looks like you've added kidnapping to your long list of crimes which include murder, exhortation and environmental rape."

"Haha! Jamila, you have such a vay vith vords! Quite delightful really."

"Why did you do it Nemo? Why did you kill her? I know why you killed all those sharks. Capitalist psychopaths like you only care about money. But why Moheet? What did she ever do to you?"

"Moheet got in the vay. She vas ready to go to the Shamandura and tell them vhat I vas doing. There vas no vay I could allow that to happen."

"She loved you. She was loyal to you. You rewarded that by murdering her."

"Moheet vas a fool! She vanted to change the vorld vith her vapid dreams! Her love for the environment got in the vay of profit! I made sure she vould never vreck my plans!

"Your plans are wrecked thanks to Dark Shark. It's finished, Nemo. It's over. Why don't you give it up, before anyone else gets hurt? Dark Shark is going to do more than wreck your plans when he gets here."

"Ha-ha! I love your optimism Jamila. I can understand vhy Dark Shark likes you so much. You are far too good for that skint hippy."

"Dark Shark is special. He is passionate, intelligent and he wants to make the world a better place. I've never met a better man."

"Ahhh... how sveet! I hope your last few minutes together vith him vere meaningful; because they are going to be the very last you ever had."

"You are pure evil, Nemo."

"Nein! Nein! You misunderstand me, Jamila. I am simply doing vhat needs to be done."

"You're never going to succeed. It's over."

"My dear Jamila. You have no idea, you silly girl. Now, I'm getting bored with this conversation. I must get ready for vhen our guest arrives. Soon I vill return vith food and vater. Be a good girl, Jamila. Don't try anything stupid, othervise I might have to kill you even before your lover arrives."

With that, Nemo walked towards the door, opened it and walked out the room leaving Jamila alone.

She waited a few minutes to make sure he did not return. Jamila looked around her. She was in a large room, poorly lit. There were no windows and only the one door. She couldn't see any tools, but she did spy something interesting lying on the floor in one corner. Tensing her feet, Jamila strained and realized she could lift the chair up, even if only ever so slightly. Using all her strength, she managed to move the chair by two inches, before setting it down again. The effort exhausted her, but she was determined to carry on. Readying herself she repeated the exercise, moving the chair another two inches. Breathing hard, she looked across to the object on the floor and sighed deeply. This was going to take a bloody long time.

In the office of the Dahab Shamandura, Dark Shark was sat on the opposite side of the desk from Adel. On his right hand side, Moheet's parents Mojave and Gobi had accompanied him. Adel was filling them in on the latest developments in the case.

"Yesterday, I got a call from the Madame of the Golden Wadi Massage Parlour, Pai Mai. She rang me to tell me she was going to spill the beans on who was behind Moheet's murder and the shark fishing. She said she had a name and evidence. She demanded I meet her at the Golden Wadi. When I arrived there ten minutes later, I found her dead. Murdered."

"Jesus."

"The Shamandura together with a specialist forensic team we had brought in from Cairo secured the scene and is currently investigating the circumstances of the murder. So far we have failed to come up with anything. The scene was completely clean of evidence. We found nothing incriminating. Whoever it was had done an excellent clean up job by the time we arrived."

"What about Salah?"

"He is with his mother at Sharm el Sheikh Hospital. The doctors tell me he is doing well, despite losing a fair amount of blood. When he is strong enough, he will face trial."

"It's incredible. Who could've imagined that the shark fishing dhow would get attacked, blown up and sunk by a pirate ship that had travelled over 2,000 miles from Somalia? What an astonishingly random event. Still, solved a rather large problem for Dahab did it not?"

Adel's stare at Dark Shark was so hard, the poor English diving instructor thought those eyes were going to bore right through him.

Adel shifted nervously in his black, camel leather chair.

"Yes, well. I suppose it was quite fortunate. Now we will go to Neptune dive centre and finish this story once and for all."

"Adel, you can't do that. If anyone else goes there apart from me, Nemo will kill her."

"Dark Shark, do I detect a distinct lack of trust in the capabilities of the Shamandura?"

"Adel, with all due respect, yes."

"Fair enough. I will admit we have been a little off our game of late..."

Dark smiled inside.

"Of late? Try the last forty years."

Adel continued, luckily unable to read Dark Shark's mind.

"... Nevertheless, I can't let you go up there completely alone. It's not possible. It would be irresponsible and illegal of me. I understand your concern however. Let's do like this. We can put a wire on you. We will provide back up. At the right moment, we will turn up at the dive centre and apprehend the criminal, Nemo."

"Okay. I can agree to that. Just make sure the wire wasn't made in China please."

"Ha-ha! Dark Shark you are such a joker."

"It's not a joke Adel."

"Don't worry, Dark Shark, we will fit you the best wire available in Egypt."

It was close to the middle of the afternoon when Dark Shark arrived home and began to get ready for Gebril Bint. He tried hard to focus on what he needed to do. He kept telling himself that it was going to be okay, that nothing bad was going to happen to Jamila, but the self-reassurance wasn't really working. Sitting on the edge of his bed, Dark Shark cleansed the shrapnel wound and applied new bandages. Next he dressed himself all in black. Black jacket, trousers, and shoes. He took a push dagger and placing it inside a black sheath, tied it to his left shoulder. It hung upside down, allowing for quick access with either hand. The knife was only three inches long and made entirely from titanium. Razor sharp, the blade was triangular, ending in a two pronged metal handle, and as the name suggested, it was designed only for stabbing, not slashing. The knife was small, but very deadly. Dark Shark felt like a Ninja preparing for a secret mission, but with the wound in his leg forcing him to double over, the reality was closer to a penguin with osteonecrosis.

Finishing his preparations, he flipped open the clam shell and dialled Adel's number, informing the officer that he was ready. Adel grunted his acknowledgement.

"I'll send the car round. Wait outside the house."

Lying fifteen km south of Dahab, Gebril Bint, like Ras Abu Gallum, is inaccessible by road. The most popular method of access is by boat. Unlike Ras Abu Gallum, it is a barren, remote place, the harsh desert meeting the sea and nothing else. Only the Bedouin pass through on their way along the coast, camels carefully treading the steep slopes and narrow paths of the mountains. Gebril Bint. Grave of the Daughter. Uninhabited and untouched.

Dark Shark stepped out of his house at precisely the same moment as Jamila reached the interesting object lying in the corner of the room. She was exhausted. The effort to gain the distance needed whilst tied tightly had all but drained her, but she had made it. Now, all she needed to do was to stretch out a hand, reach down and claim her prize. Jamila paused. It had taken her three and a half hours to reach this point. Three and a half hours of exhausting work lifting the chair a few inches at a time. During that time, she has struggled to breathe, the cloying dust, stifling heat and the gag in her mouth making the task that much harder. As she rested and gathered her remaining strength, her mind wandered and she analysed her predicament.

Dark Shark was walking into a trap. Whether or not he realized this, it didn't really matter. He would have come anyway. He had no choice. Jamila shuddered, but it wasn't cold. She realized with a stab of fear that Nemo intended to kill them both. He had been planning this from the beginning. Panic gripped her. She struggled to banish the negativity from her mind, to focus instead on the task ahead. Jamila didn't want it to end this way, was determined that having found love the second time around; she wasn't going to lose it again. No way was a psycho like Nemo going to get between her and her mate. She was from South London, goddammit!

Jamila steeled herself and stared down at the object, calculating the distance, angle and effort required, to not only lift it off the floor, but to use it effectively. She closed her eyes and began a series of deep breaths, readying herself for the task ahead. Wriggling her left wrist from side to side a few times in an attempt to gain even incremental flexibility from the restrictions of the rope, she leaned over to her left and reached out to carefully lift up the object. Her hand stretched to its limit. Her fingers shook with the effort. Sweat trickled down her brow, along her hairline and down her neck. She was sure Nemo would return to find her trying to escape and the though terrified her. To her horror, she realized she wasn't going to reach the small shard of broken glass that was her target. Exasperation gripped her; she was felt as if she would burst at any second.

"Just a little more... a little more... that's it...almost there... C'mon! For once, just gimme a frigging break here!"

Stretching beyond limits she believed possible, Jamila's fingers closed around the edge of the glass shard. At the same time, the dusty floor came rushing up to meet her and with a loud thump, she and the chair fell sideways. She winced audibly a pitiful, muffled sound. The glass she had been striving to pick up for over three hours cut deeply into her fingers. She lay on the floor unmoving, sobbing silently and overwhelmed by hopelessness whilst blood slowly formed a pool under her left hand.

In the office of the Shamandura, Dark Shark sat in a chair on the other side of the desk to Adel. Another member of the Shamandura was fastening a wire to Dark Shark's chest with all the skill of a seasoned professional. The man clipped a microphone to the inside of Dark's

Shark's jacket, then taped the length of wire before finally fitting the small transmitter. The equipment certainly looked first rate, though Dark Shark was hardly an expert on such devious devices. The man fitting the wire nodded to Adel that it was ready, who responded by saying:

"Good. Now we test it."

Both he and the other Shamandura agent placed

headphones on and with Adel indicating all to remain quiet; he flicked a switch on a console located on the front of his desk. Instantly, the microphone inside Dark Shark's jacket crackled loudly a few times, then most bizarrely, what came next sounded distinctly like commentary from a football game between arch rivals Al Ahly and al Masry. Thousands of football fans could be heard chanting and a commentator was describing the action at a hundred miles per hour. Adel threw off his headphones and swore. The Shamandura technician, who had fitted the wire, did his best to look like he was trying to fix the problem by fussing and fiddling around Dark Shark's insides.

When he was confident the problem was solved, he nodded to Adel, who glared at the poor man, placed the headphones back on his head and flicked another switch. This time the crackling was followed by a loud recording of the call to prayer from the local mosque. Adel was furious. He threw off the headphones again, jumped up and began berating the unfortunate Shamandura technician. Dark Shark raised his eyebrows, sighed deeply and slumped in his chair. Thankfully the proceedings were interrupted by the phone ringing on Adel's desk. He stopped shouting at his subordinate, gathered himself and angrily grabbed the phone.

"Aiwa?"

"Mr Adel of the Shamandura?

"Aiwa. Who is this?"

"It's me, Nemo. Put Dark Shark on the phone."

Adel's face was a picture. Angry indignation had turned to shock in an instant and his face fell. Now, frowning deeply, he passed the receiver to Dark Shark who sensed immediately who it was.

"Yes."

"Dark Shark, finally ve get a chance to talk… "

"Listen Nemo… "

"Shut up! *YOU* listen and listen good! Jamila is my guest here and at 8pm you vill be too. Make sure you come alone. Obviously I know you are vorking vith the Shamandura and if any of them attempt to follow you here, the voman you love vill look like one of your beloved sharks on the end of one of my hooks!"

"Nemo, if you touch one hair… "

Dark Shark stopped before finishing his sentence. The line was dead.

Adel took the phone from Dark Shark.

"What did he say?"

"He says I have to come alone. He says if any of you try to follow me, he is going to kill Jamila."

"He is going to kill you and Jamila anyway, Dark Shark."

"I know. But I don't want to make it easy for him. He has spies everywhere and knows our every move. Keep your men well away Adel. For now, I need to do as he says and act alone. Let me get Jamila, the evidence you need and get the hell away from Gebril Bint. Then and only then, do you move in."

"Don't worry, Dark Shark."

"Worrying is what has kept me alive so far."

On the other side of Dahab, in the sprawling ramble of Assalah, two women were meeting to discuss urgent matters. They both sat Bedouin style; on cushions, cross legged and drinking tea. They were not, however, drinking Bedouin tea. The tea they were consuming was a secret herbal concoction.

"Sinai is gripped with fear and pain. Death has come to the desert."

"I know, Sprilina. I have felt it for a long time. I sensed these events would happen long before they occurred."

"Dark Shark is walking into a trap. He is in terrible danger. Do we allow this to happen? Do we leave him to his fate?"

The woman opposite Sprilina gave no response. She stared into space, saying nothing.

Lying on the floor, tied up, gagged, bleeding and desperate, Jamila was down but she was not out. Fighting back the tears and the pain, she gingerly repositioned the shard of glass in her left hand. When she was able to grip the edge, she strained her hand towards her arm and started to saw at the rope around her wrist. Progress was painfully slow in more ways than one. Blood from her fingers covered the glass making it extremely hard to grip. The angle she was trying to saw at was very acute, but finally with a huge effort, she managed to cut through the rope. The effect on her hand being free caused her to wave it around in disbelief, unable to register that she could now move it after all these long hours tied to the chair. Her entire arm throbbed as the blood finally flowed freely again. She could feel the familiar tingling feeling of 'pins and needles' in her arm as normal circulation resumed. Putting down the piece of glass, she wiped the blood from her hand on her trousers, then picking up the glass again, she feverishly cut the remaining rope holding her hostage.

Freedom from the chair did not, of course, mean freedom. It had taken her nearly four hours to merely extricate herself from the chair. But she had done it. She had taken the first vitally important step and the success buoyed her. She was so happy she almost shouted out loud. Even if she didn't manage to escape the room, she now had a fighting chance. Whoever came through that door would find a surprising new situation. Her resolve strengthened, Jamila padded noiselessly over to the door and tried the handle.

The black craft sped across the top of the water, spray drenching the stern-faced crew member. Dark Shark stood stark still at the back of the Zodiac, remorselessly gunning the engine. He wasn't planning what he was going to do once he arrived in Gebril Bint. He wasn't even thinking about Jamila. He merely stared straight ahead, his face set in stone, eyes blazing, his determination cutting through the waves with the same efficiency as his mode of transport. He had been travelling now for just under an hour and his journey was almost over.

Twenty minutes into the trip from the naval jetty, the radio microphone clipped to his chest had suddenly started blaring modern Egyptian dance music; causing a shocked Dark Shark to promise to himself that if it happened again, the whole contraption would end up in the drink. The contraption must have realized its perilous position because after that it remained silent for the remainder of the journey. Up head, the black looming mountains of Gebril Bint grew larger. Dark Shark glanced at his watch. 7.50. He had ten minutes to make landfall. Ten minutes and he would be face to face with his arch enemy. The man who wanted to kill him. Nemo.

Dark Shark's Zodiac was now approaching the beach. He slowly relaxed his grip on the throttle and the boat slowed. Ten meters from the beach, he cut the engine completely. The Zodiac, still moving, sailed up onto the beach before coming to rest in the sand with a crunching sound. Dark Shark glanced nervously around, quickly taking in his surroundings. He was on a small, semi-circular beach no more than forty meters at its widest point. The beach stretched back about a hundred meters and all around, huge mountains bore down on the man who glanced back at their dark flanks. In front of the mountains, Dark Shark could just make out a number of buildings, dark brown in the evening light. To his left, a rickety wooden jetty jutted out across the top of the reef plate. Two Zodiacs, one black, one orange were tied to the jetty and although they were seemingly empty, they looked as if they were readied to leave at any moment. Dark Shark took all this in one hurried glance. As far as he could tell, he was completely alone. Leaning down to the right and putting his hands on the edge of the Zodiac, he swung his legs over the side and landed on the beach. He checked everything was still in place, especially the push dagger, and made his way silently towards the closest of the buildings.

When Jamila tried the door handle, much to her astonishment, (and conveniently for the author) the handle had turned. Slowly and carefully, not believing her luck, she opened the door and found herself in a dimly-lit corridor. She was shivering with adrenaline; furtively she looked from left to right, up and down the corridor. No one came. No sounds could be heard. She saw no other doors nor windows, only a long, dirty white corridor speckled in places with brown stains, green mould and broken tiles. To her left, at the end of the corridor, she could see a doorway and beyond that, the unmistakable outlines of the desert. To her right were only more walls. Taking a breath she half ran, half walked as quietly as she could towards the door way. Reaching it, she exited the building and found herself in a large open space; a space she realized instinctively was a wadi.

All around her, the mountains imposed their ominous

presence. There was no moon; the sand around her was dark brown, almost black. Despite that she could make out shade, outlines and shapes. Many, many shapes. Gripped by curiosity she stood rooted to the spot, staring at what looked like thousands and thousands of triangles lying randomly on the sandy floor of the wadi. Suddenly, with a gut wrenching, sickening stab of pain, Jamila realized what she was looking at. The triangles were not lying randomly, but had been placed there deliberately. They were not merely triangles. They were shark fins. Thousands upon thousands of shark fins left out to dry in the sun. They were being dried before their long journey to Hong Kong for the shark fin soup trade. Jamila's stomach turned and it was all she could do to stop herself from retching. It wasn't her will power that stopped her; however, it was the voice behind her.

"Ah Jamila. You are so resilient. My, you never give up, do you?"

Jamila spun round. Standing a few paces behind her, brandishing a gun aimed at her head and sporting a wonderfully evil sneer on his mush, was Nemo.

"There are thousands and thousands of fins here! How many sharks died for your greed!?"

"There are thousands of dollars here, Jamila, thousands of dollars! But then I vouldn't expect you to understand. Now come along, Dark Shark is almost here. Ve must get ready."

The figure in black padded silently towards the first

building. He moved unseen, his footfalls even and measured. He was a wraith in the night and would enter the building unnoticed. He passed through a door way and into a large room. So far, so good. He surveyed the room, taking in the whole space with one sweep of his keen eyes. The room, like him, was dark and silent. It promised much but gave nothing away of its secrets. He could make out black shapes adorning the walls. Large rounded objects with jutting serrations lined the walls; their number too many to count. Dozens of ropes hung down from the ceiling, curled up in piles or strung across the room. On the floor, stacked up in places right up to the ceiling, were numerous boxes. The labels were barely discernible, their contents unknown. Amongst all these strange sights, it was the figure standing in the middle of the room that caught the silent intruder's attention.

The figure was standing on a chair. The figure had a rope around what was obviously a neck. Hanging at the end of other ropes were large, ugly looking hooks, swaying perilously close to the figure standing on the chair. Dark Shark stood dumbstruck, shock and horror filling his every fibre as the true realization of what he was seeing dawned on him. When a light was suddenly flicked on, Dark Shark's worst fears were confirmed. The figure standing on the chair was Jamila.

Just at that moment, two things happened at the same time. Dark Shark giving out a guttural scream, rushed forward towards Jamila. The man who had turned on the light was quicker and he intercepted Dark Shark before he could reach her. The man rushed him fast, armed with a two-foot long, three-inch thick, metal bar. The unknown assailant swung wildly, but Dark Shark ducked just in time and the weapon whistled millimetres from his head. Allowing the momentum of the swing to bring him back around, the man brought up his left leg and kicked Dark Shark hard, his heel striking Dark Shark's wound. Dark Shark grunted and crumpled to the ground. Holding the bar with two hands, the man raised it above his head ready to bring it down with the motion of a sword. As he brought the bar down for the last terrible blow, Dark Shark caught the man's wrists at the last moment, and the two of them rolled over and over.

Both men cursed and dust flew up as they wrestled on the floor. The man was stronger and Dark Shark, wounded. Dark Shark felt his strength ebbing away and he struggled to locate the push dagger on his shoulder. With awful strength the man pinned him down with his knees, and then lifted his arms above his head for the final blow. Dark Shark stared helpless in horror as he looked death in the face. But the blow never came. Instead, from the doorway of the room, a stern woman's voice said loudly:

"That's enough! Put down the bar now!"

Startled, the man looked up in amazement at the woman standing in the doorway. She was tall, blond and in her right hand, she lightly held what looked like a thin staff.

"You have to be fucking jok… "

The man never finished his sentence. All Dark Shark saw or rather felt and then heard, was a loud whoosh of air and an even louder 'THWACK!' The 'THWACK!' was accompanied by a 'CRACK!' The man leaning on Dark Shark crumpled like a soggy piece of cardboard in a car crusher. He moaned softly and lay on his side, his arm a crooked mess. Dark Shark was once again dumbstruck.

He looked across weakly and saw the woman, his rescuer, kneeling beside him, still in the pose that she had used when she struck the man. She was holding the staff across her shoulders and it was still quivering from the impact of the blow. Her eyes stared back at Dark Shark, warm, bright and steady. She smiled at him warmly, and Dark Shark was sure he could see fires of mischief lurking deep in those astonishing orbs.

"Guess you weren't joking."

"C'mon, let's get you up. Jamila needs our help urgently."

"Thank you Harmonica. Thank you for coming to help me."

"You're welcome. You needed help. I should have helped you sooner… "

"It doesn't matter now. I just… "

"Later. We can talk about this later. C'mon."

Harmonica placed her arms under Dark Shark's armpits and lifted him on to his feet as if he weighed no more than a Rizla.

"Can you stand? Walk? How is the leg?"

"It's feels like it's made of cast iron, but it can take my weight."

"Good."

Satisfied that he was okay, Harmonica rushed over to Jamila. As she ran, she held the staff in her left hand. From nowhere, she produced a long, curved knife which she held out with her right hand. In three bounds she had reached Jamila and with the fourth, she suddenly jumped high into the air. With a motion too fast for Dark Shark to see, Harmonica cut the rope around Jamila's neck. She landed on the floor and held out arms just as Jamila crumpled into them. Dark Shark reached them and together, they gently laid Jamila on the floor. She was unconscious, but breathing. Dark Shark gazed intently at the woman he loved, deeply disturbed by what he saw. Holding both her shoulders, Harmonica gently shook Jamila whilst both she and Dark Shark said her name repeatedly. Jamila moaned and her eyes flickered open momentarily. Placing her hand's on both sides of Jamila's temple, Harmonica closed her own eyes for a moment, furrowed her brow, then opened her eyes again and said:

"She's drugged. She is okay, but she needs to get medical help immediately. I will pick her up. C'mon. We need to leave now."

Harmonica gently picked up Jamila and the three of them made their way towards the door. But standing in the doorway, blocking their escape, and holding a gun, was Nemo.

"Salaam, Dark Shark... Harmonica... so glad you could drop in. I see you have met up vith Jamila... Good."

Nemo was tall, muscular, blond, and very Aryan. His hair was cropped short and neat. Not quite Gestapo, but almost. There was the obligatory look of madness in his eyes and he was sweating profusely. At the top of his left eye socket, a small blue vein throbbed. Beads of sweat ran trickled down his face and not very reassuringly, the hand holding the gun trembled.

"Velcome to Neptune Dive Centre."

Nemo's voice was cold, metallic, and harsh, it sounded like it with was being strained through a sieve, an unholy blend of Darth Vader and Ariel Sharon.

"You can't carry this on, Nemo, you have to stop now."

Dark Shark winced, playing for time, his face contorted in pain.

"Nein! Dark Shark Nein! It vill not be over until I have completed my task. You vill all die and the fins will go to Hong Kong. Then I can sit back and count my money on my money farm!"

"You killed Moheet!"

"Yes! Of course I killed her! And now I am going to kill you all! You are all fools! Do you really believe anyone cares about sharks? They are just fish and I am just a fisherman! And a very good one too! Hahaha! What's so important about them that you are villing to die for them? Eh? Eh? No, you are far too ideological Mr Shark; you are far too stupid and simple to understand the complexities and realities of the modern vorld!"

Whilst Nemo was doing his impression of Dr No, ranting on with his ridiculous monologue, Dark Shark had surreptitiously placed one hand over the handle of the small push dagger hanging from his shoulder whilst all the time keeping his eyes firmly fixed on the rabid megalomaniac standing before him. Dark Shark focused. Tensing his muscles ready to move, he silently resolved not to die by the hand of a man who was incapable of pronouncing the letter W. It simply vouldn't do.

"The 'CusAmac' are on their way, Nemo."

"So vhat? By the time they arrive, you vill be dead!"

Just as it seemed as if things couldn't get more surreal, they did. From outside the sound of sirens came, followed by screeching tires, engines running and a loudspeaker announced the arrival of the men in black.

"This is Inspector Adel of the Shamandura! Nemo, put down your weapon! Don't try to escape! You are surrounded! Come out with your hands up!"

"Looks like you are vrong again, Nemo."

Nemo spun round, eyes flashing with psychotic intent. He saw the police outside, then spun back round, bringing the gun to bear on his enemies. Nemo screamed, squeezing the trigger.

"Nein! Nein!"

The gun flashed and Harmonica reeled, whirling from

the force of the blast. Nemo pulled the trigger again, but this time nothing happened. The gun had jammed. Cursing, he threw the gun on the floor. Excited by the noise of Nemo's gun going off, several of the highly strung Shamandura agents also fired their weapons at the buildings only to be immediately stopped by a gruff order from Adel. Nemo, his way blocked, charged towards Dark Shark. His speed and strength were frightening and he reached his adversary before Dark Shark could gather his wits and prepare an adequate defence. Nemo lifted his right foot aiming towards Dark Shark's head for what would have been a devastating blow, but as he did so, his left foot slipped on some of Jamila's blood, causing him to lose balance. Luckily for Dark Shark, the blow that connected was far from full strength and only served to give him a nasty swipe. Nemo was not about to stick around and try again. He rushed on, heading out the opposite door from the onrushing agents of the Shamandura.

Lying on the floor, Dark Shark gathered himself feebly and stumbled over to where Harmonica and Jamila were lying. He went straight to Harmonica who, as fortune would have it, had taken the bullet in her shoulder. She was alive, seriously wounded, but very much alive and conscious. Jamila was still sleeping, oblivious to the drama unfolding at break neck speed all around her. Kneeling over Harmonica and wandering how to stem the bleeding from her shoulder, the men of the

Shamandura rushed into the room with weapons.

Wasting no time, Dark Shark struggled to his feet and made to move in the direction the noxious Nemo had just taken. Adel ran up to him and asked him if he was okay.

"I'm fine. Thanks for coming when you did. Listen; take care of Jamila and Harmonica. I'm going after Nemo."

"Are you up for this, Dark Shark, you look like hell."

"I feel worse."

"Let me go with you."

"No. I have to do this alone. Please stay here and take charge of the situation. Make sure Harmonica and Jamila get the care they need."

"Okay, habibe, I will do this."

Dark Shark looked at the agent of Shamandura with disbelief. He shook his head, smiled and thought to himself.

"Old Adel is beginning to come good. El Hamdul'allah!"

"Is there anything else I can do for you?"

"Yes, there is. Call the Navy and tell them to send a patrol boat here."

"It is already done. The Navy has two patrol boats on their way here now. They may already be here. Nemo and Bent Bob will not get far."

"Bent Bob?"

"Yes. Bob was waiting for Nemo on the beach by the Zodiacs when we arrived. He was evidently getting the boats ready to leave. We wanted to intercept him but were afraid if we did, it would place you in great danger."

"I need to go."

"Be careful, Dark Shark and good luck."

"Thanks Adel. Really, I mean it. Thank you.

"Afwan, habibe, Afwan."

Dark Shark half ran, half stumbled back down the beach to where his Zodiac was. Accompanying him were two agents from the Shamandura, and together they hauled the boat out on to the water.

Just then, Dark Shark noticed the lines. Glinting silver in the pale light of the stars, were the shark fishing lines. They lay in a huge semi-circle and may have been ten kilometres long. Running along the entire length at regular intervals and dropping down a meter into the water, were the smaller lines that held the hooks. The thick, barbed, razor sharp, three inch long killing hooks. There must have been hundreds, perhaps thousands of hooks dangling down just a meter below the surface. Dark Shark instinctively recoiled. He felt like he was standing at the gates of Auschwitz. As far at the sharks were concerned, this was the Holocaust. Nemo must have recognized the look of horror on Dark Shark's face, because he smirked with insidious satisfaction. No matter what happened, he would take pride in that for the rest of his life. Dark Shark flinched staring into the despotic eyes of his enemy. He couldn't take it. Such deep rooted hate. Somehow an understanding was reached by both parties. Dark Shark seemed to sense the satisfaction taken by Nemo and he resolved to make the satisfaction as short lived as possible. All of this transpired between the protagonists in a matter of a few seconds.

Noticing that he was being ignored by Dark Shark for a split second, Bent Bob decided to take advantage. He turned the throttle on his motor hard to the right and as far as could. As if startled into action, the orange Zodiac sat almost bolt upright in the water, then proceeded to roar towards Dark Shark's boat at high speed, guided by a maniacal man hell-bent on his target's destruction. Bent Bob was wrong, however. Dark Shark had not ignored him, even for a split second. Quite the contrary, Dark Shark could sense very strongly that the overweight American was going to do exactly what he was now doing.

So it was that at the exact moment when Bob turned his throttle, Dark Shark did the same thing. Unlike Bob, Dark Shark not only turned the throttle all the way, he also turned the whole stick, causing his Zodiac to not only jump, but to jump and turn abruptly. His quick thinking saved him. Dark Shark's Zodiac roared off to the right, swiped Nemo's Zodiac and shot passed it. Frantically adjusting for Dark Shark's erratic manoeuvre, Bent Bob lost complete control of his boat and ploughed headfirst into Nemo's Zodiac.

The impact was huge. A huge boom sounded; an extraordinary noise for two such small rubber boats. Bent Bob's Zodiac stopped in its tracks and almost upended out of the water. Stunned by the force of the blow, Nemo was lifted straight out of his Zodiac and with an almighty crash, landed in the water. Dark Shark steadied his boat, relaxed the throttle and turned to see what had happened. Nemo's Zodiac was now between himself and Bent Bob. The orange Zodiac was still for half a minute as Bob, having also been stunned by the impact, tried to gather his wits. This still wasn't over. Looking up to the horizon, Dark Shark was mightily relieved to see the approach of the two naval patrol boats. The cavalry were finally on their way. Almost there. He just needed to stay alive a little longer.

Dark Shark looked down towards the water. He could just make out Nemo who appeared to be in a terrible state. The man was flailing around, clearly in dire straits. He appeared to be stuck, unable to escape. Dark Shark couldn't understand what was wrong. Nemo was a strong swimmer and although the impact from the Zodiac was impressive, it hadn't directly injured him. No. Something was happening in the water. Something was very wrong. Dark Shark realized with a shudder what had happened. Nemo had been hooked on one of his own shark hooks. Possibly more than one hook. With a start, Dark Shark revved the engine and drove the boat round to where he could reach Nemo. The man was a murderer, evil beyond belief, but even he didn't deserve this. Dark Shark had been here before, knew what it was like. Just as he reached the speared Nemo, Dark Shark looked up to see Bent Bob bearing down on him at full speed.

"Bob! No! Nemo is hooked up! Stop! Stop!"

But Bent Bob didn't know, care or hear. He just wanted to kill Dark Shark. Again he was gunning his boat towards Dark Shark and again Dark Shark was forced to take evasive action. Moving his boat quickly out of the way prevented the impact Bent Bob craved - but it meant the end of Nemo. Not even noticing his friend in trouble at the surface, Bent Bob sped past him at full speed. A rope dangling from the speeding vessel caught Nemo under the arm and dragged him through the water. Having avoided Bent Bob again, Dark Shark, desperate with frustration, stopped his boat and turned to watch the grim tragedy unfold, utterly powerless to prevent the grisly, inevitable horror.

Bent Bob's Zodiac dragged Nemo's already hooked body parallel with the lines. The effect on Nemo was devastating and fatal. As he was pulled along, he became caught on more and more hooks. Time and again the thick, metal barbs entered his face, neck, shoulders, arms, and legs. Finally; after twenty metres, Nemo's body was completely and utterly torn apart.

The whole time, Bent Bob never noticed nor cared. When he turned his boat round yet again to attack Dark Shark, he instead looked up to see the machine guns of the Egyptian Naval patrol boats looking right back at him.

# 18

## *Safety Stop*

In the cold crispness of a winter's early morning in Dahab, two dull, metallic grey Egyptian naval patrol vessels carefully hauled out from the sea kilometre after kilometre of fishing line. The ships had methodically worked throughout the night, retrieving the lines of death, rectifying the insanity of humans. Soon their work would be done. Soon the sea and its infinite variety of life would be free of the horror once again. Already a trained eye could spot the difference. The clues were small at first, but for those who knew what to look for, the signs were obvious. Sinai was returning to life.

Life too was returning to Dahab. All along the bay, a gentle, fresh breeze was causing the waves to gently lap the shore. The sun beat down was but not oppressive. Quite the opposite. This morning the sun was kissing Dahab, the day was embracing a new found joy.

In his office at Just Another Dive Centre, Mohammed was practically skipping. He couldn't remember a time he'd been so happy. For what seemed like an eternity, a nightmare had descended on Dahab, covering the sleepy sea side town in a blanket of dark foreboding. Now, the veil had been finally lifted. Mohammed was so excited, he could barely contain himself. Sally the counter chick was exactly the same. She kept bounding in every few minutes, half laughing, half demanding to know if Mohammed had called the hospital yet. He had kept replying that it was too early. Finally, at ten o'clock, they could wait no more. Mohammed picked up the receiver on his desk and dialled a number.

Sitting on a bed in the hospital in Sharm el Sheikh, Dark Shark glanced at his clam shell, smiled and flipped it open.

"Aiwa, Mohammed. Innta tamam?"

"Walla-hi habibe, Anna Helwa, sucran awy, awy, awy!"

Dark Shark laughed and not even the pain in his leg could diminish the joy and happiness he felt at that moment.

"Mohammed, you are coming down here?"

Sally screamed from somewhere just outside the office.

"Dark Shark! Good on ya mate! Coming to see you soon!"

"Ha! Tell Sally, I love her very much."

"Walla, of course. We are coming down, should be there in a couple of hours. Osama is going to drive, so we will bring bananas and shakshuka!"

"Meir, Meir, Mohammed. Meir, Meir."

"Yalla bye!"

They hung up. Dark Shark returned to the task being

performed on his leg by the distinguished Dr Adel. Sewing stiches in Dark Shark once again, Dr Adel gave him a look of mock concern. In his bright intelligent eyes, Dark Shark could clearly make out small fires of mirth.

"Dark Shark, I should give you a loyalty card for this hospital."

"Dr Adel, you give me the impression that you think I somehow look for this to happen to me, or that perhaps I am an accident waiting to happen."

Dr Adel did not deem the response merited a response. He merely smiled enigmatically and continued to sew up yet another hole in Dark Shark's leg. Threading the last stitch, he tied off the end, cut the excess thread, snapped off his gloves and strode over to the wash basin. Dr Adel lathered soap over his hands and spoke to Dark Shark as he did so.

"There, I am done. Same advice as usual. Come back in a week to have the stiches taken out or do it yourself as usual and as usual risk infection and scarring. Have a nice day. See you again soon no doubt."

With that, he dried his hands thoroughly and was gone.

Dark Shark smiled. He swung his legs off the bed, pulled on his pants and hobbled to the door. In the corridor, Sprilina sat on hard plastic bench, reading a newspaper. She looked up when she saw Dark Shark approaching. He acknowledged her presence with a question.

"Where are they?"

Sprilina looked him and up and down. She appeared satisfied by what she saw. Turning abruptly, she lifted one hand and waved for him to follow.

"They're together in the same room. It's just down here."

Sprilina glided down the corridor so quickly, it was all Dark Shark could do to keep up.

"Wait, Sprilina. Slow down. I need to ask you something."

She slowed to a halt and waited for him to catch up.

"Salah is here isn't he? Did you see him?"

"No."

"No, what? You haven't seen him or he's not here?"

"He is here, but I haven't seen him. I asked the doctors if it was possible to see him, but they told me he was refusing to see anyone."

"Don't' give up on him, Sprilina."

"Of course not. He is my son and on top of that I believe there may be hope for him yet. I sense the possibility that he is capable of change."

"What will happen now?"

"When he is strong enough they will put him on trial and he will almost certainly spend a long time in prison. How long? Well that all depends… "

"On what?"

"On how much the judge does or does not hate

Bedouin."

They passed two white doors. An elderly orderly was mopping the floor. The passed another door. At the fourth door on the right, Sprilina stopped and placed her hand on door. She pushed it open and they stepped into a large, white room. On one side, to the left of them, Jamila lay sleeping in a bed. She had two tubes attached to her arm, one to monitor vital signs and the other to keep her hydrated. She looked pale, but thankfully, Dark Shark also thought she looked peaceful. Turning to the other side of the room, he saw Harmonica sitting up in bed, gazing at him intently. She had a large bandage wrapped around her neck and underneath her arm, forming a large white triangle which covered her entire shoulder.

While Sprilina glided over to Harmonica, Dark Shark hobbled.

At the edge of the hospital bed they paused, pulled up chairs and sat down.

"Hi, how are you Harmonica?"

"Hey Dark Shark, Sprilina. So good to see you. Thank you for coming."

"How do you feel?"

"Weak. Drained. And if a lot of pain. Somehow though, despite all that I feel light and very happy."

She smiled. Dark Shark marvelled at her fortitude.

"How's the shoulder?"

"The doctors tell me I'm very lucky. The bullet passed cleanly through without damaging any bone. It is, as they say in the movies, only a flesh wound. They stopped the bleeding and last night operated on me to remove damaged tissue. So far, so good. They are going to keep me in for a few more days to check on the healing and keep an eye out for infections which is the only real danger at this point."

"That's fantastic news, Harmonica."

"What about you Mr Shark? How are you coping with the events of the last few weeks?"

"My leg hurts. My shoulder hurts. Most of the people I love are in this hospital. But! I haven't been so happy in all my life! I might have to change my name!"

Sprilina and Harmonica laughed. The action caused Harmonica to wince sharply in pain. Dark Shark, feeling guilty, offered to avoid humour in her presence during the recovery period.

Sprilina began asking Harmonica questions, mainly regarding the techniques used by Harmonica during her fight with the man. Harmonica was reluctant to relate the details, not believing them to be important. Only the safe outcome of all concerned was her priority.

"Yeah, but Harm, c'mon, what did you hit with him? Your staff? Did you use the Kuji In? Did you invoke the Kobudera?" C'mon Harm, spill the foul."

Harmonica sighed deeply and Dark Shark, unable to suppress a cheeky grin, took the opportunity to take his leave of the two female warriors currently discussing deeply mystical esoteric killing techniques in a Sharm

El Sheikh hospital. Standing up, he picked up the chair and slowly hobbled over to where Jamila lay sleeping. He gently placed the chair on the floor and sat down facing her. She lay on the bed, her chest rising and falling with the movement of her lungs.

Dark Shark carefully placed his hand in hers. She stirred and briefly opened her eyes.

"Hi" he said.

"Hi" she replied.

"How are you?" he asked.

"Thank you for coming for me." she replied.

And with that, she fell asleep again. Dark Shark sat motionless for a long time, holding her hand and gazing in happy silence at her peaceful countenance.

Two hours later, the hospital was a somewhat different and far busier place. Ten o'clock saw the arrival of Mohammed and Sally from Just Another Dive Centre. Twenty minutes later, Gastro and Hymen turned up accompanied by Mojave and Gobi. At eleven o'clock Osama rushed in with armfuls of fruit, mostly comprising of bananas. At eleven thirty, the Sexy Scandis, along with Shwaya Shwaya, made an appearance. With each new arrival, Dark Shark felt happier and happier. He was happy to be alive. He was happy that his friends were alive and he was happy that the genocide of sharks in Dahab was over. For the first time in a long time, he didn't entertain demons or grapple with dark thoughts. Dark Shark was simply able to be in the moment. As the afternoon wore on, the visitors began to leave the hospital. Dark Shark drove back to Dahab with Hymen, Gastro, Mojave and Gobi. It was five o'clock when he took off his clothes and flopped into bed. Three minutes later and he was fast asleep.

It was morning when he woke up, but Dark Shark wasn't sure exactly which morning it was. He had the familiar headache from dehydration which told him he had been sleeping for a long time. Apart from that, he felt remarkably good. He felt light. He felt unburdened. It was uncharacteristic, but profoundly enjoyable. He showered, dressed and made coffee. As he was sipping the hot invigorating liquid, his clam shell blared its polyphonic nonsense. It was Adel of the Shamandura. Dark Shark flipped open the phone.

"Salaam Adel."

"Walla, Dark Shark, how are you feeling? You been sleeping?"

"Yeah, just woke up not long ago. What day is it?

"Ha! You don't know what day it is? It's Saturday."

"Shit. I have been sleeping for a day and a half."

"You must have needed it. I'm not surprised. Listen, I hope you are strong enough now. I need to talk to you. I will send the car. Take your time, though, relax, eat some breakfast then come to my office, okay?"

"Sure. I will be there soon."

An hour later, Dark Shark found himself once again sitting in Adel's office. This time though he wasn't worried in the slightest about his visa.

"What's happening with Bent Bob and Salah?"

"Bent Bob is currently sitting in prison. Salah, as you know, is in the hospital in Sharm and will shortly be joining Bob."

"And the Navy boats?"

"They have completed their work. The sea of Dahab is completely free of lines."

"What about all the shark fins at Neptune?"

"We gathered them up and are holding them in a secure location. We will burn them."

"I have a better idea."

"Which is?"

"Let's get a local artist to make a memorial to Moheet and all the sharks that died, using the shark fins."

"Okay... That's a good idea. I like it. I will talk to the Governor about it."

"Sucran."

"Afwan."

"The memorial can stand somewhere appropriate in Dahab. It can stand there as a reminder of what happened here and why it's so important to protect what we have. It can serve as a reminder, so that people do not forget this story."

"Dark Shark, I do not believe that people will forget this story in a hurry."

"Mmmm. Time will tell, Adel, time will tell."

"So what happens now?"

"With what?"

"With you and Jamila."

"Her work is finished here. When she is well enough, she will return to the UK."

"You are letting her go? I thought you had more Yiddisher Kop than that."

Ignoring the rather surreal feeling of hearing a member of the secret Egyptian intelligence services speaking Yiddish to him, Dark Shark replied thus:

"She is better off without me, Adel. And she is better off with PADI in the UK."

"At this point I must disagree with you Mr Shark. She is neither better off without you nor you without her."

Dark Shark said nothing. Adel continued.

"When you have something that special it is unwise to let it go so easily."

"It's hardly easy."

"Change her mind and stop her getting on that plane."

Dark Shark decided to change the subject instead.

"Thank you for coming out to Neptune when you did. If you hadn't I wouldn't be sitting here now."

"Ha! You are welcome. You see, Mr Shark, we are not all bad at the Shamandura as you think."

"Adel, I really didn't... "

Adel waved away the reply with his hand.

"Don't worry! The past is the past. It is history. The main thing is that this awful business has been resolved and that you, Jamila and Harmonica are okay."

"Yes, you are right."

"I will let you know about the artist and the memorial. I can't see there being problem with it."

"Thanks again Adel, for everything."

Dark Shark got up to leave.

"You are most welcome."

Dark Shark walked over to the door and opened it.

"One more thing before you go, Mr Shark."

Dark Shark paused, holding the door open.

"Stay out of trouble, eh?"

Dark Shark said nothing in reply. He smiled, closed the door and was gone.

It was a beautiful day in Dahab. The sun was shining and the alluvial fan that forms the base of the town was basking in the giant orb's warmth. It was a perfect winter's morning. When the wind stopped and the sun was mild, Sinai was its best. So it was, that Dark Shark decided to refuse the offer of a lift back into town by the Shamandura and instead elected to walk. Refreshed by the gorgeous weather, a feeling of lightness came over him. He was in this positive mood, almost hovering above the pavement, when his eyes beheld a strange spectacle. A procession was slowing moving down the road in the opposite direction in which he was travelling. The cavalcade included two black cars, a large group of people and strangest of all, a band playing loud, traditional Chinese music. The band came first. They were playing loudly to frighten away bad spirits and ghosts. Behind the band, a small group of people were walking dressed in black and white. Amongst this group were six small children all wearing blue. Next, one of the cars, a hearse, slowly followed. Inside, a large black coffin adorned with flowers, filled the interior of the vehicle with ominous finality. Laid almost across the entire width of the hearse's windshield was a giant portrait of the deceased, but from this distance, Dark Shark could not yet see who it was.

Behind the hearse, the second car followed and the reminder of the people, also wearing black and white, brought up the rear. On the right arms of each person, a cloth band had been sown to signify they were in mourning. The position of the cloth on the right, rather than the left arm, signified the deceased was a woman. Additionally, each mourner carried a lit joss stick. Thin wisps of smoke spiralled up from each stick, adding to the surreal nature of the scene. As the funeral cortege slowly went past him, Dark Shark realized the portrait was of Pai Mai.

"So... " He thought. "She's not going back to Beijing after all. She will stay here."

Inside his jacket pocket, his clam shell rang and Dark Shark returned once again to the land of living. It was Gastro.

"Hey, you're on your way to Slow Down, yes? I have prepared a *huge* banquet, everyone is gonna be here."

"I wouldn't miss it for the world."

"Good. Yalla."

Half an hour later, Dark Shark walked into Slow Down. Finding Gastro, he approached his comrade and the two friends embraced.

"There is someone here to see you. She was released from the hospital while you with Adel. Osama and Sprilina went to pick her up. Harmonica is still in hospital, but I understand she is coming out in a few days."

Thanks, man."

"De nada."

"Where is she?"

"By the pool."

Dark Shark followed where Gastro was pointing and saw Jamila sitting alone at one of the tables. He sighed softly and strolled over to her.

"Hey."

"Hi."

"How are you?"

"I feel great. It's so good to be out of the hospital."

"I know. You look great Jay."

"Thank you. I am just so happy and relieved that things turned out the way they did."

Dark Shark relaxed and gazed at the woman sitting opposite him. He had been telling the truth. She did look good considering her recent ordeal. He got the feeling, however, that it was not all roses. Alongside her obvious happiness and relief, Dark Shark got a sense of sadness. He was an old soul by now and he knew why she was sad. Gastro was as reliable as his word. He had indeed prepared a banquet. Laid out on the tables were dozens of plates heaped high with all manner of wonderful delights. Around the table sat Jamila, Dark Shark, Gastro, Mojave, Gobi, Hymen, Mohammed, Sally, Sheikh Hassan and Sprilina. They laughed and ate for many hours, savouring the company, the food and the copious amounts of alcohol.

When all had had their fill and were beginning to slump in their chairs, Mojave and Gobi rose up holding glasses filled with wine. It was Mojave who spoke, raising her glass to the assembled friends. There was silence as all listened.

"When I arrived in Dahab three weeks ago, I was completely devastated at the loss of my daughter Mojave; as of course were Gobi, and my daughters back home in America. It was impossible for us to come to terms with the loss of our loved one. We were simply unable to fathom how someone could do this to our beloved Moheet, who was the sweetest and gentlest of souls. I have to admit that for the first time in my life, I doubted my ability to find any hope or solace in this world. During my time here though, I have been truly amazed by the courage, dedication and passion of all of you sitting here in front of me today. I never imagined for one moment that after the horrors I faced when I arrived here, that I might leave having a large measure of hope and solace restored to both myself and my family. Although nothing can ever replace my daughter, on behalf of me, my husband and my daughters, I want to say thank you to Dark Shark, Gastro, Jamila, Sprilina, Hymen, Mohammed, Sally and Sheikh Hassan, to all of you, for giving me back hope. Thank you, from the bottom of my heart."

It was Dark Shark who spoke next.

"You are most welcome, Mojave. We did not know your daughter for long, but she touched us all in the short time we did know her. Moheet's spirit was strong, burning brightly; she represented everything good in this world. There will always be a place in our hearts for her, and we will never forget her."

Standing up, all assembled raised their glasses and drunk a toast to Moheet, may she rest in peace.

As the groups of friends were getting ready to depart, Shanti came running from the entrance to Slow Down.

"Hymen! Gastro! Hymen! Gastro!"

"Shanti, what's up?"

"There are many police here! Army! Big men have arrived!"

Perplexed, the group of friends looked on as Slow Down was filled with a large group of very officious men, all dressed in a variety of fear-inducing uniforms and all sporting the regulation over-the-top firearms. At the head of the group was Adel side by side with the Governor of South Sinai. They looked deadly serious. Adel strode right up to the table and stared at Dark Shark.

"What's going on Adel? Why the need to bring in the

goon squad armed to the teeth?"

"For security."

"Security? From what?"

"The question is not from what, but for whom."

"Adel, what on earth are you talking about? What the hell is going on here?"

"Please allow me to introduce to you, His Excellency, the President of the Arab Republic of Egypt, Hosni Mubarak!"

Dark Shark thought he was tripping. But he wasn't. Sure enough, just at that moment, another large group of men showed up. They looked even tougher and certainly more serious that than the first bunch. There were forty in all. They were the bodyguards of the President himself. They checked the entire area again and again. When they were satisfied that all was safe, a humongous, black, stretched limousine pulled up outside the back gate. Immediately, a smaller group of body guards rushed over to the car and surrounded the vehicle in superbly efficient military style. One of the guards put on white gloves and opened the car door, but not before wiping the handle with a cloth. The car door swung wide open and much to the astonishment of the assembled friends, out stepped President Hosni Mubarak. Every one stood up.

Hosni was looking most dapper. He was wearing an immaculate black Brunello Cucinelli suit, a white Stefano Ricci shirt, and was finished off with a pair of Ermenegildo Zegna shoes made from the finest Nile crocodile skin. All the civilians present were wearing shorts, t-shirts and sandals, except for Sheikh Hassan who was looking not so dapper in his white jelibyah. Adel and the Governor walked over to President in such a manner that it could have only have been learned at a college for governmental sycophants. Bowing before him, they talked to him for a minute before escorting him over to the table where Dark Shark and the others were standing with open mouths. The President was evidently used to it. He beamed at them.

'Ah Salaam, Salaam how you all are?"

"Salaam Aleichem, Your Excellency" They all replied, bowing low in respect.

Chuckling softly, President Mubarak waved his hand in a gently dismissive motion.

"Please, please. Rise, rise. All of you. As you can appreciate, I am very busy. Therefore, I must be brief. Dark Shark, in recognition of your efforts in thwarting the efforts of the desperate shark-fishing brigands, helping the environment and saving the tourist industry, the Arab Republic of Egypt would like to present you with a gift. It was little large to bring here, but she is waiting for you in Sharm El Sheikh and I have a photograph of her."

The president held out his hand. He offered an envelope for Dark Shark to open. Dark Shark took the envelope and humbly thanked the President. He stared at it, unsure what to do with it.

"Open it, young man, open it."

With trembling fingers, Dark Shark tore open the envelope. Inside was a photograph of a boat. But it was not just any boat. It was a 32m steel hull Live-Aboard. Attached to the photo were a work permit and a license to dive anywhere in the Egyptian Red Sea.

"Wow, I really don't know what to say your Excellency. This is beyond belief. She is beautiful. I am filled with happiness and gratitude."

"It is a small token of our appreciation for all that you have done for us. Take good care of her and use her well. She is your Calypso now."

Dark Shark just stared at the image of the incredible boat. For the second time in three weeks, he fell in love again.

Turing to Jamila, President Hosni Mubarak took out another envelope and spoke before handing it over to her.

"Jamila. Your efforts were also extraordinary and we thank you most graciously. Please allow me to present you with a key to the city of Dahab. It is also the key to our hearts."

"Oh wow. Thank you so much your Excellency. Dahab and Egypt will always be in my heart too."

Everybody present clapped and cheered.

Nodding his approval, the President addressed them all.

"I must go now. It's a long journey back to my plane." He chuckled. "Thank you to all of you for your work, your courage and your love for my beautiful country,

Egypt. Good bye."

Five minutes later, President Hosni Mubarak and his forty bodyguards had left Slow Down.

Another five minutes and Adel's company of men has also left. Only an astonished group of friends remained. Slow Down had returned to normal, but only as normal as Slow Down can get. Unable to suppress his delight any longer, Gastro grinned a huge, toothless grin.

"I think this calls for a party!" he exclaimed.

Later that night at Slow Down, the party was in full swing.

Dark Shark sat with Jamila. They were drinking and laughing, happy and carefree, unrecognizable from only a few days before. Sally was chatting up the barman and Mohammed was sampling the delights of the buffet. Poi and her sister Flake were spinning fire in beautiful, hypnotic circles. Peter and Heidi were sitting in-between Megaphone and Frank Zappa, the four of them engaged in a very surreal conversation. Kim, Simon, and Paul with his EFR dummy were also there. Wesley was arguing with Shanti about Pan-African politics. Hymen was sweating in a corner, drunk as a skunk and trying to sell a diving safari to a Russian pimp. The delicious smell of bacon burners wafted from the kitchen. Inside, Gastronimica was licking whipped cream off the black leather of Eva, who was lying on a counter with her legs in the air and hitting Gastro with a riding crop. Gastro's face was a picture of pure pleasure. The Slow Down party lasted well into the wee hours.

Dark Shark slept most of the next morning and at lunch-time woke up to accompany Mojave and Gobi to the airport. He was accompanied by Jamila and Gastro. Osama was driving. The journey to Sharm El Sheikh was quiet, with little conversation. Occasionally, small talk was made. There were reminders that everyone should stay in touch. For the most part though, there was only quiet reflection. At the airport, the goodbyes were highly charged with emotion. Mojave and Jamila were crying. Everyone hugged everyone else. They promised they would meet again soon. Mojave again invited the three of them to visit whenever they wanted. Just before they left, Mojave took Dark Shark to one side and presented him with a gift.

"This is for you."

She handed him a cloth bag containing something small, but heavy.

"What is it?"

"It's a much prized fossilized tree resin, also classified as a gemstone. In First People's culture it is revered as a sacred stone, prized for its colour and beauty. It's amber. This particular piece of amber is extremely rare. It is blue amber and is from the foothills of New Mexico. I found it over thirty years ago and gave it to Moheet when she was but a young girl. It was her favourite when she was growing up. The German word for amber is Bernstein. I brought it with me, because it was the thing that brought us closest together, but now I would like you to have it. I think Moheet would have wanted that too."

Dark Shark tentatively removed the amber from the cloth bag. He rolled it over in his hands and stared. It was truly stunning. The size and shape of a small bird's egg, it had been worn smooth over millions of years. It was almost iridescent, glowing blue in the afternoon's winter sun. Dark Shark had never seen anything like it.

"Wow, Mojave, it's incredible. Thank you so much. I am deeply touched and honoured."

"You are most welcome Dark Shark. And now I fear, the time has come for us to part company. I will miss you very much, all of you. Fare thee well, my friends, fare thee well. Until the next time we meet!"

"Good bye Mojave, good bye Gobi. Take care of yourselves and have a safe journey home! Get in touch with us when you land in the States."

"We will! See you! Bye!"

Dark Shark, Jamila, Gastro and Osama watched as Mojave and Gobi put their bags on the conveyor belts, had their passports checked and with a final wave, they disappeared into the departure lounge.

As they left the airport, Dark Shark informed his friends he was going to pick up Harmonica from the hospital. Osama would drop Jamila and Gastro off in Dahab, and then return to Sharm to pick up Dark Shark and Harmonica. Saying ciao for now, the three friends spit up.

Dark Shark watched his friends depart, then jumped in a taxi and headed south towards the hospital. When he arrived, Harmonica was looking much better. The hole in her shoulder was healing well and remained clear of infection. She was in a wheelchair as crutches would have been impossible with her type of wound. Dark Shark helped her gather her personal belongings whilst the doctors and nurses gave her instructions. Harmonica was told to have new bandages put on every day by her doctor in Dahab and return to the hospital in one week. After that, if all went well, she would liaise only with her doctor in Dahab. The medical professionals were amazed at her recovery. Dark Shark knew her better and was not in the least bit surprised.

Finishing all the necessary formalities, it was a much relieved Harmonica that was guided from the hospital building by her friend. There was still time before Osama arrived, so Dark Shark suggested they go for a walk and grab some coffee.

"You walk. I'll drive."

"Ha! It's a deal."

They set off down the street, Dark Shark pushing the chair bound Harmonica. After a hundred meters they came across a reasonably reputable coffee house where they stopped to order refreshments. Harmonica ordered herbal tea, whilst Dark Shark had his usual poison. Sitting in the mild afternoon sun and sipping their drinks, the two friends had their first chance to talk properly since the terrible events at Neptune Dive Centre.

"I am very proud of you Dark Shark."

"Thank you. I am proud of you too. I can't tell you how much it means to me that you turned up when you did. I rushed in, bit off more than I could chew and almost paid the ultimate price for it."

"You did what you had to do. I am truly sorry that I did not intercede far sooner. If I had, maybe the whole thing would not have panned out the way it did. Maybe less people would have died."

"Perhaps. We can speculate forever on what might have been."

"What will you do now?"

"That is good question. I want to organize an artist to make a memorial for Moheet. I was thinking it would make ideal use of the dried shark fins which the Shamandura have stored in a warehouse somewhere."

"Wow, great idea."

"Yeah, it's a good one."

"And after?"

"After? I don't really know. I suppose I would like to just enjoy teaching diving again. To get into the water knowing there are no hooks down there!"

"Yes, I can understand that."

"I might leave Dahab and travel some more. There are lots of places I still want to dive. Tiger Beach, Guadalupe, Cocos and Malpelo. There still many delights to sample."

"Leave Dahab? Leave the Sinai? Why? You have so much to offer, so much to teach about the place. Sinai needs you to help the people protect the environment, to show them how. And anyway, I never met a Hawager who was so at home in the desert, not to mention underwater."

Dark Shark smiled.

"Dahab is going to be very lonely when she's gone."

"Dark Shark, you have to learn to let go of the things you fear to lose the most."

"Ah yes, that old Yogic chestnut."

It was three days later, that Dark Shark received the call he'd been dreading since the day Jamila arrived back in Dahab.

"Everything is ready. I got my ticket."

"When are you leaving?"

"Tomorrow evening. 6 o'clock. I have to be at the desk two hours before departure. Will you come with me to the airport?"

"Of course."

"Okay, great. Pick me up at around two. That way we will have a bit of time before my flight leaves."

"Are you sure about this, Jay?"

"No. I'm not sure about anything anymore."

Dark Shark recalled Harmonica's words from the coffee shop.

"Jay, it's the right decision. I know it hurts now, but everything will turn out fine, you will see."

"Really? Did you get that piece of spiritual shit from a

Yoga teacher by any chance?"

"Jay, what do you want from my life?"

"What do you think?!"

Jamila hung up. She threw her phone on the bed, and then followed it by throwing herself on the bed. For a long time she lay still. The only movements came from the tears which gently trickled down her cheeks. Fifteen minutes after Jamila hung up on Dark Shark, he received another call, this time from Gastro.

"So?"

"So, what?"

"When is she leaving?"

"Tomorrow night. Six o'clock."

"And you are just going to let this happen?"

"What am I supposed to do?"

"God, you really are a schmuck when it comes to women."

"Adel tells me not to let go. Harmonica advises me to let go. What do you think?"

"For the first time in my life, I am going to have to go with the Shamandura."

"I don't know. It's Jamila's decision at the end of the day."

"Only a fool would believe that."

"Thanks, G. You've been a great help."

"That's what I'm here for. Stop being a fool and do the right thing."

The next evening, as Dark Shark was stepping out of

his house to hail a taxi, Adel pulled up next to him.

"C'mon. Jump in. I will take you guys to the airport."

"Walla. Thanks."

At Sharm El Sheikh Airport, both Dark Shark and Jamila sat in silence, each thinking about the other. For over an hour they waited for Jamila's flight, lost deep in thought, time the only enemy. Jamila broke the difficult silence first.

"I'm not going."

"You have to Jay… "

"No, I don't… I can stay… "

"But your job… your home… "

"Screw the home… screw the job… screw everything...!" She sobbed.

"Jay… no matter what happens… you have to get on that plane… I don't know much in this crazy, mixed-up world of ours, but I do know that you have to get on that plane… people like you need to keep doing what you do… for the sake of all of us. People like me don't add up to a hill of beans… if you don't get on that plane now… you're gonna regret it… maybe not now, sure… but some day and for the rest of your life… "

"But what about us?"

"We'll always have the Canyon, Jay."

"I'm gonna miss you Dark Shark"

"I'm gonna miss you too, Jay."

They embraced and Dark Shark bid her farewell. He walked slowly across the terminal. Before he passed through the main door, he paused and turned back to look at Jamila, one last time.

She stood near the back of a long cue, frozen, her blue eyes wet with tears, watching his departure. She waved weakly to him one last time. Heartbroken, he returned the wave before disappearing through the main door.

On the return journey to Dahab, Dark Shark sat in the car staring at the passing scenery in silence. Adel smirked.

"Don't worry Dark Shark, she'll be back. I know it."

"How do you know that?"

"The Shamandura know everything."

"I thought the Bedouin knew everything?"

"The Bedouin? Please don't talk to me about the Bedouin."

"Listen Adel, you guys really need to start treating the Bedouin properly. Sinai is the Bedouin's home, they have been here forever. This is Egypt, but it's also Sinai, and the Bedouin have a right to be treated properly and with respect, just like everyone else. Sinai is not Sinai without the Bedouin. You know this as well as I."

"It is true what you say, Dark Shark, but we Egyptians don't forgot so easily that the Bedouin helped the Israelis during the wars."

"Adel, that was over forty years ago! First of all, not all the Bedouin helped the Israelis. Secondly, most of the Bedouin alive today had nothing to do with what happened in those terrible times. They are far too young. Must the unborn pay for the sins of their fathers? C'mon Adel, this is 2005. Enough already."

"Maybe you are right, Dark Shark. Maybe it is time for a new relationship. Perhaps we all need to work together to make Sinai successful for everyone."

"Wow, Adel. I think this is the beginning of a beautiful friendship."

The next morning, Dark Shark woke to the sound of his clam shell blaring its polyphonic nonsense. It was Gastro.

"C'mon, get your shit together."

"Good morning to you too."

C'mooonnnn... get ready... we go dive!"

"No G, I really don't feel up for it."

"That might be true. Right up to the moment you enter the water. Then after that... C'mon. I wanna go to the Canyon."

"Oh yeah, the last site I want to visit right now."

"Exactly. I will pick you up in fifteen minutes."

Two hours later, Dark Shark and Gastro emerged from the Canyon and swam to the sandy slope to make a safety stop. Gastro had been right of course. The moment Dark Shark had submerged below the surface, he'd felt wonderful once again. It almost never failed to happen when he dived. That feeling was always there. The dive was fantastic; the Canyon was in all its glory.

At the slope, Dark Shark hovered perfectly a few inches

from the sand. Suddenly, in the corner of his mask, he saw another diver swim over the saddle and head directly towards him. Dark Shark was puzzled. They had not seen any other divers so far. Another second and he recognized the diver. It was Jamila. She swam straight up to him, grinning a huge grin through her regulator. She settled down on the sand beside him, pulled out a plastic slate from her BCD pocket and handed it to an incredulous Dark Shark. Scrawled across the slate in large letters, were the words:

"Kiss me you twat!"

Dark Shark took out his regulator and Jamila did the same.

They kissed passionately, hugging each other whilst spinning around and around and around.

# *Epilogue*

Dark Shark and Gastronimica occupied the main room in Dark Shark's half a house. Blue smoke curled its way slowly up, hitting the ceiling then spreading out in soft waves. Bob Marley was singing:

"Exodus! Movement of Jah people!"

Dark Shark and Gastro were incapable of movement. The pair sat crossed legged on cushions, Bedouin style. Separating them was a metal box with legs. The box contained warm coals, a pot of tea and two small glasses. For a long time neither spoke. It was Dark Shark who broke the silence first with a question.

"What's the difference between God and a diving instructor?"

"I don't know. What's the difference between God and a diving instructor?"

"God doesn't think he's a diving instructor."

They both giggled.

Gastro somehow managed to find the strength to lift his arm and beckon Dark Shark in a slow, lazy motion.

"Oi! Pass that joint, Bogart."

On his lap he had a copy of Dark Shark's book which he had just finished reading.

"What do you think of the book, Gastro?"

"You're gonna get soo deported!"

"No, seriously."

"Well, I've been reading Ian Rankin… "

"Ian Rankin?! That's not fair!"

"Oh shut up you middles class liberal."

"I rest my case."

"Look, I'll compromise, which is something I rarely do. Let us agree that the book is better than anything by Dan Brown, okay?"

"Deal."

"When is the film coming out?"

"It's still in pre-production. But…! The great news is that Daniel Day Lewis has agreed to play you and he's even agreed to have real dreadlocks implanted!"

"Fucking eshta!"

"Indeed!"

"But if they're implants, then they're not real of course."

"I don't think anyone will notice, G."

Gastro broke into a wry grin.

"No one'll ever believe this story."

"I don't care. I have a new Live-Aboard and tomorrow Jay and I are going to the Brothers islands to see the last remaining Red Sea sharks!"

"Fucking eshta."

"Indeed!"

"That Mubarak is a character. Really nice what he did for you. Not a bad guy for a thieving dictator."

"Yeah, Mubi's a character alright."

"Can't imagine an Egypt without him and when he does finally pop his clogs, his son will probably take over."

"You never know G, Egypt might change one day, the people might rise up and call for democracy"

"Yeah right. Anyway, enough about Egypt… C'mon, c'mon tell me, what is the sequel called?"

"Well… That's a good question. After much deliberation, heartache and numerous meetings with the publishers, I've decided to call it: …"

# *Afterword*

Every day around the world, 300,000 sharks are killed. The vast majority of the sharks are killed for their fins which are used in a Far Eastern delicacy - shark fin soup. A genocide of 100 million sharks killed each year is occurring right now, a genocide that is going to have devastating consequences not only for the marine environment, but also for the human race. This genocide is far away from the eyes of humanity, indeed most people have no idea that it is even happening. Sharks are the apex predators of the sea, playing a vital role in keeping it clean and in balance. They have swum the oceans for 420 million years. They predate the dinosaurs by many millions of years. Many scientists believe that after their arrival, the sharks' almost perfect design rapidly forced evolutionary change in all other forms of marine life. In so doing, sharks were responsible for shaping all life on Earth from that moment on. In the last twenty years, shark populations across the world have been decimated. In some species, numbers have been reduced by as much as ninety per cent. After nearly half a billion years on the planet, sharks are being wiped out in an instant. It is vitally important that humans end this genocide now and do everything in their power to save and protect these magnificent creatures. For more information on Fins4Fins, please go to www.fins4fins.org and help support efforts to do just that.

*AB*

*Glossary of scuba diving equipment*

| | |
|---|---|
| BCD | Buoyancy Control Device. A jacket worn by the diver to enable buoyancy to be adjusted. The jacket is in effect a bag of air and works by receiving gas from the cylinder via a regulator. The diver can put in or take out gas as required. The jacket also holds the cylinder, normally on the diver's back. |
| Regulator | A precision mechanical device assembled in two stages. The first stage takes high pressure gas from the cylinder and reduces it to an intermediate pressure. The second stage takes the gas from an intermediate pressure to ambient pressure, allowing the diver to breathe at the same pressure regardless of depth. |
| Wetsuit | A suit made from neoprene containing millions of tiny bubbles. The suit keeps the diver warm by allowing a certain amount of water inside which is then warmed by the divers' body heat. |
| Fins | Elongated attachments added to a diver's feet to allow greater propulsion through the water. Often constructed from plastic polymers. Frequently mistaken for flippers. They're not. |

| | |
|---|---|
| Booties | Neoprene footwear worn by water users to provide comfort, warmth and protection. |
| High-pressure gauge | Instrument connected to the regulator's first stage displaying cylinder pressure. |
| Depth gauge | Instrument displaying equivalent depth in water |
| Snorkel | Plastic tube inserted into the mouth allowing the wearer to breathe whilst the face is submerged in water. Swimmers floating on the surface use the snorkel along with mask, fins and booties during an activity known as 'snorkelling'. |

*Glossary of transliterated Arabic terminology*

| Arabic | English |
|---|---|
| Salaam | Peace |
| Salaam aleichem | Peace unto you |
| Aleichem a salaam | Right back atchya |
| Sabah el kheer | Good morning |
| Sabah el full | Good morning to you |
| Mishkela | Problem |
| Mafish mishkela | There is no problem |
| Quayas | Good |
| Halas | Finished or that's it |
| Habibe | Friend or brother |
| Kabeer | Big |
| Aiwa | Yes |
| La | No |
| Kol a tamam? | Is everything okay? |
| Yalla | Let's go |
| Walla | Really |
| Walla-he | Yes, really or really?! |
| Mastool | Stoned or high |
| Mershi | Okay |
| Insha'allah | If God is willing |
| Afwan | Welcome |
| Bukra | Tomorrow |
| Eshta | Cream or the best of the best |

| | |
|---|---|
| Meir | One hundred |
| Meir meir | One hundred per cent, the top |
| Shwaya shwaya | Slowly, slowly or softly, softly |
| Sucran | Thank you |
| Afwan | Welcome |
| El hamdul'allah | Thank God |
| Helwa | Sweet |
| Jelibya | One piece gown worn by Bedouin men |
| Kefir | Traditional Arab head dress |
| Mag'ad | Place of seating |
| Maharama | Place of women |
| Shabbaba | Bedouin flute |
| Rabbaba | Bedouin violin |
| Koshary | Spicy Egyptian dish made of beans and noodles |
| Shakshuka | Bedouin dish made of tomatoes and eggs |
| Sahlab | Drink made from milk and coconut |
| Foul | Egyptian dish made of beans |
| Maya | Water |
| Wadi | Dried up river bed |
| Sharm | Bay with deep, narrow entry |

| | |
|---|---|
| Ras | Cape, promontory, or headland |
| Marsa | Open bay |
| Dahab | Gold |
| Sha'ab | Coral reef |
| Jebel | Mountain |
| Hawager | Foreigner |

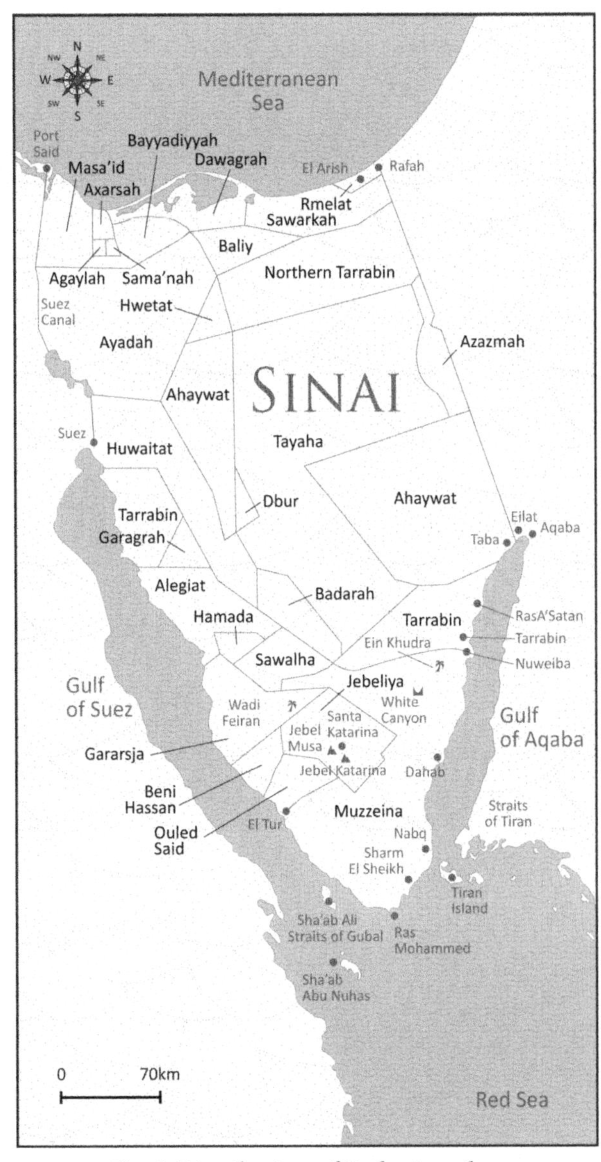


Fig. 2 Distribution of Bedouin tribes

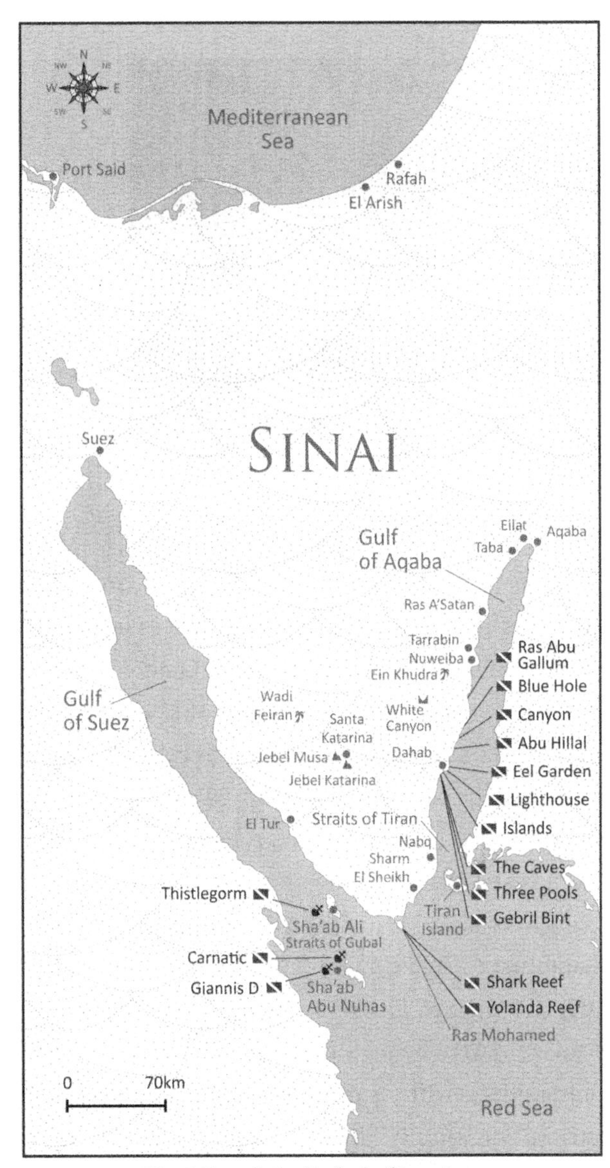


Fig.3 Death in Dahab dive sites

## *About the author*

Avi Bernstein was born not too far away from where the events in this book take place. When he was four years old his family moved to West London where he spent his formative years. At the age of twelve he did he his first ever scuba dive; but although he finds this fact fascinating, he has no idea whether it had any impact on his decision to become a dive professional. For the last fifteen years, Avi has made a living working as a PADI diving instructor. He has lived in the Sinai for nine years in addition to India, Costa Rica, Cyprus and Israel. In 2012; Avi founded Fins4Fins, an organisation dedicated to saving sharks by providing subsistence shark fishing communities with economic alternatives based on tourism, specifically diving. Death in Dahab is Avi Bernstein's first novel.

Made in the USA
Middletown, DE
18 September 2021

48544228R00308